FRANNY

NORMAN MALAMUD

Barringer Publishing, Naples, Florida
www.barringerpublishing.com
Cover, graphics, layout design by Lisa Camp
Editing by Carole Greene

ISBN: 978-0-9896338-9-5

Library of Congress Cataloging-in-Publication Data
Franny / Norman Malamud

Printed in U.S.A.

CHAPTER 1

Franny Goldsmith Pagliara was beside herself. Marrying Detective Nick Pagliara was the highlight of her thirty-one years on earth. Having been known as crafty, flighty, and outspoken, with a mouth that could cuss up a storm, she managed to stay afloat when chaos was cast upon her. The gods that be put stumbling blocks in her path, and, although she was knocked down and stepped on, she managed to pick herself up, utter a few offensive words, and regroup. Franny was a survivor.

Today she could forgive anyone anything. In one week it would be her husband's thirty-fifth birthday and with the inheritance she had received from Elaine, her dear friend who had passed away, she bought a red 2003 fiftieth-anniversary edition Corvette convertible to surprise him.

Franny, her chum Lily, who was a concert pianist, and Lily's newly acquired husband Lew went car shopping. Franny bargained, flailed her arms, cussed and carried on until the exasperated manager in charge of the dealership said, "Give her what she wants! Just close the damn deal."

But Franny wasn't through with them. "And don't forget the freaking free oil changes and car washes," she said, then added, "And put it in writing, Buster!"

After Lew made sure the aggressive salesman hadn't taken advantage of Franny, he winked at Lily, threw up his hands and retired to the showroom lounge where he poured himself a double espresso, wishing it was a double vodka.

❧

The Corvette was delivered a week later, just before Nick arrived home from the precinct. An oversized red ribbon tied in a huge bow was wrapped around the convertible. As Nick pulled into the driveway, his mouth dropped open and his eyes bulged with awe as he spotted the automobile.

His head jutted out the window of his old Volvo P 1800. Flabbergasted, he pointed a threatening finger at Franny and said, "You didn't!"

Tossing her long, kinky hair to one side, Franny let fly the car keys at Nick. "Fucking A, baby. Happy birthday."

Lily squeezed Lew's hand. Married just over a year, they were still adjusting to the suicide of his late wife, a task that did not come easily for either of them.

Franny couldn't wait to get Nick off the "most desirable bachelor" list and, being the unconventional ditz she was, opted for a beach wedding at sunset, formal attire, knee-deep in the Gulf of Mexico at the Ritz Carlton, Naples, Florida.

❧

The sun's rays bounced off of the shiny Corvette as Franny darted for the oversized ribbon and pulled at the bow. "Here, Lily," she said, "you can wrap this around your Steinway at your next concert."

Franny, overjoyed, turned towards Nick and ate up the surprised joy his face exuded. "C'mon Nick," she said, "don't sit there looking like you never saw a Vette. Get outta that old piece of shit and set your ass down in your new baby."

His heart thumping with excitement, Nick shut off the motor of the Volvo and tossed the keys onto the passenger seat. "You two," he called to Lily and Lew, "are in a lot of trouble. Couldn't you at least have given me a heads-up?"

"And go up against Franny?" Lew countered. "Are you out of your mind?"

"See you later, kids," Franny chanted to Lew and Lily as she opened the passenger door, plopped in and fastened her seat belt. "I'm going to take a ride with the birthday boy. Mm, I just love the smell of leather," she purred as she caressed it and then shouted at Nick, "Move it, Nick! Since they shifted you from homicide to narcotics, you're reacting a lot slower."

"You didn't complain last night, kiddo," he teased. "And what has one thing to do with the other, may I ask?"

"I'm in too good a mood to get into that. C'mon, get in here and take me for a drive, and put the top down before it starts to rain."

He exited the Volvo and walked to the Corvette. As he reached for the door handle his beeper buzzed and his hand froze in mid-air.

The expression on Franny's face showed the tears in her eyes before the words formed in her mouth. Staring hard at him, she yelled, "Don't even think of answering it!"

Avoiding her eyes, he glanced at the caller ID and hit the send button. He listened, then bit down hard on his lip, mouthed "Fuck!" and answered, "I'm on my way!"

Narcotics agent Oscar Greene peered from under the bill of his NYC Yankee cap as Nick approached the unmarked police vehicle. "Looks like we're in for a shakedown," he said, his Brooklyn accent evident. "Too bad about you having to shoot back down here. I understand you were on your way home."

Nick growled. "You won't believe what I left back at the house. I'm telling ya, Ossie, I shoulda stayed in homicide."

Oscar turned the ignition on as sheets of rain splattered the windshield. "Get in before you get drenched," he said. "Yeah. I heard the missus was planning a big surprise for your birthday. Did you get it?"

"I got it—right between the eyes. How did you know about me getting a present?" Nick asked as he opened the passenger door, sat down and wiped the rain from his face.

Oscar harumphed, "C'mon, Nick. There are no secrets among the women. Marsha told me what Franny was planning to get you for your fortieth last week. You're one lucky guy."

His expression rigidly impassive, Nick shook his head. "I'm so bummed. I didn't even get to drive the Vette before I got the call. Shit! Oh, and before I let you get by with that crack, it's my big three-five, not four-oh."

Oscar chuckled and pulled away from the curb. "Seat belt, Nick, and you better settle down. We might have hit the jackpot. Pete the stoolie gave me the tip we've been waiting for. Cost me a C-note but it might just pay off."

"Where and when is it going down?"

"At the Ansonia, just a few blocks from here." Oscar checked his watch. "If the info Pete gave me is legit—in thirty minutes."

"What about backup?"

"All taken care of. I've made sure the desk clerk at the Ansonia was retired for the evening and replaced by one of our boys."

Three undercover agents sat peering over their newspapers as Nick and Oscar cautiously walked into the hotel lobby.

Upon spotting Nick and Oscar, they nodded, stood, folded the newspapers, placed them on the coffee table, and followed behind Nick and Oscar.

It might have been the look on Franny's face or the disappointment with the Vette that dampened Nick's spirits, but an eerie forewarning nagged at the back of his mind. Turning to Oscar, his voice filled with concern, he said, "Ossie, I got this real bad feeling."

❧

Startled by the ring of her cell phone, Franny dropped her fork. Nick had given her only a nod and a grim expression when he left her and the Vette to meet Oscar for what was evidently, she thought, a call to action.

Lily eyed Franny, aware of the fear she read in her friend's expression. "He's not even gone an hour and you're carrying on like…"

Franny sulked. "C'mon, Lily. He's not calling to say hi. They were close to a narcotic bust, and a big one too. I'm not going to answer it."

"Maybe it's not him."

Franny pressed the off button and threw the phone across the room. The phone hit the leg of the table and fell to the floor, the back cover flipping off. "I don't want to know, Lily. Stop pressuring me."

Lily sighed and rose to retrieve the phone. She wondered if changing the conversation would help the situation but, knowing Franny's temperament, decided to wait until her friend cooled down.

Franny shouted. "Leave it!"

Lily sat down next to Franny and put her arm around her. "Listen," she said softly. "Getting all worked up isn't going to help anything. I have an idea. The Vette is still outside. Why don't we give it a test drive? I always wanted to get into one. Please, Franny, you're scaring the shit out of me. You haven't carried on like this in a long time."

Franny gave Lily a long, concerned stare. "I wiped away all my problems when Nick and I said the I do's. But since he was switched from homicide to this fucking narc-job, I'm constantly walking on eggshells. I don't sleep well and am afraid of what will happen to him—and to the happiness we've found."

"I know, I know, Honey. But you can't live like this. You'll be heading for a nervous breakdown. Maybe you should talk to someone."

Franny laughed out loud. "Lily, that's the funniest thing I have heard in a long time. See a shrink?"

They both started to laugh, thinking back to the experience they had endured with the perverted Dr. Jonathon Kent.

Wiping the tears from her cheeks, Franny sputtered, "Okay, Lily. Let's rev up the wheels and break it in. After all, a virgin would not fit into this family, would it?"

"Now, that's the Franny I know and love," Lily said. "Loan me one of your scarves. Let's put the top down and cruise the town, since it's stopped raining. Can I drive?"

"Since you're off the sauce, you sure can."

Lily tied her hair back with the scarf, took hold of Franny's arm and led her into the foyer. She swung the front door open, only to be taken aback by the inscrutable face of Oscar Greene.

There was no need for words; the look on Oscar's face said it all. Franny grabbed at Oscar's lapels, her eyes searching his for a sign, a ray of hope that Nick was not dead.

CHAPTER 2

The stillness of the hospital was broken by the painful scream of the patient in room 302. Franny bolted to her feet as a wave of hopefulness swept through her mind. Wide eyed, she bent down and shouted. "Did you hear that? Oh my God! Get the nurse! He's coming out of the coma."

Lily stood, placed her hands on Franny's shoulders and spoke firmly. "Get hold of yourself. That wasn't Nick. Nick's room is down the hall. Besides, he has a private nurse."

Franny crumpled into her chair and put her head in her hands. "Christ," she said through her tears, "it's been over two months, and he just lies there, his eyes open—waiting to wake up—waiting to come back to me. I'm going in. Maybe I'll read to him."

Lily took her seat beside Franny and put her arm around her friend. It hadn't been easy for her or Lew to keep Franny from going over the edge. Lew had suggested that they take a break and go to a restaurant, but

Franny wouldn't leave Nick's bedside for more than a shower or to use the restroom. Lily made sure Franny had a change of clothes and Lew had a chaise moved into Nick's private suite. She had to constantly argue with Franny in order to get some food into her.

Lily rubbed her friend's arm. "Let's sit a while. I want to talk, okay?"

Franny raised her head and eyed her friend. The nervousness in her stomach felt like the onset of panic. A more devoted friend than Lily was not to be found, and although she felt she was drowning, she lacked the will to overcome the depression that enveloped her—or perhaps she wanted to wallow in it.

"I cancelled two of my scheduled recitals."

Franny started to speak but Lily cut her off. "I can make them up later on. I don't want you to be by yourself. Anyhow, I needed a break." Shifting nervously in her seat, she leaned closer to Franny. The silence throughout the hospital made it harder for Lily to go on. "You have to face things, Franny. You heard what the doctors have said. Nick could awaken at any moment—a week from now, a month, or ..."

Franny nodded. "Or never."

If ever there was a time I needed a drink it's now, Lily thought. But having successfully abstained for two years, she shook her head to shake off the thought and focused back to Franny's plight. "Think of it this way. Would Nick want you to stay at his bedside day and night waiting for him to come out of the coma? Think of what he would want you to do. I hate to sound like my mother, but do it for him, not for you."

Franny sidled closer to Lily, half smiled and took Lily's hand in hers. "You know, Lily, when you're going to lose someone you love, there's an aching hole that you can't seem to fill. Like quicksand, it keeps pulling you under. It's been over two months and I wish I could go on with my life, but I just can't get it together. I hear what you're saying and I know Nick would want me to go on living..."

"We can try, Franny. You've been through hell. Think how happy you'll be when Nick comes back. I've been talking to Lew and he says they miss you at the showroom. Since you're not there, it's just like a morgue. Oops, sorry."

"It's okay, Lily. I'm lucky to have you and Lew as friends."

"Anyhow, Lew's been working on some ideas and would like to run them by you."

"Yeah. He probably wants me to get back to work—get my mind off of..."

"Well, Honey, how about giving it a shot."

"You think I'm feeling sorry for myself, don't you?"

"You want the truth? After over two months, yes."

"What's on his mind?"

"I'm sure you're aware that Lew has been thinking of opening a new division—a line of younger teen fashions, from twelve to twenty-two."

"Teens only go up to nineteen, Lily. Remember?"

"Stop nitpicking. Age is not important nowadays. Every generation loses three years. You know what the kids are into at ten, eleven and so on."

"Yeah, the ages we call 'tweens.' So where do I come in?"

"You could head it. Some of the outfits you put together are insane. And you know the designer, Matt? Lew says he's a natural to run it with you." Pleased with momentarily distracting Franny from Nick, Lily said, "I think it would work for you and for Nick, too."

"Well, I have to hand it to you, pal. You have piqued my interest. Except, Lily, my dearest closest friend in the whole world, there's just one little problem."

"And what might that be?"

"I'm pregnant."

CHAPTER 3

The muffled voices of the nurses' conversation in the corridor did not faze Franny in the least as she sat on the hospital bed, leaned over, kissed Nick on his forehead and took his unresponsive hand in hers. Not taking her eyes from his, she caressed his fingers and spoke to the nurse. "Annie, how about giving us a little private time."

"Sure thing. I could use another cup of coffee. Only had four since this morning. Can I get you a mocha latte and a sandwich? I'm going across the street to Starbucks. The stuff they have in the vending machines is ersatz and the cafeteria coffee is even worse. Gives me diarrhea. I'll knock when I get back."

The shake of Franny's head and the wave of her hand was her answer. She stared into Nick's fixed blue eyes, his expression one of blank, cold steel causing Franny's breath to catch in her throat. Then for several minutes there was no sound from inside or outside the room except for the sound of the respirator's squish, squash, squish, squash, echoing in

Franny's ears. Tears splashed from her eyes onto Nick's extended arm.

Inhaling deeply, she let the air out of her lungs with a slow, agonizing sigh. "C'mon baby. Talk to me. I know you can hear me. I can feel it. Did your finger just twitch? Squeeze my hand, blink your eyes—give me a sign. Please, Nick, just one sign, one little movement."

But there was no reaction from Nick. Frustration ran through Franny's being. Not one to have patience in the best of times, she lifted her sweater and held his hand to her breast. "Here," she said. "Squeeze it—you love that. You always said you were a tit man." She raised her voice. "Go ahead! I dare you! I double dare you! I triple dare you! I …"

Overcome with grief, Franny placed Nick's hand down at his side, adjusted her sweater, covered her face with her hands and sobbed.

Her ears were deaf to the repeated rapping at the door. "I'm coming in, Franny," the nurse called.

Franny raised her head and dabbed at her eyes with a tissue.

"You've got visitors," the nurse said, as in walked Clancy, Nick's former sidekick in homicide, followed by Oscar Greene, Nick's NARC partner. Without hesitation, Franny sprang up, embraced Clancy and waved hi to Oscar.

Holding her tightly to him, Clancy, his voice hoarse, his sorrow showing in his eyes, asked, "How you holding up?"

She blew her nose then shrugged. "The same as when you asked me the other day and the day before that. Want to say hello to Nick?"

Clancy leaned over Nick's body and smiled. Jokingly, he said, "Is that the way to greet your pal? It took me an hour to get through the traffic even with the siren blasting, and that's all you have to say to me?" He turned toward Franny. "Have to teach that husband of yours some manners."

Oscar walked closer and pecked Franny on her cheek. She surmised that he had something to say. "If you're afraid to talk in front of Nick, don't be. We have no secrets. Who knows, he may just surprise us and tell us how to get those sons of bitches that did this to him." She handed the flowers Oscar brought to the nurse. "Thanks, Annie," she said. Facing the men, she asked, "Anything going down, guys?"

Clancy grimaced. "Nothing concrete yet, but we're getting closer." He had been working with Clancy on off-hours trying to get a line on the man who shot Nick.

Franny saw red. "That's what you said last time, Ossie. What the fuck is wrong with you guys?" She looked at Nick then turned to the men and shouted, "For God's sake, if it were your kin you'd already have the fuckers who did this behind bars. What have you been doing all day, playing with yourselves?"

Clancy moved towards her. "Franny…"

She stopped, half smiled and shook her head. "I'm sorry, guys. I didn't mean it. I know how you care about Nick. It's been such a strain. I just lost it. I can't get used to seeing Nick lying there so helpless."

Conscious of Franny's grief, Clancy shifted uncomfortably from one foot to the other, his eyes taking in Franny's messy pinned-up hair to the bedroom slippers she wore. "Gotta make tracks, Franny," he said." He nudged Oscar. "I'll give you a ride downtown; wanna talk to you about a couple of ideas I've been knocking around." They pecked Franny on the cheek, said, "See ya, big guy," to Nick and with hunched shoulders shuffled to the door.

If there had been a faint ray of hope in Franny's eyes it now dimmed and flickered out as she watched Clancy's and Oscar's forlorn demeanor as they left the room.

Her face scrunched up, her hair in disarray, the little makeup she had applied without care now smeared onto the dark circles under her eyes gave her a ghostly façade as she caught a glimpse of her face in the wall mirror. Taken aback by the grotesque person she saw, she ran to Nick's side. Her rage boiled over and she screamed. "It's not fair! It's not fucking fair! What am I going to do with a baby? I can't even take care of myself!"

CHAPTER 4

Matthew Carpenter partially opened Lew's office door and poked his head in. "Got a minute, boss? I'd like you to okay some changes I've made to the new spring line." Without waiting for an invitation, he shouldered the door open, walked briskly to the tufted, upholstered lounge chair and plopped down. He brushed back hair that fell over one eye, slumped in the chair, his long legs spread-out haphazardly in front of him.

Lew set the phone in its cradle and shook his head. "Make yourself at home, Matt. If it's okay with you, Mr. Hotshot, I could move into your office and you could take this one over. And sit up straight, will ya?"

Matthew pulled himself up. "No thanks, boss," he said indifferently. "I'm happy with the view in mine. I don't need an office you can land a plane in. And I don't think I'd enjoy taking on the responsibility of running the show—too much pressure—not enough play time. And besides, you're doing a good job." He chuckled at his own compliment.

"I'm so happy you approve," Lew countered. "Let's see what's so earth shattering. You know I hate changing anything at the last minute. It's bad karma."

Matthew's wide grin and warm, blue eyes belied his sarcastic wit. He owed his success to Lew and, although he constantly teased him, he respected and worshipped his boss as a son would a father. It was Lew who discovered Matthew at a competition for the best designer of the year at New York's Fashion Institute of Technology, and although he was not a finalist, Lew recognized the raw talent and flair for design Matthew had exhibited.

At that time, shortly after losing his daughters to a drunk driver, Lew realized his paternal instincts had surfaced, and he decided to take the fledgling designer under his wing.

"Karma, shmarma," Matthew said. "You're the one who changes styles at the last minute."

Annoyed, Lew raised his Mont Blanc fountain pen and pointed it at Matthew. "Listen, you little shit, if it weren't for me you'd still be emptying the trash and drawing decals for Hallmark. Your mouth is getting bigger than Franny's, and that takes some doing." The minute the words had left Lew's mouth he wished he could take them back.

The pen fell from Lew's fingers and his eyes dropped to the scattered papers on his desk. Feeling remorse for Franny, he thought *not nice, Lew—that was not nice.*

Matthew stood. He knew of Franny's close friendship with Lew's late wife Elaine, and his current wife, Lily, and he felt Lew's pain. "We can do this later," he said apologetically. "I still have to clean up the sketches."

"We'll do it now, Matt! Never put off..."

"...till tomorrow what you can do today," Matthew finished. Ignoring the chill in Lew's voice, he picked up the portfolio of sketches, walked around to Lew's side and spread them on the desk. *He's playing boss,* he thought as he tapped his foot, impatiently awaiting Lew's approval. "Well?" he asked. "There can't be that many corrections."

Frustrated by Matthew's cockiness, Lew rose from his armchair, looked down at Matthew's tasseled Gucci loafer and stepped down hard on the toe of his shoe. Matthew gritted his teeth but would not give Lew the satisfaction of uttering a sound. When Lew removed his foot from Matthew's shoe, he snarled and said, "Ya know, kid, sometimes your smart remarks are out of line."

Matthew walked back to the upholstered chair, sank into it and sulked. He removed his loafer and massaged his bruised big toe. Slipping into his loafer, he limped to the window, gazed down onto Broadway and watched the lunch crowd queue up at Sabrett's. The hotdog vendor stuck a fork into the boiling water, plucked out a hotdog, laid it on a bun, slapped mustard and sauerkraut on it, and handed it to the next hungry customer.

Once again, his hair fell over his eye and he instinctively brushed it away. Turning to Lew, he said, "You didn't have to do that, ya know. I paid big bucks for the loafers."

Lew scoffed. "You'll survive, kid. Just wanted to make a point. It's your ego that's bruised, not your foot." Scanning the sketches on his desk, Lew silently nodded, noted a few changes and closed the revised drawings. *Well done. The kid's got talent. Real talent. Just have to knock some of the attitude out of him.*

Pointing to the tufted armchair, Lew motioned to Matthew. "Sit, Matt. I have something I want to discuss with you." He pulled a chair alongside Matthew and sat down. "Put your listening ears on and pay close attention. Here's the deal. Are you man enough to put your trust in me and carry out my instructions, no matter what it is that I ask you to do?"

Matthew was taken aback.

Lew's mouth tightened as he locked eyes with Matthew. Then he continued. "It will be well worth your while, I assure you."

Lew stood, walked to his desk, removed a Corona from his humidor, nicked the tip off with a clipper, lit it, and blew a perfect circle of smoke in Matthew's direction. Raising one brow, a chill in his voice, he stated, "You will have thirty seconds to give me your answer. If it's negative, you have my word that nothing will change as far as your position with the company goes." The armchair gave out a groan as Lew settled into it. "Here's the deal, Matt." He carefully explained his proposal.

Lew puffed on his Corona while studying Matthew's puzzled expression and then cast his eyes on his watch. "Okay, Hotshot, time's up. I know you have the chutzpah, now let's see if you've got the balls to back it up."

CHAPTER 5

Why *shouldn't I go along with Lew's proposition? Will I ever get another chance to make such easy money?*

Those questions revolved in Matthew's brain as he closed the door of his office and headed for the elevator. *It's not like I'm doing anything wrong. It's just a matter of the way you look at it—your point of view.*

The taxi stopped a few feet short of spraying Matthew from the puddles that covered the rain-laden street.

"Sorry, Mista," the cabdriver bellowed. "Da windshield wipers ain't woikin' so good." Matthew closed his umbrella, threw his portfolio onto the seat of the cab and ducked in. The cabby continued. "I've been busier than a one-armed paper hanga."

After shutting the door, Matthew removed a tissue from his raincoat pocket and wiped the portfolio that held the sketches on which he planned to work that evening. He had intended to finish up at the office, but after his conversation with Lew, he changed his mind.

"Columbia Presbyterian Hospital," he called to the driver. *Only fitting to pay my respects to Franny. Should have done it before this.*

At the flower shop in the hospital, the clerk, a woman with Betty Boop eyes and short frizzy hair, ogled Matthew. Resting both hands on the counter, she leaned forward to accentuate her cleavage, gulped down her gum, approached him and flashed her pearly whites. "Good evening," she purred. "How may I help you?"

Matthew swallowed a smirk. "I was thinking of something special. Something that has all four seasons in one bouquet."

She walked around the counter to Matthew and took hold of his arm. "If you'll come this way," she said, "I think I can arrange to give you just what you're looking for."

Unable to shake her arm loose with his hands holding the umbrella and portfolio, he deliberately dropped the umbrella. "This is a special occasion, my first wedding anniversary."

Her mouth immediately soured, and disappointment crossed her face as she retrieved the umbrella and handed it to him. Pointing to an array of flowers, she regrouped. "Here they are, all four seasons. Daisies, chrysanthemums, lilies, roses and harvest wheat. What do you think?"

"Outstanding," he answered.

In the elevator on the way to Nick's room, Matthew thought about Lew's proposal; visions of Ferraris, Lamborghinis, Maseratis and Lotus Esprits whirled around his brain.

The nurse answered Matthew's light tap, stepped out and closed the door behind her. "I'm sorry," she said, "but Mr. Pagliara is not receiving visitors at the moment. Are you a relative?"

Matthew balanced the portfolio against his leg as the umbrella hooked on his arm swung precariously. "No, I work with Mrs. Pagliara." He thought. *This calls for a bit of diplomacy.* "Can you at least tell me how he's doing? Everyone at the office is concerned for Franny, uh, his wife. I understand she is taking his condition quite hard, and I thought perhaps I could be of some help and cheer her up a little." His tone made it sound like a request. "You must have your hands full with taking care of Mr. Pagliara, and I'm sure your heart goes out to his wife." Smiling brightly at the nurse, he rubbed a finger across his brow. "Franny and I have had a good working relationship, so I thought if I could see her perhaps I could distract her from her sorrow."

Folding her arms in thought, the nurse stared out, unseeing. *Well I'll be. This gentleman could be a good messenger. He's got the gift of gab and the poor woman has been grieving non-stop.* Her lips relaxed as she took the flowers from his hand, motioned for him to wait, headed for the door, and then sharply turned on her heels. "What is your name, Sir?"

A smile of satisfaction crossed Matt's face. He could barely stifle his grin. "Matt," he said, confident things were going just as he had planned.

CHAPTER 6

Franny sensed Matthew's presence as he neared. With a slight sign of recognition, she glanced up at him, heaved a sigh, and then looked back down at Nick. "Matt?" she mumbled.

The barrette that kept her hair from falling over her eyes fell to the floor as she attempted to brush it back.

After arranging the flowers in a vase, the nurse placed them on the nightstand. "Aren't they just beautiful?" she commented. "I'll be outside if you need me." She eyed Franny. "Is that all right?" Franny waved a goodbye and the nurse left, closing the door noiselessly behind her.

The dark circles under Franny's eyes and her disheveled appearance surprised Matthew, but he said nothing. In the showroom she always flitted around, never stood in one position or place for more than a minute. Her energetic, vivacious, high-spirited personality, brash sense of humor and good looks captivated her co-workers and rendered her irresistible to the buyers.

Matthew remembered how Lew often remarked that he was unsure if the buyers bought the line because of the salability of the product or because of Franny's persona. To see her in a state of disarray caused him concern, but only for the moment.

With a ghost of a smile, Franny forced her eyes from Nick and cast a half-weary glance at Matthew. "Thanks for coming, Matt, but I'm in no mood to socialize. I'm a fucking mess."

Shoulders hunched, eyebrows furrowed, he met her gaze. "Understandable," he said. "My dad died one year ago on this very date." His frown deepened as he forced tears to cloud his eyes. Not waiting for an invitation, he pulled a chair next to hers. "You know, Franny, I would give anything to have him back, even..." He glanced over at Nick and then back at Franny, "...even if he were in a coma. At least there's a chance Nick will recover." He cast his eyes down at the floor. "Dad is gone and I'll never see..." he muttered, his words fading away.

Franny straightened in her chair. She had grasped the reality of Matthew's words. For one instant she looked apprehensive. Then compassion overcame her. "I guess I'm not the only one that's feeling heartache," she said.

He inclined his body closer to hers. "It's twice as hard doing it alone, Franny." He stood, walked over to Nick, and stared down at his unconscious form. "You're going to make it, Nick," Matthew said. "You have to—Franny's depending on you."

Neither Lily her best friend, or Lily's husband Lew could divert Franny from languishing over Nick's condition; but Matthew's unexpected sympathetic visit set off a twinge of release within Franny.

With a tender smile, Matthew focused on Franny and cocked his head boyishly to one side. "You're not helping Nick or yourself by being so inconsolable. The nurse mentioned you never eat and God knows what else. Do you think Nick would want to see you carrying on like you are?"

He held out his hand to her. "Get up! Let's take a walk, or get something to eat." His tone made it sound like an order. "If you won't do it for you, at least do it for him." He spread his arms out to her.

Momentarily sidetracked from her present problems, Franny took hold of his hand and looked up at him. "Give me a minute to pull myself together."

CHAPTER 7

Franny stared vacantly out of Matt's Mitsubishi Eclipse at the neon sign that flashed *Mel's Diner, Open 24 hours*. Looking around the automobile, the restaurant and then Matt, she wondered how and why she had left Nick's bedside. "Take me back to the hospital, Matt," she urged.

"Sure," he said. "If that's what you want, but it wouldn't be a bad idea if we ordered something for you to take out." He opened the window and let in the tantalizing aroma of hamburgers and grilled onions. He took a deep breath and exhaled noisily. "Mmm, mmm. Breathe in that delicious smell, Franny. Now don't tell me that doesn't make your mouth water."

Franny shut her eyes tight. "Makes me want to throw up."

His down-turned mouth showed disapproval.

"Okay, okay," she said. "Do whatever you want. I'll wait in the car."

He paused.

She raised her voice. "Go already!"

He shook his head. "Come with me."

She met his gaze. "Look, Matt, you got me out of the hospital. For that I thank you. But I'm not going to sit in a restaurant and enjoy a meal when Nick is lying there comatose." Her face softened. "I know that you're trying to get my mind off of things, but it's not going to work." She sighed. "In fact, I don't know what is going to work for me."

He returned her gaze, exited the car, walked around to her side and rested his elbows on the open window. "I know what would work for you."

Wrinkling her nose, she scoffed, "Now, you're not only a designer but a shrink too? Okay, so tell me, smartass. What's your prognosis?"

Suppressing a grin, Matt blurted, "I could take you to my place and give you the fuck of your life!"

Shocked and momentarily distracted by Matt's sudden outburst, Franny froze. The aroma of hamburgers and fried onions rings that hovered over Mel's Diner suddenly became more appealing than before, and once again her better judgment was put on the back burner.

Matt sang along with Elvis Presley's rendition of "You ain't nothin but a hound dog," that blasted from the loudspeaker's amplifiers outside the diner. He held fast to Franny's arm as he escorted her up the steps and steered her into the entryway, fearful that she might unexpectedly have a change of heart.

Home to its many regulars, Mel's Diner was decorated in a sixties' motif. It sported a jukebox full of golden oldies on each table that played nonstop. Mel's, famous for home cooked, three-course meals that fit a workingman's pocketbook, was considered the most popular eatery in the downtown neighborhood.

The overhead faux Tiffany shade cast a shadow across Franny's pale face as she settled uneasily into the glossy, red leatherette booth. Women servers, identified by names like Flossie, Mamie, Bertha, Dora and Kay, none under sixty, stood behind a stainless steel counter, pencils wedged in their hair, taking orders from customers who sat on vinyl swivel stools.

Restless, Franny looked down at the chrome-trimmed, multi-color flecked Formica table, and then up at Matt's anxious face.

He resisted the temptation to reach across the table and take her hands in his. *Rushing things was counterproductive and would not help him achieve his goal,* he thought. His relationship with her in the showroom had been cordial at most, and although he thought of bedding her, Lew had laid down strict orders about employees socializing in or out of the office, and Matt knew Lew would not hesitate to fire anyone on the spot if he got wind of anything untoward.

Matt toyed with his fork. "This is one of my favorite places to go when my head is jammed up." He waited to see her reaction; when she didn't speak, he continued. "Before Dad passed away we used to come here. Just being here grounds me."

She inclined her head and for one instant looked intrigued. Sensing her interest, he decided to take advantage of the situation and changed to a more upbeat topic. "The world is a sad enough place, Franny. Can I ask you something personal?"

She couldn't quite stifle an impish grin. "'Taking me to your place and giving me the fuck of my life' isn't personal?"

She's opening up, he thought. "You know I only said that to shake you up." His mouth formed a half smile. "I wanted to ask if you would consider helping me with a project Lew asked me to undertake."

"So you don't want to take me to your place and fuck?" Her shoulder hunched and she sighed teasingly. "What a bummer."

As he thought that he had broken the ice, the corners of his eyes crinkled up. "We both know Lew's rules, Franny. Without them to hold me back, I'd bed you in a blink of an eye."

"Funny, Matt, no offense, but for the longest time I thought that you might be gay."

"Yeah. Since I can remember, I've been fighting one bully after another. Becoming a designer only made it worse. After I came home a few times with bruises, Dad got disgusted and had me enrolled in Karate classes. Have to tell you, Franny, that changed my life!"

She brushed aside a lock of hair that had fallen onto her lashes. "Being good looking didn't help either, I bet."

"You got that right."

Franny felt some of her tension dissipate as she listened to Matt's problems. *His life hasn't been as trouble-free as I once assumed*, she thought.

The waitress approached and nodded at Matt. "What can I get you guys? If you're hungry I suggest the meatloaf. Nothing like it from here to eternity." She winked at Franny. "Ask Casanova, he's had it. Comes with a green salad and garlic-mashed potatoes...to die for. No substitutions. Sorry about that."

"Do you like meatloaf, Franny?" Matt asked.

"Yeah, but I'm not really hungry. You eat, I'll watch."

Matt picked up the menus and handed them to the waitress. "Flossie, we'll have two orders of the meat loaf, hold the bread and butter, and two Amstel Light. And extra ketchup, please."

Franny eyed him. "Pretty sure of yourself, aren't you?"

He settled in his chair, casually flipped through the jukebox music selection, then folded his arms across his chest and looked thoughtfully at her. "I've watched you in the showroom, Franny. You're a dynamo. The way you handle the buyers is so cool."

"Tell me something I don't know."

"It's more than that. I caught you and Lew going over some sketches I had submitted."

Her lips twisted wryly. "Feel threatened, Matt? Just because I'm tops in sales at the place doesn't mean I don't have an eye for designing."

"Threatened? Not in the least."

"You're so full of shit. You designers are the bitchiest phonies in the marketplace." Noting his offended look, she added, "So, what's your point?"

"Can I tell it like it is?"

"Sure. I can always tell you to fuck off."

He broke into a grin. "That's what I love about you, Franny. What's on your mind is on your tongue." He threw his shoulders back. "You asked me what the point is and I'm going to tell you." The moment Matt started to speak his cell phone rang. His expression toward Franny was one of May I?

She nodded.

"Hello," he answered.

"I'm Lily, Franny's friend. Is she there?"

"Sure thing. Hold on." He held the phone out to Franny." It's your girlfriend."

"What's up?" Franny said.

Lily's voice sounded uneasy. "Are you all right? I was at the hospital and the nurse said you left with a man. What's going on? I haven't heard from you all day."

"I'm okay. How did you know to call me on Matt's phone?"

"Lew told me Matt was going to visit Nick. I figured he was the man the nurse said you left with, and Lew, of course, has Matt's number. Really, Franny. You promised you'd keep in touch. You know how I worry about you."

"I know, Lily. I'm sorry. Matt schlepped me to Mel's Diner and is force-feeding me."

"Good, as long as you're okay. I have to rehearse for the San Francisco concert. I hate leaving you," she said, feeling relieved that at least Franny was not crying at Nick's bedside.

"I'm fine. I'm fine. Stop carrying on. Go practice. Love ya. Later."

Handing the phone back to Matt, she said, "She's the best."

"You're lucky. A true friend is hard to come by."

"You were saying…" Franny had started to say as the waitress set the dinners in front of them.

"You were lucky. You got the last two servings. Can I get you anything else?"

"Looks real good," Matt said, as he took the fork and knife into his hands. "No, thanks." He eyed Franny, stared at her utensils and waited for her to pick them up. "Now, be a good girl and eat your din din."

"Or else you'll hit me with a wire hanger?" She forked a portion of the meatloaf and held it up to him. "See?" she teased. "I'm going to make all gone."

Surprised but pleased that he caught a glimpse of the old Franny starting to emerge, he felt the time was right for him to present his proposal. "I think you are going to like what I have to tell you."

"I'm all ears. Shoot." She munched on a small forkful of the garlic-mashed potatoes.

"You are aware that Lew has asked me to design a…what one might call, an up-to-date, cool, hip young mother-to-be line."

"You thinking of giving 'Peas in a Pod' a run for their money?"

"Why not? That's where you come in. You're trendy, actually off the wall when it comes to fashion and…"

"I get it. And since you heard through the grapevine that I'm going to be blessed with a newborn, and since Lily must have talked to Lew, and Lew must have talked to you, you are now trying to get my mind off Nick."

"Okay, so even if you're partially right, what's so bad about the idea? You're a natural. And what's more, you'd be more than just a salesperson;

you'd be the merchandiser and I'd be the designer. We'd be a team. I tell ya, Franny, the more I think about it the more excited I get. And Lew has given his approval." He placed his fork on his plate and stared seriously at her. "There's another thing to consider, Franny. I'm a bit OCD about placing eating utensils on a table. I see how it's cleaned and don't want my fork to rest on it for a second."

"I'm listening."

The words rolled off his tongue as he spoke. "Money! And I mean M-O-N-E-Y. Sooner or later you're going to have to face the facts. No one knows if or when Nick will come to. We, of course, pray that he will come out of the coma. There's going to be a lot to deal with ahead. Think of the future. At least you'll be prepared. You'll be accumulating a nest egg for when he does come back."

She pushed her plate away from her, stood, and placed her napkin on the table. "You're coming at me pretty fast. My head's jammed. Let's get out of here."

"Want me to drive you back to the hospital?"

"Not yet," Franny answered. "How about we take a walk?"

The dim streetlights gave little protection to the couple as they walked silently out of Mel's Diner and away from its *Open 24 Hours* flashing neon sign. From the shadows of an alley adjacent to a boarded-up building, two men—one in a black hooded sweat suit, the other sporting a knitted, woolen cap—stealthily approached Franny and Matt.

The crackling of broken dried twigs alerted the couple to impending danger. Then another sound, a whirring hum came from the clutched hand of the assailant with the knitted cap. He sneered, as he whipped a link chain wildly in the air. Franny, barely able to draw a breath, smothered a scream, as the second man in the sweat suit moved behind her, thrust his arm across her neck, and brandished a knife to her throat.

The cold steel of the knife's blade pricked her skin, sending a shuddering reaction through her body. Her first impulse was to cry out for Nick, but the thought quickly faded. The glint of the whirling chain circling over Matt's head caught her eye. Franny gasped and panicked. *This isn't happening,* she thought.

The chain wielder's hood fell backward, exposing a swastika tattooed on his shaven head. Still whirling the chain, he snarled. "Money. We want your money!"

The assailant spoke with a Jamaican accent. "Dontcha be playing wid me, mahn. Me hands is bery itchy." He reached down with his other hand and cupped Franny's breast. The space between his teeth shown large as he spoke. "Do id now or I mess up your liddle coochi lady."

Matt's adrenalin kicked in. The old urge to protect himself from bullies that had plagued him all his life took over. Eyes filled with anger and face taut with intent, he crouched, swung around, kicked the legs out from under the chain wielder, and chopped him in the throat.

Taken by surprise, the choking offender reeled backwards, but before he could hit the ground Matt swiftly swung around and kicked the man squarely in the face. Loose teeth dangled from the man's mouth and blood oozed onto the skinhead's tattooed swastika, his eyes staring lifelessly into oblivion.

Franny, taking advantage of Matt's actions, caught the knife wielder off guard and elbowed him in the ribs. The knife fell from the man's hand. She moved out of Matt's way. Matt began a karate dance, turned swiftly, spun around, and caught the man above the ear with a kick.

Not fully satisfied, Franny proceeded to knee him in the groin. All her moral compassion for mankind vanished. She bent down, picked up the Jamaican's knife, gripped it tightly and then tilted her head at Matt. "How about I finish off the cocksucker? I'm on a roll."

CHAPTER 8

4 *:00 AM*. The numbers on Franny's digital clock radio appeared huge to her fully awakened eyes. She sat in bed, her hair tousled, a pillow clutched between her knees and chest, and rocked back and forth. The confusion within her mind was so intense she felt that her throbbing head, at any moment, was going to detach from her neck and spin into outer space.

She thought, *This fucking brain of mine is out of control.* The television droned on but she was oblivious to both the picture and the sound. Unsettled guilt feelings about Nick and desire for Matt fought each other within her mind.

She tossed the pillow onto the floor. "Lily! I'll call Lily!"

Upon hearing the telephone ring, Lew covered his ears with his hands and nudged Lily with his rear end. "Honey bun," he yawned, "Phone's ringing."

Rolling over, she replied groggily. "So pick it up."

"It's your phone. It's on your side."

One eye opened grudgingly. She read the time on the nightstand clock and panicked. "4:15 AM!"

Throwing the covers off of her and Lew, she leaped out of bed and grabbed at the phone. Recognizing Franny's number on the caller ID, she shouted, "Franny! What's wrong?"

"I can't sleep."

"It's 4:15 in the morning."

Franny eyed the clock. "Yeah, I've been staring at the clock all night and into the morning and I still have no idea what time it is. That's funny."

"Funny? I'm not following you. I'm getting dressed. I'll be there in ten minutes."

"Hold it! I want to talk."

Lily stepped into her bedroom slippers. "Can't we talk when I get to your place?"

Franny eyed the clock. "No! Didn't you fucking hear me? I want to talk now!"

"Franny, have you been drinking?" Turning on the lamp, she placed the phone on the night table. "Hold on a sec."

Squinting at the lamp's light with a wary eye, Lew growled, "Lily, do me a favor and take it someplace else, will you?"

Lily tied the sash of her robe around her waist, whacked Lew on his behind, turned the light off, picked up the phone and walked into the living room.

Lew pulled the covers back over his head and settled into a comfortable position, wondering if Matt had made any progress with Franny. Then he drifted off.

Cell phone in hand, Lily listened to Franny's ranting. The front door slammed shut as Lily hastily exited.

Lew stirred. "Crazy broads."

Franny attempted to distract herself. Since speaking to Lily, she loaded the laundry into the washing machine, lightly vacuumed, and was about to take out the trash. She tried removing both Nick and Matt from her thoughts but to no avail. The guilt of deceiving Nick and the feelings she had for Matt jammed her head.

The doorbell buzzed.

Franny swung the door open. "Well!" she huffed. "What took you so long? Did you stop to get laid on the way?"

"Get a grip, Franny. You wanted a Starbuck's macchiato and biscotti. I had to wait until they opened, then I had to stand in lines. It's busy this early in the morning. I also got myself a bagel and cream cheese."

Franny's mouth twitched to one side. "I could go for a bagel and cream cheese too, ya know."

Food in hand, Lily stood in the kitchen doorway watching her friend mouth off and was struck by a sense of loss. *Handling Franny's sudden emotional flare-ups has always been a problem,* she thought. *When Elaine was alive, at least I had someone to soak up the outbursts, but now there's only Lew, and it's just not the same. How can I help her? Nick in the hospital; she's pregnant...and now, her sudden involvement with Matt...* She sighed. *It's not like I'm dealing with a norm...*

Franny interrupted Lily's thoughts. "You gonna just sit there and stare at me like I'm standing on the ledge?" She took a sip of her coffee. "Boy, this will wake up the devil! And, I'll take half of your cream cheese and bagel. I hope it's toasted. You never finish it anyhow. Always watching your weight. What's with the graveyard looks?"

"I'm just waiting for you to get it all out. I've got all day." She brushed the crumbs of sesame seeds into a cluster, licked her index finger, dabbed at the fallen sesame seeds and put them on her tongue.

"If I had done that," Franny scowled, "you would have surely called me on it."

"What's with the drawn shades?" Lily asked. "And why only one light lit in the entire apartment? It's still dark outside." She walked to the light switch.

"Don't!" Franny cried. "I look like hell."

Lily rolled her eyes. "You have to be kidding. I've seen you at your best and your worst."

"All right, all right, you have," Franny acknowledged. "I don't know what to do. The fucking walls are closing in on me." She pushed the food aside, put her elbows on the table, placed her hands on her face and sobbed.

"That's good," Lily said. "Cry it out; then we'll talk."

"I'm all cried out. There's nothing left. Nick's not showing any signs of coming out of the coma, and to make things worse I think I'm becoming attached to Matt." She shook her head. "I don't know, Lily, last night I was so into Matt, for a while I almost forgot about Nick. I feel so guilty…"

Lily stood and put her arms around Franny. "You're not going to give up on Nick. You're confused."

"It's not only Nick and Matt, Lily." Her eyes darted around the room as she thought of a dignified way to soften what she wanted to say. "I can hardly cope with life now, much less raise a kid. I don't think I want to have the baby."

"You're not thinking rationally. As soon as things fall into place you'll feel differently. You have me and Lew, and we'll make sure you and the baby are taken care of." She went to the sink, soaked a towel in cool water, and walked back to Franny. "Here, this will relax you." Franny tilted her face up to Lily. Lily brushed back the hair that masked Franny's face. Startled to see Franny's bruised cheek, dark eyes and scratches, she stepped back to catch her breath. "What the hell happened to you?"

Franny's expression changed to one of enthusiasm. "Matt and I were attacked by a couple of hoodlums last night and man oh man, did we lay them out."

Lily's eyes widened. "Don't tell me that you and Matt are the two victims of the assailants that we saw on the TV news last night? Oh my God. Are you aware that the police are asking anyone who has any information to contact them?"

Franny smiled. "I wouldn't exactly call us victims. Matt is a black belt or something like that in karate. And if I may say, I did a pretty good job on one of them myself."

Lily collapsed onto the couch. "Let me catch my breath. Are you telling me that you fought one of the men?"

Puffed up with her own power, Franny strutted around the couch. "Yep! Elbowed him in the ribs and after Matt kicked the legs out from under him and the fucker hit the ground, I planted my platforms in his balls." She grinned. "Yeah! Have to check my shoes. I want to keep them as souvenirs; maybe they have some of the bastard's blood on them. Did they show any pictures on the news?"

Lily inhaled deeply and let out a long, wistful sigh. "I wouldn't take this too lightly, kiddo. They were both in bad shape. One of the men that the medics carried on a stretcher to the ambulance, the announcer said, might be dead."

"Must be the one I put down," Franny said.

Lily shook her head in disbelief at Franny's careless attitude. "Franny, you and Matt should go to the police and report what happened. If one of them survives they might identify you and Matt. True, you both were innocent victims and had to defend yourselves, but why take chances?"

She sat on the couch, sucked in her lower lip and focused intently on her hands, trying to figure out a response. "If Nick were here he'd know what to do. Jesus, Lily, I got so used to having him take charge of everything."

"Truth be told, Franny, if Nick were here you wouldn't have gotten so chummy with Matt and you wouldn't have run into those hoodlums. You'd be in the showroom schmoozing the buyers, and more important, you would be thrilled to have the baby. But, unfortunately, it is what it is. Why don't you call Clancy, Nick's old sidekick? He'll know what to do."

"Crazy world, isn't it? I'd have thought there was enough shit thrown at me in my life. Like my mother used to say, 'When is it going to be my time to live?'" Franny stood and walked into the kitchen. "Yeah, I could call Clancy. I'm going to get a beer. How about a soda, or some of that raspberry diet iced tea you like?"

If I ever needed a drink, it's now, Lily thought. She took a deep breath and followed Franny with her eyes taking in her every movement, wishing she wasn't so damn impulsive. "Iced tea works for me. Easy on the ice cubes. Have to stay strong."

Franny called from the kitchen. "Talk about staying strong. When I think of Elaine giving me her eyes so that I could see again—wow, that took courage. And you, Lily—have to hand it to you. Since Elaine passed, you haven't had a drop."

Lily blinked back tears, trying to wipe away the vision of Elaine's crippled fingers, and remembering how close the three of them had been. "Nope, not a drop. You're right when you said it's a crazy world. It took Elaine's death to make me stop drinking. When I think of the bottles I had to dispose of…"

"…And the money you must be saving," Franny cut in, as she handed Lily the iced tea. "Look, I even stuck in a straw and added two stuffed olives. I ran out of cherries." She took a deep pull on the bottle of beer and sat down next to Lily. "I can't think! The shit's hit the fan all at one time. Tell me what to do."

Lily moved her head from side to side. "Whoa!" she shot out.

Her brows arched in surprise, Franny said, "What's with the whoa? Who else is there? You are the only one I can spill my guts to."

Fearful of hurting her friend's feelings, Lily took a sip of her iced tea, set the glass down and faced Franny, aware of the anxiety she conveyed. "Look, Franny. I don't have to tell you that you're like a sister. Let's take it one step at a time. What's your biggest problem?"

"Nick."

"Of course, but we have no control over his condition. What else?"

"I guess going with Matt and my guilt for feeling good with him while Nick is in the hospital."

"You're hedging. Think. What is really making you crazy?"

"Okay, you've got me trapped. The baby." She gave a shudder. "I want it, and I don't want it."

Lily smiled reassuringly. "See, now all you have to do is think of having the baby. You can deal with Matt later on."

"Easy for you to say." You know what my father did to me when I was young." As her anxiety grew she felt hatred and disgust for her father's actions. It sent a cold chill through her. "It still haunts me." She stood and planted both feet solidly on the floor. "I don't care what anybody says, I'm not going to raise a baby by myself!"

"I told you, Franny. Lew and I will be there for you. Even have a twenty-four-hour nurse for the baby. You can go to work. You love the showroom."

Taking Lily's hands, Franny pulled Lily to her feet, drew her close and hugged her. She nestled her face on Lily's shoulder and started to cry. "There's something you have to do for me." She briefly tightened her grip on Lily's arm. "I've been thinking about this for a while, so don't say no right away.

"Tell me, what is it?"

"I want you and Lew to adopt the baby and raise it."

CHAPTER 9

Matt Carpenter never thought of himself as a hip or macho guy, but after having overcome a childhood of being bullied, he set out to show the world he could stand on his own two feet. Blessed with his father's good looks and his mother's charisma and flair for the arts, he discovered opening doors came easily for him.

Lew thought back to the time he had met Matt while attending a competitive design contest at New York's Fashion Institute of Technology. He immediately recognized Matt's flair for fashion and asked him to join his Manhattan design staff. Showing himself to be exceptionally talented, within six months Matt was promoted to head designer of women's sportswear. Although Matt's cockiness and at times obnoxious behavior irked Lew, his designs proved to be exceptionally successful, so Lew overlooked his eccentricities.

Franny, on the other hand took an immediate dislike to the new employee. Complaining to Lew, she said, "I'm not saying the fag isn't gifted, Lew. But does he have to upstage me when I'm presenting the line?"

Lew, acting as employer and mediator, responded. "Franny, I'm surprised at you. You're too smart a lady to let him upset you." He waved a warning finger at her. "And he's *not* gay. So please, cool it with the name-calling. It's beneath you."

Hands defiantly on her hips, she started to answer, but he cut her off. Arms raised, he huffed. "That's it! I'm the boss! I pay your salary! When *you* take over you can run the show like you want. Meanwhile I don't want any goddamn bitchy shenanigans when you two are presenting to the buyers. I hear the little digs you spit at each other. It has to stop! We're a team!" He eyed her. "Am I clear?"

He didn't wait for her answer. Softening his features with a smile, he continued. "Look, Franny. You know I love you. You and Lily and me, we're family. And like family, business arguments over trivial things always come up. What *is* important is the firm. We're on top now and I intend to keep it that way. My job is to steer the business in the right direction. But just as important are people like you and Matt, who keep this ship afloat."

He glanced toward the wall at a picture of the four of them—he and Lily, Franny and Nick. He remembered asking his chauffeur to snap the picture before Nick untied the humongous ribbon Franny had tied around the red convertible Corvette she had surprised Nick with for his birthday—the same day that Nick had been called to go on a drug bust, the same day he had been shot—and since then remained in a coma.

Franny pouted.

"Okay!" Lew conceded. "I'll give in a little if you give in a little. You're one of the best salespersons in the market, and I'm lucky to have you." Beckoning with outstretched hands, he broke into a wide grin. "C'mere, big mouth," he said. "Give us a hug. Let's forget all this nonsense. Okay?"

She scrunched up her nose. Taking criticism was not her strong suit. Reluctantly, she accepted his hug. "Yeah, I guess you're right." She pecked him on his cheek and walked towards the door, then turned on her heels and said, "But the fucking guy…"

Lew ran to the door, swung it open and yelled. "OUT!"

❧

Conscious of keeping his body in tiptop shape, Matt, a metro-sexual and avid cyclist, worked out at Gold's Gym every morning before he left for work. The K-cup was loaded into the Keurig coffeemaker the night before. At six AM he stood at the kitchen counter, poured hazelnut coffee creamer into a mug, watched while the coffee dripped and viewed the news on the flat screen TV.

Clad in his Chrome shorts, Nike sneakers, Under Armour wife-beater, non-sweat T- shirt, he gulped down the java, grabbed hold of a yogurt honey peanut Balance Bar, reached for his Eddy Merckx Track cycle—one of four he had acquired—lifted it off the ceiling rack, and headed for the elevator. Aware of bicycle thieves, he kept his precious bikes in his apartment and cycled to the gym carrying his Polo sweats, Balance Bar and water in a messenger bag.

At the gym he kept his bike in the trainer's office. After exercising he showered and rode the bike downtown to his office where he changed into a Dolce and Gabbana T-shirt and True Religion jeans.

Tessa, Matt's assistant designer, knocked, peeked in, and then flung the door open, just as Matt zipped up his fly. Disappointed that she missed the opportunity to catch him with his shorts down, she revealed, "You'll never guess who just went into Lew's office."

Knowing full well it was Franny, he hissed, "Tessa, we've got a shit load of work to get done today. Let's get started before Lew starts his Monday morning rant." He threw her an annoying look. "And I'm not in the mood for guessing games."

Tessa, smitten with Matt, walked to where his shoes lay, picked them up and walked back to where he stood. Holding them up playfully, she said, "Want these?" Although he was flattered by Tessa's attention, Matt forced himself to keep his eye on the big picture. He was not about to jeopardize his relationship with Lew for a quick piece of ass.

"Okay, Tessa. You can drop the act. What's the hot news?"

Tessa slurred. "Sheeeee's baaack,"

He nodded. "That's a good thing. She's been having a hard time. Nick's in a coma and she had a helluva scare the other night. Getting back to work is the best thing for her."

Taken aback by Matt's sudden defense of Franny, Tessa grinned knowingly. "The whole place is abuzz," she said." Her eyes flashed resentment as she brushed back her blond bangs. "Word is that you and Franny, the karate kids of the garment center, had an encounter with gang bangers. I shouldn't wonder if you and Franny get written up in the next edition of *Women's Wear Daily*."

Having had enough of her brashness, Matt pursed his lips in anger and raised his hand. He pointed an intimidating finger at her, then paused as the door suddenly flew open and Franny, all keyed up, swept in. She waved her hand with an impatient gesture at Tessa. "Take a hike, Tessa. Matt and I have to get this fucking show on the road."

CHAPTER 10

"**W**atch it, lady!" the Hispanic worker yelled at the woman; his rolling rack loaded with garments barely grazed her stiletto heels.

"*You* watch it, asshole," the woman called back at him. "The streets are for walking, not for pushing racks."

"Tell it to my boss, bebé," he countered and steered the garments into the street where a parked truck waited to load the merchandise. He gestured lewdly with his tongue, and then yelled to his sidekick who maneuvered the other end of the rack. "Mamacita, did you see the tits on that one?"

Franny and Matt, walking down Seventh Avenue, overheard the verbal exchange. "Some thing's never change, do they?" she said. "I've got a good mind to tell the fucker off."

"Wouldn't do any good," Matt said. He tugged at her arm. "Let's get moving. We've got a lot of scouting to do. I want to cover Macy's and if there's time, Bergdorf's, Saks and Bloomies. Let's see what they're showing. And I hate to tell you, Franny, but the two men who were pushing the rags—they work for us."

"They won't be if Lew gets wind of their behavior." She pulled at his arm. "Slow down, will ya. We're not running a marathon."

"Four inch heels were not designed for traipsing around the city. I told you to wear sneakers!"

"I know you did."

"So?"

"So I don't like the way you said it. Like you're giving me orders. I don't like taking freaking orders."

He chuckled.

"What's so funny?"

"'Freaking'? Cleaning up our act, are we?"

"Don't be a fucking wise guy," she said, taking hold of his arm to keep up with his brisk pace. She thought: *He seems concerned about me, but is he really concerned or is he playing up to me for some extra-curricular activity?*"

"We'll go to Macy's first," he said. "We can check out Peas in The Pod and Motherhood Maternity. Have to keep abreast of what the competition is showing. We can do the high-end stores later, if there's time, and you're not too tuckered out. Let's stop at New Balance and get you a pair of sneakers."

"I just told you, Matt. Stop giving me orders." But this time her tone was softer and more engaging. "And don't tell me what kind of sneakers to get!" All the while she held tightly to his arm.

At Macy's, Matt searched the racks, held up what he thought were interesting garments and waited for Franny's opinion. Although he had innately more experience than she, Franny was actually their target customer, being young, trendy, and pregnant to boot. With an armful of clothes, he accompanied her to a dressing room, where she hung the clothes on separate hooks and snapped pictures of them while he waited outside schmoozing with the saleslady.

Franny stacked the clothes she wanted to buy in one arm and the discards in another. "I need help here," she shouted. The saleslady quickly entered the dressing room and took the discarded garments that Franny held out to her. "I'll take the ones I'm holding," she said, knowing that the garments were too intricate to be photographed and that the overseas manufacturer would need to see them in order to knock them off.

Matt paid with a company credit card while Franny browsed the infant's layette and nursery departments.

The saleslady smiled at the handsome young man. "Your wife is lucky to have a husband who treats her so well."

Matt signed the slip and picked up the packages. "She's not my wife. She's my daytime lover, and the clothes aren't for either of them. They're for my mistress."

Matt, loaded down with packages, snuck up behind Franny. "Thinking of the baby?" he asked.

Startled by his sudden appearance, she quickly turned toward him. Their noses almost touching, she shouted. "Jesus, Matt! You scared the shit out of me."

"Sorry," he said, swallowing a chuckle.

Flustered at the stirring of unwelcome desire she felt, she turned away. "I'm hungry. Let's eat. Okay?"

She held onto the escalator railing as they ascended to Macy's Bistro. At the top of the escalator, Franny came to an abrupt stop, causing Matt to crash into her. She stumbled and lost her balance as Matt dropped the packages to grab her arm.

"Whoa," he called out. "You all right?"

"Thank you," Franny said, as bystanders helped to retrieve the scattered shopping bags.

Concerned she might be having one of her anxiety attacks, Matt guided Franny off to the side of the escalator and set the packages down.

"And you want to know something else? She said. "I'm thinking very seriously about giving the baby up for adoption. And what's more, I just might have an abortion."

Matt paled. *Shit,* he thought. *There goes my Lamborghini.*

In the restaurant, he held the chair for her as the waiter filled the water glasses. His mind abuzz, he thought, *you dumb bitch, you're not giving the kid up for adoption or aborting it. I'll make sure of that!*

Aware of her high-strung temperament, he feigned a reassuring smile, reached across the table and caressed her arm. "Your mind is working overtime. For now, let's concentrate only on Franny and what makes *her* happy. Let me help you. Working together on the new line is going to be so exciting. You'll be using your talent to do something that *you* created. Just think of the thousands of young mothers who will be wearing the clothes we design."

She lifted her chin and listened intently.

Satisfied that he had her full attention, he paused, looked away, and then back at her. Leaning closer, he said, "I didn't want to tell you this, but Lew has given us *carte blanche* to scout Europe and check out the latest fashions."

Her mouth dropped.

"Think, Franny, Paris, London, Italy's Via Veneto." He licked his lips. "My God, the food in Italy!"

Her eyes lit up and her lips parted slightly. "Us? You mean, me too?"

"Of course you too. We *are* a team."

"Well, fuck me!" she exclaimed.

Pleased with his shrewd insight, he shrugged off thoughts of how he would convince Lew to agree to this unanticipated plan. *Lew is smart,* he thought, *but so am I. The time will pass in the blink of an eye and before she realizes what's happening, it will be too late to abort the baby. And I'll be home free. Yeah!*

CHAPTER 11

Yesterday, she was drowning in her sorrow. Yesterday, all she could think of was Nick—but that was yesterday. Today, a whole new world had opened up to Franny.

Dr. Benjamin Levens, his face expressionless, dragged the hospital chair alongside Franny, who sat on the bed holding Nick's limp fingers. Her head swayed from side to side watching Nick, his eyes wide open, staring into oblivion.

"Oy," the doctor groused as he set the chair down, "my back is killing me." He eyed her. "You look a lot better than last week. I guess you've been taking the Ambien I prescribed?"

"I gave the pills to my cleaning lady. She has trouble sleeping."

He rolled his eyes. *Some things never change.*

"I went back to work, Benny. A lot's been happening."

"Glad to hear it, Francine. Best thing you can do is to keep busy. You know the old saying, a…"

"Cut the shit, Benny. We have to talk."

Dr. Benjamin Birthchild, Franny's family physician for as long as she could remember, was not in the least offended by her eloquent usage of the English language. The Van Dyke he sported was the only remembrance of the old days when he had studied at the Tel Aviv University in Israel and had worn the traditional peyis. His bushy eyebrows almost met over his black eyes as he raised them. "I can see that you're back to normal." He raised both hands with two pointed fingers suggestive of a quotation and teased. "But we won't go into that."

"Huh? Still with the Jack Benny jokes," she quipped. "I think it's time for you to retire, Benny. Didn't you say you and the missus wanted to settle down someplace where it's nice and warm. You must have stashed away more gold ingots than Fort Knox."

Uncertainty flashed through his eyes and once again his bushy eyebrows met. "We've been thinking about it. The years are flying by. I'll be having great grandchildren soon." He pulled at his Van Dyke. "Yes, I think I'm ready. I know Dolores is. And it's hard to keep up with the young doctors."

"Maybe your trouble is that you can't get it hard and you can't keep it up."

He nodded. "You could be right, Francine." Breathing out a long, wistful sigh, he eyed her cautiously. "Francine, you're not by any chance pregnant, are you? Do you need an examination—or maybe some fatherly advice?"

Thinking that Nick might possibly hear their conversation, she motioned with her thumb at the doorway. "You're right on target, Doc. I do need some fatherly advice."

ॐ

Frightened and trapped, Nick listened to their voices—sometimes muffled, sometimes barely audible, sometimes clear. He wanted desperately to let them know he could hear. His brain sent messages to every nerve in his body, but the messages, unable to connect with their source, came back marked *return to sender, mission cancelled.*

The floodgates in his mind opened and closed, allowing only segments of the world above to materialize. The harder he fought to reach them, to tell them he was aware of what was going on, the more the undercurrent dragged him down, the more disheartened he became.

His mind seemed to be imprisoned in an eddy of swirling, tumultuous seawater, sucking him downward, teasing him with a brief moment of lucidity, only to pull him under once again as his brain strained to make contact with the voices from above.

Franny, it's me! What the hell is wrong with you? Why don't you answer? Stop fooling around. This is not the time for your crazy games. It's me! Nick. What's wrong with you? Why can't you hear me? No—stay. Don't go with the doc! Listen to me, Franny! I'll give you the fatherly advice you need. Franny, please! Why don't you answer me?

And there he remained, bewildered and frustrated…waiting… waiting.

CHAPTER 12

Matt held his breath, wondering how Lew would react. When Lew's jaw dropped, his face turned beet red and his eyes bulged in their sockets, Matt knew he was in deep shit. *Oh boy*, he thought, *is he pissed*.

"You what?" Lew growled. "Do you know how much it will cost the company for you two to shop overseas?" Furiously, he threw open the lid of his thermidor, grabbed a Havana, crinkled it between his fingers until the cigar was in shreds, and then flung the pieces into Matt's face. "Stupid! Stupid! Stupid!" he yelled. Hands clasped behind him, he paced back and forth, walked to the window, looked down at Seventh Avenue and reflected.

Matt drew back, mindful that Lew was not upset about the cost of the trip. The merchandisers and designers traveled overseas twice a year and Lew never blinked an eye at the expenditures. "You're right, Boss," Matt, conceded. "I didn't think. But she was so depressed I didn't know what to do. I'm sorry. You're right. I am stupid."

Lew turned and faced Matt. "I'm not saying *you're* stupid. I'm saying *I'm* stupid." The armchair groaned as Lew sank into it. "You're out of control, Mister." He reached for another cigar, clipped the end and lit it.

There was a sudden hush in the room.

Matt waited until he could read Lew's demeanor.

Eventually, Lew's mouth softened, but he said nothing.

Wanting to give the impression that he was contrite, Matt spoke in a gentle voice. "Can I talk to you man-to-man, Boss?"

Lew threw a suspicious glance at Matt and then nodded grudgingly.

"It hasn't been easy living up to our arrangement," Matt offered. "Franny may be hotheaded and at times ditsy, but she's one sharp cookie. I have to be careful." He hesitated. "Can we shelve Franny for the moment?"

Lew uttered, "Ha! That's a laugh."

With his customary determination, Matt spoke. "Hear me out, Boss. I don't have to tell you how important it is to have the jump on our competitors. Especially since we're starting a brand new division. They've been around for years. They already have a solid customer base. I was going to ask you if I could take Franny with me before I blurted it out. Then I thought of the fit she would throw, not to mention the language she would discharge, when she found out she wasn't going overseas."

Lew shrugged. *The kid's over the top,* he thought, *but I tied my own hands.*

Feeling he was winning Lew over, Matt relaxed in his chair. *I'm on a roll,* he thought. *This is going better than I had hoped. Still, the man's nobody's fool. I better watch my step.* Inclining his body closer to Lew, his face thoughtful, he said, "You're upset because you wanted to tell Franny yourself, aren't you? And you're right. You *are* the Boss. I got carried away. I'm really sorry."

Lew nodded.

"I have to tell you, Boss, I've been watching her, and on our sample shopping sprees she surprised the hell out of me. The lady has a natural flair for what the young mother-to-be should be wearing."

Lew stared fixedly at Matt, blew a few perfect circles of smoke into the air and flicked the ashes off the cigar into an oversized ashtray. "Knowing your chutzpah, I suppose you've already planned the trip, purchased the tickets and made the hotel reservations? Should I check with the accounting department? First class all the way, I presume? I do remember your last trip, you know. "He pointed his cigar at Matt. "I'm going to check and double check every damn receipt." He gave Matt a sidelong glance and tapped his fingers on his blotter. After pausing for a moment, he allowed a faint smile to crease his mouth. "Okay, hotshot, where do you plan on going and when?"

Matt stood and walked to the standing world globe that stood in the corner, spun it, and then stopped it on the city of Paris. "Paris," he said, his eyes wide with enthusiasm. "The Prêt a Porter will be starting in three weeks. But first we'll do the New York show at Lincoln Center. Europe should take a solid month. We can do the Far East trip after we get back. We'll meet with our manufacturers in Hong Kong, China, Singapore and Dubai, visit factories, negotiate prices and so on."

Matt's eyes locked with Lew's. "All in all," he continued, "that should take a good two months. By then our mother-to-be will be too wrapped up in work to think of an abortion. He rotated the map slowly to the south of France. "Now, Franny would just flip when…" he started to say, as Franny breezed into the office.

"Is someone using my name in vain?" she asked.

"I was just going to call you," Matt lied. We need your input on the overseas trip. What do you think of starting in London or maybe Paris?"

She cringed. "London? I don't think so. My hair will frizz. They have the worst weather."

Lew swallowed a nervous laugh. *Let them fight it out,* he thought; *they deserve each other.* Watching the pair spar, Lew rose, rolled his eyes, picked up his jacket and slung it over his shoulder. "You have two days to get your itinerary finished," he said. "If I think it's workable, I'll sign off on it, but only after I see what you two mavens have worked out. I'm meeting Lily for lunch at Sardis and, as usual, I'm late. Want me to pick something up on my way back? Looks like you're going to be eating in for a while."

· Matt looked at Franny. "Thanks, Boss," he said. "We'll figure something out."

"I pass a Subway," Lew teased. "I could have my chauffeur stop for a foot-long meatball hero. They can slice it in half and you can share."

Franny grimaced. "Thanks, but no thanks. My boss was kind enough to extend me a company credit card. I'm covered."

Lew called Lily on his cell phone. "What? You're already there?" It's what time? I'm sorry, Lily, we were in a meeting. I'll be there in ten minutes!"

The door closed and Franny spun the globe then suddenly stopped it.

"What?" Matt asked.

"I'm so wound up," she said, "I forgot about clothes. What am I going to wear?"

"One thing at a time. I've got everything worked out. You can take the essentials and pick up what you need when we're abroad. I'll help you. I'm methodical. A born organizer."

"I'm glad you are. I'm a fucking slob."

"No comment."

"You think we should do London first?" she asked. "My hair will frizz anywhere I go."

"Your hair is one of the best things you've got going for you, Franny." Slowly moving closer to her, he pushed the hair off her face and gently blew into her ear, circling the lobe with his tongue. He lowered his hand; his fingers lingered a few seconds on the nipple of her breast. She moaned at his touch. He couldn't hide the grin that curved his lips. Finding no resistance—he locked his arms around her waist—he surrounded her with his arms, pulled her tightly to him and kissed her.

Instinctively, she returned his kiss then suddenly pulled away.

He looked at her for a long moment, his expression, one of surprise.

"No," she said. "I can't. I shouldn't. I…"

CHAPTER 13

On the flight from Kennedy Airport to Paris, Franny had second thoughts concerning Matt. He was his usual, charismatic, and attentive, smooth-talking self, ensuring her how important her input was to the new line. Still, she had reservations and wondered if beneath his bullshit compliments there was an ulterior motive. She listened attentively but guardedly.

At the showroom, buyers—some owners of mom and pop stores, others executives of huge department store chains—adored and respected her. A born salesperson, she made the garments she held up come alive. They leaned forward in their chairs as she performed her spiel. They were her captive audience, amused by her use of profanity—they expected it; this was Franny. On the phone when she called to make appointments for the next seasonal line, she asked about their husbands, wives, children, and at times discussed their personal problems. In the showroom, Franny was in control.

But this was Paris, not the showroom. The doubt that she might not be as talented as Matt told her she was intermingling her mixed feelings for him, adding to her guilt over leaving Nick in the hospital in a coma. That fact more than just nagged at her.

The flight attendants gushed over Matt, but he ignored them, focusing solely on Franny. But, through the pretense of trying to win her over, he began to feel more vulnerable and found himself being drawn to her. He was at a loss. Had he lost his modus operandi? He couldn't read her behavior or her body language, and worse, he felt he was losing his influence over her.

Sitting under a Cinzano patio umbrella, people-watching at the Marché Malik flea market, Franny chomped on a *croque monsieur* while Matt tongued away the mustard that dripped on his mouth, savoring *un hot dog avec frommage*.

He patted his lips with a paper napkin, tasted the Pinot Grigio, swallowed, then sighed and set the goblet on the red and white-checkered tablecloth. "I don't know what the magic is, Franny, but there's something here that's different."

She pushed the Cinzano ashtray to the side. "If we're in Paris, how come they're advertising Italian products? Yeah, that's what they say: Paris is magical. Maybe it's my Big Apple background, but between me and you and the Eiffel Tower, it doesn't hit me…" she placed her hand to her heart…"right here!"

"You have no soul," he whispered, sinking his teeth into the sandwich, the mustard dripping onto his rolled-up shirtsleeve. "Shit!" he exclaimed.

"What a slob," she said. "And how can you say I have no soul? I have more soul in my little pinky than you have in your entire egotistical, macho carcass. You think you're so damn cultured just because you had four years at the Fashion Institute. Well. I had a year of college, and at

CCNY, so there!"

He chortled, knowing better than to answer her.

The tightness of her mouth made obvious her annoyance. She jumped up, ran to the vendor and returned with a rag soaked in water. "Here, let me get the mustard out before it sets in, Mister Fucking Soul searcher." She shook her head. "And look, you dripped mustard on your arm too." After applying the wet rag to the stain of his sleeve she started to rub at the mustard on his arm, but he jerked it away.

"What?" she asked. "You want to save it for later, or are you going to lick it clean?"

He sent her an inviting glance. "Works for me."

"Forget it, Romeo. But since you're feeling so chipper, it's a good time for us to set the record straight."

"Clean the arm," he whined. "I know what you're going to say. Why are you getting so uptight? I was just kidding around." He rolled his eyes. "Okay, give me the rag and I'll do it myself."

She pouted. "Never mind. I'll finish the job. It's hard to do it by yourself."

"Oh, yeah! I know what you mean!"

Ignoring his remark, she removed the mustard from his arm, all the while feeling a twinge of excitement.

"Let's go shopping," he said. "Lunch break is over."

"Well, if you didn't masticate each bite twenty-seven times and swallow each morsel like you were having an orgasm, we would have finished an hour ago."

"You're in France, Franny. You just don't sling your food down like you do in the States."

Having dined in the finest restaurants in the States, she teased. "And why not, may I ask?"

"Because you're supposed to enjoy and savor each bite."

She grabbed hold of his hand and pulled him towards the clothing stalls, hoping the sensations she felt for him would go away. "C'mon, Wolfgang Putz, we'll compare recipes later."

The market was bustling with shoppers. In the clothing stalls, women flipped through the racks searching for that one special article of clothing. "Reminds me of Neiman's Last Call sale that they run twice a year. You wouldn't believe the grabbing and fighting that goes on at that high-class event." Checking out the women's attire, she turned to face Matt. "And they're not too style-conscious here, are they?"

"You're looking at the average woman. That's not the woman we want to attract. Think of you, the young hip mother-to-be. Better yet, think of a protruding basketball."

"What the fuck are you batting your gums about?"

"You don't want to hide it. You want to make it a fun thing." He placed his hand on her stomach. "There's a cute, little baby in there; you're happy—proud. You want the little darling to be covered in the latest fashion. Think trendy. Think of what *you* would wear." He studied her indifferent expression. "Franny, what's changed? You had a handle on it in New York."

"That was then and this is now."

"You're hedging. What's wrong? Have I said something to upset you?" He took her arm and steered her to an upholstered banquette. "Let's sit a moment." He sat down beside her, reached across her shoulder and rested his hand on the outer rim of the banquette. "We are going to be working together for at least two months. I was hoping for more. Now is the time to lay all our cards on the table." Holding her gaze for any length of time was difficult. He looked away and then back at her. "I know you're having a rough time. I won't go into that; it's not really my business. But you yourself just said it."

"Said what?"

He shook his head. "A few minutes ago—and I'm quoting you—you said, 'Let's set the record straight.'"

"It's not like I thought it would be."

"And how did you think it was going to be?"

Looking into his face, she tried to set aside all thoughts of right or wrong. She lowered her eyes and sank back into her seat, struggling for the right words. "It's not Nick. I've come to terms with that. The problem is my fucking feelings for you."

CHAPTER 14

Matt calmed Franny's anxiety regarding her feelings toward him. He began with a list of all the reasons for her emotional tension. There was Nick's illness, her pregnancy, and the stress of the career adjustment. Matt pleaded with Franny to vent about these issues with him. Who better than he, so close at hand and so understanding?

He knew he had to deal with their situation, and swiftly. *Take hold of yourself,* he thought. *She's just another conquest. You've had these temporary crushes before and worked them out.*

He took her to the hotel, quelled her fears with his smooth chatter and escorted her to her room, lightly kissed her on her mouth and held her at arm's length. From her expression it was evident that her anguish had evaporated. "After tomorrow's shopping for the line, we're going to do the town. I'm going to make reservations at the best restaurant in Paris. We'll do it up like it's New Year's Eve. Wear the Dior you bought and I'll wear my tux."

"You're full of surprises, Matt."

Mentally, his gaze caressed her body.

❦

It was going to be the most perfect evening. The doorman grinned, greeted her, and extended his hand to help her out of the taxi as a playful breeze lifted Franny's strapless black chiffon creation above her thighs.

The six-story Restaurant de La Tour D'Argent, the oldest and one of the priciest five-star eating establishments in Paris, was lit up like a Christmas tree. It welcomed the elegant epicureans and bourgeois tourists alike who delighted on gourmet food and paramount wines; 400,000 bottles in the famous wine cellar waited to have their corks popped.

"Garçon," Matt said to the waiter who hovered attentively at their table. "Une bouteille de Cristal, s'il vous plait."

Franny's brow wrinkled. "Are you sure we should be having Cristal? Lew is going to skin us alive."

He leaned across the table and whispered. "Fuck him."

She pursed her lips. "Tsk tsk, Matt. Watch your language."

He ignored her comment. "We are going to make the man wealthier than he already is. I tell you, Franny, I'm just beside myself. This new line is going to be bigger than we can imagine."

Caught up in his excitement but a bit hesitant, she said, "I think it's great that you're so enthused, but we haven't even done anything yet."

Pointing with his crooked index finger to his head, he smiled with assurance. "I have it all in here, Franny. It's already designed and planned out. And with *your* help, it's a done deal." He reached across the table to take hold of her hand as the waiter approached.

Leaning back in his chair, he withdrew his hand. He wondered if living up to his commitment with Lew was worth the effort. On one hand, he thought of the Lamborghini and the amount of money he would stockpile; and on the other hand, Franny was no day at the beach. Getting the spitfire to acquiesce and go along with what he had in mind was not going to be easy. *But it would all take shape and slowly fall into place.*

Their eyes met as they toasted then dined on an appetizer of *foie gras* accompanied by toast points. Franny let out a low, slow whistle as the waiter lifted the padded Limoge cover that exposed the restaurant's signature dish: roast duckling in orange sauce and gingerbread croquettes.

The waiter offered a wine list, but Matt refused, telling him that they would stay with the champagne.

"From the way his eyebrow lifted," Franny said, "I think he's not too happy about it."

"Well, ordinarily I would agree with him. Wine with the meal is the proper etiquette. Did you catch the wine list? It must be eight inches thick. We could order wine or are we happy with the champagne?"

She nodded. "Champagne works for me. I see what you mean about the French savoring every morsel. The man over there is swishing the soup around his mouth. Must be a food critic."

"No, he's just a lover of food," Matt said. "Do you know that each duck served has a serial number all its own? See," he said as he lifted a postcard that was placed on the side of the serving dish. "You can get the same food at half the price down the street, but you wouldn't get the view of Notre Dame, the Seine, the service, or the elegant décor and greatest ambiance in all of Paris. This is class."

"I don't see an empty table. How did you get reservations so fast?"

"They are usually booked up months in advance. It's not what you know but who you know."

Scanning the room, Franny took in a deep breath and let it out slowly. "What a crowd. Looks like anyone who is anyone is here. From royalty to movie stars."

"You're a match for any movie star, Franny." He reached across the table and pressed his thumb into the palm of her hand.

The titillating sensation sent a chill through her and she let her mind roam. *Oh my God, fire down below!*

They waived the fromage platter, and opted for dessert and coffee as the waiter refilled their champagne flutes.

Flustered, Franny withdrew her hand. The waiter placed a linen napkin over the empty champagne bottle, turned it upside down, and quickly removed it from the table. "Did we finish the entire bottle?" Franny asked. She tried to contain herself. "Do you realize we're here over two hours? I am stuffed, weighted and sated."

"We can leave anytime you wish. How about a walk along the Seine? Or we can go to the hotel. They have a real cool bar—we could catch a few dances—have a nightcap." He frowned. "There is work tomorrow."

"Shit. Work? Well, we still have tonight, and I'm feeling wired. Must be the champagne. Let's go to the hotel bar."

"I'll get the check," he said, wondering if it was a good idea for her to keep drinking while she was pregnant.

His arms held her firmly to keep her from losing her balance as they danced to a throaty chanteuse singing "La Vie en Rose." "I think you've had enough of the bubbly," Matt whispered in Franny's ear. "You're three sheets to the wind."

Despite the fact that her hand held tightly to his neck for support and the champagne flute tipped precariously in the air from her other hand, Franny was feeling no pain. "Party pooper," she slurred. "The night's just starting and you're acting like an old fuddy-duddy."

"Well, this old fuddy-duddy is taking this smashed beauty to bed."

"Oh, Mr. Carpenter. Surely, you're not going to take advantage of this pure, innocent maiden?"

He grabbed hold of the flute, set it on the tray of a passing waiter and steered her to the elevator. "That's a good girl," he teased, holding her around her waist. "Just take one step at a time. You don't want to trip."

"I can walk a straight line," she said and freed herself from his grip. "See?" she said as she attempted to walk a straight line. She swayed, and once again he clasped his arms around her waist to steady her. "Well, maybe I do need a little help," she slurred.

At her door, she asked, "Is this my room or yours? I know what you're after. I'm not as far gone as you think." She stumbled. "Well, on second thought, I could use a little assistance. I know I can trust you."

He slid the key card into the slot of her door. "But Franny, my pet, can I trust you?"

She flailed her arms into the air. "What kind of a frigging question is that? Hey, it's fucking hot in here. Turn on the air-conditioner."

He led her into the bedroom. "It's on. We better get you undressed before you…"

She plopped down on the bed and patted the cover for him to sit next to her. "I didn't mean to act so crazy, Matt. It's the champagne talking."

"And what is it saying?" He moved closer and touched his lips to hers.

"It's saying that I better get out of this Dior before I ruin it."

"You'll need help."

"Boy, do I need help." She stood and faced him.

Quickly, he undid his bow tie, removed his jacket, flung them onto the armchair, kicked off his patent leather slippers, pulled off his socks, unbuttoned his shirt, dropped his pants and briefs, walked to the wall console and turned on the stereo system. Soft music instantly streamed through the room. He leaned over, spread his arms out and she fell into them.

The sensation of being within his protective arms was pleasurably comforting.

"Now it's your turn," he said as he drew back. "Don't move. Don't do a thing." Facing her, he reached around and gently lowered the zipper of her dress and held her gaze as the dress slid to the Oriental. She attempted to step out of it, but he stopped her. "No Franny. I told you—it's my turn. I'll undress you."

"I need a drink!"

Covering her lips with his finger, he smiled. "Shush. Just enjoy."

Her excitement rose as he lifted her and tenderly placed her on the glossy satin coverlet. As he removed each article of clothing, he kissed her with sensitivity on that part of her body. She gasped with excitement. Aware that she was fading fast, he said, "Not yet. You're still not allowed to move."

CHAPTER 15

The aroma of Matt's cologne lingered on Franny's pillowcase, jogging her memory back to the previous evening when she and Matt dined at Tour de Argent and afterwards danced at the George V.

Making a determined effort to sit up, she groaned. "My head. It's exploding!"

Matt slipped into a guest bathrobe and ran out of the lavatory. "What's all the racket?"

She covered her eyes with her hand and peeked between her fingers. "The damn light—it's blinding me. Pull down the shades, will you?"

"Hangover, huh? Some hot coffee, a couple of aspirin and a nice cold shower and you'll be back to the old Franny." He swallowed a laugh. "You'll get used to the light."

She winced. "It's not funny, Matt. How come you're not feeling anything?"

"Some people can hold their liquor while others don't know when to stop."

"How about the aspirin?"

"I've already called down for aspirin and coffee, and breakfast is on the way." He picked up the clothes he had flung in a heat of passion the night before, tightened the robe and headed for the door. "We have one hour to get out of the hotel and start earning our salary."

She wrapped the bed sheet around her still naked body. "Not so fast, Sonny Boy," she called. "I'd appreciate your take on what, and if, anything happened last night."

He turned towards her. "Oh, so you don't remember anything?"

"I remember. I remember. Well, up to the time when we danced at the hotel bar and you helped me to my room." She screwed up her face. We didn't …"

"Have sex?"

"Stop playing with my head, Matt!"

He couldn't resist. Taking in a deep breath, he let it out with a long, sensual sigh. "Ooh—oooooh, Fraaaanny. It was awesome." His eyes shut tight. "I can't begin to describe it. The earth moved, the angels wept. Wow!"

He stepped out into the hall and called back to her. "I had no idea you were that good," then quickly kicked the door shut, avoiding the pillow she had thrown at him.

"Bastard!" she yelled as his door closed.

There was a rap at the door and Franny, thinking it was Matt, shouted, "Get lost, you piece of shit."

"Madam, it's the waiter with your *petite dejeuner.*"

Embarrassed, she let the waiter in, watched while he arranged the table, tipped him, and after he departed, hurriedly washed down the aspirin with the orange juice. Quickly taking a bite out of a buttered croissant, she forked some scrambled eggs into her mouth, gulped the coffee, and ran into the bathroom to bathe.

Matt's voice reverberated as he sang in the shower. Shaking his head, he laughed out loud, his thoughts remembering last night with Franny. *The lady is not to be believed. True, she has a potty mouth, but she also has a hell of a lot of redeeming qualities. For sure, she's one of a kind. I'm not going to tell her that nothing happened—keep her guessing.* He laughed again, thinking of how he had worked her up to a frenzied state of sexual bliss, kissing her over every inch of her eager body, as she lay naked, yearning for his skillful fingers to find the place where she longed to be touched. And when he did, he watched her draw a shuddered breath, gasp, and climax.

Matt turned the shower off, feeling an inkling of bittersweet compassion, recalling her tears tumbling onto the satin pillowcase, her voice sighing, "Nick, oh Nick," as she fell asleep.

CHAPTER 16

Franny had been unable to sleep. She was wide awake at 4:00 AM, and still feeling off balance by last night's episode and Matt's indefinable devil-may-care attitude. She dialed Lily in New York.

"What's wrong?" Lily asked.

"What makes you think something's wrong?"

"I haven't heard from you for God knows how long. I've thought of calling you but I didn't want to interfere with your hectic schedule."

"I suppose that's meant to be sarcastic?"

"You *could* say that."

"Why are you being so bitchy?"

Lily huffed. "If you have to ask me, then there's no sense in answering."

"Lily, what the hell are you talking about?" Franny threw the cover off and slid into her slippers. "Are you or are you not my best friend in the whole world?"

Trying to reason with Franny was at times frustrating, so Lily decided to overlook what was destined to become a war of words. "It's just that I've left messages with your hotel and haven't heard back. Naturally, I was concerned. Lew's been in touch with Matt but…"

Franny overrode Lily's words. "That's why I'm calling you, but if you're going to get all pissy on me, forget it. And stop rolling your eyes. I may be in Paris but I can just see you as plain as day."

"You're right! You're right! You're right! I give up. What's the problem? From what Matt has told Lew, you're doing extremely well. By the way, has the lover boy gotten you into bed yet?"

"I'm tempted to divorce myself from you, Lily. That was a bitchy thing to say. You don't think I'd sleep with anyone, knowing that Nick is sick?"

Silence.

"Well, I'll overlook your silent callousness this time. I'm serious, Lily. That's my dilemma."

"I'm all ears, Franny."

"Is Lew within earshot?

"No."

"Good. I wouldn't admit this to anyone else but you, Lily—but last night we had a little too much to drink. Well, I did, anyhow. He took me to my room and undressed me."

"And you let him?"

"I didn't exactly let him. I bought this sensational Dior cocktail dress and I didn't want to mess it up. And since I was a little tipsy…"

"He suggested that he help you take it off, right?" Lily finished for her.

"I'm not sure how the scenario went, but it went pretty far… I think. Trouble is, I don't remember how far."

"Was he with you this morning? What did he say?"

"He was in the shower and when he came out he ordered aspirin and breakfast for me and started to leave when I confronted him."

"And?"

"The bastard just picked up his clothes and said, 'the earth shook and the angels wept.' But I couldn't tell if he was really serious."

"Great line. Not to worry, Franny. You're not a virgin and you're already pregnant. So who cares?"

"Lily, I'm scared. I'm so confused." She fought the urge not to break into tears. "I love Nick, but I have this crush on Matt, too." The tears broke through. "I hate myself. I hate my life. I hate what's happening to me. I hate being pregnant. And worst of all Lily...I hate the baby."

"I'm getting on the next plane and flying to Paris."

"No, Lily. Don't come. I'll get through this."

CHAPTER 17

By the time Lily cleared Customs at the Charles de Gaulle Airport it was 9:00 PM. The plane sat on the runway for over forty-five minutes because of a deranged passenger who had locked himself in the lavatory.

Shuddering, she thought, *this is not a good omen. Lew was upset with me for going—Franny is freaking out, and now this. Damned if I know why I did come.* But she knew why: Franny would have done the same for her.

No sooner had she stepped out of Customs than the media converged.

"Here on a vacation, Ms. Fitzgerald?"

"Are your magic fingers going to perform in Paris?"

She held her hands up. The press had always been kind to her, and she gave them the same respect.

"I'm giving my magic fingers a sabbatical. This is simply a holiday."

Spotting Lily, Franny placed two fingers in her mouth and blew out a shrill whistle. "Lily! Over here!"

After hugging and kissing, Franny asked, "You're bunking with me, right?"

Lily stepped into the limousine, plunked down and exhaled noisily.

Franny patted her best friend's arm. "What's with the heavy sigh? Want your own room?"

The driver started to turn onto the highway as Lily took hold of Franny's hand. "I came to help you get back on track. We'll find a solution. Right?"

Franny turned a disheartened face out the limo, staring but not seeing the impressive Paris skyline in the distance. It was as if the tension of the last few days drained all the life out of her. "Right," she answered robotically. "We'll find a solution."

Franny slipped the key card into the door of her suite at the Hotel de Crillon. "I suppose you and Matt have adjoining suites?" Lily said.

"Well, it's convenient, since we are constantly exchanging ideas."

"Franny, you know that I love you to death, but if you're not going to be on the level with me, I'll stay the night and be off in the morning."

"I'm sorry! I'm sorry! I'm sorry!" Franny cried. "Don't be cross. I need your strength. It's all closing in on me. Nick in a coma, my being pregnant, the new line—and my feelings for Matt."

Lily opened her arms to Franny. "Listen, I'm starving. Let's order something a la Françoise, loaded with a tray of fattening, creamy *éclairs, macarons, pain au chocolat* and *petits fours.*" She smoothed Franny's hair. "To hell with the calories. Let's eat on the terrace. The view must be breathtaking."

Franny lifted her head, then with renewed confidence drew herself up and faced Lily. "How about we change into our PJ's and have an old fashioned sleepover like we used to? I'm beginning to feel better already. We can talk later."

Lily's eyes narrowed at Franny. "Later? The time to talk is now! You need to make some decisions."

"After the desserts. Okay?"

The telephone rang. "It's probably Matt," Franny said. "I'll get rid of him."

"New York City calling Mrs. Pagliara."

"This is she, operator... Lew? How are you? How come you're calling me? Yes, Lily's here.... You don't want to talk to her?... You want to talk to me? Is something wrong?... What about Nick?" She paled. "He's awake but he's not all there?"

Lily approached Franny. "What?" she mouthed.

The sofa made a swishing sound as Franny dropped into it. The phone dangled from her hand and she shut her eyes tight. "Fuck this!" she yelled. "Why is all this happening? You talk to him, Lily. It's too much—too fucking much. I can't handle this."

Grasping the phone from Franny's hand, Lily almost shouted. "What's going on, Lew? Franny's about to go into shock."

"Nick started to gain consciousness. When he first woke up, everything seemed to progress well. His arms and legs twitched, then moved. He spoke a few words—and then..."

"Spit it out!"

"And then he relapsed."

"Is he comatose again?"

"Not exactly. When he first awoke the specialist said he could improve but it was too soon to tell. We'd have to wait and see how he progresses. The second day he made remarkable strides. It was unbelievable. I stayed with him all night. But the third day he faltered somewhat. And the fourth he was almost his old self, joking around; even said he wanted to wait and surprise Franny with his quick recovery. The specialist tried to explain Nick's condition in laymen's terms. It's like wiring that has a short circuit. Sometimes it works and when it disconnects it doesn't. He could regain complete control of his senses—or maybe not."

"Why are you speaking in the past? When did all this happen?"

"A month ago."

"A month ago! My God, Lew! You kept it a secret from us all this time, and especially from Franny?"

"It was touch and go. One minute he was okay and the next…" The doctors felt he might snap back at any moment. And we know how hypersensitive Franny is. What good would it do if she knew?"

"You had no right to keep it from her, Lew."

"I know. But it's done. Wait, there's more." He hesitated.

Lily glanced at Franny, now holding her head in her hands and swaying back and forth. "Dear God, don't tell me there's more."

"Nick left the hospital on his own and we don't know where he is."

CHAPTER 18

Three weeks later. The sun shown through fluffy cumulus clouds as they darted in and out of the snow-capped Rocky Mountains, indicating another hot day for the inhabitants of Santa Fe, New Mexico.

Esmeralda Rosa Sofia Jacinta Macarena Duarte stood in line at the checkout counter and watched the grubby, unshaven man slip a wrapped ham, lettuce and tomato sandwich into his jacket pocket.

"Hey you," a clerk called out, "this isn't the Salvation Army. Put the sandwich back and get out of here before I call the cops. Ya bum." He leaned over the counter to see if the man replaced the sandwich.

"Just one minute," Esmeralda said. "Who you calling a bum? That's my brother. I'm paying for the sandwich along with the other items in my shopping cart. You know me. I work for the Sinclairs. And I expect an apology or I'll be taking Mrs. Sinclair's business to your competitor."

Embarrassed, the clerk shrank back. "I'm sorry."

Prodding the homeless man with her elbow, she snatched the sandwich from his hand and placed it into her shopping cart. "Wait for me outside, Alberto," she said, "and don't get lost, you hear?" She turned to the waiting customer who stood in back of her. "Sorry to hold you up, but my brother—he needs attention."

The lady smiled compassionately. "Tell me about it. I have the same trouble with my father. I spend half my life looking for him. I…"

Esmeralda rode over the woman's words. "I know. I know. Please, excuse me, I've got a million things to do and I'm already late." She signed the bill and smiled at the clerk. "It's okay, Miguel. You didn't know he's my brother."

The homeless man stood outside the store as Esmeralda steered the shopping cart through the sliding electronic doors and parked it by the store's bench. A look of confusion crossed his face. His searching eyes stared blankly at her as she approached him. Eyeing him with reservation, she barked, "Sit!" Parking the shopping cart alongside the bench, she sat down next to him, unwrapped the sandwich and held it out to him. When he hesitated, she insisted. "Go on, take it."

The soiled shirt, ill-fitting pants and unlaced sneakers were self-explanatory. "When was the last time you ate?" she asked.

The man just about swallowed before he chewed. After gulping the sandwich he answered. "Haven't eaten…in f-f-few days. I hopped a freight train…the guards-s-s-potted me. I r-r-ran for it."

"Running, huh? From the law? How long are you running?"

"Law? No…I don't think so. S-s-s slept in…box car."

She took out a six-pack of soda, removed one, flipped the tab, and offered him a Dr. Pepper.

"Drink. The way you stuffed down the food, you're liable to choke. And I'm not too good with that 'Heimlich remover' thing." His indecisive manner of speaking and the rapid blinking of his eyes suggested to Esmeralda that the man was in need of a helping hand.

"I want to…th-th-thank you…m-m-miss…"

Esmeralda nodded thoughtfully, bringing to mind the time she and her brothers almost drowned when they journeyed in a homemade boat they had put together, attempting to flee Cuba. Her eyes watered as she once again relived the vision of gasping for air after the waves had capsized the dinghy; and how they had held on to the boat in the ice-cold ocean, praying, expecting to drown at any moment, until they were picked up by local Cuban American fishermen. Luckily, the men were sympathetic to their cause and helped them elude the law and locate their relatives in Miami.

"Thanks are not necessary. My real name is Rosie Duarte. I wanted so much to be American, I dropped the Esmeralda plus the other four names." She crossed herself. "Everyone calls me Rosie." She tossed her hair to the side and threw back her shoulders with pride. "I'm an American citizen, too. I study the English language all the time. But don't misunderstand me. I'm proud of my heritage."

"You should be," the homeless man said. "It's the land of the free. That's what it says on the Statue of Liberty. Give me your tired, your poor, your huddled masses, yearning to breathe free. And so on and so forth."

Searching his eyes, she said, "You don't sound like a hobo, and all of a sudden you're not stammering."

"I'm not sure what a hobo sounds like, Rosie. I've met well-educated men from all walks of life on the road, and they prefer living a free, *au natural* lifestyle."

"And they're hobos?" She eyed him with surprise. "You didn't trip over your tongue."

His look became distant. "I didn't? I hadn't noticed."

She shook her head. "Well, I have to get back to the house before the food melts."

"Defrosts," he corrected.

"Okay. Defrosts. Could you give me a hand with the groceries?"

After the groceries were loaded into the station wagon, he opened the driver's door for Rosie. "Th-th thanks…uh…f-f-for the d-d-drink…and s-s-sandwich," he faltered, and turned to leave.

She rolled down the window. "Where are you going?"

"I'll be…all…r-r-right."

"Wait! I can't just let you walk away not knowing if you will have a place to stay or something to eat. Come in the car."

He shook his head. "No. I'll b-b-be…f-f-fine."

"I gave you a sandwich; at least you could do what I ask. Come, sit for a minute."

He opened the passenger door, put one foot inside the car, then stopped. "I could be a convict. You shouldn't trust anyone you've just met. Especially someone that's as seedy looking as me."

"Let me worry about that. Come on, I have to get back. I'm a cook and the madam has company tonight. I'm already late."

He cocked his head to one side. "What are you thinking?"

She smiled again, taken aback by his change in speech. "I'm thinking that you need to get off the road and into a shower. The Santa Fe police don't have a lot of tolerance for vagrants." Her smile deepened. "The house is so big you could land an airplane in the living room. And besides, I have my own cabana away from the main house and staff. It's just a *pequeno cabaña*. I mean a cottage. It has a small kitchen—one bedroom and an alcove with a bed that hides in the wall and comes down and opens up. I sleep in it when my brothers come over and they sleep in my bed." Not being able to read his expression, she paused. "Funny, but I can't get over you talking straight again."

"You want me to go home with you? You're crazy. You don't even know me. And what about your husband or boyfriend?"

"Put your seat belt on. Have a good meal, get cleaned up and stay for one night."

His look was questioning.

She nodded. "Don't worry. No fooling around. I'm seeing someone. You're pretty big, but he's bigger," she chuckled, knowing that there wasn't a husband or man in her life except for her brothers."

His eyebrows furrowed. "Why do this for me, Rosie?"

Her lower lip covered her upper lip. Reflecting, she said, "My brothers and me, we almost died in the ocean trying to get to Miami from Cuba. God sent three angels disguised as fishermen to save us. At that time I swore that if someone ever needed help I'd do the same for them."

The engine made a grinding clatter as she shifted the gear into first and sped away. "What's your name?"

He stared out the window then back at her. His frown deepened as he heaved a frustrated sigh. "Honestly, Rosie, I don't know."

CHAPTER 19

A virgin Bloody Mary in hand, Lily walked from the terrace of Franny's suite in the Hotel de Crillon into the living room to confront Franny.

Before she could say a word, Franny spoke up. "Stop with the faces, Lily. I know what you're going to say."

Lily put her glass on the cocktail table, sat down alongside Franny and folded her arms across her chest. "Glad to hear it. You'll save me a lot of aggravation."

Silence.

Lily's brow puckered. "I'm all ears."

"You know, Lily, you and Lew treat me like I'm some hypersensitive, airhead, scatterbrained ditz."

"Yes, you are all of the above and then some. But to be perfectly honest, your virtues way outshine your shortcomings. There's a world of goodness, talent and brains, in addition to an amazing sense of humor lurking behind that wacky façade you display."

Frustrated, Franny munched non-stop on a plate of *pommes frites,* doused them with ketchup, shoved three at a time into her mouth, chewed, swallowed and then continued. "Thanks for the eulogy, but I'm not about to jump off of the terrace, Lily. I love myself too much." She sat up straight, displaying more self-assurance than she had exhibited in a long while. "Nick's situation is fucking driving me nuts. They can't find him and I don't know if he's safe or just wandering the streets like he's on Golden Pond." She shoved the plate of fries to one side then mindlessly retrieved them. Continuing to nosh, she said, "Matt and I have finished shopping for samples for the new line. We'll be going home in two days."

Lily's face was expressionless. "I knew that. Lew told me."

"I know that I've been a real ball buster, upsetting you and Lew. I'm sorry. But with what's been going on, I needed an outlet—and Matt's been here for me. He's really a sweet guy."

"Uh, huh," Lily said.

"Okay, so we screwed around a little. Well, maybe more than just a little. But, hey, so what? If it weren't for him, I would have fallen apart." Her head bobbed up and down, affirming her assertion. "Yep, I would have."

Lily shrugged with indifference.

Franny scoffed. "You gonna just fucking sit there and not say anything but 'uh, huh'? Did you, or did you not come all this way from the States to give me support?" She screwed her mouth to one side and smiled wistfully. "You don't approve of Matt, do you?"

"I'm not here to judge. None of us are angels. I just wanted to make sure that you weren't falling apart."

"You think I'm a heartless bitch, that I've just put Nick on the back burner. Is that what you think?"

"You said it. I didn't."

"Look, Lily. Matt's been a lifesaver. You weren't around and he was. So, as I said before, I may have acted irresponsibly but I'm coping."

Lily swallowed hard. "From the way you talk, Franny, you seem quite capable of handling things yourself." She fell silent for a second. "By the way, isn't it time for a visit to the doctor? You are starting to show, you know. But I have to tell you, Kiddo, you look great in spite of what's been going on." Lily glanced at Franny's set face. "We've never kept any secrets, no matter how personal, have we? Is there anything you want to tell me? Something you've been holding back?"

A knock at the adjoining door prevented Franny from answering.

"Hi, in there," Matt called out. "I haven't had a chance to say hello to Lily. Are you ladies decent?"

Franny's face brightened at the sound of his voice. She let out a sigh of relief. *Saved by the bell.*

CHAPTER 20

The night before, Rosie had insisted that he shower and shave. He followed her with his eyes as she scurried around the kitchen, warmed up a hefty plate of meatballs and spaghetti, set it in front of him, grabbed a brightly colored serape off a wall hook, snatched an embroidered carpetbag and waved a hasty goodbye. Without turning towards him, she barked, "You better be here when I get back. I have enough to worry about. The madam is entertaining tonight, and I'm already late getting the dinner in motion. I left my brother's pajamas on the chair for you." The screen door whacked as it closed behind her. He listened to the gravel scatter as her espadrilles skimmed onto the path that led up to the main house of the estate.

Upon her return to the cottage, Rosie gently pulled back the hand-sewn curtains that enclosed the hide-a-bed, peeked in and studied the sleeping hobo to whom she had given refuge. She watched his chest rise and fall as he inhaled and exhaled steady slow breaths. *He's peaceful now—*

but in the morning, who knows? Good-looking, in a macho sort of way. Could be Italian. I wonder what his life was like before he lost his memory—where he lived—is he married? A thousand questions only he can answer. It took all her will to close the curtain and walk into her bedroom.

As she undressed for bed, she reprimanded herself. *What are you thinking? You did a good thing, but don't get carried away.*

The following morning lying in bed wearing Rosie's brother's pajamas, the man stared fixedly at the pale blue stucco ceiling and pondered the unsolved doubts and uncertainties of the last few days. For as long as his memory allowed him to remember, it felt good to have cleaned up, slept in a bed with clean sheets covered by a handmade patchwork quilt and with a soft feather-pillow beneath his head. He laughed silently. *I know I'm not a basket case. Aside from the stuttering, the occasional blackouts and dizziness, I feel okay. But who am I? What happened to me? Where did I come from and where was I going when they ran me off the railroad boxcar? No name. No means of identification. And then there's the law. Could I be a criminal?*

The sound of bacon sizzling in a frying pan piqued his attention as the aroma worked its way up his nostrils. He drew the curtain to one side and watched Rosie in the kitchen, flipping bacon, humming a Spanish song.

Aware he was awake, she turned toward him. "Buenos dias, Alberto."

Her invitation, generosity, acceptance of him, even naming him Alberto, touched him deeply, but with it came a litany of warnings.

He dropped the 'o' from Alberto and suggested that he have a first, middle and last name until his real identity could be established. She suggested Albert B. Center, but from the sour expression on his face Rosie could see he was not happy with the choice.

She asked, "You're not happy with the names I picked?"

"I-it's f-fine."

"Then you pick."

"I l-l-like Al."

Smiling shyly, Rosie lowered her voice. "ABC. Albert B. Center. I did that in case you forget who you are. Comprendo?"

At the market, Rosie picked up a head of lettuce, peeled the top leaf off, nodded with approval and placed it in her shopping cart. "Mrs. Sinclair wants one of the help to do the shopping for me. Says I have enough to do with cooking the meals. I told her, if I cook, I shop. What's the sense of my cooking when I can't trust the person who picks the food?"

Al answered with a shrug of his shoulders.

"It's good for you to be seen with me," she said. You've been a great help. This way people will get to know you as my brother." She faced him. "You don't have to talk unless you feel it's necessary. "I'll talk for the both of us."

He laughed. "Yeah," he said without stuttering. "I like the name Al. But you should reconsider your boss's advice. You can't do everything. And I won't be here forever, you know."

"Don't jump the gun—one thing at a time. You're here only a week.

Rosie signed the bill as Al steered the shopping cart into the street and started to load the groceries.

Once seated in the car, she said, "I told Mrs. Sinclair about you."

"Y-you w-what?" His eyes shut tight and his head fell back onto the headrest.

"Suavacito. Take it easy. She's like a mother to me. I can swear for her. Believe me, she is a wonderful lady. She won't give you away."

Silence.

"Al, What's wrong? Talk to me."

Blinking his eyes rapidly, he shook his head then straightened up. "Guess I had one of my dizzy spells."

Starting the van, she cried, "I'm taking you to the emergency room."

He placed his hand over hers, preventing her from shifting gears.

"You're not doing anything but driving back to the house, Rosie. I just had a brief blackout. I'm okay. Really. And if I go the emergency room I'll have to give some sort of identification. No. Let's go home. What were you saying about Mrs. Sinclair?"

"I was telling you that I told Mrs. Sinclair all about you." Before he was able to get a word in, she held up a hand to stop him. "Please, just listen to me." She steered the van onto the shoulder of the road, trying to avoid a pothole. "The citizen's committee has been after the county to fix this road for the longest time." Leaning closer to him, she said, "Good. You have your seatbelt on."

"You shouldn't have said anything to Mrs. Sinclair. I'm sure she's already called the authorities."

Rosie eyed him then turned her attention back to the road. "I thought about it for a while and decided that she can be trusted. She took me in when I needed a job. I was lucky, I had a lot of cooking experience. You're better off taking a chance with the Sinclairs. You would be picked up by the police sooner or later."

"I'm not so sure."

"Trust me. Mr. Sinclair is a very rich man. He is president of the Santa Fe National Bank. He has a lot to say about what happens in Santa Fe. And Mrs. Sinclair does a lot of work for the charity organizations."

Al smirked. "Have him do something about this messed up road."

CHAPTER 21

After the guards at the main entrance to the Sinclair estate checked Rosie and Al, they clicked the remote control and the fifteen-foot iron gates, scrolled in the design of musical notes, opened. The road leading up to the Sinclair estate was lined on either side with imported forty-foot Ethiopian Panola trees that reached skyward, seemingly into outer space. The main house and the grounds that encompassed the extensive landscape stood on a hill overlooking the Santa Fe River. The estate had been highly praised by *Architectural Digest* and *House Beautiful* as one of the "Havens of the Rich and Famous."

"Wow!" Al exclaimed. "This is *living!*"

Rosie drove along the gravel path that led to her cottage, pulled up the handbrake and stepped out. "That's the way I felt when I first got here," she said. "My cousin works as a server when Mrs. Sinclair entertains and introduced me to her. No one gets hired until Mrs. Sinclair checks him or her out. I had to take a cooking test to see if I was good enough. I was so scared; my hands shook so bad I spilled the sauce I was preparing."

"But you're in charge of the meals. How did that happen?"

"The head cook became pregnant and she gave three months' notice. She saw that I knew what I was doing and spoke to Mrs. Sinclair. She trained me for three months and I proved that I was capable of cooking and running the kitchen. At first I was going loco because of the gourmet dinners, but eventually I caught on. I have plenty of help. But it was not easy winning them over, you know, being an outsider and a foreigner. But I did."

"How do you manage getting all the meals scheduled on time?"

"The second cook takes care of breakfast and lunch. The marketing I do is only for special occasions. That's why I like to shop for the particular foods and delicacies by myself. The bulk of the food is delivered and accounted for by the sous chef."

"The what chef?"

She giggled. "The sous chef. He's second in command and is responsible for checking in all the food deliveries. You should see him. His belly is bigger than Papa Noel."

She waited for him to open the door for her and then entered. "Hungry?" she asked. "One thing I had to get used to is the amount of food we use. The Madam makes sure the homeless are taken care of."

Annoyed at her having told Mrs. Sinclair about his living there, he walked into the living room and sat down. Brooding, he said, "I think I should leave."

Rosie hung her serape on the wall hook, sat down beside him and placed her hand casually on his arm. "You can't leave. You're getting better. The last few days you haven't stuttered. Not once. And you seem more normal. You yourself told me you're feeling better."

He ran his hands over his face. "You're sounding like my mother or, worse yet, a nagging wife."

She pulled back and removed her hand from his arm. "I'm only trying to lend a hand."

Sensing he hurt her feelings, he sat wordless, sulking. Lifting his face up to hers, his eyes searched her eyes. "Believe me," he said, "I appreciate what you've done for me. But my being here is not going to make it easier for you. You could get into trouble."

"Look, you must be in your middle thirties, maybe younger, right? I'm thirty-eight. If I sound like I'm mothering you it's because I care. I want to make sure that you are okay. You shouldn't be alone—not yet." She struggled to get the words out. "I like you, Al. I mean—I really like you."

"I like you too, Rosie," he said, realizing his interpretation of liking differed from hers. His was one of appreciation not of affection. "And didn't you tell me you had a boyfriend who was bigger than me?"

"I was only joking." Embarrassed at admitting her affection for him, she blushed and quickly changed the subject. "I haven't said anything to you, but Mrs. Sinclair said she would find a place for you on her staff."

"Rosie, aren't you going a little too far? I'm not one hundred percent—I haven't a legal name, an ID—nothing that makes me a legal citizen."

"The Sinclairs will take care of that."

He shook his head. "What are you talking about?"

"Mrs. Sinclair would like to meet you."

He hated feeling helpless, and although he was powerless to do anything about his situation, his instincts told him he hadn't any choice.

CHAPTER 22

On Saturday morning Jeremiah Jenison Sinclair III, formerly Jerome Jesse Slivovitz, neatly folded the *Wall Street Journal* and held it up for the butler to take.

"Thanks, Bentley," he said as he placed a linen napkin across his lap.

"Will you be breakfasting with Mrs. Sinclair this morning, Sir?"

"Yes. Mrs. Sinclair should be down shortly."

"Shall I pour the coffee or serve it when Madam arrives?"

"I'll wait, Bentley. Hand me the rest of the newspapers. I want to see how fast the country is going down the tubes. I'll have my usual breakfast."

"Madam has already made out the breakfast menu for this morning, Sir."

"Where does that woman find the time to do everything she does?"

"It would seem that Madam is quite capable."

"You got that right, Bentley. She's one in a million."

Mr. Sinclair, thought back to when he was nicknamed J.J., president of the most prestigious bank in New Mexico and board member of every prominent corporation in Santa Fe. *I hadn't always enjoyed the lifestyle of the rich and famous. Fact be known, I was born among a potpourri of Italian, Irish and Jewish ghetto inhabitants in the lower Eastside of Manhattan and raised by a widowed, alcoholic mother. At the age of eight I headed a gang of young hoodlums who led a sordid life, stealing items from shopkeepers and taunting the police.*

Realizing that this life of transgression he led was not going anywhere, Jerome Jesse Slivovitz decided to become a law-abiding citizen. While working his way through his last year in college, he met debutante Ce Ce—Celia Chase Morgan—whom he relentlessly pursued. The Chase clan balked at a Jew joining the family but the love-struck couple threatened to elope if the family did not accept them. Jerome won them over with his charm and good looks; eventually, they swallowed hard and gave in.

As a wedding present the Chases had their lawyers legally change Jerome's name, sent the honeymooners on a world cruise, and bought them a mansion. Upon their return, they discovered a Rolls Royce awaited them and Jerome was made vice president of the Chase Bank. To be more acceptable in banking circles his office door read Jeremiah Jenison Sinclair III.

Bentley cleared his throat. "Mrs. Sinclair will be down presently and suggests you start without her." He signaled for the maid to bring in Mr. Sinclair's breakfast.

"She must be on the telephone arranging or rearranging something or other," J. J. said.

The butler stood at the sideboard, poured coffee into Mr. Sinclair's favorite mug decorated with a decal of the New York Giants in action. He added two lumps of sugar, milk, stirred and placed it in front of his employer. "As a matter of fact, Sir, the madam is speaking with a young man in the anteroom."

"Hmm."

The scent of Joy drifted in the air as Mrs. Sinclair entered the breakfast room all atwitter. Waving her hands in the air, she said, "J.J., I want you to meet someone. A thousand pardons for interrupting your breakfast, my dear, but I have a million things to attend to today and I wanted to get this out of the way before I get bogged down. I knew you wouldn't mind. The man is…well let's say, shy. I did want to brief you before I introduced him.'

"Settle down, Ce Ce. How about breakfast?"

"I'm absolutely swamped this morning."

J.J. shrugged. "So what's new? I sense this gent you are touting needs employment and you want my approval?"

"Yes."

"Since when do you need my approval?" Recognizing the gleam in her eyes, he smiled at the woman he worshipped and respected. "Ce Ce, Honey Bun. For you, I have all the time in the world." His eyes narrowed. "This isn't one of your rehabilitation-sponsored projects, is it?"

"He's a friend of Rosie's. Well, sort of."

"Sort of? Uh, huh."

Taking a seat next to him she said, "Your food will get cold. I'll talk while you eat."

"This is going to be worse than I thought. Shoot. I'm listening."

"The man is, or rather, was a hobo. Rosie met him at the supermarket. He was taking a sandwich and Rosie paid for it."

"You mean he was swiping a sandwich."

"Yes. Anyhow, the point is that the man has no memory."

He shook his head. "And you took pity on him and want to play doctor until his memory comes back. Are you serious?"

"I know it sounds crazy, J.J., but if you just talk to him…you'll see that he is not a derelict. There's something…I can't put my finger on it. I'm sure he's a responsible person who's lost his way."

"And you're going to help him find his way back, Mother Teresa?"

Her expression spoke for her.

"Okay, he said. Where is he?"

"Waiting in the anteroom."

"Bentley," J.J. called, "show the gentleman in." He turned up his face and with his index finger pointed to his lips. "Honey Bun, plant one here and say goodbye. I'll see you at dinner."

CHAPTER 23

J.J. gave the man a sidelong glance and motioned for him to take a seat. Bentley immediately pulled the chair out and waited until Al sat down.

Extending his hand for Al to shake, J.J. said, "I'm Mr. Sinclair."

Al sensed warmth in the man and began to relax. He said, "Al. Albert B. Center," then shrugged. "It's a temporary name that Rosie gave me until I…"

"I'm not going to interrogate you, Al. I just want to get a line on where you could fit in, here at the estate. If that's what you want." He smiled. "That is, until you get yourself together. Have you any idea as to what you would like to do? How much do you remember from your past?"

"Not very much. The last thing I remember is being run off a freight car here in S-Santa F-fe and meeting Rosie in the market."

"Don't be nervous, Al. I'm on your side."

"I'm not nervous. The stuttering comes and goes. Otherwise I feel fine."

The phone rang. "Excuse me, Sir," Bentley said. "Head of security says it is urgent he speak with you."

J.J. listened intently as the chief in charge of security for the estate spoke. In the middle of his sentence, J.J. cut him off. Shouting into the phone he blasted the man. "Are you telling me that with all the state-of-the-art security we have on the estate, no one knew there was an intruder lurking around? Listen, you fucking moron; this is the third time something like this has happened. I'm putting you on notice." He flung the phone at Bentley, who adeptly caught it.

Turning his attention to Al, J.J. shook his head. "I have the most sophisticated network of cameras and doohickeys ever invented and still someone gets through. Unbelievable!"

Al straightened up in his chair, then leaned forward. "Ya know, Mr. Sinclair, there's always going to be a guy smarter and more knowledgeable than you. The trick is to keep one step ahead of them. Someone's always trying to think of a way to build a better mousetrap. If you got it, they want it. You have a lot of employees working on the estate. More staff equals more problems. More problems means more chances of a perpetrator doing damage. Sounds like an inside job to me. Could be your security needs overhauling." He cast a pensive look across the room then focused back on J.J. "You might consider planting a mole on the estate."

His jaw setting, J.J. stared fixedly at Al. "You think so?" Startled by Al's seemingly knowledgeable discourse relating to safety measures, J.J. probed further. "Seems to me you know something about security. What prompted you to say what you did?"

"Haven't the slightest idea. It just popped out."

J.J. studied Al. "Just popped out, did it?" He rose from his chair, placed his napkin on the table, walked to the window and thoughtfully gazed down at the gardeners nurturing the well-manicured gardens. He lifted the window and inhaled the scent of the roses the breeze carried through the air.

Al scanned the room, taking in the lavish furnishings, the artifacts and the paintings done by the masters Renoir, Gauguin, and Lichtenstein. *These are no fakes.* His mind assessed J.J.'s tough, cogent demeanor with the warm, caring tone he used towards his wife when Al listened through the partially open door in the anteroom. He smiled inwardly, remembering how J.J. had laid the security chief out in no uncertain terms, and how affectionately he had spoken to his wife before she left, imparting the words, *"Plant one here, Honey Bun."*

J.J. walked to where Al sat. Al started to stand but J.J. gestured for him to remain seated. "I'm interested in what pops into your head, Al. What's your take on the security malfunction at the estate?"

Al hesitated, squirmed in his seat. "I couldn't give you an answer—not right now. I'd have to investigate." He hesitated. "I'm not sure I'm qualified, Mr. Sinclair."

J.J. stared him down. "I don't think you know how qualified you are. Listen, Al. I know what I'm talking about. I didn't come from nothing to amass a fortune without knowing something about people and what makes them tick. You're a blank piece of paper, a mind without a memory."

The hair on Al's neck bristled. "I could give it a try. But I can't promise anything. It's all so new to me."

J.J. stood and Al followed. "No pressure, Son. Take your time. Get back to me when you've worked out something you think has merit." He clapped Al on the back. "Yes, everything is brand new to you. Look at it this way. How many people can start their life over? Think of all the opportunities that are open to you and all the mistakes you've made that you can now avoid. My God, man. It's like being reborn!"

CHAPTER 24

The windshield wipers could barely keep up with the rain that sloshed onto the truck's windows as Rosie pulled up to the cottage. She turned the ignition off and almost tumbled out of the car when the door flew wide open. A smile crossed her face as she caught sight of Al, umbrella in hand, a smile on his face, standing in the rain, his hair sopping wet.

In her haste to avoid the rain, she stepped onto the running board. The heel of her shoe caught on the edge of the grooved rubber step and threw her off balance. Al dropped the umbrella and reached out to grab her. She fell into his arms, their faces almost touching. Her arms locked tightly around him. It was all she could do to restrain herself from kissing him.

Alarmed by the flirtatious glint in her eyes, he pulled back. Promptly, she said, "Carry me into the house before we both get soaking wet."

Once inside, he lifted her from him, put her down, walked directly into the kitchen and reached for the teapot. His mind deliberated whether to mention his conversation with Mr. Sinclair, or to tell her that her feelings for him were not reciprocated. Instead, he asked, "How about tea, or coffee, or maybe hot soup?"

Sensing his discomfort, she took a long painful sigh and released it audibly. "Soup," she said. "Hot soup will warm us on a dismal day like today."

Her downcast expression told him that revealing his conversation with Mr. Sinclair was the way to go. *If the new undertaking with security works out,* he thought, *I'll probably have to live at the estate full time and she'll eventually lose interest in me. I'd be foolish to turn down this opportunity. It feels so right.*

CHAPTER 25

Ｎew York in winter has a distinctive characteristic all its own, Franny thought. She sat at a table sipping a hot chocolate at the Wollman skating rink in Central Park and watched the skaters glide by accompanied by the perennial skaters' waltz. The clock on the bistro wall told her it was after 1:00 PM and that Lily was late. She pulled up the collar of her new mink coat closer to her neck and focused on the skaters.

The launching of the new *Bun in the Oven Maternity* line was a huge success. Five months of time-consuming, tedious, endless hours in the design room, sketching, adding and discarding ideas, flew by for Franny and Matt.

Casting her eyes down at her baby bump, she sighed, thinking that in less than three months a little stranger would materialize.

"Thinking of a name for the baby?" Lily asked, approaching the table. Franny screwed up her face. "You're late."

Lily took a chair and sat down. "I guess not. You don't know if it's going to be a boy or a girl."

"I don't want to know and I don't care."

"Sure you do."

Franny squinted at her friend. "Don't fucking tell me if I care or I don't care."

Heads turned. Ordinarily, Lily would be embarrassed, but, knowing Franny, she was immune to Fanny's outbursts and cursing. "Aren't we in a cheerful mood today," she said. "Lew is over the moon with the success of the new line. It's blowing out of the stores. You seem to have adjusted as well as can be expected to Nick's disappearance, and you and Matt are hitting it off. Come on. Give."

"Want to have something to eat? I do."

"That's why we're here. The chicken salad is to die for and you go ape over their fries."

"Yeah."

Uh, oh. Another crisis, Lily thought. *Why don't they give her a break?* "Lew suggested the four of us do the town tonight. Celebrate the great job you and Matt did."

Franny stared into space. "He wants to marry me."

"Whoa, there lady. You *are* married. Is that what's on your mind?"

"Among other things, yes."

"Let's have it."

"I don't know where the hell to begin."

"Start with Matt, then Nick and then the baby. That should cover all the bases."

"There are four bases, Lily."

Pleased Franny was getting back to the old Franny, for the moment anyhow, she said, "Start with Matt. First of all, you can't marry him. I think the spouse has to be missing for seven years in order to be declared legally dead. So that's one down and two to go. Let's take Nick."

The waiter served the food. Franny dipped a french fry into the ketchup and sprinkled it with salt. Catching Lily giving her the eye, she quickly shoved it into her mouth, chewed, swallowed and proceeded to lick her fingers. "Best part of eating fries," she said. She wiped her fingers with a napkin. A grim expression crossed her face. "Funny thing—well, maybe not so funny, I have to tell you, Lily—as time goes by, I'm starting to forget about Nick. The longing for him, the sleepless nights when I cried non-stop—even what he looks like—they're fading. Is there something wrong with me?"

Lily put her half-sandwich on her plate and faced Franny. "Personally, I think it's normal. It's been…how long? Almost five months since Nick came out of his coma and disappeared. Listen, it's easy for me to give advice, but you do have a life to live and a baby to think about. When and if Nick shows up, that's the time to deal with it."

"I guess you're right. That's what Matt says." She reached across the table and took Lily's hands in hers. "You know, Lily, you're the closest person I have in this upside down, crazy world. I once asked you something and we never finished the conversation. About you and Lew adopting the baby."

Lily sank back in her chair, her hands falling away from Franny's. "At the time, I did speak to Lew. He was thrilled. He said he would do it in a heartbeat."

Franny let out a sigh of relief. "Good! That's a load off."

Lily inclined her head to the side, avoiding Franny's eyes. "But I said…no way."

CHAPTER 26

Mr. Sinclair decided to override his sophisticated security system and employ Al to help flush out the problems that had surfaced at the estate. He planned to house Al in one of his tastefully decorated ultra-modern units that included a living room, fully equipped kitchenette, bathroom, screened-in lanai, heated swimming pool and spa. To ensure the utmost privacy, high shrubs isolated the cottage. Located on the east wing of the Sinclair estate along with a group of similar guest cottages, it was intended for the unanticipated government official, the alcoholic celebrity who had crashed at the previous night's festivities, or relatives who unexpectedly just happened to be in the neighborhood. In other words, those individuals the Sinclairs did not want staying at the main house.

With Al's approval, Mr. Sinclair devised a plan to introduce Al as part of the family to avoid suspicion from the staff or security. They were already on high alert because of Mr. Sinclair's prior admonitions towards them.

Amazed at Al's insight into security procedures, he conceived a plan to use Al as a mole at the estate. "How about this for a cover-up?" he suggested. "This buddy of mine and I did a stint in Vietnam."

Mr. Sinclair frowned and cleared his throat. "We've been close for many years. I was lucky. I got away with minor injuries, but shrapnel took its toll on Mel. I've been trying to get him to live with us on the estate since his wife passed, but he refuses. His son, a doctor, works in a remote region in Africa rehabilitating third-world children.

"You would be Mel's son, paying us an extended visit. You'd have your own living quarters; and, what's more important, as our guest, you would have the freedom to roam the entire estate. Keep in mind that security checks out everything and everybody on the grounds, relatives included. I'll give them a heads-up on you."

"I don't know. I'd have to use the son's name. And I'm not too sure about taking on the role of a doctor." He looked up inquiringly at his boss. "In the short time I've lived as a nonentity, I've already been given two names."

"That could be worked out. You've already a head start. The son's name is Alexander. We could cut it to Al. As my guest, you won't have to answer to anyone and you would have your own living quarters. Incidentally, my daughter Cassandra, 'Cassie,' will be coming back from Europe today. She's a chip off the old block. Real sharp. She's the youngest partner in the firm of Brewster, Pinkerton and Sinclair."

A tinge of excitement crept through Al as he listened. *I could do my snooping while I'm pretending to be this man's son—have my own living quarters, and best of all, a reason to exist—not be just a blank piece of paper.* "Yes, it sounds doable, Sir," Al replied, thinking, *it'll probably be the closest I'll ever get to having a family.*

"Call me J.J."

Al drew a cautious breath. "There's only one hitch, uh, J.J."

"What's that?"

"Rosie. She knows my story."

J.J. waved a hand of dismissal. "Leave it to me."

Al's brow furrowed. "That may not be as easy as you think."

"How so?"

"It seems Rosie is a little…well, taken with me."

"So I've heard. Mrs. Sinclair did mention something about Rosie having a crush on you. Not to worry. She can be trusted."

Al said nothing. But the thought that J.J. hadn't any reservations about Rosie disturbed him.

CHAPTER 27

Cassandra Chase Sinclair sat in her Ferrari convertible sports coupe a half-mile from the entrance to the Sinclair estate. She turned off the ignition, leaned her head against the headrest and stared up at the forty-foot high Panola trees. *What am I going to do now that I'm back?* she thought. *Did I make the right decision, breaking off with Preston? He wanted a wife to entertain, raise a kindergarten of brats. I'd rather have a good argument in court than change diapers. Settling down, having kids, attending garden parties, boring socials, not to mention the Friday night get-togethers, is not why I spent all those years in school. I'm just as confused now as when I left for Europe. Dad will be happy. He didn't like Preston; and Mom—she'll give me that same old spiel about family ties.*

Her sandy blond hair caught the breeze as she drove up to the gates of the estate. Jose the security guard gave her a snappy salute and pressed the button on the remote, his eyes following the fifteen-foot iron gates as they parted. "Welcome home, Miss Sinclair," he said. "Have a pleasant trip?"

"There's no place like home, Jose," she lied. "Anyone at home?"

"Your father's here. Your mother is out."

"Figures," she snapped.

He stepped closer to the car. "My wife and I want to thank you for taking care of my daughter's problem in court and for not charging me."

"No es nada, Jose," she said, and waved at the other guard, who tipped his cap at her. As she drove through the gates she called back, "Have someone pick up my trunks and baggage, will you, please? And don't alert my father that I'm back. I want to surprise him." She drove towards the main building, her words fading into a whisper as they succumbed to the gravel's clatter. "As if that's possible with all the security guards and cameras lurking about."

Cassandra knocked at her father's bedroom door.

"Come in, Cassie. I've been expecting you." Unable to hide his expression of delight, he spread his arms out to her. "Get over here and give your dad a fitting hug."

Rushing to him, she pecked him on his lips and tightly embraced him. "Is that fitting enough, Dad?"

He pulled back, held her at arm's length, and smiled at his pride and joy. "Let me look at you. Yes. You're more beautiful than ever but..."

"But nothing," she said. "If you're going to give me one of your 'what's wrong' lectures, forget it."

Spoofing, he said, "And when did I ever lecture you?"

"Forever," she replied. "You're glad I pulled the curtain on Preston, aren't you?"

He walked to the nightstand and poured coffee into his mug. "Coffee?" he asked. She shook her head. "You know damn well I didn't like that loser. The only reason you continued seeing him was to aggravate me. You took a month in Europe to get your head together; you came back and it seems to me you're no better off than when you left." He waited for her to answer. When she didn't, he shrugged, sipped the coffee and smiled deviously at her. "Why must there always be this rivalry between us? We're father and daughter. I'm not an adversary arguing against you in the courtroom."

She stood her ground. "Could have fooled me. You're the one who made me this way."

He drew back. "I what?"

"Don't bait me, Dad. Ever since I was able to speak, you tried to mold me into a carbon copy of you."

"You've got to be kidding."

"Look, Dad. To you there's nothing better than a down-and-out, fight-to-the-last-man brawl."

"What's wrong with that?"

"I'm not a man. If you wanted a son, why didn't you adopt one?"

A knock at the door interrupted their exchange. "Beg pardon, Sir," Bentley announced, "but the young man, Al, would like a word with you at your convenience. He's in the downstairs parlor."

"I'll be down shortly, Bentley."

Cassandra's smile showed interest. "Who's the young man, Dad?"

"No one that would interest you." He pecked her on her cheek, started for the door and called over his shoulder, "None of your business, Miss Busybody."

Cassandra waited until he was out of sight, walked stealthily down the stairs and listened at the closed door.

"My daughter is home, Al. I don't want her to know anything about what we are setting up. Understand?"

CHAPTER 28

Rosie never thought of herself as a jealous individual, but as she sat in the main house kitchen planning a special dinner for one of Mrs. Sinclair's soirees, she reflected if lately there were times when she was resentful of Al and his new position at the estate. *I've got to forget about him. He's not interested in me. If he still lived here with me, maybe in time he would change his mind. But now that he has his own place and is getting so friendly with the boss...*

Her thoughts were interrupted by the echo of Cassandra's high heels clicking on the tile of the kitchen floor.

Throwing her arms around Rosie, Cassandra smiled. "It's so good to see you. Still creating surprising menus for Mom?"

Nodding, Rosie asked, "Did you have a good time in Europe?"

"I couldn't wait to get back."

"Why didn't you just come home?"

"Good question. I'm not sure." But she was sure. Acknowledging that her father was right about Preston would be admitting he had won the round, and that was something she would never concede.

"Did you have breakfast, Miss Cassie? I could fix something."

"No. Well, maybe a quick cup. You do make the best coffee ever. It's my first day back at the office and I'm sure there's a ton of work waiting for me."

Rosie poured coffee, placed four rugelach pastries on a dish and offered it to Cassandra. "Your favorite," she said. "It will give you a good start for the day."

"You're a sweetheart, Rosie." She munched on the pastries, sipped the coffee. Sighing she said, "Mmm, mmm. I can't resist—maybe two more. I think you should put them on the market. The French pastry chefs can't hold a candle to your baking." After finishing the coffee and rugelach, she patted her mouth with a napkin, took out her compact, touched up her makeup and applied fresh lipstick. Leaning back in her chair, she brushed a few crumbs from her pantsuit. "So, tell me. What's been going on since I left?"

"Nada. Same old, same old," Rosie said. "Your mom is as busy as ever with her organizations and volunteer work. And as usual, your father is hard at work at the bank, with board meetings and the problems that have come up with the estate's security."

"That's odd. He didn't mention a problem about security."

"You just got back yesterday."

Cassandra eyed Rosie. *This is not the same old Rosie,* she mused. Deciding to probe further, she asked, "What gives, Rosie? You seem a bit out of sorts. Not feeling well?"

Aware she was wearing her heart on her sleeve, Rosie feigned a smile. "Just trying to catch up on your mother's to-do list."

"Well, I better make tracks to the office. We'll talk later, okay?" Starting for the service door, Cassie turned around and said, "By the way, Rosie.

Who is the stranger staying at one of the guest cottages? Al? Is that his name?"

☙

In the evening after Cassandra had changed into shorts and a tee shirt, she took her dogs for a walk. The stars sent a shaft of light onto Cassandra as she strolled the cobblestoned path alongside the guest cottages with her two Borzois, Boris and Natasha.

The dogs playfully romped about, every so often nudging her for attention. She ruffled their fur and spoke aloud. "Missed me, didn't you, you adorable creatures? Want to play?" Crouching, she picked up two sticks, held one over her head and shouted, "Fetch!" Chuckling as the branch sailed through the air, she waited for Boris to retrieve it. "Good boy," she praised, and briskly threw the other stick and watched it sail through the air. It made a sudden sharp crack as it came in contact with one of the cottage doors.

Hearing a noise, Al folded the blueprint estate security plans he had been going over and opened the front door. He stepped outside then promptly drew back as the dogs stood poised, ready to attack. He jumped back inside and shut the door.

"Sit!" Cassandra commanded. They immediately obeyed.

"You can come out now," she shouted. "It's safe. They're really the sweetest dogs in the world."

Al opened the door and stepped out. Cassandra spoke to the dogs. "He's a guest…a good guy," she said, giving him the once over.

The dogs sniffed Al, and he in turn petted them. "They sure are beauties. What are they?"

"Borzois. Also known as Russian wolfhounds."

She extended her hand for him to shake. "I'm Cassandra Sinclair. Cassie to my friends. And you are?"

Taken aback by her eye-catching good looks, he tried to appear composed. He took her hand. "I know who you are. Your father said you were coming home from Europe."

"Did he?"

"I'm Doctor Alexander Hartman, Al to my friends. Your dad and my father were buddies in Vietnam.

She peeked into the room through the open door. "Nice digs," she said. "I like this cottage. It was the last to be finished. In fact, I helped plan the décor."

He had the feeling she wanted to be asked inside.

"How come you're not staying at the main house?"

"Your father asked me to, but I prefer my solitude. I'm trying to decide where to set up my practice."

"What about Santa Fe? You'd have it made in the shade."

"How come?"

"My God, Al, with Dad's connections it would be a shoo in."

"That's all well and good, but I think I can make it on my own. Anyhow, I'm not certain Santa Fe is where I want to settle down."

She scrutinized him with a keen eye. "Independent, huh? Have to respect you for that. Planning on staying a while?"

Her probing made him uncomfortable. "I'm not sure. If you'll excuse me, I have work that I must finish."

"Me too. I have briefs to go over." Upset at having been cut short, she said, "Will you be doing us the honor of dining with us or are you going to hole up and wallow in your solitude?" She didn't wait for his answer, but abruptly turned away and called to the dogs.

Wow! What a shrew. No wonder J.J. doesn't want her to know too much. However, she is one hot lady. He watched her walk away, eyeing the wiggle on her perfectly rounded, firm buttocks emphasized by her too-tight short-shorts. He smiled, gazed down and released a low sigh of arousal. *At least that didn't go the way of my memory,* he thought.

Stretched out on the lawn in front of the main house, Cassandra rested her head on Boris while her toes massaged Natasha's furry coat. She spoke to the stars. "There's something out of the ordinary—something more than just strange and appealing about that man." The dogs whimpered a sign of agreement. Focusing once again on the stars, she said, "He doesn't know it, but I'm going to marry him."

❧

The moon had dipped into the folds of the Sangre de Cristo Mountains when Cassandra heard the gentle knocking at her bedroom door.

Mrs. Sinclair poked her head into the room, "Cassie, Darling," she called, "may I come in?"

"Yes," she said sarcastically. "I've been home since yesterday morning."

"I know, Dear. Forgive me. I haven't been able to chat with you since you arrived. You know me, always flitting around. I thought I'd take a chance and see if you were still up. Want to chat or is it too late?"

Cassandra thought. *Too late? Yes, mother, about twenty-five years too late.* But to her mother she said, "I was reading."

Mrs. Sinclair pecked her daughter on the cheek and took a chair alongside the bed. "J.J. told me that you broke off with Preston. Was that wise?"

"I think so."

"Well, you never did listen or take my advice, but when it comes to your father, that's a horse of a different color, isn't it? You and he are always at odds, but somehow you always run to him with your problems. I might as well be invisible."

Cassandra lifted an eyebrow. *She's asking for it. This is as good a time as any to set her straight.* "If you would have paid attention to me, instead of having nannies and nuns raise me, and taken the time to be there for me, instead of spending endless hours at shallow tea parties and inane women's socials, flitting around, as you so aptly put it—maybe, just maybe, I would have listened to you."

"You've had everything you have ever wanted, and more."

"Except your love."

"That's not true. I do love you."

"Is that why you waited a day to greet me? Why don't you ask me if I had a good time in Europe? Or maybe something like, you look fantastic; or, I'm so glad you're back. But no, you immediately attacked me with why I broke up with Preston."

Her mother drew back. "Let's not get into that again. I came up to welcome you home."

"You're a day late."

"So you said. Anyhow, how was your first day back at work? Hard?"

"Not as hard as yours, I'm sure."

"I was going to ask you about your trip, but you didn't give me a chance. How was it?"

"It sucked."

Mrs. Sinclair shook her head. "Why can't we have a mother-and-daughter talk, Cassie?"

"Why?"

"Because I want to, and I think you do, too, despite your hostility towards me. Let's call a truce. I'll give in halfway if you give in the other half."

"I'm not sure you want to hear my half."

""We can't undo what's done, Cassie, but perhaps we can make a new start."

Cassandra hesitated, but decided, *why not? I have to tell someone or I'll lose my mind.* "I was pregnant with Preston's child," she blurted, aware of the quiver in her voice.

Mrs. Sinclair forced herself to look inquiringly at her daughter. "My God, Cassie," she said, "How, why?"

Sensing her mother's bewilderment, Cassandra half smiled. "That's the first rational thing you've said. Don't speak, just listen."

Cassandra felt a tense contraction in the small of her back as she relayed her traumatic experience while traveling in Europe. For the first time in as long as she could recall, Cassandra grasped her mother's hands in hers. "Breaking off with Preston was not in the least upsetting," she said, "but discovering I was pregnant was an unexpected shock. Abortion was my choice since I had no intentions of seeing Preston again. I called Dr. Hodgkin. He suggested having it done while I was in London. He arranged for all the accommodations but…" Weeping, she faltered. Wiping her tears, she repeated, "He arranged for the abortion…but that night I started to bleed and was rushed to the hospital and miscarried."

Her mother gasped. "And you didn't have anyone to call?"

"I should have. They assured me I would be okay but…"

"You're scaring me, Cassie. That's a very worrisome 'but.'"

"I'll come right out with it. I was told that if I were to get pregnant again I would be putting myself and the baby at risk."

Mrs. Sinclair's breath caught in her throat. "I've got to share this with your father, Cassie. I'm going to call him." She stood.

Cassandra grasped her mother's hand. "Wait!" she said. "After all these years, we're finally beginning to communicate. Let's keep this to ourselves." She searched her mother's eyes.

"If that's what you want, I'll agree, but I'm not pleased about hiding this from your father. We have never been untruthful with each other."

Closing the door behind her, Mrs. Sinclair leaned against it and sighed. *Who am I kidding? I can swear for myself, but for J.J.'s infidelities—I'm not too sure.*

116

CHAPTER 29

The wind whirled around the terrace of Franny's new condo on the thirty-fifth floor of the high-rise complex. "How do ya like this pad?" Franny asked Lily. "Fucking class, right? It's a far cry from the walk-up brownstone in Brooklyn."

Lily popped open a bottle of Cristal, poured it into a flute and handed it to Franny, then lifted her glass of Perrier sparkling mineral water to toast. "Who would have thought last year at this time that we would be celebrating now? Here's to the new apartment, the success of the new line, and to Matt and you living in perfect harmony."

"Yeah," Franny said, "who'd a thought it? Except that the harmony between Matt and me is out of tune."

Lily said, "No one is perfect. Remember the three things we used to say? Understand, overlook and forgive?"

She shrugged. "You wouldn't be intimating that I am hard to get along with, would you?"

Lily rolled her eyes. "Answering that would be redundant."

"I didn't expect an answer. I know damn well I can be a handful." She refilled her flute with champagne and lifted the Perrier bottle towards Lily, who refused. "And don't tell me I shouldn't be drinking. Seriously, Lily, how come my problems seem so much more important then yours? Never mind. I don't want to know. I want to run something by you. Lately, when Matt and I are doing the nasty I get the feeling that Nick is watching. It's weird."

"Does it distract you?"

"No. Actually, it turns me on. I have the best of two worlds."

"Be careful you don't shout out Nick's name by mistake." She sipped her Perrier. "It takes time. It's been seven months since Nick vanished." Thinking they needed a change of subject, Lily asked, "I'm so excited. Before you know it, the baby will here."

"Yeah, that's another thing. I've been thinking and thinking, and..."

"Don't think too much. The mind can be a dangerous thing."

"You wouldn't be referring to me, would you?"

Lily rolled her eyes. "Don't tell me after all the talking we've done you're still not sure about having the baby. It's a little too late; you're in your eighth month."

The howling wind outside combined with the rain's lashing against the terrace doors, and Franny's comments sent shivers down Lily's spine. "I have to tell you, Franny, you're going to drive me back to the bottle." She gritted her teeth then forced herself to relax. "You and Matt have just finished decorating the baby's nursery and you're *still* undecided?" She frowned. "Well, at least *he's* excited. He's practically bought out FAO Schwartz."

"I wish some of his enthusiasm would rub off on me." She squirmed in her seat. "Honestly, Lily, I just can't see myself as a mother. I can just barely take care of myself never mind an infant. If you were as good a friend as you say you are, you would adopt the baby like I asked you to."

Lily opened her mouth to release a primal scream but held back. "So you said, a thousand times." She drew in a deep breath and let out a frustrated sigh. "Ten, nine, eight, seven, six, five, four, three, two and one. I never heard that, and I don't want to ever again!"

"Okay, okay, don't get fucking bent out of shape. It so happens, I'm planning to make other arrangements about the baby."

Lily covered her ears with her hands and shut her eyes tightly. Her mind spun. *I don't want to hear this. I don't want to know what she's saying, thinking or planning.* She stood. "I just remembered I have an appointment. I'll call you later."

Franny jumped to her feet. "I'm sorry. I'm sorry! You're right. I'll never mention it again. It was selfish of me to come up with such an idea." She took a seat on the couch and patted the cushion, inviting Lily to sit next to her. "You can take your hands away from your ears, Lily. I'm not going to have one of my tantrums."

Lily's frustrated look vanished and was replaced with a questioning frown. Her voice, cool and precise, asked, "You made other arrangements? I can't wait to hear this."

"I have seriously decided to put the baby up for adoption."

"Uh, huh," Lily said indifferently. "And what did Matt say?"

"Matt? Yeah. He went fucking bonkers. Don't ask. I've never seen him so furious. I thought he was going to slug me. Threatened to walk if I did. He slammed the door and stomped out. I haven't heard from him in two days. He didn't even show at the office."

Lily shook her head. "And you didn't tell me? I bet Lew knows where he is. Have you contacted any adoption agencies? Lew can have them checked out."

"Mm. It would save me a lot of running around, wouldn't it?"

"More than that. Lew's lawyers would make sure everything was done to the letter of the law. Don't forget, Nick is the baby's father. And there has to be a lot of red tape and legal ramifications that the ordinary layman is not aware of. Also, I think I heard that in certain states once you sign on the dotted line you cannot reclaim the baby under any circumstances." She tilted Franny's face up with her finger and fixed her eyes on her friend. "Listen. You don't know how you're going to feel down the road. You may change your mind once you see it, hold it. This may be the most important decision you will ever have to make. You should be certain that this is the way you want to go. Think about it. Once you sign the papers, you get no refunds, rain checks, or changing your mind. The baby will belong to someone else…forever."

CHAPTER 30

Roused by the sharp ring of the telephone, Lew rubbed his eyes, poked Lily and mumbled, "Get it, will you, Hon? I worked late into the night."

Lily turned on the bedside lamp and checked the clock. Fretful why anyone would be calling at three in the morning, she grabbed the phone.

"Lily, It's Matt. Franny's in the hospital."

Lily was already out of bed and at her closet. "What happened?"

"She's in the emergency room. She started to bleed. Luckily, I was there. I just came back to get some of my things. We had a big falling out. I'm sure you heard. Anyhow, I immediately carried her to my car and drove to the hospital. She was a raving maniac. Cursing like you wouldn't believe."

"I believe, Matt. I believe. How *is* she?"

"I don't know. I'm waiting for the doctor to come out." He sobbed. "It's my fault. I went ballistic. Even punched a hole in the wall. Why didn't I just leave? If she loses the baby I'll kill myself."

"Get a grip, Matt. I'll be right down. Which hospital?"

"Lenox Hill. 100 East 77th."

"I know where it is. Goodbye."

She hung up, turned to grab her car keys and collided with Lew. "You're dressed," she said.

"You didn't think I was going to let you go by yourself, did you? Ralph is downstairs waiting for us."

The limo tires screeched to a halt in front of the emergency entrance of the hospital. Lew flung the door open and pulled Lily out.

"Easy, Lew, I still need my fingers to play with."

"Sorry, Lily, I wasn't thinking."

"I know. We're just so anxious."

"Hang out, Ralph," Lew said. "We don't know how long we'll be."

The chauffeur tipped his cap. "Yes sir, Mr. Benjamin."

❧

In the waiting room they saw a distraught Matt. He immediately sprang from his seat and embraced Lily. "I should have known better," he cried. "I'm such a fool. She's not like ordinary people. She's so sensitive— gets upset so easily."

"Anything since we spoke?" Lew asked.

"I was just going to tell you. She's going under the knife as we speak. The doctor said he couldn't wait. They're doing an emergency cesarean." He walked to the armchair, sat down and put his head in his hands. "It's my fault, it's my fault."

Lily put her arm through Lew's and steered him out of the waiting room. "I know what you're thinking," he said. "If Franny gets through the operation and she and the baby are out of danger, it would be in their best interests if she did give the baby up for adoption."

She turned away from him. "She asked me to adopt the baby and I

122

refused."

"I know, Dear."

"I feel so guilty. We *are* more than just best friends."

He turned her towards him and lifted his hand to her cheek, then lightly caressed it. "It was a hard decision, but you did the right thing. You have your career, and I have a business to run. Nannies and strangers would be raising the child. It wouldn't be fair to the youngster. First things first. Let's pray they get through this in good shape."

CHAPTER 31

Mr. Sinclair addressed his wife, his daughter, Cassandra, and their guest Dr. Alexander Hartman. "Now isn't this better than going to some noisy restaurant where everyone talks over one another, where the service is iffy and the food just mediocre?"

Cassandra's tone was sharp and condescending. "Yes. And how many people have someone like Rosie to plan the menu, a staff of cooks, butlers, maids, and a gentleman's gentleman like Bentley to serve them?" She folded her arms across her chest. "And did I forget to mention a Rolls Royce with a chauffeur, and a plane waiting to take off at a moment's notice?"

"Whoa, Cassie," Mr. Sinclair said, "you're sounding off like one of those radical activists. Since when have you started moralizing for the huddled masses? Maybe you should get a soapbox and hand out leaflets. Or join women's lib? May I remind you that I contribute thousands of dollars to hundreds of organizations? And I can't begin to count the charities in which your mother is involved."

Trying to keep on the better side of her daughter since they had recently bonded, Mrs. Sinclair sided with Cassie. "You forget, J.J., not many people live the life style that we enjoy, or can afford to dine the way we do. We should show gratitude, appreciate what we have and remember the poor people starving in the war-torn countries. That's all Cassie was trying to say."

"For god's sakes, Ce Ce. You seem to forget I was also one of the poor working class."

"As you never cease to remind us," Cassandra added.

Al, having given in and accepted Cassandra's invitation to dinner, sat listening. *I know it may not be my place to intervene, but I think I'd better step in before this becomes a full-blown family dispute.* "If I may," he said, "people have different tastes. I'm sure there are some who like a noisy restaurant and then there are others who prefer quiet."

"And listen to elevator music too," Cassandra snapped.

"No need to get testy, Cassie," Mr. Sinclair said. "The doctor is a guest." He glanced questioningly at his wife. "Our daughter is a bit on edge tonight." He confronted Cassandra. "You didn't by any chance lose a case in court today?"

"Actually, I won."

"Congratulations. So, why the sour face and bitchy attitude?"

Mrs. Sinclair stood up. "Rosie has baked some of her fabulous desserts. Shall we have coffee and pastries here or on the terrace?"

Cassandra stood. "I'll skip dessert. If I may be excused, I'll take the dogs for a walk." Half smiling, she threw Al a fleeting look.

Al rose and faced his hosts. "Thank you for inviting me. The meal was delicious. Unfortunately, I have work I must attend to. But I'll take a doggy bag of sweets, if you don't mind. I wouldn't want Rosie to think I passed on her baking." He glanced at Cassandra. "If you'd like company,

I'll walk with you."

The Sinclairs eyed one another.

"Bentley," Mrs. Sinclair said, "would you mind wrapping up a dessert for the doctor?"

❧

"You were looking for trouble, weren't you?" Al asked Cassie as they walked beside the panola trees that lined both sides of the road. "Was there a reason you purposely baited your dad? From the way he spoke about you, to me, I thought that you and he got along famously."

She hesitated, bent down and petted Boris, then Natasha. "I guess I was a horror at dinner. It's just that sometimes he and mother both have that puffed-up mind-set—and I have things on my mind."

"I don't know them as well as you do, that's a given, but from where I sit, they seem to be top drawer. Your father has proved himself and your mother seems to be a very dedicated lady."

"You're right. I was out of line. It's me. I've been out of sorts lately."

"Trouble in Paradise?" Fighting his will to keep from taking her hand, he brushed up against her. "Oops. Sorry," he said. "I have this habit of leaning on people when I walk."

She took hold of his hand. "Maybe this will steady you."

"It may do more than that."

She ignored his remark. "Fact is, I just broke up with my fiancée."

"If you did the breaking up, why are you so annoyed?" He kicked a loose stone from the path. "I better mind my own business."

"You're a doctor, I don't mind telling you."

He flushed, knowing he was not a doctor but an imposter with a memory loss. He drew back. "Do your parents know of your dilemma?"

"Mother does."

"And not your father? You have an odd relationship with them."

"Enough about me. Tell me about yourself. I want to know all about you."

CHAPTER 32

A l sat in an ergonomic desk chair, tilting it back to its extreme limit. Sensing the chair was going to tumble backwards, he quickly leaned forward. *This is clearly the direction my life has been heading: up, down; forwards, backwards. I have a great job, super accommodations, gourmet meals, all at no charge.* He swiveled around, jumped up, ran to the bathroom and splashed cold water on his face.

The mirror's image conveyed a dejected, confused man. *Who am I? Better yet, who was I?* Toweling off, he walked back to the computer and shut it down. His eyes focused on the computer's blank, dark screen, once again reminding him of the emptiness he felt.

The ringing of his private phone linked to Mr. Sinclair's brought Al back to reality.

"Al," J.J. said, "we have to talk. I…"

Al cut him off. "Not over the phone," he blurted.

"Right," J.J. agreed. "How about your place in ten minutes?"

"Fine."

Al walked from his bedroom/office into the second guest bedroom, now converted into a state-of-the-art security facility. He spent endless hours scrutinizing and scanning the twenty-five TV cameras that captured and recorded the comings and goings of anything that breathed, spoke or moved on the estate. Placing the headphones over his ears, he viewed and listened to Cassandra lying on her bed talking to one of her gal pals.

"Did you see the creep who tried to come on to me?" she said. "What a loser!"

He would have liked to keep watching Cassandra, but his conscience dictated otherwise. *You have an ethical code to uphold,* he told himself. *You're not a voyeur, a peeping Tom. There's a job to be done. Put your private life on hold. Concentrate!*

Reluctantly, he switched from Cassandra's bedroom to Rosie's cottage to catch a glimpse of Rosie, obviously disgruntled, quarrelling with one of her brothers. He listened intently for a few minutes, but a motion detector signaled a warning of J.J.'s approaching footsteps. Against his better judgment, he jotted down the scene frame, laid the headset on its clip-hook, closed the door, locked it, and walked to meet his boss.

J.J. clasped Al's hand. "Let's walk," he said. "It's getting harder and harder to have a private conversation without the damn security listening to every word we say. Makes me crazy. I'm tempted to sell the whole kit and caboodle and downsize. I'm starting to feel like a prisoner in my own fortress. If it's not the servants eavesdropping, the guards nipping at our heels, it's the relatives mooching money."

"I get what you're saying, J.J. But you must admit, with the extravagant lifestyle you enjoy there are going to be shortfalls. The same feeling comes over me when I examine the security cameras. It's like intruding into a person's personal life. I'm practically in bed with…"

J.J. broke in: "Careful, Al. You might be saying more than you intend to."

"If you're referring to Cassie, you're overreacting. Asking Cassie if she wanted company doesn't imply I was going to do anything more than just walk with her." He stopped and faced J.J. "She *is* over 21, you know. If you want me to stay away from her, say so."

J.J. frowned in thought. "You're right. It's just that she can be so volatile. She has my temperament. One minute she's compassionate and the next, a tiger out for the kill."

Al shrugged. "I suppose that is what makes her a good lawyer." He thrust his hands deep into his pockets. "We got sidetracked. What did you want to see me about? Are you asking if I've made any headway with security?"

J.J. nodded.

"I have, but I wouldn't want to make any judgments or come to any conclusions until I have concrete evidence."

"I knew it! You *are* on to something. Jesus, man. Don't leave me hanging."

"I wouldn't be able to live with myself if I accused anyone without substantiated proof or proper evidence, J.J."

J.J.'s voice was calm and collected. "Well," he said, clapping Al on the back, "I respect you for that. By the way, I've been meaning to ask you. Anything coming to you—you know—from your past?"

"Not a damn thing."

J.J. rubbed his forehead. "It's so bizarre. You have such a propensity for sleuthing. There has to be some connection that ties you to crime from your past."

Al laughed to himself. "Think I've got a sordid past, huh? Maybe I'm running from the law?"

"Don't be foolish. I just meant…"

129

"I know what you meant and I appreciate your concern." His smile conveyed he was pleased that J.J. showed interest in his well-being. "To tell you the truth, J.J., I enjoy your company. It feels good to have someone to talk to. I need friends," he said, thinking of Cassandra.

CHAPTER 33

Al was shaken out of the arms of Cassandra in his dream by the shrill ring of the telephone. "Yes," he said, rubbing the sleepies from his eyes and checking the digital clock on the nightstand.

"Get dressed," Cassandra said. "You're taking the day off."

"Sure. Are you drunk or on something?"

"It's going to be a perfectly gorgeous day. Just right for saddling up the horses and taking a canter along the Rockies."

"Cassie, it sounds wonderful, but I couldn't even if I wanted to." Impersonating a doctor—and hiding the fact he was a mole working to find the security breech on the estate—distressed and worried him. Keeping one step ahead of Cassandra was another undertaking he had not anticipated.

"You're asking the impossible, Cassie," he said. "I'm going back to bed and you should too."

"What can be so God-awful important that can't be put off for one day? I'll pick you up in fifteen minutes. We should get an early start. Daddy has a cabin outside of the city. We'll stop at Guadalupe Street and outfit you at Kowboyz."

"Listen, I'm not going anywhere and certainly not getting outfitted in cowboy attire. Is that plain enough for you?' He thought quickly. "And besides, I've made an appointment this morning with your father to discuss my future. You're the one who said he could do wonders for me, remember?"

"I'll call my dad."

"At five in the morning?"

"He's an early riser. Tell you what, if he thinks it's more important for you to meet with him, I'll beg off. Okay?"

"You know, Cassie, I pity the guy that you get your hooks into."

Al hung up and called J.J., hopeful he would get to speak with him before she did.

Speedily explaining his conversation with Cassandra, Al waited for J.J. to speak.

The first words out of J.J.'s mouth were, "That little minx. I wish she would find a guy, get married and relocate to Timbuktu. She's ringing me on the other phone, so I'll make it short. Take the day off, and sleep over if you want to. One or two days is not going to make a difference." Mr. Sinclair hung up and picked up the other phone. "Hi, Sweetheart. What gives at this hour in the morning?"

"I thought it would be a hospitable thing to take Dr. Hartley on a tour of Sante Fe and also show him our cabin. And there's the annual fiesta going on. But he said he had a meeting with you and didn't want to break it."

"Cassie, that's very thoughtful of you. What a great idea. By all means, go. Have fun, Sweetheart." Mr. Sinclair hung up the phone, pumped his arm, and shouted, "Yes! Yes! Yes! Whoever you are, Al, you just may be the answer to my prayers."

CHAPTER 34

Sitting behind the wheel of the Jeep she had borrowed from the gardener, waiting for Al to come out, Cassandra rested her elbow on the open window and ran her fingers through her long, blond hair. She lowered her oversized sunglasses and cast her eyes in Al's direction with an impish gleam as he walked towards her.

"Good morning," she smiled. "Want to drive? Dad says I'm too aggressive with the guys and should let them do the driving."

"Well, I was kinda expecting you to open the door for me," he joked, aware that he didn't have a driver's license. He thought. *That's something I must attend to. I'll talk to J.J. He'll know what to do.* Quickly regrouping, he said, "You're the guide, and besides, I think you like to be in control."

"You're right. I do."

"What happened to the Ferrari?"

"There's no point in calling more attention to us than is necessary." She opened the compartment door, removed a scarf and wrapped it around her head.

Al caught sight of a gun and four rolled marijuana joints in the corner of the glove compartment. Conscious of his observation, she said, "It's the gardener's Jeep. He lives in an unsavory part of town and thinks he needs protection."

"And the joints?" he asked. "Is that for protection too?"

"Nosey little bugger, aren't you?" She turned the ignition on and drove away from the cottage. "I'm going to show you a good time. There are a million things to entice us."

❧

She floored the gas pedal of the Jeep and they were on their way to the family's cabin, which overlooked the Red River, at the foothills of the Sangre de Cristo Mountains. The Jeep devoured the miles at an accelerated speed, setting the mood for an adventurous and carefree day in the country.

"Why were you so shy about getting outfitted in native garb? It suits you."

Al stretched his hand out of the Jeep to catch the wind. "First of all, I don't have any money. The outfit cost you over three thousand dollars. I'm not happy about you laying out all that cash." His expression tended to be grim. "I didn't realize the merchants started business at seven A.M."

She chuckled. "They don't. The gentleman that outfitted you owns the shop. He's a dear friend of the family."

"You mean you got him out of bed to open up, just for you?"

"We're a close-knit group, Al. We care about one another. Isn't it like that with you?" Gently, she touched his arm. "Where *did* you say you lived?"

Gritting his teeth, he brought his hand back into the Jeep and clenched his fists. *This lady is nobody's fool. Sooner or later, she's going to find out the truth and I'll look like the idiot that I am.*

Becoming aware of his uneasy behavior, she asked, "Did I strike a sensitive chord?"

Shifting nervously in his seat, he slowly turned towards her. "Can we pull over?"

In the blink of an eye, she swerved the Jeep onto the shoulder of the road and turned off the ignition. "Are you sick?"

"Yes," he admitted, "but not the way you think."

"You're married."

"No. No, no, no… At least I don't think so."

"Are you going to tell me or do I have to choke it out of you?"

"I'm not who you think I am."

"That's interesting."

"I don't know where to begin."

"I'm a lawyer, I could interrogate you."

Silence.

"Okay. You're not married and you're not physically ill."

"I'm not a doctor either."

"I'm listening."

"You don't seem surprised."

"I'm not. I researched you. Sure, there are doctors that have the same name, but they don't have the same vital statistics. Actually, I didn't think you were in the medical profession. So, what's your deep dark secret, and why is my dad covering for you?"

"I lost my memory. I don't know who I am."

She reached across, grabbed hold of his cowboy jacket lapels and drew him towards her. "I love it," she shouted. "I fucking love it!"

"Let go of me and I'll tell you."

To his surprise, she pulled him even closer, held him tightly, kissed him, reveling in his innocence. "I'm not sure I want to know. I'm too intrigued."

"Don't play with me, Cassie. I'm serious."

Reluctantly, she let go of his lapels and shrank back in her seat. "Give," she said. "Meanwhile, I'll drive."

The Jeep's tires gripped the dry, hard asphalt and the car took off.

Al stared blankly into the windshield. "I was kicked off a boxcar by the law. I was starving and went into a grocery store. I tried to steal a sandwich and Rosie paid for it."

"Sounds like Rosie."

"She took me home and cleaned me up. Two days later, she introduced me to the your mom and dad. After he and I talked, your dad felt I had an aptitude for sleuthing and asked me to spy on the estate because security couldn't find an intruder seen lurking on the property."

"Why the doctor bit?"

"Your dad didn't want anyone to know who I was and made up the doctor story; he also didn't want you involved. I think, with you, it was more of a game."

"I can understand that. We have a habit of playing the game of who can outfox the other. So, Mr. Mystery, who are you, really?"

"I told you. I don't know. The last thing I remember is traveling on the boxcar and ending up in Sante Fe. And that's the story of my short life."

"Well, you must have redeeming qualities or my dad wouldn't think so highly of you and take you into his confidence. He's a Mensa man. Real sharp. Someone to be reckoned with."

"A Mensa who?"

"It's a super-high IQ organization. Who named you Al?"

"Rosie."

"Oh, yes. Mom said she has a crush on you. Should I be worried?"

He relaxed in his seat. "No. You know how I feel about you."

"Of course," she said with conviction. "It makes for a great start to our little trip."

The glove compartment snapped open as Cassandra touched the latch. She removed a joint, depressed the cigarette lighter, lit it, took two hits and handed it to Al.

Stop! he gestured. "I'm not sure I should. If I smoked before, I don't remember."

"I'd judge you're between thirty-five and forty. You must have tried it. Anyhow, if you didn't, it's a good time to start. Loosen you up." She held up the joint in his direction. "I insist," she said.

He took the joint, put it to his lips and held it there without inhaling.

"If I don't get what I want, I can be a real bitch." She laughed.

"I'll try it. But you're going to be responsible if I lose control."

"I'm willing to take the chance. A couple of puffs will not make you crazy. Inhale deeply."

Smoking and chatting happily, they found themselves thoroughly enjoying each other's company. Their inhibitions dwindled as the day progressed.

"Have you ever gone rafting?" she asked.

He gave her an inquiring glance.

"Guess not" she said. "Not with your up-to-the-minute existence. Well, there's hiking, camping, fishing…"

He frowned.

"Doesn't do anything for you, huh? Got it! The festival. You'll love it. There's every kind of ethnic food you could imagine. You can eat until you drop. We can play games, dance, ride. Oh, yes, and beat the piñata. There's a festival for everything. A wine fest, a chili fest and even a love-in fest."

"Now, that turns me on."

"Don't get peeved, but we'll have to stop and get outfitted."

"Again? Are you kidding? What did we do in the Kowboyz shop?"

"Your wardrobe leaves a lot to be desired, Al. We have to blend in with the locals at the festival. Just a few things; serapes, moccasins, sombreros and…"

"Cassie, we're spending one night, and I'm really getting pissed at your spending so much money on me."

"It makes me happy. And besides, if we're going to be an item, you can't go around in those hand-me-downs you've been wearing. Don't you want me to be happy?"

He shook his head. "Well, it doesn't make me happy. Now you're dressing me? Soon you'll be telling me what to eat and then you'll be running my life. Aren't you taking 'us as an item' for granted?"

"Al, my love. Why begrudge me a little pleasure?" She removed one hand from the steering wheel and grasped hold of his. "And the cabin has a fantastic, cozy fireplace with a real comfy bear rug."

He glanced at the speedometer. "Do you realize you're going eighty-five?"

"Oh, oh," she cried. "That's not a good thing." She eased up on the accelerator just as the siren from a police car pierced their ears. "Shit!" she said. "I'd better pull over. Don't say a word. Let me do the talking. She quickly removed the joints and revolver from the glove compartment and shoved them under her bottom.

The police car pulled up in back of them and sat for a few minutes.

"What's he doing?" Al asked nervously.

"Checking the Jeep's license plate on his computer to see who owns the car and if it has any unpaid tickets or violations."

"What about the stuff you're hiding?"

"Too late to do anything about that. Here he comes. Sit tight."

The officer approached the Jeep and surveyed the back seat, then Cassandra, then Al. He planted his feet wide apart, sniffed the marijuana that wafted in the air and shook his head disapprovingly. "Where's the party and what's the hurry?" he asked.

Cassandra smiled brightly at the officer. "You're not invited, but if you're a real good boy I'll let you have some of the cannabis."

Al, panic-stricken, shrank back in his seat, wishing he were invisible, not believing what he heard.

She winked and smiled broadly. "You flatfooted excuse for a cop," she said, "Why aren't you going after the druggies and drunks?"

The officer scowled at her, lowered his sunglasses, rested his hand on his gun holster, and put his face close to hers. "Please step out of the car, Ma'am," he drawled.

Cassandra put one foot out of the car, met the officer's gaze head-on and raised her hands. Why don't you cuff me, you big bully?"

Unexpectedly, his expression turned to surprise. "Cassie!" he exclaimed. "Is that you? Well, I'll be."

Al let out a sigh of relief.

"How are you doing, Jesse?" she said, smiling. "Last time I saw you was in court. How are Marilyn and the kids?"

"Have another on the way."

"Congratulations." Motioning towards Al, she said, "Jesse, say hello to Al, my latest."

Jesse waved a hello at Al.

Relieved they knew each other, Al half smiled and waved back.

Jesse placed a gentle hand on Cassie's shoulder. "You best be taking it easy," he advised. "Some of the boys that patrol this district might not be as gracious as me. And be careful about the pot. I could smell it a mile away."

"We dated in high school," she told Al, threw a kiss to Jesse, turned on the ignition and sped off.

Al studied her face, raised one brow and shook his head. "You know, I think I've taken on a little more than I can handle."

Somewhere in his troubled psyche a fuzzy physical feature of another lady flashed before his eyes, then instantly grayed away, taking with it a memory of his veiled past.

❧

Forested mountains with lakes, meadows, scattered hot springs and exposed rock formations, crossed by many animal tracks and few paved roads, kept Al's mind occupied as they approached the secluded cabin.

"Wow!' Al sat up and peered through the windshield. "Is this what you call a cabin? Looks more like a hotel. I thought cabins were what Honest Abe lived in."

"Dad bought it from one of his golf buddies who retired and moved to Fisher Island. It was rumored to have been a retreat for a clandestine Santa Fe elite set who were into playing bizarre games."

"Bizarre? Did your father participate?"

Cassandra pulled into the four-car garage. "Would you mind getting the luggage, Al? I want to see if Leon the caretaker is around. The front door should be open. I called him to make sure the pantry was stocked and the liquor topped off. No one has used the place for a while."

"You've piqued my interest, Cassie."

She took a few steps and turned around. Shoulders hunched, she asked, "How?"

"You didn't answer my question about the odd games you just mentioned."

Walking over to him, she leaned her backside against the Jeep's fender, drew him to her and pecked him on the forehead, the nose, each cheek, and then kissed him fully on the mouth.

"It seems the elite social set of Santa Fe were bored and needed some extra-curricular activities to get them out of the doldrums. So they did a few snorts and smoked some weed, and ..."

"And?" he asked, pressing her to him.

She held him at arm's length. "We'll have to save this for later. I must get to Leon and see what needs to be spruced up in the cabin. I'll tell you all about the elite's improprieties at dinner." Pushing him away, she slid him a meaningful glance. "And Al, there is something about me you should know before we ..."

CHAPTER 35

His arm around Cassandra, Al rubbed his naked body on the soft, furry bear rug he and Cassandra shared. A glass of chardonnay in hand, he stared fixedly into the stone fireplace, daydreaming. *Yesterday I was a hobo, a lost soul looking for a handout, traveling on freight cars, not knowing or caring where the next screech of the train's wheels would take me.* He chortled. *And today I'm lying next to a beautiful woman who professes to love me, and has the means to take care of me in the best style that life can afford. She has this magnetic hold over me. Am I in love? Why can't I give myself wholly to her? I'd be a fool to let this opportunity slip away…and yet…*

Cassandra turned to him, propped up on an elbow and looked intently into his unwavering eyes. Her voice was low and engaging. "Want to come back down to earth? How about inviting me into your mysterious world?" She cuddled up to him.

Setting the wine glass down, he surrounded her with his arms and tenderly kissed her on her forehead. "Sorry," he said. "Every so often my thoughts tend to drift."

"I know. You've got a lot going on in that good-looking head of yours. Let's put all the heavy stuff on the back burner. From now on, there's only you and me."

Nuzzling her nose with his, he laughed softly. "It's crazy."

"I like crazy. What is?"

"It's one in the afternoon, you have a roaring fire going, and the air conditioning on at the same time. I can't figure you out."

"Neither can I, Al. Neither can I. Let's not talk. Let's just chill out—get into each other's thoughts in silence. The less said the better." She deftly rolled her body on top of his.

He moaned.

"Shush."

"I have to ask you something," he said.

"You're breaking the spell."

"Please?"

She rolled off of him and propped back up on her elbow. "It better be important or you're in a lot of hot water."

"We can always continue the thoughtful silence."

"Did I tell you that I love you, Al?"

"Yes."

"Well?"

"I love you too. I've been thinking about what you said before."

"You mean the clandestine goings-on with the elite?"

"No. You said there was something about you I should know."

She sat up, pulled her negligee across her breast and sulked. "I have to tell you, Al, you couldn't have chosen a worse time to bring that up."

She quickly turned away and rose before his outstretched hand could touch hers. She walked to the window.

Pulling on his shorts he ran to where she stood, positioned himself in back of her, and encircled her with his arms. "For God's sake, Cassie, what did I say to upset you? Help me out here, will you?"

Grasping his hands in front of her, she inclined her head on his shoulder. Her reflection from the windowpane spoke to him. "It isn't you, Al, it's me."

"I'm sorry," he said. "I fucked up. But since I've already destroyed the mood, maybe it's a good time for you to tell me what you're holding back."

A tear rolled onto her cheek.

Grasping her waist, he lifted her bodily and placed her on the sofa. He picked up the glasses of chardonnay, handed one to her and sat down beside her. "Drink," he said. "You need it."

"I don't want to lose you, Al."

"Lose me? Funny you should say that. If anyone were going to lose, it would be me. What do I have to offer you? No money, no future, no memory..." His eyes held hers. "You've got it all. You're beautiful, wealthy, and a successful lawyer. Riding on your coattails would set me up for life. I'd have it made in the shade. That is, unless you're going to tell me that you murdered someone or robbed a bank. What could you possibly have to say that would make me want to leave you?"

"You're thinking just like a man."

"Excuse me?"

"You're right. I might as well come clean. All my life, I have been trying to prove myself. Always driven, ambitious, aggressive and self-confident. From kindergarten through law school I had to attain the highest grades, become editor of the school newspapers, leader of the sorority, cheerleader, top sports player, and who knows what else. I'm sure a lot of it was Daddy's constant pushing." The tears now streamed down her cheeks.

He handed her a handful of tissues. "You're on overload, Cassie. I'm sure J.J. only wanted the best for you. Parents are human but they *can* get carried away." Narrow-eyed, he stared at her. "That can't possibly be what's bothering you."

"No, it's not. I hadn't intended to spill my guts out. It just happened. I feel so comfortable with you. Anyhow, I was pregnant when I went to Europe, supposedly to break up with my fiancée. I had made an appointment to have an abortion, but without warning I miscarried." She hesitated.

"Go on."

"I had complications which required an emergency hysterectomy. As a result, I can't have children."

Sensing her fragile state of mind, he bent his head and brushed his lips across her temple then kissed her gently, tenderly. "Oh, Cassie, I'm so sorry." He raised a finger and wiped a tear from her cheek. "Still, it's not the end of the world. You can always adopt."

She glanced up at him. "You said, '*you* can always adopt.' I would have preferred '*we.*'"

Guilt and uncertainty ran through Al's mind. "I wasn't thinking, Cassie. Honestly, I did mean 'we."

"Can I take that as a commitment?"

Al swallowed a thoughtful sigh, held it in as long as he could then let it out slowly, biding for time to consider her unexpected proposal. Finding himself faced with making a decision and caught up in his own web of uncertainty, he took her hand, pulled her to her feet, held her tightly to him. "A commitment sounds like an arrangement or a written court order of documentation. I'm more comfortable with an "I do."

CHAPTER 36

Out of the darkness, something thrashed against the glass sliding door of the master bedroom. "What was that?" Cassandra called to Al.

He buttoned up the silk gaucho shirt she had pleaded with him to wear and glanced at her as she played with the ball-fringed tassels on her sombrero. "Probably a branch that fell off the weeping willow tree, or Leon puttering around the patio.

"Leon's in town. I gave him three days off."

Al huffed. "Three days, Cassie? You know I have to get back to the estate. You promised we'd be here for the festival and then…"

"That was then and this is now, Sweetheart." She walked over to him and unbuttoned the four top buttons on his shirt. "No one buttons all the way up," she said. "You've got fantastic pecs. Why keep it a secret?"

"Cassie, you're getting ahead of yourself. I'm not one of your boy toys that jump every time you whistle. Don't try to make me into something I'm not, or try to run my life. As it is, I've got a hard enough time trying to get through each fucking day."

Adjusting the handmade serape cape around her shoulders, she poured wine into two glasses, handed him one and smiled. "Jesus, Al, the last thing I want to do is make you into one of those wimpy yes-men. What I love about you is your independence, your strong character. Maybe I can be a little overbearing at times, but I do love you."

"And I love you too, Cassie. I didn't mean to go off on you. You have to give me time to adjust."

"Take all the time you want, Al. That's what true love is. A test. Two people argue, settle their differences, make up—then work it out and build a solid relationship. Don't you agree?"

A sudden shatter of glass crashing onto the terrace patio floor interrupted Al's answer. "What the hell?" he cried. "There *is* someone out there!"

"I'll call the police," Cassandra shouted.

"Doesn't Leon have a dog?"

"A Lab."

"Hold on. Let me check it out. It could be an animal. We *are* in the boondocks. Maybe Leon came back."

"I doubt it."

Al drew his gun. "Cassie," he called, "turn off the lights."

Surprised, she backed up. "You pack a gun?"

The familiarity of holding the gun triggered momentary flashes through Al's mind, but he shrugged them off. Moving toward the terrace door, he said, "Shut off the lights. I don't pack a gun; it's the one that was in the pickup truck."

Without delay, she switched the lights off. "Al, I lied," she said. "It's my gun, but I have a license."

"I guessed as much." He sidled up to the terrace door, slid it open and looked out.

At his heels, Cassandra stopped short. "I just remembered," she said, "I can light up the entire area."

"Where's the switch?"

"Right here, on the wall."

"Whoever or whatever it is, is gone by now. Turn it on, but stay inside."

At the turn of the switch the area lit up like daylight, and from the far end of the road Al could just about make out the rear-end of a pickup truck as it sped away.

"What does Leon drive?" he asked.

"An old vintage Oldsmobile that J.J. gave him years ago. It's his pride and joy. Should I call him? Maybe he came back for something."

"Forget it. That wasn't Leon." Al bent down and examined the shattered glass. "How come there aren't any cameras on the property?"

"J.J. had them removed."

"Because of the clandestine parties?"

"I don't know. It's possible. It's been years. The elite were totally hush-hush when it came to their personal lives."

"I bet they were."

"Maybe someone took a wrong turn."

He shook his head. "I doubt it."

She studied his face then raised one brow. "J.J. was right. You do have an affinity for sleuthing."

"Are you nervous?" he asked.

"Not with you here."

Al focused on the water that had spilled on the table then eyed the shattered glass vase that lay scattered on the patio floor. The flowers lay motionless, seemingly waiting to be rescued.

"It's most likely an animal looking for food. I'll turn the automatic lighting timer on. Leon can leave it or shut it off after we leave.

"I'll clean up the mess," Cassandra offered.

"Why not leave it for Leon?"

"Good idea, Sherlock," she joked. "Are we still up for the festival? Or? Let's put everything on hold for the time being."

Grinning mischievously at her for calling him Sherlock, he picked her up, carried her to the bed and gently put her down. "You're asking for trouble, lady." He climbed on top of her and held her arms down at her sides.

"Oh, Sir," she exclaimed, "I could have you arrested for taking advantage of this poor innocent girl's maidenhood. I'm barely fifteen."

"You haven't been fifteen or a virgin since Brooklyn was a prairie."

His lips found hers and she quickly responded.

I know what I want, and this is it, he told himself, as he fought to stave off the memory synapse that sparked his brain during sex.

She hesitated for a moment, listened to his breath quicken, watched the intense expression on his face—in his eyes. Smiling triumphantly, assured of his love, she prayed his memory would never return. *If it did,* she thought, *he might not know who I am and I'll lose him.*

Breaking the kiss, he drew back, jumped up and tore his clothes off.

She pulled her blouse over her head, tossed it, stepped out of her skirt and panties, and lay back on the bed, waiting.

Flushed with the heat of the moment he pleaded, "Cassie, please, I'm so hot. I can't wait. Could I...?"

Grasping Al's hand, feeling the excitement of his fingers clutching hers she cried, "Yes! Oh yes! Do it! Do it!"

Holding the Sunday newspapers, Al stood, looking down at Cassandra, admiring her angelic features while she slept. He smiled.

Aware of his presence, she opened her eyes and returned his smile. With outstretched arms, she beckoned to him. "Good morning. Forget the papers. Burn them in the fireplace along with all the dreadful one-sided interpretations those fiends make up."

"No can do, my love. Leon has gone to all the trouble to make a breakfast fit for a king and queen. In fact, he said he made your favorite breakfast dish: an egg in the hole. Whatever that is. And I've already spoken to J.J."

She sat up and pulled the top sheet across her breasts. "Is he here?"

"Leon or J.J.?" he joked.

"Leon, silly. Why did J.J. call?"

"I spoke to J.J. on the phone two hours ago. Seems we're both early risers. The problem with the guy who's been lurking about the estate has been solved. You'll never guess who the culprit is."

"I haven't had my coffee, and since you refused my advances, I'm not playing your game."

She rose, slipped into her negligee and pulled him to her. "You don't know what you're missing," she teased.

He held her at arm's length. "You're dying to know."

"I couldn't care less. Dad's spent a fortune setting up that apparatus in your cottage. Now it's useless."

"Maybe the prospective tenants who buy the estate will give it to their kids along with the video games and iPods."

"Dad's been talking of selling the estate for years. He won't."

"Want to change into something more appropriate?"

"Not until you tell me who the intruder was."

"I don't care if Leon gets excited when you appear in that see-through negligee."

"I'll change if you want me to."

Knowing she probably would have the nerve to breakfast in the sheer negligee in Leon's presence to spite him, he said, "It was Rosie's brother."

"And last night's incident?"

"The very same. Evidently, Rosie broke down and told her brothers that she liked me and they took it upon themselves to retaliate, since I shrugged her off."

"But, Al, the disturbances on the estate happened before you came here."

"I know. It seems they were planning to do something unsavory. They did have access to the estate when they visited Rosie. Anyhow, J.J. gave them a choice: back to Cuba or jail time here."

"Poor Rosie. I'm starving," she said. "Let's talk about it later. I'm really covered up and Leon is gone."

Al growled: "But *I'm* embarrassed, Cassie."

"Okay, I'll change." She ran into the kitchen, grabbed a cup of coffee, stood in front of Leon, and said, "Morning, Leon," then quickly ran into the bathroom.

When she returned she encircled Al with her arms as he sat waiting for her. "Al, Honey, you didn't have to wait for me." She took a seat opposite him and filled his coffee mug while catching a glimpse of Leon as he walked down the road. "I guess Dad spoke to Leon about the incident last night." She watched Al's every expression, trying to read his thoughts. "Can I serve you my special egg dish?"

"If you like," he said, not happy with her immodest behavior. *How much do I know about this woman I'm in love with?* he wondered. "You never cease to amaze me, Cassie."

She nodded. "That's the way it should be, Sweetheart. Otherwise it could be boring." She placed the egg concoction onto his plate. "How does it look? Good enough to eat? Now you know what Leon meant by an egg in the hole. You just cut out a circle in the bread, butter the frying pan and put the egg in the hole. I have to know these things so I can be the perfect wife when we're married."

Taken aback, he nearly choked on the coffee. "Shouldn't we get engaged first? We haven't even picked out a ring. And I'm more than perturbed about not being able to pay for it myself, which will probably be never."

"Al, my love. I have a diamond ring that would knock your eyes out." She leaned across the table, stared into his eyes, and whispered, "It is what it is. So you're not rich."

"That's a joke. Did you ever think that I might be married?"

"I've already taken care of that. Well, actually, not me, J.J."

"I can't wait to hear this."

"Later."

"You wealthy folks think you can buy your way out of anything. Why not now?"

"Because there are other matters we have to discuss and we have to face the facts. You don't know your past, and your future could present significant problems for us…that is, if your memory should return. You might not know who I am. *I'm* willing to take the chance. Do you love me enough to do the same?"

Infatuated with her and well aware of his impoverished circumstances, he sighed. "I do love you, but you have to understand my plight. We can't rule out the fact that my loss of memory could be caused by other problems, like an aneurism or brain damage. I did stutter a few months ago. I am getting better but…"

"We'll go to the most accredited doctors in the world and have you checked out. What is important is the now. You can do anything you want. Work for J.J. Take up polo. Or even retire. As I said before, we have to live in the now." His sour expression troubled her. "There is one thing I have to discuss with you."

"What's that?"

"I won't give up my practice."

"I would never ask you to do that, Cassie." A muscle in his jaw tightened. "What about children? Is it too sensitive a subject to talk about at this time? You were upset when you told me about the operation."

"Al, you don't have to be afraid to say it. The word is hysterectomy.

"I know, but…"

"I don't intend to live in the past." She nodded to confirm her opinion. "More eggs?" Then suddenly, "I'd love to adopt. Just think—our own family. A boy for you and a girl for me."

"I have to be honest with you, Cassie. This is very hard for me to digest."

"Don't tell me my eggs in the hole are giving you agita? Wait until you taste my French toast."

Ignoring her tease, he sipped his coffee and held it out for her to refill.

"At least the coffee is good," she said.

He stood, bent over, reached across the table and held her face in his hands. "You little tease," he said, "you know damn well Leon prepared the breakfast," and then proceeded to kiss her.

The chair scraped along the kitchen tile as he sat back down. "Don't be pulling your lawyer spiel on me, counselor. I'm on to you. Underneath that phony, tough exterior you put on you're as soft as mush. I think J.J. wanted a son so badly he tried to make you into a guy."

Could be, she thought. Swishing the bread and egg yolks around her plate, she placed the fork on the table and raised her eyes so that they locked with his. "I think J.J. might be wrong for once in his life. Maybe you weren't in law enforcement. Maybe you were a shrink."

She started to clear the dishes when he unexpectedly grabbed hold of her hand. "I have the strangest feeling you're holding something back, Cassie. Is there something bothering you? It's been only a few months. If we are to spend a lifetime together shouldn't we clear up any misunderstandings now?"

Her answer came quickly, as if she'd been preparing for this question. "You're right, Darling, but let's just shack up until we both feel we're ready."

CHAPTER 37

The flap on the bottom of the revolving door *whsst* to the sound of people going in and out of the Empire Diner on 34th and Fifth.

Upon seeing Lily, Matt stood, greeted Lily with a peck on her cheek and a hug.

Lily took in his unkempt appearance. His expression, usually full of energy and cheerfulness, was now downcast and sullen. The once sparkling brown eyes were clouded and lifeless. She touched his arm with assurance then let out a deep, audible breath of frustration.

"I'm being tested every damn day," Lily said.

He pulled the chair out for her. "Tested?" He sat down. "Explain, please."

"Your heavy sigh and excessive hug just sent me a message of why you wanted to meet in a place Franny wouldn't be seen in."

He nodded. "You got that right. All I need is for her to see us dining without her. What's with the test?"

"Whenever a problem comes up, and lately they've been popping up nonstop, my mind reaches for the booze."

"I'm sorry, Lily. I forgot they serve liquor. Want to leave?"

"Don't put off today, to coin a phrase, Matt. What did Franny do this time? I thought all was quiet on the western front."

"It's been touch and go. The baby is an angel. He just about sleeps through the night and giggles all the time."

"And?"

"Listen, you know Franny better than anyone, and I hate ragging on her and her eccentricities but…"

Lily gritted her teeth. "Tell Mama all about it."

The waiter approached and they ordered.

"Believe me, Lily. I dislike using you as a sounding board, but I don't know where else to turn. With all the crazy shtick she pulls, I still love her. She has that certain something that attracts, yet hurts."

Lily nodded. "I know. She stings you with honey. On the other hand, she would lay down her life for a friend." She sipped her lemonade, held it up to admire the colors. "This is better than wine! Better than wine! Better than wine! Sorry, I should have said my serenity prayers instead. What did our Franny do now?"

He took a bite of his tuna on rye toast, chewed, wiped his mouth and leaned forward. "She loves the baby but…"

Lily filled in his words. "But she's not sure she wants to be burdened with him."

"I don't know if burdened is the right word." He shrugged. "Then again, it is. Little Nicky is so good, and he's getting to look more like his father every day."

"That doesn't bother you?"

"Not in the least. Nick isn't around. What gets me is the lack of attention Franny gives the baby. The likeness bothers Franny, not me."

"What are you saying?"

"Lily, you can't deny that the baby resembles Nick, can you?"

"No."

"I'm not one to judge a woman's moods or behaviors after they give birth, but I think Franny has a deep resentment toward the baby because of Nick."

"You think? Why?"

"She talks in her sleep."

"My God!" Lily exclaimed. "Postpartum depression."

"If it weren't for the live-in nurse, and the visits from you and Lew, I'd probably have split before this. And I thought I had found the real thing," he said. "Now I want to pack everything in and take the next plane to…"

"Yes, Matt. I know exactly how you feel. But it wouldn't work. Franny did mention giving the baby up for adoption, but that was before she gave birth. And afterwards, she seemed to take on a whole different attitude. She doted on the baby."

"Not for long. A week after we brought Nicky home she stopped nursing and had the nurse put him on formula. She said it hurt when he suckled."

Lily grimaced. "I made a big mistake. I'm beginning to think I should have adopted the baby like she asked me to. I am the baby's godmother."

"I'd like to," Matt said. "But I'm not the father, a relative, or even a stepfather, and Franny would never go for it. I have to be honest with you, Lily. If Franny keeps on the way she is, I'm not sure I'll be able to stick around much longer. I've suggested she see a shrink, but then she pulls one of her tirades."

"How's she doing at work?"

"Fantastic. It's the only thing she looks forward to. In fact, she's become a workaholic. Gets up early and comes home late. Most of the time she doesn't even look in on the baby."

"I'm going to talk to Lew. Maybe I *will* take the baby for a while."

"What about your concert tours?"

"I have only four this year."

"Think it's a good idea? I mean, moving the baby around?"

"You're right. It's not a good idea. An infant picks up things from the moment they're born. Still, something has be done—and soon."

Matt clenched his jaw and rubbed his temples. "I've tried reasoning with Franny, but you know her. And arguing in front of the baby is a no-no. I count to ten and leave the apartment. I think she's blaming Nick for not being here."

Nick would have been able to handle her, Lily reflected. *Where is he when she needs him?*

His hand unsteady, Matt took a swallow of his coffee and put it down clumsily, causing it to spill onto the table.

Lily instantly grabbed for the paper napkin holder and blotted the trickle. "You're not using, are you?"

He shook his head. "No, it's nerves. I've been straight for over a year. I've got too much responsibility running the new line. Don't need the stuff. Even hang with a different crowd. I don't know what's come over me. The metro-sexual Don Juan who is always in control is suddenly becoming a train wreck." He looked profoundly upset. "You and Lew are the only ones she'll listen to. If you two took the baby as you suggested and had a heart-to-heart with Franny until things can be worked out, it would be a tremendous help."

Lily dipped the raw broccoli into the dish of low calorie dressing, held it in midair in thought, and then put it down on her plate. She wiped her fingers with a napkin, reached into her bag for her cell phone and called Lew at the office.

CHAPTER 38

Hardly visible among the scattered mountains of maternity sketches, Franny sat cross-legged on the floor of her office, intently studying the drawings.

Lily, her arms folded across her chest, stood at the door for a few minutes, silently watching her friend immersed in work. Lily's heels clicking on the parquet floor announced her arrival. She walked to Franny's desk and sat down.

Without lifting her head to see who it was, Franny mouthed jokingly, "Did you make an appointment with my secretary? I only work by appointment. Take a hike, sister." She dropped the drawings and jumped up, ran to Lily and kissed her on both cheeks. "I knew it was you. Lew told me you were coming."

"You didn't answer my phone call. What's your excuse?"

"Yeah, I know. You can see what's going on. I'm up the kazoo with work. I haven't had a fucking minute to myself."

Hands defiantly on her hips, Lily said, "Really?"

"What's with the attitude, Lily?"

"If I may be allowed to borrow some of your habitual street terminology…too fucking bad."

"Well, the fancy shmancy diva pianist has taken to cursing?"

Lily swiveled back and forth in the armchair. "We have to talk."

Franny kicked at a few of the sketches. "Don't push me, Lily. No fucking talking, no fucking preaching, no fucking nothing." She hesitated. "Excuse me if I used two negatives in one sentence. I just want to be left alone to do my work."

Lily walked to the door and shut it then walked back to the desk and picked up the phone. "Chantal," she said to Franny's assistant, "Franny will not be taking calls until further notice. Got it?"

"You have a helluva nerve coming in here and giving my secretary orders. Just because you're the boss's wife doesn't give you the right to take over," she yelled.

But within her troubled mind, a voice longing to be heard called out. *Oh, Lily. Beat me! Slap the shit out of me! Shake some sense into me! Help me lick this damn depression. I hurt so badly.* She turned away from Lily to hide the tears that fell onto her cheeks. "Okay," she whispered, "as soon as I finish up I'll give you a call, and we'll talk."

Lily stood and waved her finger at Franny. "We'll talk now! Turn around and look at me!"

Franny turned slowly, the tears evident.

Arms outstretched, Lily waited for Franny to fill them. "I'm such a bitch," Franny sniffled. "You're always there for me and I treat you like shit. What's wrong with me?"

They looked at each other and broke out laughing. "Don't say it," Franny said as she wiped beneath her eyes. She looked at the tissue. "And they guaranteed the eye makeup wouldn't run even under water."

"Ready to have a heart-to-heart?" Lily asked.

"Yeah, I'm ready."

Lily sat down on the couch and motioned with her finger to Franny. "Sit," she commanded. "Let's get serious here. Working twelve hours a day is ridiculous." She leaned closer. "Now concentrate and fill in the blanks."

Franny looked puzzled.

Lily continued. "I'm running away from...?"

"Huh?"

"C'mon, Franny, fill in the blanks. I'm running away from...?"

Franny screwed her face up. "The baby."

"And why is that?"

"I don't know."

"Sure you do. Think."

"I don't know, I tell ya."

"Frannnnny!"

"All right!" she blurted. "It's been over a year and Nick's probably dead or whatever, and even though the baby is adorable, every time I look at him Nick's face appears."

"Go on."

She struggled to maintain her calm. "And I feel real bad about Matt. He's been doing his best to be there for me—and I treat him like shit. I want to love him, but fucking Nick stands in the way. I can't tell Matt about it."

"And you're...?"

"Lost and confused. The only thing that gives me pleasure is working on the line. It's an escape, but I don't know what else to do. We even planned to take a vacation with the baby, but I chickened out. And there's another thing." She lowered her eyes. "You're going to kill me."

Lily rolled her eyes. "I can't wait to hear."

"I've been drinking."

"How much and how long?"

"Don't get crazy. I stopped two days ago. I couldn't take the throwing up and it interfered with my work."

"Are you being honest with me?"

"I sincerely am, Lily."

"Well, that's one less problem to cope with." Rubbing her finger across her forehead in an attempt to erase her frown, Lily said, "Franny, I've talked to Lew and we have decided to take the baby—just until you get your head straight."

"Oh, Lily, I knew I could depend on you. I'm beginning to feel better already."

"Not so fast, lady. There are conditions."

"Anything."

"You have to go away for at least a month."

"You're committing me? Where to? The loony bin?"

"No. Be serious. Maine Chance or the Golden Door."

"A month? No way. I have too much work to do."

"Lew said the spring line is finished—just waiting for Matt's and your approval. You need to regroup. Lew's going to pick up the tab."

"You think I'm nuts, don't you?"

Lily dropped her shoulders and raised an eyebrow. "You don't really want an answer, do you? It's well documented that you're off the wall. What do you say?"

"Will you come with me?"

"I can't. I have a concert in Chicago coming up. And I want to spend time with the baby. But I promise, I'll visit."

"I'll do it." She took Lily's hand in hers. "I love you."

Lily took in a deep breath and let it out slowly. "And vice versa, Kiddo."

CHAPTER 39

Franny tried to turn off all thoughts of people, things and events—chuck them somewhere, anywhere. Smiling inwardly, she recalled Lily's last words when she hugged her goodbye at J.F.K. Airport. "Don't forget to take the pills. Remember, you're going on a rest cure, a getaway vacation—to get away from Franny."

She popped two Valium, washed them down with a cup of water and inclined the seat as far back as possible. Comfortable in white sneakers, a New York Giants sweatshirt and loose leggings, she greeted the flight attendant with a smile and a wave of dismissal. "I'll be incommunicado until further notice, thank you," she said.

Recalling Lily's advice, she thought, *Get away from Franny? How the hell do I do that? Okay, so I go off once in a while. The last year hasn't been a day at the beach. What's the big deal? I'm entitled.*

Her inner voice reminded her. "Maybe you're thinking of Franny and what *Franny* wants?"

Okay, so I tend to overreact. Who am I hurting?

The voice replied, "You tell me."

I know where you're going with this. You're intimating that I'm a bad mother because of the kid?

"The kid? I take it you are referring to your baby."

Excuse me! Yes, the baby. Let me tell you something. I'm a person with feelings and I don't take lightly to your accusing me of neglecting my child. He has the best of care. People who adore him surround him.

"But they are not his mother."

Is that so? And I suppose it's my fault that his father deserted him and me? You think that's okay? Well, I've got news for you. I don't. I get to say what's right and what's not right for me.

"For you? What about the baby?"

Listen, whoever you are. You're trying to confuse me. I have enough to contend with. That's why I'm taking this…

"…Holiday—vacation—getaway—escape? What are you escaping from, Franny? Your guilty conscience?"

Who says I'm escaping from anything? You're making me out to be some compassionless, self-absorbed nitwit. Well, I'm not. I held a responsible job as top salesperson. All my customers loved me. Ask anyone in the garment center. And I'm instrumental in what is now a very successful business. I worked my frigging ass off. So there too!

Silence.

Guess you gave up, huh, Miss Nosybody. No response?

"I didn't give up. Only trying to make some sense out of you. Does that excuse you for running out on the baby?"

Running out? That's as much as you know. After I come back, I'm going to give the baby up for adoption. He's going to have parents that love him and give him everything he deserves. I'm doing what's best for him.

"And why is that the best thing?"

Listen, whoever you are. I'll lay it on the frigging line. Don't think I don't know my shortcomings. In case you haven't heard, I'm not fit to raise a child. I have a screw loose somewhere. I can't even cope with what's on my frigging plate now. And since you insist on prying into my private affairs and won't mind your own business, I'll let you in on a little secret. Is it my fault my husband is not around? That my boyfriend is leaving me? You think I don't want a normal life like most people have? And don't for one frigging minute think that my heart's not breaking—having to give up the baby.

The flight attendant bent down and gently touched Franny's arm. "Excuse me, Mrs. Pagliara, you were talking in your sleep." She motioned with her eyes toward the other passengers and whispered, "You were attracting attention."

"Did I say anything off-color?"

"No."

"Well, that's a first. There's hope. Things are already looking up."

CHAPTER 40

The moment she exited airport security she came face to face with a placard held by a white-gloved chauffeur. It read: Franny Pagliara. He tipped his cap and greeted Franny with a wide smile. "I am William. Welcome to the Golden Door." He escorted her to a gleaming, black Bentley limousine. "I hope you don't mind sharing, but there is another passenger already aboard." His finger touched the remote control and the limo's door swung curiously upward.

"No, I don't mind," she said, but thought *now I've seen everything.*

As if angel wings had come to rest, the doors of the limo noiselessly closed. Franny fastened her seat belt and stared at the lady sitting opposite her. *Jesus,* she thought. *Here I am in my sweats and straw wedgies and this fem is dressed to kill.* She sank back into her seat.

The attractive lady, her hair swept back in an elegant chignon, dressed in a white linen pantsuit and Jimmy Choo sandals, peered over her designer sunglasses and smiled at Franny. "You were smart," she said. "I wish I had the time to dress in jeans and a sweatshirt. I was running to make the flight."

No shit? Franny thought. *From the looks of you, you could have had your maid bring along a change of clothes.* "Only way to travel," Franny said. "Who were you running from?"

"I wasn't running from anyone." Her face darkened as she leaned forward, envisioning the argument she had had with Al, about getting away in order to sort things out before they got out of hand. "You might be right. I did leave hastily."

Franny leaned back in her seat. "Everyone's rushing around, spinning their wheels and ending up in the same place."

"You're from New York, I take it?'

"You got it. Born and bred. Shows, huh?'

"I like it. Where I come from everyone sounds like they're from the Midwest."

"Where's that?"

"New Mexico."

"Yeah. In the Big Apple, you can slice a piece of every culture and you've tasted the entire universe."

Cassandra considered Franny's comment. "Quite profound," she said.

"So, why the rush to the airport?"

"I was in court. I thought it would never end."

"Win, lose or draw?"

"I won, thank God. I'm a lawyer. I was trying a case."

"Mm… beauty *and* brains. I'm in the fashion business. Used to sell, but now I'm heading a maternity line. It's going like blockbusters."

"Good for you. I thought you might be a model."

Franny guffawed. "Are you on drugs?"

The woman laughed out loud. "Come now," she said. "You *are* very pretty."

"Yeah, I guess. But a model? You're putting me on. Now you—you're class. I can see you strutting your stuff down the runway."

"I like you. You're so down to earth."

Franny broke out laughing. "I've been told that I'm a lot of things. But more like from outer space than down to earth. I'll take that as a compliment. You're all right."

Cassandra extended her hand. "I'm Cassandra Sinclair. Call me Cassie."

"I'm Francesca Pagliara. Franny, to the world."

CHAPTER 41

A pain sliced through Rosie at the thought of her brothers.

True, she thought, *they were high-spirited boys in Havana. But to become hoodlums and steal from the Sinclairs—it boggles my mind. Wasn't it only yesterday we pushed the homemade barco into the ocean and after hours of rowing tipped over and almost drowned until the fisherman picked us up?*

Her brothers were the last people she wanted to see, talk to, or have anything to do with, and it tormented her no end.

And then the moment she dreaded happened. Simultaneously, the cell phone rang and the boiling teapot whistled, sending a shiver through her.

The statue of the Holy Virgin Mary loomed down at Rosie as she dropped to her knees. "Madre los mios," she cried. "Help me! What should I do? Give me strength."

Holding on to the mantel of the makeshift altar, she slowly raised herself, walked to the burner, turned it off and picked up her cell.

"Rosie."

"Desi," she whispered hoarsely. "I told you not to call me. Haven't you and Vidal shamed me enough? I'm so embarrassed. I can't show my face. The Sinclairs have been so good to me, and to you and your brother, too."

"We are sorry, Rosie. Really we are. We didn't think. We only wanted to get enough money together so we could send for the old folks and maybe a few relatives."

"You couldn't care less for the relatives back in Habana. And you think stealing from my boss was the right way to get the money?"

She flashed back to when they were growing up—of the times the boys were caught lying, stealing, and constantly embroiled in trouble.

"I'm not going to listen to your lies anymore, Desi. You're not thankful to be in a country where you can be free to think and worship the way you want to, not that you and Vidal ever went to church." She crossed herself. "If the Sinclairs weren't so abundante, you both would be in jail."

"You're right, you're right," he said in an attempt to placate her. "Si, they were very good to us."

"So what do you want?"

"We want to get out of here. These are not our kind of people. They treat us like peasants. Always looking down their noses at us and talk about us behind our backs, like we are dirt."

"Then go back to Habana if you're not happy here. I doubt they'll let you back in."

"We are going to Mexico."

"You think it's better there? The Mexicans are all coming here."

"We won't be safe anywhere in the States. Mr. Sinclair is making sure of that. He wants us out of here and pronto."

"So go. What's stopping you?"

"Dinero. Dinero, hermana estimada. Dinero."

She wished she didn't have brothers. *It's a knife in my heart, but I have to do what is best for me. If they go, my problems will also, and I'll have my life back to where it was.*

"Dinero, dinero," she mimicked. "And you promise to leave for good?"

"We promise on the blessed image of Candida Maria de Jesus."

Knowing Desi never stepped a foot into a church, she swallowed a gurgle. "Cuanto?"

"Two thousand."

"Usted esta' loco!"

"Half for Vidal and half for me. It is not safe for us to stay here. The boss will cut our bolas off."

She mustered her strength. "One thousand. Not a centavo more. You better take it, or you'll be sleeping in the jail."

"You drive a hard bargain, Rosie. Okay, when can we meet? It has to be soon. The boss has his dogs on our ass."

"I don't want to be seen with you two. I have to go to the bank and withdraw the money."

"Small bills, Rosie. Donde y cuando?"

"Meet me on the corner of Elm and Pine at the edge of town at two o'clock this afternoon. I'll be driving my truck. As soon as I see you, I'll throw the envelope to you. I don't even want to touch you. Understand?"

"Si, si. Adios."

Rosie closed the cell phone and knelt at the makeshift altar. Holding tightly to her rosary beads she looked up at the Madonna and crossed herself. She prayed then walked to the stove and touched the teapot to see if the water was still hot. Her eyes followed the teabag as it slowly slid to the bottom of the cup. She thought. *Al is gone—the boys are gone—and I'm alone.*

The buzzer from the main house rang, startling her. "Yes, Mr. Sinclair," she answered. "It's important? I'll be right over."

CHAPTER 42

A warm southerly breeze carried a promise of better days to come as Franny checked out the clients having breakfast under multi-colored umbrellas.

A voice, clearly precise, came from behind her. "Dining alone is so boring. Mind if I join you?"

Without turning around, Franny said, "Has to be my newfound friend, Cassie. Sure. Take a load off. I was looking over the to-do list." She shook her head. "Is this a spa or a boot camp?"

Cassandra pulled out a chair and sat down. "I take it this is your first time at the spa."

"My first, and from the looks of this schedule, my last."

"You'll change your mind. Once you get into it, you'll love it."

"I guess you've been here before?"

"I come as often as my work allows me to, or in-between mini breakdowns."

"Mini breakdowns. That's a new one. What do you do? Shake the money tree until the wheelbarrow's full? You must have an orchard of money trees. This place is *ex-pensive.*"

"I manage to keep my head above water. I'm a pretty good lawyer. But the real money is from the family." She shrugged. "You could say I'm a spoiled brat with a trust fund."

"Never would have thought it. But then, I don't know you. What does your old man do?"

"If you're referring to Daddy, he's a bank president, among other things. If you're asking about my fiancé, that, I'm afraid, would take us through breakfast, lunch and dinner."

Franny held her gaze. "Everyone's got a story, huh?"

Cassandra shifted uneasily in her seat. "I'm not sure," she said, thinking it best to change the subject. She picked up her schedule and studied it.

"How come yours is different from mine?" Franny observed.

"Clients get special attention according to their needs."

"What's with this list of therapists? Facial, massage, fitness, dietician, equestrian, swimming…I can't go on."

"If you are entertaining the notion of making your own rules, forget it."

The waiter approached the table. "Good morning, ladies."

Franny looked up at him. "Good morning. I don't have a menu but I know what I want. I'll have sunny-side up eggs, bacon well done, toasted English muffin, butter on the side, and coffee with milk, please."

He handed her a menu. "*This* is your breakfast menu, Mrs. Pagliara." He then handed Cassandra one. "And yours, Ms. Sinclair."

Cassandra reached across the table and patted Franny's arm. "Go with the flow, Franny."

"I suppose," Franny said reluctantly. "Like the decorator who did my apartment, told me, 'Live with it; you'll get to like it.'"

CHAPTER 43

"Wow!" Franny remarked. "You whacked the hell out of that ball. Guess you've been playing since you were a kid."

Cassandra handed her caddie the club and picked up her tee. "From the day I started to walk, Daddy made sure I had an instructor on just about every sport you can imagine. Your turn."

Franny bent over and pressed the tee into the grass. "I'm over-instructed out of my head, Cassie. Swimming, horseback riding, and now golf lessons..."

"No one forced you to sign up for them."

"I know, but since *you* did, and we've been 'palling' around, I thought it wouldn't hurt to catch up on the athletics. I have been sitting on my ass for hours on end at the showroom. And besides, I don't know any of these uppity ladies, and you're a regular guy."

"Yes, I'm a regular guy, all right. That's what Daddy wanted."

"What's with this Daddy talk? Sounds like you're five years old."

"Hit the ball, Franny. And remember what Tom said. 'Keep your head down and your eye on the ball.'"

The ball barely rolled off the tee as Franny's club made contact with it. "Fuck!" she cried. "You jinxed me."

Cassandra turned her head to mask her amusement. "We're not counting strokes. Hit it again. Every one tips the ball, but watch your language. It doesn't offend me, but the people on the next green heard you."

Franny crooked her head to see the people staring at her.

Curse words formed on Franny's lips but Cassandra cut her off. The caddie flashed a huge grin and a thumbs-up at Franny.

"Honestly, everyone tips the ball," Cassandra said. "You're doing okay for not having played before."

"I bet you didn't think I could ride as well as I did, did you? In Brooklyn, we used to ride in Central Park every Sunday, and we'd go to a Dude Ranch in the Adirondacks."

"Yes, you are an excellent equestrian."

"And I'll have you know I was captain of the softball team in high school and the star pitcher, too." She deliberately tapped the ball off the tee.

Cassandra quipped, "If we were playing real golf, that would be counted as a stroke."

"Stroke this!" she called out.

Cassandra chuckled. "I think we've had enough golf for today."

Franny grimaced. "Yeah. Let's pack it in." She handed the club to the caddie then faced Cassandra. "Maybe we can sneak in a glass of wine while we're discussing my athletic accomplishments."

As they rode the golf cart to the clubhouse, Cassandra shook her head. "You are one of a kind, Franny."

Franny put her arm around her newfound friend. "I know, I know."

CHAPTER 44

At dinner, Franny sipped her wine, set it down and observed the clients in the dining room. "This place is something else."

"Why?" Cassandra asked. "Because we're being stared at?"

"That, and also the fact that we are younger than they and…"

"And more attractive?"

"Uh, huh. And dig the cocktail dresses and jewelry."

"The majority of women are from old money, Franny."

"Aren't you?"

"Whatever gave you that idea?"

"You did say you were a spoiled trust-fund brat, didn't you?"

"Yes, but I'm talking about old money that's handed down from generation to generation. Like, the Rockefellers or the Vanderbilts. My father was actually a poor man who worked his way up to become a bank president. He struggled to get to where he is."

"Has to be one smart guy."

"That he is. Smart enough to build a small empire."

Franny's cell phone rang. "I'm not answering it," she said. "Ordinarily, I can't resist picking up the phone but…"

The adjoining table of ladies eyed them. "We are getting the evil eye from our neighbors," Cassandra said. "The spa does not approve of cell phones while dining. Franny, try to control yourself."

"What makes you think I was going to say anything?"

Cassandra raised her head inquiringly.

"Never mind. Well, I might have."

The phone rang again. Franny addressed the other table. "Sorry, ladies, but I forgot my phone was on." They raised their disapproving brows. Turning back to Cassandra, she whispered, "How's that for self-control?" She snuck a glance at the missed call then hit the "end" button.

"I better take this in the lobby, Cassie. Please eat. I'll be right back."

"I'll wait," Cassandra promised.

❧

In the lobby, Franny plopped into an armchair and said hello.

Matt's irate tone pierced her ear. "I don't give a damn if you talk to me, but honestly, Franny, you could at least call Lily and ask how the baby is."

"Why? Is something wrong? Is the baby sick?"

He hesitated. "The baby is fine. Thanks for asking."

"Why are you sounding off at me? The reason I'm here is to get my head on straight. I'm only gone four days."

The terminology—getting my head on straight—forced a loud guffaw from Matt.

"What's all the hullabaloo? You could ask how I'm doing, instead of climbing all over me."

"Why do I even bother?" he countered.

"Because you love me and care about me. And I care about you, too."

"Yeah, I bet. Okay. So how is it going? Ready to come home? Lily and

Lew miss you, and I do, too."

"I just told you I'm only here four days. Let me go, Matt. My dinner is getting cold."

"Lew is paying enough at that spa. You can order another dinner."

"Say goodbye, Matt. You're starting to depress me. I love you."

She ended the call before she could hear his voice say, "I might just fly out there and surprise you, Honey Bun."

❧

"That was quick," Cassandra said as Franny sat down at the dining table.

Franny fidgeted with the silverware, arranging and rearranging. "Not quick enough," she stated flatly. Staring at Cassandra with a blank expression, she folded her arms defensively across her chest and let out a sigh of frustration.

The waitress appeared and placed an entrée in front of them. "I took the liberty of ordering another dinner."

Franny pursed her lips. "I'm not hungry."

"You're upset. Want to talk? I'm the ideal person to unload on. I'll probably never see you again, so your innermost secrets will die with me."

Franny unfolded the new napkin and placed it on her lap. "It wouldn't be right. I wouldn't want to burden you with my problems. But thanks for asking."

Cassandra said, "Listen, you are the only one here that I can relate to. Your being miserable is going to put a damper on my stay. I'm not thinking of you. I'm thinking of me."

"You're so full of shit. You don't need anyone. You're self-sufficient."

Cassandra spoke impatiently. "If you want to wallow in your troubles, go right ahead," she warned. "But please don't include me." The chair made a scuffing echo as she stood.

"Wait!" Franny called. "Don't go. Please?" She reached up and grasped

Cassandra's hand.

Not surprised Franny would react to her strategy, she sat down. "Let's eat," she said. "I'm famished."

Relieved to find she had an ally, Franny smiled. "I'll eat, too."

A hint of approval in her voice, Cassandra said, "Good."

The filet mignon was so tender Franny sliced it with her fork. "You can always tell a good filet when you don't have to use a knife."

After they had eaten, Franny and Cassandra walked out of the dining room, but not before Franny winked and waved a ta-ta at the annoyed women.

In the lounge, Cassandra gave Franny a long warning look. "I would think twice before taking you on as a client, Franny."

"Funny you should say that. I do need some legal advice." Her hand flew up in a STOP! gesture. "Not free. The maternity clothes are flying out of the stores. I know you lawyers charge by the second but it would be a big help to me."

"It depends on what kind of lawyer you need. My specialty is divorce."

Franny thought: *What if Nick turns up? What if I made a commitment to Matt? And what about the baby and his future? I wish Lily would reconsider. Adoption. It's the only way to go.*

"Am I losing you?" Cassandra asked.

"I don't want to take advantage of our friendship but…"

"I'm a big girl, Franny. I'll let you know when and if you're taking advantage."

"We are scheduled for mud baths in an hour."

"We have as long as we like. What's on your mind?"

"My head is so jam-packed, I don't know where to begin."

"Answer me without thinking and before you take your next breath. Ready?"

Franny nodded.

"What's the foremost thing on your mind?"
"Nick."
"Is he your lover, husband or what?"
"He's my baby."

CHAPTER 45

From six to seven AM, Franny watched and listened to two California scrub jays chirping on the ledge outside her window. Sleep had not come easily. Her mind would not shut down.

That must be the male, she thought. *He's pecking at her to let her know that he's the boss.* Every so often the male would proudly spread his azure blue wings and pompously flaunt his ash-gray ruff of feathers at his ladylove, trying to get her attention. *Figures,* Franny thought. *The ladybird is smaller and her coloring is for shit.* She thought of feeding the birds some of the Trail Mix left over from last night's midnight snack, but as she reached for the bag, the phone on the night table rang.

Has to be Cassie checking to see if I'm ready to ride the ol' Chisholm Trail. It's the one thing I'm enjoying, except for the massages. Have to let go of my anxieties. Maybe Cassie can help.

She picked up the phone. "Don't get yourself into a twist, Cassie," she spouted, "I'll be ready! I'll be ready! Let me get myself together. I had a bad night."

"No problem. There's plenty of time. I'll be at your door in a half hour. We can breakfast in your room. I took the liberty of phoning the chef and told him to have both of our meals sent to your room. "Is that all right with you?"

"Sure," Franny said. "Just let me jump into the shower. By the way, Cassie, do you think the spa has birdseed?"

❧

Cassie and the waiter wheeling the breakfast cart arrived at Franny's door at the same time.

Upon hearing the buzzer, Franny, still in her bathrobe and toweling her hair, flung the door open. She sputtered, "Don't say anything, Cassie. I know I'm dawdling. Take over, will you? I have to blow-dry my hair. I'll be through before you pour the coffee."

"Take your time," Cassandra said, and tipped the waiter as he exited.

Franny spoke from the bathroom. "Maybe I'll leave my hair wet. It frizzes up anyhow."

"We're going horseback riding. Not auditioning for the Miss America pageant."

"Think the horse will care if my hair is frizzy?"

"No one will care, Franny, You're a natural beauty."

At last, Franny sashayed into the room, her colorful locks swept up into a turban, and took a seat at the table the waiter had set up for them. "Beauty, huh?" she said, sipping her orange juice and giving Cassandra the once-over. "Get you! You look like one of the models in *Horse and Hound* magazine." She picked up the slender Lalique vase that held a red rosebud, sniffed it and said, "L'amour, l'amour."

Tapping to remove the top from her three-minute egg that rested in the eggcup, Cassandra eyed Franny. "You're bubbling over with humor this morning. What's going on with you? You're borderline manic."

"I was watching two birds hovering outside my window ledge this morning and I was wondering."

"I suppose you want me to ask you what you were thinking?"

Franny placed her fork on the table and stared intently at Cassandra. "Did you ever wonder what it's all about?"

"Is that why you asked me if the spa had birdseed?" As if reading Franny's mind, she walked to the phone and dialed the front desk. "I would appreciate you canceling Mrs. Pagliara's and Ms. Sinclair's riding appointments for this morning."

Franny breathed a sigh of relief and continued eating. "You are very perceptive. I am sort of frustrated."

"You are not alone, Franny. Join the zillions of troubled men and women that inhabit the earth. Let's finish breakfast and then we can talk."

"You mean *I* can talk. I'm being selfish. It's all about me—Franny!" She paused and looked directly at Cassandra. You must have some skeletons in the closet you want to release."

Cassandra arched her back. "Tell you what. You start and maybe I'll come up with a few of my own trials and tribulations. Your baby would be a good place to start. Don't you agree?"

"Yeah," Franny groaned. "I guess it's as good a place as any. She tested the warmth of the coffee cup with her fingers. "It's cold."

Uneasy, Franny accidentally tipped over her coffee cup and quickly blotted the stain with a linen napkin. She followed Cassandra with her eyes while Cassandra picked up the coffee cups, emptied the contents into the sink, washed them, returned and poured hot coffee from the carafe.

Franny thought, *I should start with Nick. That's where it all began. But how can I? What's important is putting the baby up for adoption.* "The man I'm living with is not the baby's father."

"Where's the father?"

"I don't know. Gone—gone with the wind—disappeared into thin air," Franny said, knowing that much was the truth. "He's not in the picture. Matt, the man I'm in love with, wants me to keep the baby. He's crazy about the baby."

"You keep saying the baby. The child does have a name, doesn't he? Or is the child a she?"

"Nick. His name is Nick and he's three months old."

"Is Matt taking care of Nick?"

"No. Nick is staying with my girlfriend. Actually, Lily, my dearest friend in the whole world, is taking care of him. I wanted her to adopt Nick, but she refuses."

"What do you have against Nick, that you want to give him up?"

Franny picked up a half-eaten piece of toast, swished it around the yolk of an egg, and popped it into her mouth. Looking up at Cassandra, she shook her head dolefully. "Cassie, you've known me for five days; you're a smart lady. Need I say more?"

Cassandra refilled her coffee cup, set it down and focused on Franny. "You want the honest to goodness truth?"

"Of course."

"You're not a vindictive person or lacking in intelligence. God knows, you're entertaining, thoughtful, and you do have a proven track record of success."

"Can we stop there?"

Rolling her eyes, Cassandra continued. "On the other hand, you are inclined to speak without thinking. You are a tad bizarre, and your use of profanity…" She rolled her eyes. "Do I have to spell it out?"

"What you just spelled out, I already know. I've avoided facing my problems. I have to be a big girl and grow up."

"You said it, I didn't. Bottom line, Franny. You're going to make an extremely important decision. Giving up the baby might haunt you forever."

Franny grinned. "Gee, that's what my friend Lily told me."

"She's an intelligent lady. She can't take care of the baby forever. Are you that definite?"

Picking up a knife, Franny balanced it on her upturned middle finger in deep thought. Top-heavy, it fell onto the table. Meeting Cassandra's eyes, her voice firm and somber, she said, "I can't see myself raising a child. I really love the baby, but I'm not a fit mother. I don't have the attention span for it, nor do I take raising a child as seriously as I should. In fact, I don't take anything seriously. Other women dote on them, hug and kiss little kids. I just turn away. It doesn't do anything for me."

"What does turn you on?"

"Designing. Selling. The business has become my life, my world. It's more important than anything else."

"Why don't you give the final decision a little more time?"

Franny sprang from her chair. Her emotions, stirred up by Cassandra's probing, struck a nerve. Her hands flailing in the air at her newfound friend, she shouted, "Why is everyone pushing me to keep him? I'm done! Finished! That's it! As soon as I get back, I'm going to make arrangements to have him adopted. Case closed!"

Cassandra stood. For one instant, she feared she had gone too far. At least, Franny had faced her problem—for the moment, anyhow. "You have just come to terms with yourself," she said. "The case is not closed." *But there is something more*, she thought. *I might have the perfect solution.*

"Why are you smiling?" Franny asked. "I'm serious. I meant every fucking word."

Cassandra folded her arms in front of her. "Franny, dear. I'm going to make you an offer you can't refuse."

CHAPTER 46

Monday dragged its way into Tuesday. Tuesday made way for Wednesday, and when Thursday arrived, Cassie decided it was time to phone Al.

"Cassie," he said, surprise in his voice.

"I haven't heard from you," she said. "I miss you."

"I miss you, too. But you're the one who said 'give me time to sort things out. I'll get in touch when I'm ready.'" He cleared his throat. *"Are* you ready?"

"I wasn't the only one who had to sort things out, Al."

"True enough. Not knowing my past keeps me irritable and on edge."

"Are you coping with it now?"

"I'm taking one day at a time. Hey, your father has set me up with a shrink."

She huffed. "Don't you think you should have consulted me first?"

"No. I may not remember my past, but I'm quite capable of making my own decisions, madam counselor. *This* fiancé is not your client. You have to admit you didn't help my situation by constantly ragging on me to tie the knot. Jesus, Cassie, we're engaged for less than two weeks. We barely know each other."

Agitated, she drummed her fingers nervously on the writing desk. "What does time have to do with it? I couldn't love you more if we were childhood sweethearts, or met an hour ago." Her voice softened. "Al, all that matters is that I love you."

He didn't respond with an I love you. "Guess what? Your father has offered me a job."

Confused by his change in attitude, she hesitated. "Al, listen. I know you love me and I understand your hesitancy. I'm willing to wait. I want to hear something more than, 'I need more time.' Let me ask you this. Can you see yourself spending the rest of your life with me?"

Feeling cornered, he deliberated. *She has everything a man could want. Beauty, brains, wealth, and, most important, she loves me. What can I offer her? A past that could one day return and ruin our relationship. With her I would have a fantastic future. It's time to make a judgment. I do love her. I'm sure I do.*

Aware of his lack of enthusiasm, she said, "Al, I don't mean to press you. If it seems like I'm forcing you to make a decision, I'm not. I understand your predicament and am aware of problems the future might present."

"You mean if my memory comes back?"

"Exactly. I would be deeply, deeply distraught if one morning you woke up and said, 'Who are you?'" Wrapping the telephone cord around her finger, she paused then said, "But let's not talk about that now. As you said, 'one day at a time.' You think I'm capable of holding my own because I appear dominant and in control, but you're wrong. Don't for one minute believe there aren't times I'm scared to death. I need you as much as you need me."

"Cassie, I like your strong personality and our sex life is great. It's like I said a hundred times. It's me. I'm just not sure of myself."

"I can be sure for the both of us. If you *like* me the way I am, that's good enough for me. But, do you *love me* the way I am?"

"I love you," he said and thought, *Of course, I love her.*

"Oh, Al. I'm so happy. Then you won't mind if I phone Mother and Dad and tell them the good news, will you?"

"Of course not. But we have to talk about the future—I mean, getting married. Keep in mind, my past could present problems."

"Al, I'm so happy you brought up the subject of marriage. I didn't want to jump the gun. I was afraid of how you would take it."

"Well, it is a concern."

"I'm sure Daddy will take care of problems that come up. He can work miracles. Anyhow, we can live together for the time being."

"You're not suggesting we live at the estate with your parents, are you?"

"No," she said adamantly. "We don't have to. Whatever you want. Just name it. By the way, Sweetheart, I have a big surprise for you, but I'm not telling you what it is. Not yet."

"And I have a big surprise for you, Cassie!"

"If I guess what it is, will you tell me?"

"Uh-uh. Anyway, in a million years you'd never guess."

"I love you! I love you! I love you! I'm so excited, Al. I can't wait to tell the news to my new friend."

"That's surprising. I remember you telling me you never bother with other guests. You get away to have privacy and peace of mind."

"Usually, I *am* a recluse, but I met this lady. She's quite a character, and we've become good friends."

""I've never heard you mention other women. I mean, like a girlfriend."

"You're right. I don't have any. But this woman is special."

"How special?"

Cassie hesitated. "Al, all I can say at this time is that she's very special."

"Do I have to worry?"

She laughed. "You don't have to worry, Darling, but when you see her *I'm* probably the one who's going to have to do the worrying."

"When I see her? Are you bringing her home with you?"

"Not yet."

"She *must* be something else. You sound fired up. Now I'm really anxious to know what she's all about."

Knowing she had said more than enough, Cassie changed the subject. "You didn't tell me what kind of job Daddy offered you."

"Yeah. I didn't believe it, but he fired the entire security team at the estate and is putting me in charge of a new one."

"Is that the best he could offer you?"

"C'mon, Cassie. He did try to get me into the bank, but I didn't feel it was the right move for me."

"I'm not going to tell you how to run your life Al, but…"

He cut her off. "Then don't! I won't interfere with your law practice and I expect the same consideration."

Feeling she had overstepped her bounds, she backed down. "I'm sorry, Darling," she cooed. "You're right. I'll mind my own business."

"Good. Now tell me more about this mystery lady. What's her name?"

"Franny," she answered.

CHAPTER 47

Startled, Franny bolted upright in bed when the waiter accidentally dropped a tray in the hall outside her door. Remembering where she was, she rolled over on her back and stared sleepy-eyed at the ceiling, mulling over her unexpected good fortune. Tossing the covers aside, she stood nude in front of the full-length mirror, turned from side to side, and patted her flat stomach, admiring her slender figure. *Not bad for an old broad of thirty-three,* she mused. *Things are looking up. If Cassie doesn't change her mind about adopting little Nicky, my troubles are over.* Tucking her kinky, jet-black hair into a shower cap, she started for the bathroom when the phone rang.

"How are you doing?" Lily asked.

"I was going to call you. Guess what?"

Before Lily could answer, Franny came out with, "The most unexpected, amazing thing happened." She paused. "Wait a sec, Lily, I need to take this cap off. I was just going into the shower." She snapped the cap off her head, quickly slipped into a robe, and plopped onto the bed.

Lily said. "Tell, tell. The suspense is killing me."

"First things, first," Franny said. "How's the baby doing?"

Lily couldn't resist. "Well, well. What do you know? Franny's maternal instincts are surfacing."

"I'm too happy, so I'll excuse your fucking sarcasm and even though you seem to think I don't give a rat's ass about little Nicky, I do!"

Knowing better than to argue, Lily backed down. "Sorry, Franny. The baby is just wonderful. A perfect little bundle of joy. He just laughs and smiles all the time. And he…"

Franny shouted into the phone. "Stop! I don't want to hear any more!" Suddenly, her conflicting emotions regarding the adoption flooded her mind.

Lily changed the subject. "What's the amazing news?" she asked. Before Franny could reply, the baby began to cry."

Upon hearing the baby whimper, Franny's body stiffened. "Listen, I'll call you back and explain everything." She slammed the phone down.

Within seconds the phone in Franny's room rang. Thinking it was Cassie, she picked it up.

"Listen, brat," Lily said. "You have a hell-of-a nerve cutting me off when it suits you. Yes, the baby cried. They do that! Seems to me you're having a good time recuperating from your problems while Lew and I are taking care of *your* child. Having second thoughts?"

"No. You volunteered to care for Nicky. Besides, I've solved my problem."

Lily's frustrated sigh was long and loud. "Don't tell me. Let me guess. You've decided to give the baby up for adoption. That's old news."

"Yes, but not to just anyone."

"You've got that right," Lily said. "Lew and I have talked it over. We've decided to adopt the baby. You're a free agent. That's what you wanted, isn't it?"

"Yes, but…Lily you're going to hate me."

"Franny, if I haven't drowned you or put arsenic in your food by now, you must know I love you or I wouldn't put up with your nonsense."

Franny's voice was subdued. "You *are* going to hate me."

"What did you do now?"

"I promised the baby to a wonderful lady I met at the spa."

Lily, stunned, watched the nurse pick up the baby and walk into the nursery. She took a long, deep breath and let it out. "You did say you promised the baby to a lady you met at the spa, didn't you? Franny, do I have to send for the little men in white coats to come and get you?"

"Let me explain. This gal is pure class, cream of the crop. I mean old, old money. Her father is the president of a bank. They have an estate you could land a plane on. She had a hysterectomy and is dying to adopt Nicky."

"And Lew and I are one step away from the poorhouse? You are supposed to be my dearest friend, Franny, and we have been taking care of Nicky. We love him."

"I understand what you're saying. Hear me out. I was thinking about it. If you and Lew adopted Nicky, I would be involved in his life. That's too close for comfort. You know me. I might be tempted to want him back. Isn't it better that he be where I won't be able to see him? Out of sight, out of mind, so to speak? And he would have everything his little heart desires." Her voice choked as tears welled in her eyes. "I need you to be on my side, Lily. You might not believe it, but it's getting harder and harder to give him up. Isn't it enough that I lost his father? And now the baby too? You have always been there for me. I need your support."

Lily walked into the recently decorated nursery and looked down at the baby gurgling with joy in his Neiman Marcus crib. She scanned the hand-painted walls, done by a renowned artist, depicting sailboats in a blue-green ocean with white clouds. Above, the moon and stars gazed down on the luxurious surroundings. In a corner, a rocking horse waited for the infant to grow up. The setting caught her eye; once again she sighed.

"Are you still there, Lily?" Franny asked.

"Yes, I am. What does her husband do?"

"They're not married. Not yet. They're engaged. You should see the rock she sports. Bigger than the Hope Diamond."

"Just do me one favor, Franny. Don't do anything rash. Let Lew have them checked out. Can't hurt. Make me happy. Okay?"

"Of course. In fact, I'll have her call you and give you the info first-hand. Thanks for taking care of Nicky. Let's be honest. I'm not ready to raise a child. We've covered that route. I know I'm doing the right thing, but I do need your support."

"I'll always be there for you. It's your decision, Kiddo, although I have to tell you I'm not happy. The baby has grown on me, like it was my own." She paused. "But then again, I guess it makes sense. What are their names? Where do they live?"

"They live in Santa Fe, New Mexico. Her name is Cassandra Sinclair. I don't know anything about her fiancé, except his first name, Al."

CHAPTER 48

Poolside, Cassie reclined in a lounge chair in a one-piece bathing suit, under an oversized multi-colored umbrella, and chatted with Franny. "I can't tell you how excited I am. I've discovered the reason I've been so touchy lately. It's not because Al and I have been at odds, but because I can never have children."

Franny, stretched out on an air-cushioned lounge chair, sunned herself next to Cassie. Clad in a two-piece Band-Aid bikini, she shaded her eyes with her hand. She had worked like crazy to regain her pre-pregnancy figure. "What's the beef with the boyfriend?" she asked. "Matt and I argue all the time. It's natural."

Hesitating to relate too much to Franny regarding Al, Cassie chose her words with care. "He can be unsure of himself and unyielding at the same time."

"So what's new? Men want to be the boss. Comes from their mother's spoiling the hell out of them."

"Trouble is, I'm strong-willed too."

Franny waved a hand of dismissal. "Men never bother me. They have to be really nuts about me to put up with my shit. I can be a real pain in the ass. I've been called an enigma. Bet your guy is a knockout. What's he look like?"

"Well, he's tall—has dark brown hair that falls over one eye—is well built, but he's not what you'd call movie-star handsome. More like a young, rugged John Wayne."

Franny sipped at her iced tea, then placed it back in the pocket of the cushion. "Sounds like a movie star to me. Got any pictures?"

"No. I was in court and just about made the flight. I've been meaning to put one in my wallet."

Franny turned her nose up. "I don't carry pictures with me. Brings back too many unpleasant memories."

Cassie turned towards Franny. "I think we're going to be good friends, Franny. I don't want to rehash the adoption subject again and I promise this is the last time I will bring it up, but being of a legal background, and also wanting to clear my conscience. I have to ask…are you definite about the adoption?"

The lounge cushion *whished* as Franny sat up. "You're the second person today who has asked me that. Look, Cassie, I think you're the best thing that's happened to me in a long time. Let me make it real clear. As much as I'd like to be your friend, I can't. It's not you. It's just that I'm not—well, let's put it this way—I know my shortcomings. I'm a dynamo at work and I can sell anyone the Brooklyn Bridge; but when it comes to raising a child," she motioned a thumbs down, "I'm a total mess. Once the deal is done I don't want to have any contact with you or the baby." She turned away as her eyes filled with tears.

Cassie reached over and embraced Franny. "Whatever you say, Franny. I swear I'll do everything possible to make sure the baby is loved and taken care of. Can I ask you one more thing?"

Franny returned Cassie's embrace. "Sure. What?"

"Do you want me to keep the baby's first name?"

Franny smiled. "Sure. What's your dude's last name?"

"Center. Albert B. Center."

"Mm," Franny said. "Think you could add a middle name? Maybe Albert Nicholas Center Jr. Classy huh?"

CHAPTER 49

Al hummed to the music as he drove the Land Rover along the highway, mulling over his conversation with Cassie. He thought. *I know J.J. meant well, but it's not my thing. Vice president on my first day at work. Talk about nepotism. I'd be kowtowing to J.J. But what else do I have? And it will make Cassie happy.*

It all happened in the blink of an eye. The oil tanker, avoiding a deer, skidded out of control, overturned and slid into the oncoming traffic. His body engulfed in flames, the driver leaped from the cab and ran from the oil tanker. Within seconds, a thunderous crash followed by an explosion sent masses of billowing black smoke and fire roaring skyward.

Al steered to avoid the tanker, but it was too late. The Land Rover hydroplaned off of the oil-slicked road and launched uncontrollably into the air. Foliage, branches, and strewn debris scattered over the area as the vehicle continued its wild plunge down the steep ravine. It crash-landed onto the swampy earth, rolled over, and came to an abrupt stop in a rivulet. His seatbelt secure, his face crushed against the airbag, Al lay unconscious, bleeding profusely.

Retired Mayor Mason Eldridge of Fairmount County and his wife Martha, driving behind the Land Rover, could not believe their eyes.

Instinctively, Mason steered his model T Ford Flivver onto the shoulder of the road, pulled up the hand brake and shouted at his wife. "Martha!" Quick! Call 911!"

Fumbling nervously in her straw pocketbook, she pulled out her cell phone. "Is this 911?"

Mason pulled the phone out of her hand. He boomed. "Listen, emergency, ya best be getting the fire department, an ambulance, and the police to Highway 475 and Tequila Junction on the double. There's an oil tanker overturned and it's afire. A car went belly whopping down the ravine. All hell's bustin out. The road's like holdin' onto a greased pig, and the cars are piling up faster than a stack of wheat cakes. My name? Elmer Fudd, you dang idiot. Get some help out here and pronto!"

The Fairmount County Ambulance Rescue unit and sheriff's team arrived within minutes, followed by the local TV news people.

Mason Eldridge approached Sheriff Milford. "Listen, Tom, the medics best be seeing to the truck driver. He's been toasted real bad. And there's a vehicle flipped over down the gully. Didn't see no fire but ya can hear the horn a-blarin."

Sheriff Milford shouted. "Brandon, Carl, and you—Flossy—and the medics get your asses down the ravine. See if the occupants are still alive. Fred, you and Ambrose help the medics with the people in the wrecked autos. Mortimer, get on the horn and alert Santa Fe and Los Alamos. Tell them to send as many emergency crews and volunteers they can dig up. Make sure the traffic is stopped going east."

The sheriff's cell rang. "Chief, Flossy here. The man in the driver's seat is hanging upside down. He's unconscious—dripping blood like a leaky faucet. The medics will have him out of the seatbelt in a jiffy and on a stretcher as soon as we cut him loose. Carl's working on it."

"Anyone else in the vehicle?"

"No."

"Smell any liquor?"

"No. But I checked the license plate."

"Stolen car?"

"No. The plate tag is ABC 1000, but it belongs to Jeremiah Jenison Sinclair III. Isn't he your Friday night poker buddy?"

"Not J. J.? What the hell is he doing in a Land Rover?"

"It's not him, boss. From what I can make out, a younger guy was driving."

Sheriff Milford ended the call and speed dialed his poker partner, J.J. Sinclair.

❦

J.J. and Ce Ce waited patiently in a private room at the Christus Regional Medical Center. She wiped a tear from her cheek. "This is not happening. J. J. Tell me it's all a nightmare."

Frustration spread across his face. "Nothing would give me more pleasure, Ce Ce. It's not a nightmare. It's happening." He shook his head. "Never know what the next minute will bring."

She shifted uneasily in her chair. "Why isn't Cassie here?"

"I sent the jet for her. She'll be here within the hour."

Mrs. Sinclair said nothing; her expression said it all. When she found her composure, she sniveled. "I can't face her. She's going to be devastated."

"Cassie's strong," he said. "It's you I'm worried about. If you fall apart, you'll only make things worse."

She shuddered. "It's been over three hours."

"We won't know anything for a while, not until the doctors finish the preliminary examination." He bit his lip. "I'm sure they'll operate, if they haven't already started."

"You make it sound like he's on his last legs."

"You didn't see him. I did." His eyes shut tightly as he tried to erase the vision of his future son-in-law, his face unrecognizable, lying comatose on a stretcher when the medics wheeled him into the hospital. "Pray he pulls through, Ce Ce."

Staring at her husband with intense fear, she gasped. "Pulls through? You didn't tell me it was that serious."

"I didn't want to upset you. I had a consultation with the doctors before you got here."

"My god, J.J. Are you saying he might...?"

He nodded. "Why do you think I had the best team of surgeons flown in?" He took hold of her hand. "Ce Ce, his face... He'll need a lot of facial reconstruction. That is, if his brain isn't damaged...and if he pulls through."

She turned pale. "That's a lot of ifs, J.J." The damp tissue shredded in her hand as she nervously clenched it. "Why doesn't someone come out and tell us how he's doing? Are we supposed to just sit here and wait—and wait?"

Losing his patience, he shook his head disapprovingly. "Ce Ce, you're getting on my nerves. An operation of this magnitude, if successful, could take four or five hours at the start just to keep him alive—maybe longer—and that's just the beginning. There are world-renowned specialists in there, and God only knows how many doctors and nurses. There's nothing you or I can do. Why don't you go home? I'll wait for Cassie. I promise, I'll call you as soon as I hear anything."

"I *am* rather shaky. You won't mind if I go?"

"Ce Ce, I know you. You'll be better off at home." He leaned over and kissed her.

She hesitated.

"Go," he urged. "Please, Sweetheart. I feel your pain." As she started for the door, he called to her. "I love you, Ce Ce."

After she left he called his physician to make sure the doctor would be there to attend to his wife when she arrived at the estate.

CHAPTER 50

Cassie did not greet or look in the direction of the chauffeur as he held the door of the limo open for her, but climbed in, tossed her bag inside and grabbed for her cell phone.

"How are you holding up, Cassie?" her father asked.

"I'm on the ledge, Daddy. What's the latest with Al?"

"Same as I told you just before you landed. Teams of specialists are working on him."

"How's Mom? She must be half crazed."

"I made her go home. She was falling apart. The doctor is probably with her now."

"I had so much to tell you, Dad, but it all seems so insignificant now."

"At this point, any news that's uplifting would be a blessing, Cassie. What's going on?"

"I adopted a baby."

"The connection is bad, Cassie. We're lucky we can talk. I have this suite and I guess it's set up so that it doesn't interfere with the hospital's acoustics. Come again."

"I said I adopted a baby."

"That's what I thought you said but, knowing you, it's probably true."

"I'm not going to go into the details, Dad."

"Why not? I need a break from the tension."

Doctor Willis wrapped lightly at the door. "Mr. Sinclair, may I come in?"

Unconsciously, J.J. turned off his cell phone and sprang to his feet. "What?" he said.

The doctor's tone held more than a hint of cold steel. "Sit down, Mr. Sinclair. We have to talk."

J.J.'s heart skipped a beat.

CHAPTER 51

The hospital was silent except for the clock's second hand that ticked away the seconds.

Behind a sliding door in a VIP suite, two nurses and an attending physician listened to the monotonous sound of the ventilator's woofing hum.

Comatose, Albert B. Center drifted from one sleeping configuration to another, aware of the outside world but unable to communicate with them. *Why?* he grieved. *Why is this happening?*

But his dilemma did not end there. Another person challenged him: his alter ego, Nicholas Pagliara.

Within the realm of his brain, Al and Nick fought for control.

Get lost, Al said. *I was here first.*

No, you weren't. I was. You don't remember. You showed up after I was shot.

Al tsked. *Big deal. I had the accident. You died and I took over. I was doing a good job getting my life together.*

I didn't die, idiot!

Could have fooled me. In reality you did, Al countered. *You had the world by the balls and you fucked it up playing cops and robbers.*

I can make it right. I know I can.

Al winced. *Get real. When I wake up I'm the one that's taking over. You had your chance. Stop kidding yourself.*

It wasn't my fault that I got shot.

And it wasn't my fault I woke up in your body. You can bet your phony existence, if I had a say, I would have done a hell-of-a lot better.

Better than what? You were a bum—a hobo—making that nice lady Rosie fall for you and then brown-nosing your way into the Sinclairs' good graces by pretending to love their daughter Cassie. What a sham! My love for Franny was real.

Al snorted. *That's as much as you know, brother. I do love Cassie. You don't have an inkling of what she's about. And besides, I don't know this Franny person you're talking about.*

And I don't want you to, Nick shot back. *Let's keep it that way. But one thing for sure, you phony impersonator, when I come back you are history. And don't call me brother.*

Al's voice sing sang. *I don't think so.*

I'll let you in on a little secret, Al. I've had flashes of your Cassie lady.

"*So what does that prove?*

It proves I'm getting stronger. I just might start to take over. And then you'll be just a speck of my imagination, if that much.

Dream on. Meanwhile, Nick ol' boy, I'm going to concentrate on sweeping you under the rug. I know what you're trying to do.

And what's that? Nick asked.

You're trying to demoralize me. Use your strong-arm police force tactics to intimidate me. It won't work. I'm not afraid of you.

The hospital door opened.

Who's that? Nick asked.

I don't know, Al replied. *You'd better disappear.*

Why don't you?

I had the accident, stupid. They don't know who you are. Someone's paying me a visit. Do it!

You mean visiting us, don't you?

Fade! Al demanded.

Okay, for now. But I'll be back. You can count on it.

CHAPTER 52

Franny clasped her hands around Matt's neck, smothering him with kisses. "Mm, you feel so good," she said. "I missed you." Holding him at arm's length, she smiled. "So much has happened; I don't know where to begin." Eyes bright with anticipation, her face glowing with exhilaration, she said, "I didn't know how much I missed you until just now."

He touched the tip of her nose playfully. "Until just now?" His eyes narrowed. "If I had said that to you, you'd be all over me."

"Are you fucking with me? Matt, I'm serious."

"Whatever. I'm too happy to argue with you. I never win anyhow." He pulled her close. "Tell you a secret."

"What?"

"I missed your craziness and your potty mouth."

"Turn me loose and I'll tell you something, you brute. I met a classy lady lawyer at the spa and I've decided to clean up my act."

"The lady who's adopting Nicky?"

"Fucking A," she said.

He shook his head. "Uh huh," he said. "Cleaning up our act, are we? What about the adoption? Is it definite?"

"Damn! If one more person asks me if it's definite I'm going to punch their fu—freaking lights out."

"That's using control," he laughed.

"Be serious. Cassie—that's the lady's name—her fiancé had a horrible accident. He's in a bad way."

"I'm sorry to hear that. Did she change her mind?"

"No. She's going through with the adoption anyhow."

He sulked.

She put her hand on his arm and squeezed it as he steered her toward the limo. "Come on, Honey," she cooed. "We have each other. That is what's important. Let's start fresh, a new chapter in our lives."

The chauffeur opened the door. Franny climbed in and waited for Matt to sit beside her.

He avoided her eyes and gazed dejectedly out the window, staring blankly at the New York skyline, making no attempt to mask his coolness.

Franny tilted his face towards her and caressed his cheek. "It's for the best, Matt. We have so much to look forward to. The business is going gung ho, and we will be traveling the globe. And, most important, we'll be together. Isn't that what you want?"

He stared lovingly into her eyes. "You've changed," he said. "Is it possible you've grown up?"

"You think so? I hadn't noticed. Like the new me?"

"Totally!" he said. "But I love the old screwy Franny, too. Don't get too normal."

"That, my love, is not possible," she said.

He studied her eyes, her face, and took her hands in his. "You laid out a very tempting plan of bits and pieces, Franny. You've convinced me that we could have a fantastic life together. Are you proposing?"

Taken aback, she stuttered. "I…I…"

He cut her off. "Maybe it *is* time to think about making it permanent."

"Marriage? I don't know…it never occurred to me."

"Why not? Is there someone else?" He hesitated. "I mean besides Nick."

"Get real, Matt. Where am I going to find a guy like you, who puts up with my shit? Maybe I didn't know how much I love you, but I am certain of it now." *I did say that, didn't I?* she asked herself. "At the spa, I talked non-stop about you to Cassie. I have to be honest. Nick was on my mind for the longest time, and it drove me crazy. But honestly, he's slowly fizzling out."

"Fizzling out?"

"I talked it over with Cassie and she made some calls. I did tell you she's a lawyer, didn't I?"

He showed surprise. "So you have been thinking about marriage?"

"I guess with all the hoopla over the adoption and my usual state of confusion, I sort of got lost."

"I can see that," he teased. "Go on."

"In New York State you don't have to wait seven years if a judge decrees the spouse legally dead on the record."

"Then we have clear sailing? Why didn't you tell me this before?"

"I don't know."

"Figures."

The limo pulled up alongside the curb of Franny's condo. Matt grabbed for the door, but Franny took hold of his shirtsleeve. "Hold it!" she said. "Bob, the doorman will get it. We're living on the Upper Eastside now."

In the elevator, Matt bumped her playfully with his hip. Raising his eyebrows ala Groucho Marx, he said, "When?"

"Can we put the wedding nuptials on hold?"

His face soured. "You're the one that did all the pursuing, Baby Doll. Maybe I was wrong about your growing up. You still don't have the balls to make a commitment."

She inserted her keycard into the slot of the door and flung it open. Once inside, she kicked it shut with her heel and shouted, "Get the hell over here!" She jerked him towards her and grabbed at his crotch. "You want commitment, Buster? I'll show you fucking commitment!"

CHAPTER 53

Where Cassie spent the night was not typical of a hospital room, but reminiscent of a five-star hotel suite. When the daylight peeked through the blinds, Cassie woke up. For the moment, she had forgotten where she was. The bed made a prolonged squeaking noise as she sprang to her feet. She ran to Al then stopped dead in her tracks. The bed was empty. The tension within her intensified and she gasped. Her eyes wild with fear, she asked, "Where is he?"

The nurse called to her. "Mr. Center is off the ventilator. He's breathing on his own."

Cassie collapsed into a chair. Her mouth opened but the words would not come out. When she regained her composure she confronted the nurse. "Why didn't anyone wake me?"

Her father scurried into the room. "We caught a break, Cassie. Al came to."

"I heard," she said. "So why can't I get a straight answer? Where is he?"

"I'm sorry, Baby," he said. "Your door was closed and before I could get to you the orderlies had him on the gurney and were wheeling him out of the room and into radiology. I wanted to get to you sooner, but everything happened so fast. The doctors and nurses were hovering over him, and there was so much commotion."

She released a long-drawn-out sigh of relief. He stretched out his arms and she fell into them.

"Oh, Daddy, isn't it wonderful?"

"Someone was watching over him, Cassie. But I did hear him say, "Where's Cassie?""

"He did? I wish I'd heard that."

He hugged his daughter again. "This is just the beginning, Cassie. He'll have to have a sequence of facial reconstructions."

"I know, Dad, but he's a fighter. He'll make it."

"I hope to God he does. I've been wondering, Cassie. Are you still planning on going through with this adoption business? You can't be serious."

"Don't lock horns with me, Dad, not now. I made a deal and I'm going to stand by it."

"You're as stubborn as I am," he said. "Will I at least get to meet the mother and father of this child?"

"The father is not in the picture. She's engaged to someone else and they're planning to marry. I've invited them to the estate as soon as they finish their seasonal line. They're manufacturers of maternity clothes in the garment industry in New York. The baby boy is staying with her best friend for the time being."

"How old is the boy?"

"Three."

"Months or years?"

Her mouth tightened. "Months!"

"And why, if I'm permitted to ask, is she giving him up?"

"Dad, stop right there. It's a done deal. I don't want to be disrespectful, but I'd like to keep the details between the mother and Al and me. I've made all the proper inquiries."

He raised both hands in self-defense. "Okay! Okay! I'll mind my own business."

Her eyes narrowed. "Dad, I'm serious. I know how you can manipulate. Promise me you won't interfere. I've thought it through. It will give Al time to heal from his preliminary surgery and by then the adoption should be finalized." Glancing sidelong, she eyed her father. "I was also thinking that Al and I should get married now."

He tried to keep the tension he felt at bay, but he felt his blood pressure start to rise. "Aren't you getting a little ahead of yourself?"

She kissed him on his cheek. "I told you, Dad, I've got everything under control. Remember, you said you would not interfere. And besides, I know you love me."

He shook his head. "That I do, Cassie. That I do. And now, I better call your mother. She must be on her third Valium by now."

"Daddy, be happy for me. You and Mom will be grandparents."

His voice faded as Cassie's mind pictured an adorable three-year-old ring bearer, a flower girl sauntering down the aisle scattering rose petals onto a red carpet and the guests oohing and aahing with delight as J.J. escorted her down the aisle at St. Patrick's Cathedral in New York City.

CHAPTER 54

The summer maternity collection blew out of the stores; the fall collection followed and before they realized it, six months had flown by and it was time for Franny and Matt to work on the spring line.

Her hands gently resting on his shoulders, Franny stood behind Matt and watched as he sketched a maternity dress.

She huffed. "No, Matt. That's not right. The draping should be on the other side. You're making her look bigger. The idea is to flatter the woman not inflate her."

He sighed. "Franny, why don't you trot over to your desk and finish the pull-on shorts you were working on, and get out of my hair?"

"What's the matter? Am I crowding you? Can't take a little corrective criticism?"

"I don't mind criticism," he snapped, "but not when it's counter productive. I think it's time for us to have separate design rooms."

"Watch yourself, Buster. You're cruisin' for a bruisin'."

"And that's supposed to be funny?" He tossed the drawing pencil onto the sketchpad and turned around. "What's eating you, Franny? Everything was going great guns, but the last few weeks you've been acting like…"

"Like what? The old Franny? Why don't you just come out and fucking say it?'

"Okay, I will."

She covered her ears. "No, don't! I don't want to hear."

He stood and approached her. Placing his arms around her waist he drew her to him. "C'mon, Baby," he said. "Let's talk it out. We're at the happiest time of our lives. The business is going great—we have everything we want—you have a diamond the size of Cleveland and…"

"I know you're right. I don't know what else I could ask for. You've been so good to me…so good *for* me. You're the best."

"But?"

She sulked. "Matt, I can't hold back."

His face turned ashen. "Whatever it is, Franny, we can deal with it." He led her to the couch, sat beside her and looked intently into her eyes. "Want me to guess?" he asked.

"No. Yes."

"Is it about the baby?"

"No, not really." She avoided his eyes. She toyed with the tassel that hung from the arm of the couch. "You do know that I love you, Matt."

He searched her eyes. "And I love you, too. If it's not the baby, Franny, I can't imagine what it could be."

"I've been having strange dreams."

"How strange?"

"It hasn't anything to do with you." She hesitated. "Well, in a way it does."

"You mean you've had the same dream more than once."

"Yes. I've been dreaming that I'm having sex with Nick."

"Better than with me?"

"That's not funny, Matt."

"I think it is. And you want to know the damn truth? I don't care. I *really* don't. You and Nick had a good thing going, but it's over. We're not living in the Stone Age, you know. I dream about Nicole Kidman all the time. As long as you don't shout out Nick's name when we're having sex, I don't care." He tilted her chin up with his finger. "I think there's something more. C'mon, what is it?"

"You said it before."

"Then it is the baby." He shook his head. "You're heading for heartbreak, Kiddo."

"I don't think so. I've been doing some thinking."

"That's trouble. What?"

"Just hear me out before you start yelling." Her arms crossed defensively across her chest. "I want to get pregnant!"

For a long moment he stared at her, not believing what he heard.

"If I have another," she continued, "all this guilt I feel about giving up the baby will go away."

His brows arched and his jaw dropped. He thought, *here we go again.* He stood over her. "You're the one who said you have no motherly instincts, you're too crazy, too unpredictable, too nutty, and too off the wall to have a kid. Now, after you gave Nicky up and signed the documents, you want to have a baby?" He clasped his hands to his head. "I need a drink!" He went to the shelf, reached for the vodka, unscrewed the cap and drank from the bottle.

"Hey," she shouted back. "Don't hog it all. Let me have some of that."

He handed her the bottle. "Okay," he said. "Take a swig. We're taking the rest of the day off."

"What's going on, Matt?"

He seized her coat, grabbed her hand, slammed the door shut with the heel of his shoe and pulled her to the elevator. "Let's get started," he shouted. "Times a-wasting!" His fist cut through the air. "Yes! Yes! Our very own baby. Wow!"

CHAPTER 55

Born of Jewish parents, J.J. did not argue with Ce Ce when she suggested a Roman Catholic wedding for Cassie at St. Patrick's Cathedral in New York City, nor did he blink an eye when she proposed they fly the guests and put them up at the Waldorf Astoria. He simply shrugged and said, "Ce Ce, I don't give a damn about religion, or the expense. They can have a Greek Orthodox wedding, a Voodoo tribal ritual, or take vows parachuting off the Eiffel Tower. What I do have reservations about is Cassie's hasty decision to adopt the baby before they're married. What the hell has gotten into her? As a rule, she has the intelligence and common sense to think before she acts."

Mrs. Sinclair stood in back of her husband and massaged his shoulders. "Now, J.J.," she said, "you *did* promise Cassie you would mind your own business."

"Yeah, yeah," he growled. "I just can't let it go."

"From the day Cassie brought the baby to the estate you've done nothing but dote on him. I don't understand you. You can be so compassionate and generous, but as soon as someone opposes you..."

He overrode her words. "Ce Ce, save the sermon for Sunday."

She walked around the end of the sofa, sat next to him and rested her hand on his arm, aware that confrontation was not one of her strong points. "It's more than the adoption," she said. "Are you upset because Al refused to take the job at the bank? You're the one who said he has a natural talent for law enforcement."

"I know, I know," he said. "I have a lot on my mind."

Her mouth turned downward as she removed her hand from his arm. "Anything you might want to discuss with this mundane housewife?"

"Not now, Sweetheart," he said. "You know I'm always willing to hear you out. I know where your heart is. But now is not the right time."

She frowned.

"Ce Ce. Would you mind? I'd like to be alone for a while—clear my head." He turned up his face and waited for her to kiss his cheek. "Love ya," he said.

She responded with a peck, knowing full well that conferring with her regarding business happened rarely. She busied herself with women's clubs and volunteer work. Although there was more than enough help to keep the household running smoothly, she kept to her responsibilities and he kept to his. Secretaries, women associates, and even Ce Ce's friends often hit on the distinguished, wealthy banker, but he stayed true to the woman he loved. "Love you too, Dear," she replied.

He moved to a recliner. The soft leather cushion felt good as he tilted his head back and touched a button that put the chair into position. He closed his eyes and meditated, his thoughts drifting to the time Al entered his life.

Cassie parted the curtains of the French doors, peered in, then tapped on the glass. "Dad," she called, "guess who wants to visit."

CHAPTER 56

The eyes *were* his. It was the only feature on his face that had remained unchanged. Implanted hairy follicles taken from his armpits shaped dark, bushy eyebrows. A widow's peak of sprouting hair plugs, guaranteed by the plastic surgeon to grow into a full head of hair, dotted his scalp. His nose, straight and masculine yet turned up slightly at the tip, was numb to the touch, as was the rest of his face. More pronounced than before, his chin sported a cleft, and newly implanted cheekbones lent perfect symmetry to his man-made face.

Al held the hand mirror up and stared at his image. It was a man he did not recognize. *I lost my memory and my past and now my face. My life was finally starting to come together and now this?*

Blown away by the unfamiliar gentleman who attempted to smile normally, Cassie stared at Al. Suddenly it struck her. *Who is he? Is he the man I fell in love with?* Doubt began to cloud her mind.

From her puzzled expression, his voice, huskier and deeper than before, faltered. Enunciating each syllable, he said, "What's the matter? This is as far as my mouth will open. It will take a while before I get full usage. Are you disappointed?"

"Of course, I'm not disappointed, Darling. They did a fantastic job! You're more handsome than before. I'm just so thankful you're alive."

"The doctors are releasing me tomorrow. I can't wait. I heard that J.J tried to sneak little Nicky in to see me but he got caught. Knowing your father, I'm surprised he didn't use the emergency entrance or bribe security." The straw fell to the side of the plastic cup as he attempted to sip orange juice.

"Let me help you," she said.

"No, Cassie. I've got it. It'll take some time until my mental and physical sensations get acquainted again." He put the plastic cup on the tray and took hold of her hand. "But the other organs are raring to go. By the way, you look beautiful. I guess the baby is the reason you're glowing."

She kissed his fingers. "You're the reason I'm glowing. I would be lying if I said the baby isn't the love of my life, but you are the rhythm of my heart. And I won another case in court. That's always an upper."

"Are you still thinking of a big wedding?"

"Only because you said it was okay. I don't care. It's actually more for Mom."

"Whatever you want, Cassie."

The intimacy she felt for him started to work its way back. "But if you don't think you're up to it, I'd just as soon cancel. We can get married anytime—even elope."

"With the baby?"

"Why not?"

"I'm fine with the wedding, Cassie. Your mother's been like a guardian angel during this time. I wouldn't want to disappoint her." A muffled chuckle escaped from his mouth. "I understand St. Patrick's holds about two thousand people."

"There won't be an empty pew, what with Daddy's business associates, Mother's contacts and friends, and then all the relatives. On second thought, I *am* beginning to get a little overwhelmed." She covered her face with both hands.

"You're lucky," he said. "You don't have to lift a finger."

"Are you intimating that I'm a spoiled brat?"

"Well?" he said.

"I'm not going to argue the point. Not now. I'm going to save it for when I can slug you. By the way, Nicky's biological mother phoned me yesterday."

"I thought she cut off all ties with you and the baby."

"She's pregnant. And guess what…"

"She wants the baby back?"

"Over my dead body, Al. *That* is written in stone! She wants to resume our friendship. I've invited her and her fiancé to visit us at the estate. We don't have any friends our age. I think it would be fun. She's quite a character. And her language! I wanted to get your okay first."

"You're all keyed up. It's all right with me. When are they coming?"

"In two weeks."

"I look forward to meeting her. What's this character's name?"

"Franny."

CHAPTER 57

Acluster of puffy-white cumulus clouds floated above the sprawling Sinclair estate. Bumblebees buzzed around the lilac and jasmine bushes that filled the air with their fragrant perfume.

Franny and Matt sat arm-in-arm, viewing the grandeur of the palatial setting. Matt gently poked her. "Your mouth's open."

"Fuck," she exclaimed. "Did you ever see anything so beautiful?"

The chauffeur's eyes darted to the rearview mirror as he suppressed a chortle.

"Sure is impressive," Matt said. "I'd hate to pay the electric bill. But when you're in the financial bracket of these people, it's just a drop in the ocean."

"Guess so. I remember Cassie telling me her family was well off."

"Well off? More like filthy rich."

"Whatever. She didn't come off like one of those snobby society females. More like a regular guy."

"I've been meaning to ask you, Franny..."

"So ask!"

"You won't get upset, will you?"

She faced him. "I haven't felt this normal in years. And that's saying a lot for me. There isn't anything short of your leaving me that would fuck my head up. Shoot!"

As he gazed out the window, his mind drifted to the day he drove her to the lawyer's office to sign the adoption papers.

It was a grey day. She wore a grey dress. He wore a grey pinstriped suit—and it had rained.

"Stop with the dramatics," she had said. "I'm the one doing it, not you." And with the same breath, she apologized. "I'm sorry, Matt, but I can read your mind. It's a done deal. Let's get this over with and get on with our lives."

But when the lawyer placed the documents in front of her and held the pen out to her, she wavered, took a deep gulp of air and, with a trembling hand, signed the certificate of adoption.

Snapping back to the present, he turned back to her and half smiled. Cautiously, he asked, "How are you going to…take seeing the baby?"

"It won't be easy. But I made a commitment, and now that we're going to have our own, I don't foresee a problem."

He raised a heavy brow.

She met his eyes. "It will be a real test for me. Don't you agree?"

He squeezed her arm and pecked her cheek. "Of course," he said. "I'm so proud of you. You've come a long way." *This is too good to be true,* he thought. *God, please, help me out here, will you? Watch over her.*

The chauffeur drove the limo up to the marble steps of the estate's front entrance and opened the limo door.

Cassie dashed out of the door, the Russian wolfhounds, Natasha and Boris at her heels. "Sit," she commanded. With outstretched arms, she hugged Franny. "My good friend, I'm so glad you're here."

Cassie caught sight of Matt standing alongside the limo. "And this must be Matt," she said.

"Isn't he gorgeous?" Franny asked.

"I'm *so* glad to finally meet you," Cassie said, clasping both his hands in hers. "At the spa, Franny spoke nonstop about you."

"And," he said, "Franny spoke about you, too."

"Let's go inside, I'd like to introduce you to my parents and my fiancé Al. You already know he was in a horrible accident and is recuperating from plastic surgery."

"Yeah," Franny said. "How's he doing? The last time we spoke he was swathed in bandages."

Cassie escorted them into the entrance hall. "He wanted to welcome you, but he is not allowed to go out in the daylight. Not for a while. The sun is not his friend. At first, his face was one big bandage. Imagine the invisible man with only eyes staring at you."

"Must have been quite a shock," Franny said.

"Shock? It was like waking up next to your husband and seeing a stranger."

"How long have you two been together?" Matt asked.

"Just about a year."

Matt blew out a deep breath. "At least he's on the road to recovery."

Cassie began to answer, but Al, standing on the landing of the staircase interrupted. "Talking about me behind my back?" he chided. "Not nice." He walked closer to them and held out his hand to Matt. "Glad to meet you, Matt."

"My pleasure," Matt said. "So you're the invisible man?" He moved closer to Al. "Wow! I can't believe you had all that work done. Fantastic."

Al turned towards Franny. "So this is the infamous Franny Cassie keeps talking about."

She smiled. "The one and only." She stared intently at him.

As he took her hand, a frisson of sensation tingled throughout his body—and hers.

CHAPTER 58

Matt and Cassie flanked Franny as they climbed the winding staircase to visit Nicky in the nursery. Al, a few steps behind, held onto the banister.

What the hell is wrong with you? Franny thought. *Get a grip.*

Matt tightened his hold on her hand. "You all right?" he asked.

Aware of Franny's hesitancy, Cassie stopped short. "We can do this later."

Franny shook her head. "No. Have to face up to seeing him at some point. Why not now?"

Al spoke. "I agree. Better to get it over with. You do have one of your own in the oven."

"Yeah," Matt chimed in. "I'm hoping for a girl. He laughed out loud. Arms outstretched, he announced, "I can see it."

"You can see what?" Franny said.

He faced Franny. "Just think, Honeybunch—a clone of you. A little Franny! And guess what her first words will be?"

The banter relieved the tension, but only for the moment.

Nurse Riddle stood alongside the bassinette as they entered the nursery. Franny avoided making eye-contact with the baby, instead commenting about the decor. "What a lovely room."

Cassie, sensing Franny's discomfort, said, "The decorator had an artist paint the nursery rhyme characters on the walls. The rocking horse was Mom's idea and the car bed was Al's." She shrugged. "It is a bit premature for an infant, but for some reason he had it designed as a miniature Corvette." Al smiled complacently. "The blue and white wallpaper," she continued, "was Daddy's brainchild. He said that since I was going to raise Nicky in the Catholic faith, the least I could do was have the blue and white colors of Israel's flag to give the baby a hint of his Jewish heritage.

At a snail's pace Franny edged her way forward until she had no choice but to look down at the bassinette.

Nurse Riddle picked up the baby and placed him into Franny's reluctant arms. The baby smiled and gurgled. Franny, startled by the baby's resemblance to Nick, froze. Her breath caught in her throat. *My God! It's a miniature Nick!*

Memories flooded her mind.

The day she had first met him when he was the detective investigating the murder case she was involved in...their eccentric wedding when they took their vows...the ocean waves circling their knees, the guests sopping wet, laughing and clapping...the day she had surprised him with a vintage Corvette for his birthday...the very day he was shot commanding a drug bust.

Her face ash white, the baby still in her arms, Franny started to sway. Then her knees buckled.

Reacting quickly, the nurse snatched the baby as Al instinctively grabbed hold of Franny.

Cassie and Matt stood mute, stunned.

Franny looked up at Al. "Nick?" she said.

CHAPTER 59

In her cottage, Rosie sat, her elbow on the table, her chin resting in her palm, going over the dinner menu she had prepared for the Sinclairs' guests. The crush she had on Al was evident by the blush that colored her cheeks at the thought of him. The times they had bumped into each other, she had masked her feelings, greeting him politely. Their conversation limited, aware of his indifference towards her, Rosie kept a low profile but seethed within. *If it weren't for me he'd still be riding freight cars. A hobo—a man without a memory. It was I who gave him his name, a place to stay and introduced him to the Sinclairs. And now it's "How are you Rosie? How're you doing?"* Tears of outrage ran down her cheeks.

She picked up the menu then laid it back down. *It's my brothers' fault. If they hadn't prowled around the estate, stealing things, this never would have happened.* Hearing the teapot whistling, she walked to the stove, poured the brew into a cup, set the cup and saucer on the table and dabbed at her tears with a tissue.

She picked up the menu. It was in her handwriting.

Champagne - Cristal 1990   Dom Perignon 1996

Appetizer. Escargot.

Salad. Belgian endives. Miniature tomatoes. Yellow beets. Grilled radicchio.

Soup. Vichyssoise with snipped chive served in iced bowls.

Entrée. Individual Beef Wellington.

Vegetable. White asparagus with turnip/parsnip galette.

Between courses. Palette cleanser. Make sure the lemon ices in miniature martini glasses are chilled properly.

Imported cheeses and fruits with after-dinner wine.

Dessert. Cherries jubilee flambé over the chef's homemade gelato.

Coffee, tea.

To stave off her dejected thoughts, Rosie tossed the damp tissues into a wastepaper basket, took a shower, dressed and walked to the estate's kitchen to check on the dinner arrangements.

Out of the corner of his eye, Al saw Franny staring at him. Suddenly, a blinding jolt to his memory burst in his mind. An image of a red convertible tied in an immense bow with a hazy figure of a woman holding a shiny object up to him. He shook his head to clear it and turned away.

"I'd like to apologize for my unseemly behavior this morning," she said. "Seeing the baby gave me a weak moment. But I'm over it now."

All eyes were on her.

"I mean it. Now that we're going to have our own, I couldn't be happier. Our business is thriving and we have new friends." She reached over and took hold of Matt's hand. "I'd have to be fu—uh, crazy to think otherwise."

"Apologies are not necessary," Mr. Sinclair said. "We understand."

"You did what you thought was best for the child, my dear," Mrs. Sinclair added. "And we are so grateful for your wonderful gift to Cassie and Al."

"I want this to be the best weekend, or week, or however long you and Matt decide to stay," Cassie said. "Right, Al?"

Al's eyes were on Franny. His head spun back to Cassie. "Yes, by all means. Here's to Franny and Matt, our most welcome guests."

After they drank, Al stood. "And," he said, his glass held high, "to our gracious hosts, my future in-laws, Ce Ce and J.J."

"Thank you," Ce Ce said. "And let us not forget the lady who made this fantastic meal possible. We have Rosie to thank for her culinary expertise." She called out to the butler. "Bentley, Rosie is in the kitchen. Please summon her." Turning to Franny and Matt, she said, "We just adore her. In fact, we sent her to Le Cordon Bleu Culinary Institute in Paris. She is like family."

"She is not *like* family, Ce Ce," Mr. Sinclair corrected. "She *is* family."

She responded, "You're right, J.J."

Rosie gave a brief nod to the guests as she entered.

"Bentley," Mrs. Sinclair said, "please make room for Rosie." She motioned towards Al. "Over there. Next to Mr. Center."

Reticent, Rosie sat down.

Al placed his hand on her arm. "Rosie," he said, "you outdid yourself."

Feeling the warmth of his hand on her arm, Rosie looked down and wrung her fingers. She looked at him, her eyes large and watery. A silent sigh escaped as he removed his hand from her arm. Taking a deep breath to regain her composure, she said, "I hope you enjoyed the dinner as much as I enjoyed planning it."

"A toast to Rosie," Al called out.

Everyone stood and toasted.

"Thank you," Rosie said. "And now, if you will excuse me, I must attend to the kitchen."

J.J. raised his hand. "You just sit right back down, Rosie. It can wait."

She stood up. "I'll be right back," she said. But she didn't. She scurried past the cooks and the chef and ran to her cottage.

After dessert was served and the last drop of coffee consmed, Ce Ce rose. "I know J.J. is dying to have one of his Havanas. Whoever cares to join him you are welcome to accompany him to the rose garden."

The springs groaned when Rosie plopped onto the bed. She pounded her fists on the pillow. "It's not fair! It's not fair!" she yelled. "I'm the one who breathed life back into you. Now you have everything and I have nothing! Slowly, she got up and walked to the kitchen table, tore the dinner menu into shreds, threw the bits of paper into the air and watched as the pieces fell to the floor. She walked to the window, parted the curtains and looked up at the sky, unseeing. "You're not going to get away so easy," she said. "Oh, no!"

CHAPTER 60

He was gone when she woke up. On the nightstand, a note leaned against last night's half empty glass of water.

Out jogging with Al – didn't want to wake you.

Love ya, Matt.

Franny swung her feet to the floor and sat up. No sooner had she slipped into a robe than Cassie tapped at the door.

"Franny, are you awake?"

"Come on in. I was just getting up. What time is it?"

"A few minutes past eight."

Franny's brows knitted. "What is this, boot camp?"

Cassie chuckled. "You're free to stay in bed all day if you wish. The men are out jogging and I thought you might…"

"Go jogging? Forget it. I have a hell-of-a-time getting Matt off my back in the city. He wants me to get up at six and schlep around Central Park. I go to the gym once a week. That's about the most fucking muscle-building I can manage. And that's a struggle. Anyhow, I think I'm in pretty good shape."

Cassie sat down beside Franny. "I told you, you're free to do anything you like."

"Listen, Cassie. You don't have to sweet talk me because of the baby."

"I wasn't, Franny."

Franny ran her fingers along the smooth satin sheet. "Well, I'm getting uncomfortable vibes."

"Last night at dinner you were…"

"So pleasant and apologetic?"

"Why the Jekyll and Hyde attitude?"

Franny picked up a pillow and hugged it to her chest. "I wanna go home."

"Not until we have this out! Running away is not going to solve anything."

"Okay, counselor. The truth is…it is the baby."

"The *baby* has a name. And what is the baby's name?"

"Don't cross-examine me. I'm not one of your clients."

"Thank God."

"What's that supposed to mean?"

Matt and Al's voices cut into their conversation. Cassie jumped up and locked the door.

Matt jiggled the doorknob. "Hey," he called, "what's going on? I'm sweating like a pig. I'd like to take a shower."

Cassie spoke up. "Al, take Matt into the other guest room and give him a change of clothes. Give us a half hour and we will join you on the terrace for breakfast. We're doing a makeup thing. Okay?"

"Okay," he answered.

Cassie waited until she heard the guest bedroom door close. "Now," she said to Franny, "talk."

"I have to brush my teeth…and I have to pee."

Cassie tapped her foot impatiently. "Stop stalling. I'll wait. Meanwhile, I'll have coffee sent up."

In less than three minutes, Franny scampered back into the room and faced Cassie. "I'm okay now. I thought it over and there's really nothing to discuss."

"Sit!" Cassie commanded.

"Shit!" Franny said. "I had a feeling you were going to trap me." She sat down on the chaise and folded her arms across her chest. "Truth be told, I'm glad you're pinning me down. I needed someone to sit on me, get me to open up. Matt's a real sweetheart but he's just a man. There's Lily, but she's not here. And a telephone conversation won't work for me."

"Then I'm your woman, Franny."

Franny unfolded her arms. "It's not only seeing the baby…uh, Nicky. I'm worried that Matt's getting tired of my shenanigans. I have been known to lose it."

"He's crazy about you. Anyone can see that. He hangs on your every word."

"I'm not so sure."

"Insecurity. It's getting the better of you."

"Ya know, Cassie, I'm starting to doubt myself. It was so clear in my mind. I could see Nicky and not feel anything, and then…"

"And then what?"

"I became deeply affected emotionally.

"How so?"

"Promise you won't laugh?"

"I promise."

"I felt like I was Alice in Wonderland."

"How so?"

"I was boxed in. The room grew smaller and smaller but I stayed the same." She uncrossed her arms and leaned forward. "I've been having disturbing dreams…nightmares."

"What about?"

"Matt and I are jogging. After a while he disappears and I'm jogging alone in a strange neighborhood surrounded by high, chainlink fences. And to complicate things, there aren't any gate openings. Again, I'm boxed in. Suddenly a man appears on the other side of the fence. He motions for me to come to him, but when I try he fades away. The man seems familiar, but I can't make out who he is."

"Dreams tend to fade rather quickly," Cassie said.

"Ya know, Cassie, my husband, Nick, the one who disappeared, was the only man I truly loved. He understood me. Whenever we'd have an argument he'd say, 'It doesn't matter who's wrong or who's right, we have to understand, overlook and forgive.' Something I could never do. When Matt came into my life he helped ease the pain, and the loss of Nick gradually slipped away. I could breathe easier. He's the best. Success with the maternity line gave me some support, and I finally came to terms with your adopting little Nicky— or so I thought—until the other day when I held him. And what did I do? I fell apart. The resemblance to his father hit me like a ton of bricks."

Cassie studied Franny's face with suspicion. "I understand what you're saying but I have to tell you, Franny, I think there's something more. Can I ask you something personal?"

"You mean spilling my guts out to you isn't personal? Or do you want to know about Nick, the baby's father?"

"No, not at the moment. Something more important. Are you on medication?"

"I…I…"

"I'll take that as a yes."

Bentley knocked at the door. "Your coffee, Ms. Sinclair."

Cassie took the tray from the butler and set it on the cocktail table. She relocked the door and poured the coffee. "Cream? Sugar? Both?"

Franny shook her head. "Coffee makes me hyper. I'll drink water."

"How about an honest answer?"

Silence ensued.

"Come now, Franny. You said you wanted to open up, get it off your chest. Don't shut me out."

Franny half-filled a glass with water and drank it. "Yes, I'm taking medication. You didn't think I could get through all this damn stress without some kind of help, did you?"

"What are you taking, and who has been prescribing the meds?"

"Ya want them in any specific category? By doctor? Alphabetical?"

Silence.

"I'm sorry," Franny said. "I'm being an ass. There are two doctors in New York that I use. I'm taking Xanax to keep me on an even keel and Ambien to sleep. Don't ask me the dosage; I don't keep track. When I feel I need them, I take them."

"They're not candy, Franny."

"No shit, Sherlock."

"Did you ever think that you might be overmedicating? I'm sure Matt is aware."

"We had some big blowups. But he gave up." She picked up an empty glass and drank from it. "Oops," she said, then shrugged and set it down. "Anyhow, Matt said that I was becoming an addict and should look into getting therapy."

"How long have you been on the medication?"

"If you're worried about Nicky, you don't have to. The pill popping started after I gave birth."

"Aren't you being selfish? What about the baby you're carrying? If I were you, I would seriously think of easing off the stuff. I have a terrific gynecologist."

"Yeah, you're right. Trouble is, I can't stop cold turkey."

CHAPTER 61

Matt stepped out of the guest bathroom and into the living room, toweling his hair. He heard a knock at the door; he grabbed for the bathrobe Al had given him and tied the sash. Thinking it was Franny, he said, "It's open, Honey."

"It's Al, Matt. They're still holed up doing whatever it is they do."

"Come in," Matt called.

Al stepped in and closed the door. "Since the ladies have locked us out, we'll just have to fend for ourselves. The answer from Cassie when I knocked at Franny's door, was "'Entertain Matt, Sweetheart. We'll see you later.'"

Matt folded the towel and draped it over a chair. "What the hell are they doing in there?"

"Ours is not to question why," Al joked. "I brought you a tennis outfit. I think we're about the same size. That is, if you're up to playing a set after breakfast. We can't count on seeing the ladies any time soon. Do you play tennis? Or maybe golf?"

"Tennis, yeah! Golf is one sport I've never been able to get into."

"Great. I've been dying to play. Tennis was not one of my chosen sports, but since I have an instructor I'm really getting into it. Cassie is pretty good, but when she loses she pouts. Something about losing to a guy, I guess."

Matt shrugged. "Figures. I know exactly where you're coming from. I'm used to Franny's shtick. Living with her is like being a contestant on a reality show. You never know what she's going to come up with next. It used to drive me nuts, but she wore me down. She *does* have a lot of redeeming qualities."

"Yeah," Al agreed. "She's a firecracker all right. The other night at dinner I could've sworn I had met her somewhere."

"If you had met her, you'd remember. That's for sure." He took the clothes from Al. "Good man. You thought of everything, down to the underwear. Let's pray the sneakers fit." He held one sneaker up. "Good choice, man. These Nike Zoom Vapor 9s are the best." He stepped into the bathroom to change.

Al sat at the bay window and looked down at the manicured grounds. "I didn't pick the clothes. Bentley the butler did. My taste in clothes is for shit. Cassie has to lasso me into the stores. Now she just buys them and has Bentley hang them in my closet. Like you, I caved in. No sense fighting it. We can't win."

Matt spoke from the open bathroom door as he dressed. "Since I've been in the fashion industry, clothes are a big thing with me. "I don't get you on this. I should think that with your lifestyle clothes would be important."

"I don't know how much Cassie's told Franny, but I don't have the social background of the Sinclairs. Far from it." He shook his head. "Very far from it."

"How'd you meet Cassie?"

"I headed up security for her father here at the estate and we hit it off."

"Just like that? Wow!"

"There's more to it, Matt. A lot more." Hazy images flashed through his mind. Shaking his head to clear the cobwebs, he said, "It would take a lot of time to go into detail. Maybe another time. Do the clothes fit?"

"Like a glove. If my pants split at least no one will be around."

"What about you?" Al asked.

"I used to be what you'd call a chick magnet. A typical jock that schmoozed the gals at the bar, then took them back to his macho pad. I'd hit the remote control and the drapes closed, the bar came out of the wall and the Bose sound system filled the room with mood music. The stage was set for seduction. With everything...including an oversized waterbed and mirrored ceiling."

"I'm not into the chick magnet and typical jock scene, much less the romantic setting you describe, but it sounds like something I might like to fanaticize about."

"Why?' Matt asked. "Maybe I'm crossing the line but from where I sit, you've got it made."

"Yeah, I know. But still..."

Matt frowned in thought. "Forget it. It's overrated. You get off work, head over to the local watering hole, have a drink, head home, nosh on some leftovers, take a two-minute shower, put on a fresh shirt, sports jacket, True Religion jeans, and head back to the bar. After a while it's like a hamster spinning its wheels: the same damn scene night after night." He bent over and laced his sneaker. "I have to tell you, Al, I was one selfish son-of-a-bitch. But when I seriously started dating Franny all that became ancient history. Except for the duds. Love the clothes. I'm ready."

"Do the sneakers fit?"

Matt clapped Al on his back. "Like we were twins, Al. Like we were twins."

CHAPTER 62

A t 1:00 the lunch crowd at Santa Clara's Bistro was jam-packed.

The hostess greeted Cassie. "Buenas tardes, Senorita Sinclair. Como esta usted?"

"Good afternoon, Tatiana. Very well, thank you."

She escorted the couples through a maze of beaded curtains, through a cove with a gushing fountain, to an area of tables with vinyl-checkered cloths. Her bosom overflowed her low cut peasant blouse; her well-rounded buttocks jiggled back and forth in time to the lively cha cha of the three-piece combo.

Checking out the hostess, Matt motioned with his eyes then nudged Al. "I like this bistro. It has great ambiance."

"I know what you mean," Al said. "And the food is lip-smacking too."

Franny spoke up. "Keep it in your pants, boys. Concentrate on us."

"I have to admit it, Cassie. It's great to get away from the estate," Al said.

"Do you mind if I order for us?" Cassie asked. "We dine here quite a bit."

Franny said, "Whatever you decide is fine with us. Matt and I will eat anything as long as it's not walking."

Cassie nodded. "Drinks. We have to start with cocktails."

Franny's nose scrunched up. "Stop eyeballing me," Cassie said. Make mine a *virgin* Bloody Mary, okay?"

"Tatiana," Cassie said. "One Virgin Bloody Mary, three Margaritas straight up and easy on the salted rims. You may take the menus. We will begin with salad and the chef's unbelievable Cilantro-lime house dressing. For the entrée, a Quesadilla combination of pork, cheese, and chicken, rice and refried beans. And for dessert, caramel crepes."

A dark-haired, pretty Spanish chanteuse dressed as a toreador joined the musical combo. Shaking maracas, she started to sing.

Franny hummed with the music. "There should be a dance floor. The music is to die for."

"In a few minutes people will get up and dance," Cassie said."

Franny looked around the crowded room jammed with tables. "Where?" she asked.

"In the aisle, at their tables, anywhere there's space for a body to gyrate. Watch. You'll even see people dancing by themselves."

"Love it!" Franny said.

A couple stood at their table and swayed to the rhythm of the music. At another table a well-endowed lady rose, rolled her hips and began to dance by herself.

Franny jumped up. "I wanna dance!"

Matt made a sour face.

Al took a swallow of his margarita and spoke up. "I'm game if you are, Franny."

"Go on," Cassie urged.

Al extended his hand and led Franny to a small space between two tables just as the song ended.

Still holding onto his hand she exclaimed, "Shit!"

"They play nonstop," he said.

She felt the warmth of his hand on hers. Gazing up at him, she hauled in a breath. "Good."

The floor overflowed with dancers as the combo played a slow rumba. He held her firmly in his arms, his mind wary but his body willing.

"You smell good," he said.

"It's Paris," she replied.

"It's Santa Fe," he countered.

"It's a perfume, you ninny," she said, resting her head on his shoulder.

"I told Matt I thought you were a firecracker," he said. "But you have a calming effect on me."

"It's the music."

"Maybe."

Impulsively, he tightened his grip on her.

For a second, she took pleasure from the closeness, but his hold on her was painful. "Easy, Al," she said, "you're squeezing the life out of me."

Intermittent flashes of recall emerged. He loosened his grip. "I'm sorry, Franny. I didn't realize I was doing that." His head befuddled, he shook it. "I don't know what came over me."

"Must be my pheromones. Matt says I give them off like flowers to bees. Didn't Cassie tell you I'm a little eccentric? I love to tease."

He became serious. "Don't tease me, Franny. I have had these weird sensations about you from the moment we met."

"Yeah. Like you've met me before, huh?" She looked up at him and nodded. "Me too. Maybe we were soulmates in a past life."

His eyes locked with hers as a current of electricity ran through him.

Beads of perspiration dotted his forehead. "Past life... I..." His voice trailed off.

"You don't look so good, Al. Let's go back to the table."

A myriad of past visions flashed though his mind. Suddenly he drew a shuddered breath, his body stiffened and he fell to the floor.

CHAPTER 63

The wind howled. Sheets of rain lashed relentlessly against the master bedroom windows, but Al lay motionless, unaware of the world around him.

The dreaded day Cassie had feared had come. It hit her squarely between her eyes—and her heart.

Please wake up, Al, Cassie muttered to herself. *Please!* The nights when she was unable to sleep worrying about his memory returning took its toll on her, haunted her. *What if? What if? What if he doesn't know me?* Stroking his hand, she mumbled. "No. Don't wake up. Not if you're going to be a ghost, a stranger. When you do come back…come back to me as Al. Please! Please!"

Her father placed his hands on her shoulders. "Time for you to lie down, Dear. It's been two days; you're falling apart. Please take the sleeping pills the doctor prescribed. You need to rest."

She shook her head. "No. What if he wakes up and I'm not here?"

"At least drink the tea. You haven't eaten or had any liquid." He held the teacup out to her. "You don't want him to see a haggard old lady when he wakes up, do you?"

Franny paused in the open doorway. "I'm sorry, but I just had to know how Al's doing." Feeling guilty for interrupting, she retreated. "I'm sorry, I'll go."

Cassie turned toward Franny. "It's all right, Franny. Come in. You *are* family."

Franny stepped in and walked closer to Cassie. She looked down at Al. Deja vu of Nick's coma flashed in her mind. "I know exactly how you feel, Cassie. I've lived through the same trauma."

"You never mentioned it," Cassie said. "Was it Nicky's father?"

"Yes."

"What happened? Or is it too personal?"

"Jesus, Cassie. This isn't the time to unload my tale of woe."

"Might be just the right time, my dear," Mr. Sinclair said. "I'm going to attend to Ce Ce. I'll leave you two. Franny, it might be a good idea if you get some liquid and food into her. I haven't been successful. The nurse and doctor are staying close by in case Al comes to."

Franny half-smiled. "I'll do my best."

"Let's make a deal, Cassie," Franny said. "What's happening to you now is almost like what I went through. If you eat, I'll tell you my sad story. Maybe we can both profit from it."

"You trying to bribe me?"

"If that's what it takes, yes. How do I get to Bentley?"

Cassie pointed to the intercom. "Dial double zero and he'll pick up."

Franny lifted the phone and dialed. "Bentley, rustle up some breakfast …whatever you think…yes…in Mr. Center's bedroom but in the far alcove by the fireplace. Thanks."

"Let's sit over there," Franny suggested.

Cassie hesitated to let go of Al's hand.

"You can't eat with one hand and I'm not about to feed you," Franny said. "We can see him from the table." She eyed Cassie. "C'mon."

Reluctantly, Cassie placed Al's hand at his side and stood. Franny put her arm around Cassie and led her to the settee.

Sitting beside her, Franny let her mind focus on Nick's loss to her. *Where to begin? Where to begin? The drug bust? The bullet? The coma? His loss of memory? His fleeing the hospital?*

Bentley cleared his throat as he approached the women. The aroma of the coffee filtered through the room. "Doesn't that smell good?" Franny poured coffee for Cassie. "Let me serve you. I insist." She placed a napkin on Cassie's lap. "Black, right?"

"The coffee does taste good," Cassie admitted. "I didn't realize how good."

Franny tore a croissant apart, buttered it, placed three strips of bacon and two fried eggs on a plate and placed it in front of Cassie. She took the fork and held it up to Cassie. "Eat!"

Cassie's face paled. For a moment her thoughts were on Franny's story, not on Al. Suddenly, she sat up straight. "It's unbelievable," she said.

"Yeah," Franny said. "They seem to have a lot in common. Except, Nick lost his memory and Al knows who he is."

Cassie shrieked. "Oh, my God! It's not possible."

"What's not possible?" Franny asked. "That we're living through a similar situation?"

"Franny, don't you get it? Al doesn't know who he is."

"You're losing me, Cassie."

Blinking his eyes wide, Al took a few minutes before he became conscious of where he was. His eyes searched the familiar room then focused on a night table with Cassie's picture and a vase of overflowing red roses.

He heard a husky voice. "He's coming around."

Cassie rushed to his side and stood frozen, waiting breathlessly, praying he would recognize her.

Smiling broadly he said, "Cassie?"

She sighed with relief. "Oh, Al, you're back, you're back."

"Where have I been? Last thing I remember, I was dancing at the bistro. No, I was on a drug bust. Or was I…?"

Franny edged closer.

Taken aback at the sight of her, he mouthed, "Franny?" He squeezed his eyes tightly. Slowly his head swiveled from Franny to Cassie, and then back to Franny. "Something's not right," he said. "You're both here? What's going on?"

Sympathetic to his state of mind, Cassie said, "You should rest now. You've been through a lot."

"Franny? Is that really you?"

She threw a cautious glance at him and stepped back.

"It's Nick," he explained. "Your Nick."

She looked at him with a mix of bewilderment and irritation.

He looked back and forth between the two women. Frustrated and confused, he covered his eyes with his hands and shouted, "Will someone please tell me who the hell I am?"

CHAPTER 64

Dr. Fillmore Prentiss rested the clipboard on his knee and fiddled with his Mont Blanc fountain pen. "You know, young man, if I didn't know the Sinclairs personally, I never would have taken you on. Your story has the making of a Hollywood B Movie. You're right up there with the most bizarre case studies I have come upon."

"What do you mean a Hollywood B movie? This isn't fiction. It's my life! Everything I've told you can be verified. Mr. Sinclair's lawyers have given you all the proof you need. I don't need a screenwriter. What I need is a shrink that can help straighten me out." He tapped his fingers nervously on the arm of the leather chair. "I'm about to lose my mind. Can you help me or do I have to look elsewhere?"

Dr. Prentiss put his pen down and raised his hand. "Relax. We've hardly begun. This is your first step."

"I suppose the next step is to say anything that comes into my mind? Isn't that what shrinks usually ask?"

Dr. Prentiss smiled. "If you don't feel like talking, don't. But before we get started, it would be nice if you had a name. You can call me Fill, if you like," the doctor said."

He eyed the plaque on the desk. Dr. Fillmore A. Prentiss M.D. *What a nerd*, he thought. *I wonder if he's Fill or Phil?* "Are you taping my conversation?"

"Yes. Does that bother you?"

"No. Just wondering."

"About what?"

"You read my history. I used to record a suspect's testimony when I was a detective."

"What was your name then?"

"Are you playing games?"

Dr. Prentiss leaned forward. "I don't think so. Not me anyway." He half-smiled. "Not at $250.00 an hour."

He frowned. "Okay. Nicolas Salvatore Pagliara. Is the Rorschach test next, or would you like me to close my eyes and touch my nose?"

Dr. Prentiss ignored his remarks. "Fluctuating between Nick and Al can present a problem. Take your time."

"I don't know if I can."

"Who would you like to be?"

"I'm not sure."

"Close your eyes and concentrate. Who comes to mind? Which one stands out? Who do you see? Nick or Al?"

He closed his eyes. "My alter ego Al seems to be gone. But he's a part of me. At least I think so. I'm Nick. Yes, definitely Nick. Except you wouldn't know it to look at me."

Dr. Prentiss nodded. "I read about your accident and the reconstructive surgery on your face."

Nick's fingers pressed his temples hard. "If only it were that simple.

I'm getting these damn headaches. Sometimes I can't see straight." He heaved a sigh. "As Al, I began a new life with new people. As Nick, I have a wife I adore who doesn't recognize me. As Al, I have a fiancée who loves me." He put his face in his hands and started to sob. "It's too much. I can't do this. It's just too much!"

Dr. Prentiss placed his hand on Nick's shoulder. "We'll work this out," he said. "Little by little, we'll lick this problem. Trust me."

Nick raised his face and met the doctor's eyes. "I don't see how, doctor. I love them both."

CHAPTER 65

❧

"You're supposed to be my best friend in the whole world, Franny. I haven't heard from you since you and Matt flew into Santa Fe," Lily said. "Lew and I have been worried. Fine friend you are."

"Don't fucking come down on me, Lily. Not now."

"Your taste for the English language hasn't changed any."

"Will you shut up and let me talk?"

"You sound frazzled. What's wrong?"

"Everything."

"I take it seeing the baby upset you."

"Yes, but that's not the half of it. Are you sitting down?"

Lily held out her other hand for Lew to take. "I'm sitting, I'm sitting."

"Nick turned up."

"What?" Lily shouted. She turned to Lew. "They found Nick." Back at Franny, she asked, "How? When? Where?"

"Here, in Santa Fe."

"Keep going."

"He's living on this grandioso estate and is engaged to the owner's daughter. The one I made friends with at the spa."

"What are you talking about? Not the same lady, the one who adopted Nicky?"

"The very same, Lily."

"So his memory—it came back?"

"It did. Boy, oh boy, did it ever. Well sort of."

"Sort of?"

"Oh, yeah. He knew me but I didn't know him."

"Okay. There's got to be more."

"He had an accident and had to have his face reconstructed. He doesn't even sound the same. But there's something about him that's so Nick."

Lew grabbed the phone from Lily. "Franny, Honey, enough with the talk. I'm hiring a plane. We'll be in Santa Fe in a couple of hours. Don't worry about a hotel. We'll make the arrangements."

"Don't make arrangements. Don't come."

CHAPTER 66

Cassie seemed to have lapsed into a stupor.

"I have to tell ya, Cassie," Franny said, "this is one hell of a mess." She bit into a buttered croissant, talking as she chewed. "It's fucking unbelievable." Annoyed by Cassie's withdrawn behavior, she reached over and shook her. "What's with you?" she barked. "You're supposed to be the strong one. I'm the unbalanced ditz who's incessantly in la la land."

Cassie lifted her head. "I know. It's just that the shock of Al being Nick and..."

"And Nick being Al? Give me a break. You don't think I'm in shock too? At least you have only *one* to contend with."

"What are you talking about?"

"Matt! What am I going to do about Matt? The guy's been a saint."

Cassie sat up and straightened her shoulders. "You love Matt, don't you? Enough to..."

"Give up Nick? That would clear the way for you with Al, wouldn't it?"

"Let's not argue. You said you wanted me to come up with a solution. I'm trying to think of one." She picked up a cookie and munched at it then let out a minute chuckle.

"What's so funny?" Franny said.

"I was thinking that we should be at each other's throats, and here we are…"

"Like sisters? What good would a catfight do? Like you said, Cassie, we're family. You've got Nicky to take care of and I… Anyhow, you're the lawyer, so you should be able to think of a way out for us."

Cassie shook her head. "Uh-uh. This is a joint undertaking."

Franny nodded. "Okay, you start."

"You realize if we're truthful we may become emotional and say hurtful things. And once it's said, it may be too late to retract it." She pulled in her lower lip. "Or we could take it a step further and leave it up to the patient to decide."

"And let the cards fall where they may?" Franny said. "What if he picks me? How are you going to take it?"

Cassie's voice cracked. "I guess I'll have to face up to it, same as you will. Personally, I don't think he's in any condition to make decisions at this time, even if he did tell the shrink he wants to be called Nick."

Franny raised her voice. "Now *you're* playing shrink! I don't think so. Looks like we've already hit a roadblock." Staring into Cassie's face, Franny saw an expression of determination not to give in. Momentarily lost in thought, she picked up the knife and went back to buttering the other half of the croissant. *This is the time to speak up,* she thought.

"Let's face the facts," Cassie said. "There aren't any roadblocks unless we create them. Nick's experiencing mood swings, headaches, and personality changes. This does not sound like he's recuperating. And you know as well as I do that Dr. Prentiss wants him to see a neurological specialist."

Franny dipped her fingers into the water glass then wiped them dry with a napkin. "Honest to goodness, truth be told, Cassie, I have this weird feeling both of us are going to lose out. You're right. He's not getting better."

Cassie squinted at Franny. "Don't tell me you're giving up."

"Let me put it as simply as I can. You knew him as Al from the first time you met him. His identity and memory loss didn't come as a shock to you. You took him for who he was. Look at it from my point of view. I don't even know if he's the same man I married. I see him as a ghost—a ghost of Nick. Sure, he has the same build—maybe the same walk—but if he didn't tell me who he was I wouldn't know him from a hundred other guys in a crowd. I don't recognize the man. It's not the face I knew or even the same voice."

Cassie looked at her dubiously. "Are you telling me you're not going to lay claim to him—that he's mine?"

"I'm not committing to anything, Cassie. I just wish he would have chosen to be Al, not Nick."

"But he professes his love for both of us."

Franny spread her arms. "Yeah, that's what he professes. C'mon Cassie, you're a sharp cookie. Don't let your heart rule your head. With all the hoopla he's exhibiting can you honestly tell me he's rowing with both oars in the water?'

"You're not only unfeeling but unreal."

"And you're supposed to be the levelheaded one," Franny said. "Let me lay this on you. What if Al, Nick's alter ego, shows up again?"

Cassie smiled. "I'd embrace it."

"Yeah, I suppose you would. Listen, I've got a better idea. How about we don't give him a choice?"

CHAPTER 67

Nurse Riddle cast a guarded eye at Nick.

The baby gurgled happily as Nick held the infant high above his head. "I didn't mean to leave you, Son," he said. "I'm going to make it up to you, I promise."

"I wouldn't advise tossing him, Mr. Center," Nurse Riddle advised. "He may throw up on you."

"Yes, you're right," Nick said. "It's just that I'm so excited to finally spend time with Nicky, I got carried away." He placed the baby into his crib and stared down at his son. "I missed the first six months of your life. You can bet I won't miss any more."

"It's time for his nap."

"Okay. Just a minute more."

She turned up her nose and exited.

With glazed eyes, he leaned over the crib, brushed strands of hair away from Nicky's forehead and smiled. "The shrink is so full of shit. Wants me to see a neurologist and get an MRI, and God only knows what else. Thinks I might be showing—what did he say? oh yes—signs indicating non-specific cerebral dysfunction. Have to keep one step ahead of him. I see the way he eyes me. Can't take any chances. He might be thinking that I'm not competent and keep me from seeing you, Son. What a crock! I think he should look into retiring. Next thing he'll be telling me is that I'm schizophrenic. What an idiot. I'm just about rid of Al. That means I'm getting better."

Still staring down at little Nicky, he continued. "We know better, don't we, Nicky? So what if I get migraines and have some issues? I've lived through a lot. A lot more than most. You're all the medicine I need. You know what I'm saying, Son?"

Aware of Nurse Riddle reentering the nursery, Nick straightened up, pointing a finger at his son. "I have to concentrate on us. I'll be back later. Then we can have a real father-and-son chat."

"He's all yours, Nurse," he said, but thought, *but not for long, you suspicious bitch.*

CHAPTER 68

When J.J. stopped talking, the group was silent except for the sound of the rain splattering against the library's stained-glass windows.

"What are you saying, Dad?" Cassie asked. "You spoke to Dr. Prentiss about Al? You know about patient/doctor confidentiality, don't you?"

"We're not in court, Cassie. So stop with the legal mumbo jumbo. And you better get used to calling him Nick."

She didn't answer, but the expression in her eyes spoke volumes: not on your life, Daddy dear.

"The reason I asked you all to this get-together," J.J. continued, "is to come to some kind of understanding as to how to deal with Nick's situation."

"Al," she mouthed.

He shook his head. "Nick! Al! It's enough to make *me* want to see a shrink. I've been through a lot in my time, but this takes the cake."

"I know what you mean," Franny said. "Matt and I thought we were riding high until Nick showed up. Anyhow, J.J., what did Dr. Prentiss tell you?"

"I don't want to hear," Cassie said. "I'm sorry, but I see him as Al, not Nick."

"You don't want to face the facts, Cassie," J.J. said. "And I understand. Finally you found the man of your dreams and…"

Matt spoke up. "I'm Franny's fiancé. I'm not linked to the man as you all are. But I think J.J.'s on the right track. He has been acting strangely."

Cassie took offense. "How do you expect him to act? For God's sake, he's been through hell." She turned towards Franny. "Back me up here, Franny."

Franny rubbed her arms. "I've got the chills," she said, looking at the rain splattering against the windows. She turned back to the group. "When I first saw Nick in the hospital I didn't have any idea who he was. Then he called to me. 'It's Nick,' he said—'your Nick.' My emotions were coming from every direction. Ya could've knocked me over with a feather. The times we spent together came at me like a tsunami." She shrugged. "Like I said before, he was a stranger." She took hold of Matt's hand. "Matt's the only man in my life."

"That's all well and good," J.J. said. "I'm happy for you and Matt, but there's more to contend with. There's the baby…." He hesitated. "And even if I didn't speak with Dr. Prentiss, surely we have all seen a change in Nick. His reticence—his suddenly spending so much time with Nicky and…"

Cassie looked pained. She jumped from her chair. "You're just plain callous and heartless! Can't you see what the man is going through? Well, I for one am going to do whatever I can to help him."

J.J. shook his head. "Face it, Cassie. The man is folding up inside himself."

Bentley interrupted. "Beg your pardon, Sir. The limo has just pulled into the driveway. The gentleman has returned."

CHAPTER 69

No sooner had the limo door closed and the chauffeur pulled out of the driveway than Cassie allowed herself a sigh of relief and turned to him. "At last," she breathed. "I didn't think they were ever going to leave."

"You're amazing," he said.

"Getting rid of Franny and Matt was easy. They needed a change. Getting Mom and Dad to go was the challenge. Dad is nobody's fool. I've got a sneaking suspicion J.J. wanted us to be alone. Thinks I'll change my mind if I spend time with you."

"I agree. He's a pretty sharp guy."

"I don't care. The important thing is we are alone. I don't remember the last time they dined out. Usually it's with Dad's business associates or for one of Mom's charity affairs."

He ran his hands over his face. "Matt and Franny seemed eager to go." He lowered his voice. "Especially Franny. She's not the same woman I married. She keeps avoiding me, like I didn't exist."

"Franny loves to go out on the town. You know that. And besides, you don't look anything like the Nick she knew. She doesn't recognize you. Don't you look in the mirror?"

Feeling her skeptical gaze on him, he said, "Of course I do, every goddamn day. That's what gives me these migraines."

She took his hand and led him to the couch, but he refused to sit. "I don't care about anyone or anything—if you're Nick or Al or the man in the moon," she said. "Being with you is all that matters to me."

He drew her close. "And you're the only one that matters to me. You've stood by me. The others…I'm not too sure about."

He sat and she followed.

"We have to be careful," he said.

"Why?"

He took her hand in his. "Everyone is scrutinizing me. I feel like some kind of bug being analyzed under a microscope. And Dr. Prentiss. I have to be real careful around him."

"Careful? Why?"

"It's hard to explain. He upsets me. The way he stares at me with that smug, holier-than-thou look of his—just waiting for me to slip up and spill my guts out. You'd think a shrink would make you feel at ease."

"How do you expect him to help if you hold back?" His flushed face warned her to back off. "Let's not rush it. I'm here for you. You can tell me anything. I'll understand. I love you. I'll do anything to help you."

"Anything?"

Her face took on a puzzled look, but she acquiesced. "Anything."

For an instant he thought he would tell her who he really was but suddenly changed his mind. "Okay," he said. "Get rid of Nurse Riddle. She gives me the creeps. Always snooping around." Thinking he might have pushed her too far, he lifted her chin and kissed her gently on the cheek. "Let's not worry about her now," he said. "We don't have much time. They'll be back in about three hours. I have a key to one of the guest cottages. We'll finally be alone. Tell me again how much you love me, and this time tell it to me—Al."

CHAPTER 70

D r. Prentiss extended his hand to Al, but Al ignored him. Muttering incoherently, he took the chair furthest from the doctor, sat down and stared down at the Oriental rug.

"Good morning," the doctor said.

Al gritted his teeth. He pulled at his sleeve and tossed his jacket onto an adjoining chair, loosened his tie then struggled to unbutton his shirt collar. Raising his voice, he said, "It's hotter than hell in here. Saving on the air-conditioning? For the prices you charge at least you could keep the place cool." Unable to unbutton his shirt, he tore at it until the button popped.

The doctor's face remained impassive. *He's irritated. Good. I'll sit patiently and wait for him to open up.* He walked to the thermostat and checked the temperature of the room. *Mm. Sixty-five. Any colder and I'll have to get my cardigan out of mothballs.* He walked back to his desk, picked up his pen and clipboard and sat down. *Imagine*, he thought, *complaining about my fee. As if he's paying for the therapy. J.J. and Ce Ce must be having their hands full. And Cassie. Whoever said love is blind hit the proverbial nail on the head.*

Slowly, Al lifted his head. "What do you do for fun, Phil, besides play with yourself? Hit on any of your lady patients?"

Silence.

Al stood, walked to the doctor's desk and picked up a framed picture of the doctor's wife. "Nice looking lady."

The doctor's eyes followed Al's every movement. "Thank you," he said complacently, and added, "I'm fortunate to have her."

"Yeah," Al said. "That's what Nick keeps telling me. All this shit about how he and Franny had this unbelievable love affair going on."

"When did he tell you this?"

Beads of perspiration formed on Al's forehead. Frustrated, he shook his head. "A few days ago—maybe yesterday, maybe this morning, maybe an hour ago. I don't know. What's the difference?"

Dr. Prentiss made a note on his clipboard. "Two days ago you told me Nick was gone."

"Gone! Gone! Gone!" Al shouted. "Don't you understand English? Gone!" He stood and grabbed his jacket. "That's enough for today. I'll be back when you have the good sense to understand me."

Dr. Prentiss stood. "Hold on a second. Just one more question and you can go. Please?"

"What?"

"Does Nick want to talk to me?"

Al's hand reached for the door, grasped hold of the knob, turned it and held the door open. The corners of his mouth tightened and his eyes narrowed. He turned toward the doctor and sneered. "You bet your sweet ass he does, but I'm not going to let him. There's no fucking way he's going to take over."

CHAPTER 71

"Good Evening, Bentley." Cassie handed him her briefcase. "What a day!"

"You do look a bit under the weather, if I may say, Miss Cassie."

"I had the most dreadful day in court."

"I'm sorry to hear that."

She looked into the hall mirror and fluffed her hair. "Who's home?"

"Your mother and father are having an early dinner. Your guests are playing pool in the game room. They asked to be informed when you arrived. Mr. Center is in the nursery with Master Nicky."

"And Nurse Riddle?"

"Last I noticed she was sitting outside of the nursery."

Cassie rolled her eyes. *It never ends.*

"Shall I bring you your usual?"

"No, thank you, Bentley. Inform my guests Mr. Center and I will be joining them for cocktails at 6:00 and dinner afterwards." She took a step up the staircase, paused, and turned toward Bentley. "That is, if they haven't made other arrangements." Deep in thought, she held tightly to the circular banister as she climbed up the solid hardwood staircase. *Maybe Franny and Matt are thinking of going back home to New York. I do love her; after all, she did give me Nicky. But with her gone it would ease the burden Al feels about Nick's unrelenting presence. And with the doctor's sessions and my support, it will work. It just has to.*

CHAPTER 72

Nick hid behind the alcove outside of Franny's suite. *I've got to catch her alone. I need to let her know I don't want to be Al any longer. I want to be Nick and be back where we were, just she and I, and now with Nicky.*

Franny came out of her suite and called to Matt. "Don't be futzing around all night. I don't want to keep them waiting. Ya hear me?"

"Keep your shirt on," he yelled back. "Just have one more e-mail to write to Lew. I'll meet you downstairs."

She walked casually to the staircase when suddenly she collided with Nick. "Al," she cried, shaken. "Where did you come from?"

Holding on to her in order to steady her, he lied, "I was going to pick up a deck of cards from the game room. I'm sorry. Are you all right?"

Startled, she lifted his arm from her waist and stepped back. "No. But you scared the shit out of me." She turned to leave but he grabbed hold of her arm.

"Please don't go," he said. "We haven't had a chance to talk."

"What's there to talk about, Al?"

"I should think you owe me five minutes, Franny. After all, we were more than just friends." He stared hard at her. "Franny, this is Nick talking. What about all the good times we had, the times with Lily and Lew, the times with Elaine? You do remember Elaine. Don't you? Or is she erased from your brain like you're trying to erase me? Open your mind...and your heart."

A tear rested on her eyelid as she thought back to the close friendship the three women had before, during, and after Nick and how deeply she had loved this man. The thought tugged at her heart. For a split second she felt a splash of the old electricity return, but as quickly as it had come it vanished. *He's right. I do owe him at least that much. I can't just walk away. But I don't love him or know him anymore. At the moment, he thinks he's Nick—but for how long? He's so confused.*

She took his hand and led him into the game room. Flooded with guilt and past memories, she motioned for him to sit and took a chair alongside him.

He looked at her with wounded eyes. "Put yourself in my place, Franny. You can't imagine the hell and pain I've gone through—and am still going through."

"Pain?" she questioned. Her fingers gripped the arm of the chair. "Look, I know it must've been hell. What about my pain?"

"You weren't shot. You didn't wake up in a hospital disoriented, without a memory, and then have to bum around the country not knowing where your next meal was coming from."

The laughter of Cassie and Matt rose from downstairs. "But Nick, look how lucky you are. You survived. You have Cassie, who loves you, and a new, handsome face."

He winced. "I want the old face back, and you with it."

"Let me lay it on the table. There's a problem you haven't mentioned."

"That's a laugh. Only one? And that is?"

She was silent for a short moment. "You've got this Al/Nick thing going on."

"I can fix it. If only I had stayed in the hospital in New York, none of this would have happened.

"That's a huge if. We can't turn back the clock. If I went with you we'd have to make too many adjustments. After a while we'd be at each other's throats. You know how unstable I can be and you're…."

"A misfit," he filled in for her.

"In time, you'll work out your psychological problems. Cassie loves you. Give yourself a chance. In time, you'll get better. Think of all the advantages you have with Cassie."

He stood and unexpectedly pulled her up and into his arms. "You don't get it, do you? Why do you think I'm spending so much time with my son—our son?"

She pulled away, knowing to argue with him was pointless. "You have our son. And when you marry Cassie, it will be a done deal."

"Cassie loves Al. Can't you get it through your head? I'm not Al. I'm Nick. I don't want Cassie. I want you!"

CHAPTER 73

Dressed in an argyle sweater, Armani plaid long-sleeved shirt with sleeves rolled up past his elbows, a Hermes belt looped through his jeans and Gucci loafers, Al sat there. With each breath he took, his frustration increased. His face flushed reddish purple. The armchair's leather cushion squished as he shifted uneasily, trying to conjure up words to irritate the doctor. Threatened and fearful that Nick was trying to come out, he fought to stay in control.

Doctor Prentiss greeted Al with his usual quiet warmth and patience. "Good morning."

After a moment Al leaned forward in his chair. His eyes tightened. "Stop staring at me with that superior look!"

"I'm sorry," the doctor said.

"You should be. Your probing is getting on my nerves. I'm trying to hold on to my sanity and you're taking delight by goading me. I know what you're after."

"And what is that?"

"What is that? What is that?" Al yelled. "You know damn well what that is!" He rubbed the rising pain in his forehead. "I've gotten used to living like the rich and famous and not you or anyone is going to change it. And another thing, I would appreciate your not playing favorites."

"Favorites?"

"Don't playact. I know you're taking his side. You enjoy watching me suffer, don't you?" He bobbed his head up and down. "Do you torture all your patients? I bet you even play games with your wife. Is that why you became a psychiatrist—to get off on provoking your patients?"

"It's important that you are comfortable with your therapist, Al. If you are not happy with me I can recommend someone else."

"You're not getting off so easy, Doc. I'll give you another chance. Not because you're winning out. Just so I can prove to you that I'm not giving in."

Doctor Prentiss placed his clipboard and pen on the desk, walked around to Al and sat down alongside him. "Do you know what MPD is?"

"Of course. It's when a person has multiple personalities. So what? If you're thinking that's my problem, think again. I'm the only one in this body."

"What about Nick?"

"There isn't any Nick. There's only Al."

"I know you're an intelligent man, but I can't help you if you won't trust me. You want to get better, don't you?"

Silence.

"Can I at least explain?"

Al grumbled.

The doctor continued. "The goal of MPD therapy is to achieve integration: the unifying or altering into a single cohesive whole with a single set of values and a unified memory bank. I would have to probe more deeply into your past experiences. And in order to achieve that I will have to bring your alter ego, Nick, into the scenario."

Eyes shut tight, fists clenched, Al fought with all his power. *I'm not going to let you out, Nick!* He sprang to his feet and started pacing back and forth. *You can rot in hell, Nick. You're not going to come out! No way.* He stopped short, walked to the leather armchair and plopped into it. "I'm not going to!" he shouted at the doctor. "You can't make me."

"You don't have to do anything you don't want to," the doctor said. "All in good time."

"Damn right," Al said.

Dr. Prentiss glanced at the wall clock. "I think we have had enough for today." He looked at his schedule. "Tomorrow at three o'clock?"

Al did not respond but sat staring into space.

"Three tomorrow?" the doctor repeated. "Okay?"

Al did not answer. He started to get up then sat back down heavily. A dazed expression crossed his face. He smiled triumphantly. "I just got here. What about the session? I don't understand. Three o'clock tomorrow? Okay. Anytime you say." He sucked in a deep breath and with outstretched arms waved a hand in front of the doctor's face. "Doctor Prentiss, I made it. I finally did it."

"Did it?"

He thrust his fist into the air. "I did it! I did it! Don't you understand, Doc? This is Nick talking."

Doctor Prentiss retrieved his clipboard and pen. As a rule he never gave much of a reaction, neither a smile nor a frown. Surprised and delighted by the turn of events, his lips curled up, suggestive of a smile. He flipped the page on the clipboard and wrote, The emergence of Nick.

"Well?" Nick said. "You don't seem very happy to see me. Or is it that you're surprised to see me? Do you have any idea how hard I've tried to get your attention?" He threw off the argyle sweater. "I hate that faggy sweater, the silk shirts, the designer jeans and Gucci loafers he wears. But most of all, I detest this face he stuck me with."

"It's a good-looking face," the Doctor said.

"Yeah, I guess. But it's not mine." He sighed. "Tell me, doctor, how can I disassociate myself from him?"

"All in good time, Nick. There is no instant cure for MPD."

"Don't placate me. You're stalling. I don't have time. I'm losing Franny. Every hour that passes I feel her growing more distant. This Matt fella she's engaged to, he's standing in my way. I know she would start to remember the old Nick she was crazy about if he wasn't around."

"First things first, Nick."

"And there's another problem."

"I'm listening."

"I can't talk to Al like I used to. Something's happening—changing."

The doctor raised his brows. "In what way?"

"We used to have these real knockdown-drag-out fights, practically read each other's minds. At least I'd have a handle on the way he felt and what he was up to. But since we can't communicate I don't have a clue as to what he's thinking. One thing for sure, he's trying to get rid of me."

"And you? How do you feel?"

"Yeah, I want to do the same to him."

"Would you agree to hypnosis?"

"Put me under? Go into my past? My childhood?"

Dr. Prentiss gave an understanding smile. "Yes. It has helped many people with MPD."

"Sure. Why not? I've got nothing to hide. As it stands, everyone at the estate is viewing me with curiosity. And maybe it will help me get a good night's sleep. The sleeping pills don't work anymore. My mind won't shut down. It keeps spinning, filled with ghostly characters—people I have never seen. When can we start?"

Concerned as to which personality would appear, Dr. Prentiss hesitated. "Why don't we play it by ear," he said. "We have an appointment at three tomorrow. Perhaps then."

Nick entered the limo waiting at the curb and sat. Two thoughts filtered through his mind: *Keeping Al from coming out…and doing away with Matt in order to get Franny back.*

✿

Dr. Prentiss waited behind his desk anticipating the arrival of his next patient. He wondered, *Who will show up today? Al or Nick?—And for how long?*

The man who sat in front of Doctor Prentiss at three o'clock was self-confident, and self-assured. "Good afternoon," he said, staring at the doctor. "Well, here I am. Three o'clock just as we agreed."

"Good afternoon. You seem rather chipper. Feeling better today?"

"Better than ever." He sat up straight in the chair. "I'll save you the trouble of playing twenty questions, Doc. Since yesterday an epiphany has occurred."

"An epiphany. Really?"

"Yep. I don't know how, but when I got out of bed this morning and put both feet on the floor I felt…how can I explain it? Like I was reborn. A whole man again. I ran to the mirror expecting to see the face of Nick, thinking maybe I was still asleep, dreaming."

"Enlighten me as to who this whole man is."

"Al. I'm Al. You have no idea how good I feel."

Having reservations about this sudden change of events, Dr. Prentiss said, "This all seems to have happened overnight. Maybe you'd like to tell me more of what you're thinking and feeling."

Al shrugged. "What's there to talk about? I *know* Nick is gone. I'm free, whole once again. The best thing is that I remember everything about

Nick's past." He stood and walked to the sofa and sat. "I can hardly believe it. His childhood...his life before Franny...his first marriage...working as a policeman and then a detective...what he thought of when he was shot on a drug bust...the coma...the hospital he ran away from when he lost his memory...even his childhood and the conversations he and I engaged in. It's so strange, Doc. I keep saying Nick. I keep forgetting that actually we are the same person. It's ironic."

"What is?"

"He had thirty-five years of living, and I, less than one year. It must have been torture for him to look in the mirror and see my face and not his."

"How did Cassie take the news?"

"She couldn't be happier."

"And Franny?"

"Franny and Matt, as we speak, are flying back to New York. They have a business to run. She was anxious to go, mostly because Nick was giving her a hard time and she is pregnant." He half smiled. "Or should I say *I* was giving her a hard time?"

"And all this happened since our session yesterday?" He shook his head. "And we didn't even get to hypnotize you."

"You're testing me, aren't you? It was Nick you suggested be hypnotized, Not me."

"That is true." He met Al's eyes. "Still, we have to crawl before we walk."

"Mm. Maybe so. I still want to see you. That is, if you'll let me."

"And your headaches?"

"Just a mild nudging. By the way, I was thinking of taking Cassie and the baby on a short vacation. What do you think?"

Skeptical, the doctor suggested, "It might be wiser if you didn't rush things. Fit into the scheme of things. Go to work. Keep active. Go swimming. Play golf. Adjust to the whole man you have become." He stood and opened his appointment book. "How about three this Friday?"

"You got it," Al said." He stood, walked to the door then turned around. "I'll bring Nick, just in case I need a back up." He laughed out loud.

Dr. Prentiss listened to Al's laughter as it trailed down the hallway and faded away. The elevator door closed, and the laughter came to an abrupt end.

CHAPTER 74

In a remote cabin on the slopes of a rocky incline in the Sangre de Cristo Mountains, two men sat at a makeshift picnic table drinking beer. They watched children tease a stray dog.

Esmeralda Angel de Marco Gutierrez wore an off-the-shoulder peasant blouse and a flared, multi-colored skirt. She kicked at the loose step that led up to the small house. Her large black eyes flashed anger at her husband and his brother Vidal. She spoke in Spanish. "How many more times do I have to tell you to fix this before someone gets hurt?"

"I will fix it this afternoon. I promise," her brother-in-law said.

Waving a finger at the children, she shouted, "Leave the dog alone. If he bites you, you'll be sorry."

Desi wiped his mouth with his shirtsleeve. "Angel, speak in English," and then shouted at the kids. "Listen to your mama!"

His brother intervened. "Let them play. What else do they have to do?"

"Mind your business, Vidal," Desi said. "You're his uncle not his father."

Vidal stared hard at his brother. His eyelid fluttered as it always did when he became angry. "You got a big mouth. You forget who paid under the table to bring Angel and the kids from Cuba."

"You only paid half. Rosie paid the other half."

"And what did you pay? Nada!"

Desi stood, his fists raised.

"Bastantes!" his wife yelled. "Stop with the fighting." She flung her jet-black hair to the side. "Desi, get los ninos to wash up. Dinner is ready. We eat outside. It will be cool there."

The screen door clacked as it slammed shut. "And the both of you—wash also," she called back.

Desi sent the children to wash and turned to his brother. "No problemo, Vidal. I paid off Raymond the security guard. He's going to work with us. He knows the layout. We could never pull this off without him."

"You sure?" Vidal asked. "Can we trust him? Senor Sinclair will have us buried in the Monterey Cemetery if we are caught."

"Leave it to me, bro." He clapped his brother on his back. "I see you're getting nervous. That tic in your eye is doing that thing."

"Let's go over the plan we talked about," Vidal said.

"No," Desi said. "Let's get the baby first. Then we will make a plan with Raymond to figure out the ransom."

❧

"That's a good boy," Nurse Riddle said as she laid Nicky into his crib. With a tissue, she dabbed at a drop of spittle that had lodged on the corner of the baby's mouth. She smiled warmly. "You're the best little man in the whole world." The mobile fluttered at the touch of her hand. His arms flailing, his feet kicking, Nicky gurgled with joy.

A ghostly shadow of a man with outstretched arms cast a menacing image on the nursery wall. Its shadow loomed larger and more grotesque as it neared Nurse Riddle. Startled, she turned and called out. "Who's there?"

A rough hand grabbed her and covered her mouth with a kerchief. She gasped for breath as the fumes of chloroform entered her lungs. Her eyes rolled upwards and Nurse Riddle slumped to the nursery floor.

"Desi, grab the baby and do it fast," Raymond, the security guard, said. "Vidal, leave the nurse and be quick about it. We don't have much time. The security cameras will be reactivated in three minutes and I have to get back to my station before they miss me. I only get a ten-minute bathroom break. I'll see you at the cabin right after I get off of work tonight."

CHAPTER 75

Fifty feet from the entrance to the rustic cabin in the rocky slopes of the Sangre de Cristo Mountains a man stood guard at a roadblock of makeshift tree stumps and rocks. Upon hearing the roar of a faulty muffler, he crouched, positioned his rifle to confront any intruders. As the old Fiat neared, he sighed with relief, mopped his face with his bandana and raised his rifle to acknowledge his friends.

Desi braked to a full stop and yelled. "Move your ass, Adam. Get the crap out of the way."

Adam nodded stupidly, like a bobble-headed dog in the back window of a sedan. His unibrow rose as he yelled back. "Get out and help me or send Vidal to give me a hand."

Vidal shouted at Adam as he sprang from the automobile. "Moron! Why did you put up these rocks? The tree stumps are enough."

Adam ignored him. "How did it go? You got the baby?"

"Si," Vidal said. "We got him. Did Angel shop for the diapers and baby food?"

Before Adam could answer, Desi yelled from the car. "What the fuck are you doing? Move your ass, the bebe is crying. Vidal, get Angel out here. The brat took a shit and he stinks."

Angel ran out of the cabin and down the path to where Desi sat.

Through the open car door he held the baby up to her. "Take him before I vomit."

Gently, she took Nicky into her arms. Looking disgruntled, she shook her head at Desi and said hotly, "You haven't got the brains you were born with, Desi. We are all going to go to jail."

"You don't know what you're talking about. You want to be like the peons that break their backs picking tomatoes and frutus for pennies, taking shit from the rich ones? You want to live in poverty all your life? Vidal and me and Rosie didn't risk our life crossing the ocean in that homemade piece of junk to be peasants. We could have stayed in Cuba and done that." He spit out of the open window. "You were lucky. I was able to send for you and los ninos. You came here in style."

She turned away and started to walk around the roadblock towards the cabin, then turned towards him. "Big shot," she called. "You forgot why you and Vidal left Cuba? The police were after you. You didn't pay one peso to bring me and los ninos here. Rosie sent me the airfare. You know she is the one who sends money to the old ones every month so they can have more than just crumbs the government hands out."

He revved the engine, trying to drown out her voice. "Big deal," he said. "We are family, no? Does it matter who paid to bring you over or who sends the family money? You're here." He smirked. "When we are riding in a new car with real leather seats and you can buy fancy dresses and real gold earrings, you'll change your mind. I wasn't going to tell you, but I have plans."

"What? To rob a bank?" she said.

"Don't be stupid. We could go back to Cuba and live like kings. The Sinclairs will pay to get the baby back."

She tossed her head back and released a futile sigh. *Why do I waste my breath on him? He can't see further than his nose—stubborn as a mule.* The loose plank squeaked as she walked up the stairs of the cabin. *I will have to fix it myself before the children get hurt.* Kicking the screen door open with her sandal, she held the baby close and stepped inside.

She lowered the bar on the second-hand crib she had picked up at a flea market for $2.00 and laid Nicky down. His wide-awake blue eyes sparkled up at her.

Her sons ran to the crib and looked intently at the new addition. The five-year-old boy tugged at his mother's skirt. "Where did the baby come from, Mama? Is it ours?"

"I'm taking care of him for a lady. It's only for a short while."

The seven year old spoke up. "We want a dog. Can't we have a dog? Phew, he smells."

"Go wash up, both of you! Dinner is almost ready."

Angel waited for the children to leave, hurried into the kitchen, soaked a dishrag in soapy water, rang it out, lowered the crib bar, bent over and started to remove the coverlet. Looking at the child swathed in a hand-knitted cashmere coverlet and a matching Ralph Lauren tee shirt and shorts, she hesitated.

The children reappeared. Their hands in the air, Armando, the elder child, said, "All washed up, Mama. Can we go outside and play until you call us? Uncle Vidal promised to show us how to play a new game."

"Go, but don't get dirty," she said, "and tell everyone dinner will be on the table in fifteen minutes."

She watched the children leave, mindful of their worn-out, patched-up clothes and bare feet, and gnawed at the inside of her cheek. As she cleaned Nicky and changed his diaper, a notion crossed her mind. In deep thought, she stood quietly and looked down at Nicky, then walked to the kitchen, poured milk into a saucepan, heated it, tested it with her finger and emptied it into a baby bottle. The baby sucked hungrily on the nipple of the bottle as Angel held it to his mouth.

An image of the boys outfitted in the finest clothes money could buy as they attended their first communion flashed in her mind. Her breath quickened. *Wouldn't it be wonderful if the boys could have new socks and shoes and wear clean, store-bought clothes? Imagine them going to a private Catholic school then to a university.* "Mi Dios!" she cried. Her eyes caught sight of the designer tee shirts and shorts that lay in an open valise Vidal had taken from the nursery. Aggrieved feelings pulsated within her. *Could Desi be right?* she wondered. *Just maybe?*

CHAPTER 76

"You sure you don't want to eat?"

"No, thank you," Raymond said. "I had an early dinner in the Sinclairs' kitchen."

"A shot of tequila, maybe?"

"No, thank you." Looking around, he asked, "Who resides here?"

Desi tore off a piece of the bolello bread, dunked it into the lentil stew, swished it around until it soaked up the sauce and proceeded to chew. "One thing you can say about my wife," he boasted, "she knows how to cook a real Cuban meal." He questioned Raymond. "You mean who lives in this house?" He dipped the bread into the stew again. "My two boys, my wife Angel, and Vidal, my brother. Adam sleeps in the shed in back of the house. He is a friend not a relative. Why?"

Watching Desi eat, Raymond swallowed hard. He removed his suit jacket, rose, placed it neatly on the back of the bamboo chair, unbuttoned the top button on his shirt and loosened his tie. He thought: *Desi's crude eating habits—talking and chewing with his mouth open and wiping his mouth with his shirt sleeve—are against my middleclass upbringing, but I understood that an opportunity of this nature happens once in a blue moon, and it's more important to go along with his uncouth behavior than to make unnecessary waves at this time.*

Desi asked. "Why do you ask who lives here, Ray?"

"I'll get to that in a minute. First, let me explain a few things. I told the chief of security at the Sinclair estate that it was essential I take my vacation now and not in the winter because of a personal family problem that has come up."

"And they let you, just like that?"

"They didn't question me. My performance history with the company is irreprehensible."

Vidal eyed Desi. "Some fancy English he's talking. "Irre…what?"

"It means that they trust me. I have been with them for three years—ever since the Sinclairs installed the new security system."

Vidal gestured with his thumb at Desi. "Hey, Desi," he said dryly. "This guy talks like a lawyer."

Desi barked, "Shut up, Vidal!"

Annoyed, Vidal cursed under his breath.

Raymond continued. "They weren't receptive to my wishes but I finally convinced them. They hate to deviate from their schedule." Not wanting to insult the men but trying to bring the conversation down to their level, he toned down his vocabulary. Looking around, he asked, "Where are your wife and children?"

"They're outside."

"Good," Raymond said. "From now on we will include you, me, Vidal and your wife."

"I make all the decisions for Angel," Desi said.

Raymond shrugged but was not happy with Desi's reply. Toying with the empty shot glass, he said, "I'm bringing in another man."

Desi's anger erupted. "Another man? How come you tell us about this man, now?"

"Easy, now," Raymond said. "He's been with the FBI for years. He's retired and knows the ins and outs of the law."

Desi shook his head. "I don't know. Another partner? So we have to split five ways? You took a lot on yourself, amigo. You should've spoken to us before you did this."

Raymond stood, walked to the window, pulled the floral curtains to the side and looked out at Angel throwing a ball to the children. After a long moment, he closed the curtain, returned to the table and sat down. "The first part of our plan was successful. The baby's here. As far as the money, we'll split it four ways, including your wife. That should make her happy."

Desi nodded. "Si, it would make her *veeery* happy," he said, aware he would have her share and his to boot.

"This man, we will call him Johnny, is not a partner. He'll get only twenty-five thousand. Believe me, he's worth every penny. I don't think you know how much we are going to get from this venture. We have to trust each other," he said. "Besides his vast experience with kidnappers, this man will do any dirty work that comes up. He's worth ten times that amount. Our hands will be clean."

Vidal spoke up. "You mean like taking someone out?"

Raymond smirked. "Exactly."

"What about Adam? Where does he fit in?" Desi said.

Raymond shrugged, placed both elbows on the table and leaned closer to Desi. "Don't take this the wrong way. Hear me out. Adam has to go. I have nothing against the man, but let's face it, he's a dummy."

Vidal sprang to his feet. "No way, man!"

Desi raised his arms. "Vidal, Vidal, take it easy. Let the man talk."

Grudgingly, Vidal sat down.

Raymond locked eyes with Vidal and then Desi. "This deal we're going to pull off is too important. We can't afford to have anyone screw it up. We can all be rich, very rich, but it has to be done competently and professionally. This is not like just taking a child, writing a ransom note, picking up the money and riding off into the sunset." As soon as the words "riding off into the sunset," slid off of his tongue, he knew he would have to rectify it to them. "We're dealing with people that not only have an army of police at their fingertips but have access to the media. They'll be searching under every rock to find us." He looked from Desi to Vidal and back again to Desi. "Do you want to get rich? If you do, you have to make sacrifices. We all do."

Desi thought long and hard then eyed Vidal. "He's right. We've come this far. Adam could slip up."

Vidal nodded reluctantly.

"Good," Raymond said. "Nothing personal, but what about the missus and the kids?"

Desi pushed the plate away, poured a shot of tequila and drank it. "The kids can go to my relatives," he said. "Angel is cool. She put up a stink, but she's okay now. She'll listen to me. Besides, we need her to take care of the baby. C'mon, have a shot. We are partners, no?"

"Sure," Raymond said.

Desi reached for the bottle, refilled Vidal's glass and poured the tequila. "Here's to the four Amigos," he toasted. "A su salud."

"Your wife should be joining us," Raymond suggested, thinking he should have spoken to her before.

Desi shook his head. "Angel, she doesn't drink. Not even soda."

Raymond appraised Desi's intelligence. *The man may not have had an education,* he thought. *Probably didn't finish high school, or even public school. But he is street smart.* "I don't want to come across like I'm running the show—we are equal partners, but there are one or two things we should get straight."

"Sounds like you're already running the show," Vidal said.

"Be quiet, Vidal," Desi said. "I like that you put your cards on the table, Ray. What do we have to get straight?"

Raymond hesitated then went on. "We were lucky the nurse didn't recognize us. We handled the kidnapping like a bunch of amateurs. I'm not blaming anyone. It's as much my fault. But it taught us a lesson. Careful planning and it starts with all of us. Number one—the drinking—that has to ease off. To pull this off, we must have cool heads. Agreed? After this is over we can go anywhere in the world and drink as much as we want to."

Angel knocked at the door. "I don't want to bother you, but I have to go upstairs and attend to the baby."

"Where are the kids?" Desi asked.

She called down from the top of the stairs. "Outside playing."

"Very pretty lady," Raymond said.

Desi grinned widely. "Oh, yeah! She was the Princesa of the Parade of the Roses, back home."

Raymond nodded. "One more thing before we end this get-together. I have made arrangements to move us to another location. We may have to relocate every couple of days. I suggest you have the children sent to their relatives as soon as possible."

"Done," Desi said.

"What about Adam?" Vidal asked.

Raymond put a hand on Vidal's shoulder. "Leave that to Johnny, the new man," he said. "Let him earn his money."

CHAPTER 77

It was five AM Matt tossed the comforter aside, slipped into his bathrobe and walked barefooted out of the bedroom. Sleeping was impossible. Franny's tossing and turning saw to that.

She eyed the alarm clock. "Where ya going? It's only five."

Turning towards her, he shook his head. "I can't sleep. You're moving around like a drunken sailor."

"So why didn't you poke me? I give you a what-for when you're restless."

He sat on the bed and gently caressed her cheek. "I figured since we went to bed so late I'd let you sleep."

"I wasn't sleeping!"

"Yes, you were."

"Don't fucking tell me if I was or I wasn't sleeping."

"Okay, Franny. You were sleeping."

"Don't appease me."

"It's too early to start an argument."

"Then don't!"

Knowing her shtick, he swallowed a chuckle. "I'm going down to get a glass of milk and cherry cheesecake. We can finish this discussion in the morning."

She sat up. "It is morning and we can finish it now."

He crinkled his fingers at her. "Bye bye."

She jumped out of bed. "I'm coming with you. I'm hungry."

"Only if you promise to drop this nonsensical conversation."

"I promise."

At the kitchen table," Matt faced her. "What's wrong? Why are you so stressed? Anything to do with the baby?"

"Which one?"

"The one that's in the oven. Will you stop with the jokes?"

She masked a sad-clown face.

He stared her down. "Try being serious, will ya?"

"I'm sorry."

"I'm worried about you." He cut a piece of cherry cheesecake and started to eat.

She opened the refrigerator and removed a jar of pickles, plucked the largest one with a fork and chomped at it. "Yum," she said.

He poured a glass of milk, cut another piece of cheesecake, placed the fork on the plate and hesitated in thought. He had broached the subject of marriage more times than he cared to remember, and each time she had put him off. "I'm going to ask you something, Franny, and don't get crazy."

"I won't."

"You're two months gone. I think we should seriously consider getting married."

She finished the pickle and stabbed at another but said nothing.

Annoyed, he said, "You don't fool me. I see right through you."

"So now you're a mind reader."

"Goddamn it," he shouted. "Admit it! You made a mistake by having Cassie adopt the baby and you can't live with it. The guilt is eating away at you. Say it! Say it!" The jar of pickles quivered and the glass of milk fell to the floor as he pounded the table with his fist.

She slunk in her chair, threw the fork on the table and put her face in her hands. "Yes," she sobbed. "I want him back. I want him back."

Matt lifted her in his arms, carried her upstairs, gently laid her on the bed and spooned his body against hers. "I'm sorry I yelled at you, Franny. I was just so frustrated. In seven months, we'll have our own baby." He kissed the nape of her neck. "Give yourself time. Before you know it we'll be changing diapers." His laugh was subdued and didn't come off the way he intended it to.

"You're right. I'm doing what I always do—overreact."

"To know you is to love you, Kiddo. Want me to get you the jar of pickles?"

"Uh-uh," she whispered. She reached for his hands and held them to her breasts. "What I want is for you to make love to me."

He undressed quickly and lay down alongside her. He kissed her nose, her cheeks, her eyes, her chin and then her mouth. Slowly she lifted her body and he tugged the bathrobe from beneath her. His finger passed over her lower lip then traced to her cheek, her throat, her breast, and encircled her nipple. She moaned. Their gazes locked. He kissed her and she kissed him back, his tongue invading her mouth. He drew back, letting her catch her breath as the softness of her thighs pressed against his hardness. Then she guided his hand slowly until he slid inside of her.

One hour later, the shrill ring of the telephone awakened Matt and Franny.

"Don't answer it," he said.

"I won't." She tugged the covers tightly about her.

He yawned. "Good. Let the message machine get it."

"I turned the machine off."

"Why didn't you turn everything off?"

"I forgot."

"It's still ringing."

"Matt, I'm going to pull the fucking cord out of the wall."

"It might be important. Why do you have most of the cover?"

She released a part of the cover. "Happy, Dear?"

"Franny, it's still ringing."

"Matt, I'm going to deck you. Anyhow, it stopped."

"Sleep in today. I'll go over the sketches."

She turned on her side. "I'll see how I feel."

The telephone rang. "Brrrrr…"

Matt reached for it.

"Matt. This is Cassie."

"Oh." He checked the clock radio. "It's pretty early. Is something wrong?"

"Everything's wrong. THE BABY IS MISSING!"

His eyes widened. "What?"

"Kidnapped! The baby's been kidnapped."

Franny threw off the coverlet and sat up. "What's going on, Matt?"

"It's Cassie."

"She grabbed the phone out of his hand.

"Matt is turning blue. What's up, Cassie?"

"Oh, Franny. It's a nightmare."

Franny paused only to take a deep breath, and resumed before Cassie could speak. She yelled into the phone. "Talk to me. What happened? What nightmare?"

"The baby...Nicky...he's been kidnapped. I...I..."

Mr. Sinclair came on the line. "Franny, this is J.J. Cassie has fainted. Nicky has been abducted."

"How? When?" Franny asked.

"Sometime last night or early this morning."

"How is that possible? Where's the nurse?"

"Nurse Riddle was chloroformed. She doesn't remember anything except being grabbed from behind. When she came to, whoever took the baby was gone."

"I'm catching the first plane out."

"I've already made arrangements. As we speak, a private plane is at LaGuardia waiting for you. Bring Matt if you want to. I have to attend to Cassie and Ce Ce. They're both basket cases. Al is taking over."

"Al?"

"Yes, Al. Surely you haven't forgotten that he was a detective."

"I did. This damn split personality hoopla is more than I can come to grips with." The note of anguish in J.J.'s voice worried her. Her hand trembled. "I can't believe this is happening. Why would anyone want to take the baby?"

"Money, Franny. Money. What else? Listen, Honey, I have a lot to do. That's not important right now. I'll see you when you get here. And just to fill you in, call him Nick, not Al. He said he spent a year as Al and over thirty-five years as Nick. And that's who he wants to be. Nick Pagliara."

CHAPTER 78

The rain grew heavier and seemed to pound with a vengeance at the window of the private jet.

Franny tried in vain to get comfortable in the custom leather armchair. She pressed a button and the seat reclined to a sleep position. *If it's not one thing, it's another,* she thought. *The guy who said life isn't fair must have had me in mind.*

The flight attendant smiled at Franny. "I'm Nadine. I see you're ready to get some shut eye, but I must ask you to please adjust your seat to an upright position."

"This is a private jet, isn't it?" Franny carped.

Nadine's smile remained glued on her face. "Yes, Ma'am. It's just a precaution—until after we take off. Mr. Sinclair said to take special care of you." She tilted her head. "Please."

"Okay, beam me up. Rules are rules. When will we take off? The weather isn't going to delay us, is it?"

"No." She checked to make sure Franny's seatbelt was secure. "The captain will signal an all clear. And we'll be good to go."

Franny wiped the fogged up window with a tissue. She shook her head. "Rain," she growled. "Figures. How long is the flight?"

"Depending on weather conditions, ordinarily, six hours." Aware of Franny's downcast expression, she added, "I'm sure it will be less than six hours. This plane is super fast. We clocked it at four and one half hours the last trip."

Simultaneously, a light flashed and a buzzer signaled. "We're ready to take off. I'll be back in a few minutes."

Before Franny knew what was happening she felt a forward thrust and the jet whooshed its way into the sky. She eyed the phone set on the wall in front of her and reached for it, but her hand hovered in midair. *On second thought, what would I accomplish by calling? They probably have their hands full. It's been only an hour since I spoke to J.J. I'll call Matt. No, I just left him. He wanted to come. I should have let him. The baby…those bastards! My baby—but he's not mine—not any more. It's my fault. If I had kept him, none of this would've happened. Stop it*, she told herself. *You're going off.*

"Coffee or a drink?" Nadine asked.

Franny shook her head. "Coffee? I don't think so. I'm too wired. But I could use a glass of ice water."

"We *have* food."

Franny turned up her nose and waved a hand of denial. "If I get a sniff of food, I'll throw up." She opened her purse, removed a vial of Valium, popped three tablets in her mouth and washed it down with the water. "Nighty-night, Nadine. See you in Santa Fe."

CHAPTER 79

Nadine gently touched Franny's shoulder.

"We've landed. Four hours and fifteen minutes. Looks like we broke the last record."

Franny blinked. "We're here? I just closed my eyes. The pills knocked me out."

"Mr. Sinclair has sent a car to take you to the estate. The captain will escort you."

"Forget the VIP service, Nadine. Let me have a quick coffee with a dash of milk and one Splenda." She released her seatbelt, grabbed her tote bag, stood and called to Nadine. "I'll take the coffee to go, please."

Leaning against the door of the Jeep, Nick smiled and waved at Franny as she came into view.

Confused as to why the Sinclairs' chauffeur did not come, Franny felt a little panic wash through her. She stopped short and cleared her throat, trying to disguise the discomfort she felt by his unexpected appearance.

He spoke up quickly. "I asked J.J. to let me pick you up. Give me a chance to explain. Please."

"Explain later. What's the latest with Nicky?"

"We're waiting for the bastards to contact us."

He opened the door, waited until she was seated, then walked around and entered the Jeep. "I've been a real shmuck," he said.

She tossed her tote bag into the rear seat. "No kidding? Do you know how threatened I felt—feel? I'm still not sure about you. One minute you're Al and then suddenly you're Nick."

"I know. I know. Listen, will it be too breezy for you? The top is down."

"It's okay. Fresh air is good. I slept all the way. It will wake me up." She turned towards him then quickly looked straight ahead. "Go!" she said.

He turned the key in the ignition. "Franny, put your seatbelt on."

No one spoke as he steered the Jeep out of the airport lane and onto the highway. Finally he said, "There was so much confusion; so much was going on in my head."

She covered her ears with her hands. "Stop! I don't want to hear!"

"Please, Franny," he pleaded. "I've got to get this out."

She put her hands in her lap. His words, "Please Franny, I've got to get this out," hit a sensitive chord within her. Memories of the old Nick flooded her mind. "Can't we just let it go?"

"I wish to God I could. Just this once. I promise I'll never mention it again."

"I have to tell you, Nick. I'm very fragile right now."

His voice was low and hoarse. "I can see that," he said. "But it's difficult to talk—to say what I want to—while driving. Do you mind if I pull over to the side of the road?"

Franny looked out across the Sangre de Cristo Mountains. The hills were thick with fir trees, and along their ridges, early pioneer cabins dotted the countryside. Hesitantly, she answered, "All right. For a minute."

He pulled onto the shoulder of the highway. He faced her but she kept her eyes focused on the scenery. In her mind his face portrayed Al, not Nick.

"This Al/Nick hodgepodge," he said, "has to be cleared up. You do remember me as I once was, don't you?"

"Yeah, I remember. You're not going to rehash the past, are you?"

"Just listen. I'm not asking you to take the old Nick back. What I'm trying to accomplish is getting my life into some kind of order."

She sighed. "I'm sorry. I'm jumpy. So much is happening. I'm frazzled, drained."

"Well, join the club. Want to change places?"

She turned toward him then quickly turned back to view the mountains. Shrugging, she said, "Change places? I guess not."

"I'm going to be straight with you, Franny. What I'm trying to tell you is that I've won out over Al."

"What exactly does that mean?"

"It means that he's still a part of me, but only a short-lived part." He rubbed his forehead. "I'm not asking you to come back to me. I know how you feel, and although I still love you I realize it would never work between us. You've got a good thing going with Matt, and you *are* going to have his baby. What I'm attempting to tell you is that the old Nick is still here—Nick and Al—the past and the present. Everything in my previous life is now clear to me. For instance, the days with Clancy, my sidekick back at the precinct… Lew and Lily…our crazy wedding knee-deep in the ocean…the day you surprised me with the red Corvette…the day I was shot at the drug bust…" His voice barely recognizable, he sat back into his seat. "It's like someone took a flash snapshot of my past and replayed it."

"What about Cassie and Nicky?"

"You may think I'm deceitful, that I'm using the Sinclairs and their daughter, but if you believe in the old Nick you'll believe the new-fangled one too. I do love Cassie. As for Nicky, I love him as much as I love you."

Her breathing slowed as she drifted into another place, another time. She could hear his voice from afar. The headlights of the patrol car that pulled up in back of them brought her back to the present.

With a stride reminiscent of John Wayne, the burly officer approached the Jeep. Instinctively, his eyes scanned the vehicle. He tipped his cap and drawled, "Evenin', Ma'am, Sir." His feet wide apart, planted firmly on the graveled earth, he asked, "Is there a problem?"

Nick was quick to respond. "No, Officer. I picked the lady up at the airport and stopped to discuss an issue before we arrived at our destination. That's all. Nothing's wrong, Officer."

The officer rested his hands on the outer surface of the Jeep's door. The scent of his Big Red Cinnamon gum breath hung in the air. "You should know better than to leave yourself and the young lady at risk in a parked vehicle on a main highway after dark, Sir."

"I carry a gun," Nick said. "I'm in law enforcement. Would you like to see credentials?"

"That will not be necessary, Sir. I know who you are. I checked your plates. The department is aware of your problem. Mr. Sinclair is a highly respected citizen around these parts. And…we are on the alert in regards to your son."

Fanny leaned toward the officer. "Have you heard anything?"

"I would have heard if anything broke, Franny," Nick insisted. "J.J. would have called me."

She leaned back. "Yeah, he would've."

"Want me to stay with you until you leave?" the officer asked.

Nick looked at Franny.

"Let's just go," she said. "We've nothing more to discuss. Right?"

He nodded. "Right. I've been selfish thinking of myself when the baby's in danger."

She touched his arm. "So have I. So have I."

CHAPTER 80

At dawn Nick slipped out of bed, stealthily went to the guest kitchen and opened the refrigerator door. He removed a loaf of Wonder bread, imported Swiss cheese, ham, a tomato, onion, lettuce, Dijon mustard, mayonnaise, and a jar of Granny's old fashioned kosher pickles, and started to make a monstrous "work-of-art." It took him back to a time when he and his sidekick Clancy worked at the precinct all hours of the night and well into the early morning, unaware of the beginning of another day. It was a time before Franny…little Nicky…his loss of memory…the Sinclairs…or Cassie had existed.

He knew that concentrating on the kidnapping and only the kidnapping should be foremost on his mind, but his brain would not shut down. *The mind can be a dangerous thing. How well I know that scene.*

Clearing his mind of all distractions concerning his personal life was one of the fundamental principles he had been taught at the police academy some fifteen years ago.

The sandwich parted as the knife cut it in half, causing slices of tomato to slip onto the plate. He sprinkled the fruit with salt and proceeded to eat the sandwich when a thought came to him. *Clancy! I'll call Clancy. He must be getting up by now. I bet he's made detective.* To his amazement, he remembered Clancy's cell number.

A groggy voice answered. "Detective O'Brian here."

"Clancy, you old son of a bitch. So you finally made detective."

Clancy checked the caller ID. "You have the wrong number. Go back to bed." He pressed the end button.

Nick redialed.

Clancy picked up. Before Nick was able to speak, he said, "Listen, whoever you are. You're in for a lot of trouble if you don't stop calling this number. I can trace this call and you'll be serving time before you can blink."

He was about to push the end button when Nick quickly spoke up. "Clancy, it's me, Nick."

"Yeah, and I'm Justin Beiber. I'm giving you fair warning…"

Nick cut him off. "My badge number was 96924 and we worked on the three ladies who killed the shrink a few years back."

"Anyone could get hold of that information," Clancy said. "You're fucking with me, man. It doesn't even sound like you."

"Okay, I'll prove it. When you were my sidekick and we worked all night, we ordered from All Night Arties. I had a combo of pastrami and chopped liver on rye with mayonnaise and mustard with Dr. Brown's Celery tonic and a big kosher sour pickle."

Clancy swallowed hard. "Holy Mary Mother of God, I thought you were dead. Where are you? I can't believe it's you. What happened to your voice?"

"It would take all day and then some to tell you, Clancy. So much has happened."

"The buzz down at the station is that after you got shot in the drug bust, you took off from the hospital and disappeared. Fill me in."

The voice sharing Clancy's bed stirred. "It's 3:00 AM. Don't tell me you have to go out."

"Go back to sleep, Sylvie. It's from out of town. It's Nick, my old buddy."

She pulled the covers over her head. "I thought he was dead."

"I heard that," Nick teased. "Who's the lady? Don't tell me you're married."

"Not yet, Nick. Just living in sin." He slipped into his slippers, tousled at his curly red hair, scratched his privates, leaned down and kissed Sylvia on the top of her head. "Can I call you back in five? I have to take a piss. I have your number. By the way, where are you staying?"

"I'm living in Santa Fe, New Mexico, at the Jeremiah Sinclair estate."

"Hold it. The wealthy banker whose grandson was kidnapped?"

"The very same."

"This is too much," Clancy said. "I'm not calling you back. I can take a leak while we're talking." He lifted the toilet seat. "Go!"

"I know I'm asking a lot—maybe too much—but I need someone I can trust to work with me, like we used to." His voice broke. "I'm over my head. You wouldn't believe what I've gone through since I left the hospital. I lost my memory and…"

Clancy cut in. "Say no more, Nick." He thought back to when he had been a fledgling cop from the lower Eastside of New York, how Nick, at the time a sergeant up for promotion to detective, had seen the rookie's potential. Sternly but thoughtfully, he'd trained and groomed Clancy as he would his own son.

Born of a second generation Irish-American father who, as a policeman, enforced the law to the letter, and an overly protective Jewish-American mother who asked nothing less than her son become a doctor or a lawyer, Clancy worked his way through college and graduated with a B.A. in liberal arts.

It was a black day for Patrick and Gussy O'Brian when Clancy sat at the Formica leafed kitchen table and announced to his parents that he did not have his heart in anything but law enforcement.

"Clancy, are you there?" Nick asked.

CHAPTER 81

It took a lot of sweet-talking, persuasive convincing and groveling for the captain of the New York precinct to sign an order granting Clancy a temporary transfer to the Santa Fe law enforcement special unit division. Mr. Sinclair swore he had nothing to do with it, but it was common knowledge he pulled strings with his cohorts in Washington to arrange for Clancy's transfer.

"Give me the keys," Franny said. "I wanna drive."

"Do you know how to drive a stick shift?" Nick asked.

She pulled the keys out of his hand. "Are you out of your frigging head? Who do you think drove the Corvette when you pulled your vanishing act? I think a piece of your frigging mind is still missing."

"Frigging? Cleaning up our act, are we?"

"I cleaned up a lot of things, Nick."

"I know. One of those things was me."

"Don't start. We agreed to smoke a peace pipe. My cursing doesn't offend J.J., but Ce Ce cringes every time I say fuck. Have to respect the lady. She's been aces with me. What with the baby's abduction and the media attention at the estate, the poor thing is living on Valium."

"Aren't we all?"

The gravel parted as she pulled out of the driveway. "How come Cassie didn't come?" she asked. "We talked. She knows I don't have any designs on you. She was worried because you had said you loved both of us, but I assured her you didn't." She expressed amusement with a chuckle. "Women and their insecurities. Have to tell you, Nick, I'm pleased with your attitude. Matt and I are in love and then there's the baby coming, and you and Cassie are hitting it off. I know with you and Clancy working together again, the baby will be back home in no time."

When he didn't answer, she asked, "Won't he?"

She is so full of shit. Forget her? Never, he thought, as the wheels in his head worked on overtime. "We'll get him back," he promised.

She blew out a breath. "I'm so excited about seeing Clancy, I can hardly breathe."

"Slow down," he said. "The last time we took this highway we got stopped. Remember?"

"Yeah, you're right."

"Never figured you to be so crazy about kids. You sure have changed."

"Oh, I don't know. Matt says I still have a screw loose, and he's probably right." His presence upset her, and for a moment she felt a twinge of the old feelings. She shook it off. "What did Clancy say when you told him you had a face job?"

"I didn't."

"You want to give him a fucking heart attack?" she said. "I love the guy. Remember when you and I and Lily and Lew, hung out? We tried so hard to match him up with a date. Boy, was he shy."

"Well, he's not shy any more. He's been shacking up with a lady. Looks like it's serious."

"Good for him."

Nick's cell phone buzzed. "They did?" he shouted. "Five million? Did you get to trace the call? No, huh. Listen, J.J., Franny and I are at the airport now. I'll pick up Clancy, and we'll be back at the estate in record time. No, we don't need a police escort. Let's not attract more attention than necessary. As it is, the media is crawling up our ass."

CHAPTER 82

Tension was masked by the forced chitchat and laughter. On the surface, the atmosphere in the game room seemed to be consistent with the usual Sinclair social gatherings: a group of beautiful people pretending to enjoy themselves.

Nick, with both Clancy and Captain Nate Knickerbocker from the Santa Fe Police Department at his side, huddled quietly in a far corner of the room. Kidnapping was foremost on their minds.

Clancy scanned the room. "You'd think it was an ordinary Friday night family get-together. But it's not."

Nick agreed. "Far from ordinary. If you look closely, they are holding their emotions at bay."

The captain spoke with authority and confidence. "I was a criminal investigator analyst for more years than I care to remember, and I think I'm a fairly good judge of people."

"Meaning?" Clancy asked.

"Body language," he said. "Take J.J. He appears to be unruffled, composed. But beneath the façade there is a nervous, worried man."

Nick snapped. "Why shouldn't he be nervous? His grandson was kidnapped."

Clancy asked. "What has that to do with the people who are here?"

"Yeah," Nick agreed. "Where are you going with this?"

Clancy's eyes narrowed. "Hold on, Sir. Are you thinking that someone in the room could have something to do with the abduction?"

"I'm only saying what has been drilled into our heads from the first day we were accepted into the academy."

Nick and Clancy spoke in unison. "Everyone is a suspect."

"Right," the captain said. "Don't for an instant think I'm telling you how to run the investigation, but you have to admit, Nick, you're fairly close to everyone here."

"I was married to Franny, engaged to Cassie, and yes, I am close to J.J. and Ce Ce, but I'm certainly capable of distancing myself from family ties when it comes to my work."

Feeling he might have offended Nick, he said, "Look, no one has to tell me how competent you are. You've proven that. I'm just thinking aloud."

Nick shook his head. "If I'm thinking what you're thinking, you're way out of town on this."

The captain shrugged. "Let me put it this way. If I were in charge of a kidnapping, I wouldn't trust my own mother."

Franny studied the balls on the table. "Ten ball in the side pocket," she stated.

"Humph!" J.J. cried. "Not on your life, Kiddo. Impossible. Only a pro could make that shot."

Franny picked up the cue stick, balanced it on the palm of her hand, curled her mouth to one side, and faced J.J. "How about putting your money where your mouth is?"

He grinned at her moxie. "Twenty-five bucks says you can't do it,"

Franny snickered. "Tell you what, J.J. Make it a C-note."

"I hate to take your money, Franny. Let's leave it at twenty-five."

"I hate to take *your* money J.J. A hundred Georgies or forget it."

"The lady's got chutzpah," he said to no one in particular. "Okay. You're on."

Ce Ce set her demitasse on the table. "Cassie, what's all the to-do about? I can hear J.J. shouting."

Cassie, as a rule, a self-assured, strong-willed woman who could hold her own with the best of her peers in the courtroom, was now thrown off balance by the baby's abduction, and by Nick's frank confession of his love for both her and Franny. At her mother's voice, she looked up. "What? Oh. Let's have a look, shall we, Mother?"

The players' raised voices attracted the attention of the others and soon everyone gathered around the pool table.

Rosie, frightened and nervous, remembering the repercussions when her brothers were caught stealing from the estate, fussed at the dessert table, arranging and rearranging. *Madre Mia,* she thought. *They wouldn't be so stupid.* But in the depths of her mind, she realized the possibility existed. She felt Nick's eyes penetrate the back of her head but dared not turn around. The Sinclairs considered her a member of the family, but J.J. had given the brothers an ultimatum: either leave the state and never return, or serve prison time. Every spare moment and into the early morning she knelt at her makeshift altar in her cottage and prayed to the Virgin Mother Mary that her brothers had nothing to do with the baby's abduction.

Nurse Riddle sat alone. She observed the group, thinking. *They blame me. I can see by the way they look at me and turn away. Except Ce Ce. I wish I could leave but the detective said I should stay. He can't think I had anything to do with Nicky's abduction.*

Nick turned away from his conversation with the captain and Clancy. His objective was to concentrate on tracking down the kidnappers, but Franny's presence and cool attitude irked him.

"Looks like J.J. is going to get his ass whipped," Nick said.

Captain Knickerbocker shook his head. "I wouldn't bet on it. J.J.'s pretty good at the game. Many a night I watched while he hustled the guys at the club."

"I know the lady," Nick said. "She'll set him up—let him win a few games then move in for the kill."

"Gather around, everyone," J.J. shouted. "You're going to witness the easiest C-note I ever made."

Franny shouldered him playfully, walked around the pool table and checked the position of the balls. She took the cue holder from the wall rack and placed it in front of the six ball. Her pulse quickened. *Hold it together, Franny. Concentrate. Nick will get the bastards and when he does, you'll be there to drive a cue stick right through the fucker's heart. I wish Matt was here.* With a keen eye, she took in a breath, held it, and made her shot. The cue ball jumped over the six ball, bumped the side rail and whacked the ten ball into the corner pocket. Then she let out her breath.

J.J.'s smile faded. He shook his head in disbelief. "Wow! Was I taken in. You were playing me, you hustler."

Nick's expression told Clancy it was time to get down to business. He approached J.J. "I could have saved you the C-note. She shows no mercy with the cue stick. Can we talk? I mean away from the group."

"Sure," J.J. said. "Let's go into the library."

"No. Outside. The walls have ears."

Walking along the manicured gardens, J.J. asked, "Has something happened?"

"Not yet," Nick said. "Clancy and I are working on the info, data and clues the forensic people have collected. We may be lucky. The perp's tactics appear to be amateurish. Asking for five million when they must know you're worth close to a thousand million."

Clancy's mouth dropped. "Whoa! That's a billion!"

J.J. ignored Clancy's comment. "Go on, Nick," he said.

"They're giving us time to think it over. I've got something in mind. Just have to work it out. Sit tight. You know the cottage I transformed into headquarters when the security people couldn't come up with who was lurking on the estate?"

"Yes."

"I'd like to use it as an office. We wouldn't have to schlep downtown, and all the necessary info will be at our fingertips. Captain Knickerbocker has assigned two agents to work with us."

"Of course," J.J. said.

"Let's drop the formalities," Captain Knickerbocker said. "Call me Nate."

Nick faced the captain. "Well, Nate, I hope you don't mind, but I ran a check on your men. Just wanna be straight with you."

His face somber, Nate shrugged. "Don't blame you. I would've done the same. I run a tight ship, but it is possible that a slime ball who's had a grievance with the department might slip through the cracks."

"I appreciate your candor," Nick said.

"Can I be of any help?" J.J. asked.

"Just sit tight," Nick said. "And now, J.J., if you will excuse us, Clancy and I have a mountain to climb. Nate, we'll be in touch." Clapping Clancy on his back, Nick steered him along the rows of bougainvillea to the cottage they intended to use as their headquarters. He removed his keychain and unlocked the door. "When are the men coming?"

"They'll be here later tonight," Clancy said. "I told them to pack light. Anything else they can pick up later on."

"You're staying at the main house, Clancy. Nothing but the best for you, Buddy. You've got the guest room Clint Eastwood stayed in."

"Yeah, I bet."

"No shit, Clancy. Ask J.J., if you don't believe me. I'm not kidding. J.J. pulls a lot of weight. Hungry? Yeah, you're always hungry. We could eat here or at the estate. What do you think?"

"I'd like to see Franny, but we have a ton of work to do."

"Same old workaholic, hey, Clancy? Okay, I'll call the kitchen and have them send a snack."

Clancy teased Nick. "I hope they don't have a pastrami and chopped lover combo." He chuckled. "I meant chopped liver."

They both laughed.

"Clancy, I'll need a complete rundown on all personnel now employed, or who worked at the estate in the last year, including the security staff."

"Gotcha, Boss." Clancy said. Working alongside Nick again brought back the times they had worked bleary-eyed into the early morning hours. *You'd a thought he was my Dad, not my boss, by the way he worked my ass off, trying to shape me into a dedicated detective. Boy, was I devastated when he was shot on that drug bust. The only issue I have is adjusting to his new face.*

"You with me, Clancy?"

"I've already got men working on it. Who do you want to interrogate first? And when?"

"Tomorrow. Nine sharp. First, the help." He walked to the window and drew the blinds. "Start with the head chef, Rosie Duarte."

"I spoke to her tonight. Casual conversation. Nice enough lady. Nervous as hell."

"Call her at her cottage tomorrow morning. Use your persuasive boyish charm. We don't want the help to panic. The place is in enough turmoil as it is." Staring blankly out the window, he recalled the morning he was routed from a freight car in Santa Fe. *She paid the clerk when I pocketed a sandwich, took me home and made sure I cleaned up. It was Rosie who took me in and gave me refuge. She saved me.*

"Something on your mind?" Clancy asked.

"Scratch that," Nick said. "Start with Nurse Riddle. See if she can remember anything new." He let the blind drop with a whack. "I'll talk to Rosie myself."

CHAPTER 83

Clancy slammed the phone down. "Who was that?" Nick asked.

Clancy plopped into his chair. "I don't believe it."

"What?"

"It was New York. There's been a series of bombings and they need me back."

"After all the finagling it took to get you out here, now they want you back? Are they nuts?" Slamming his fist on the desk, Nick yelled, "Never a break. With you here, I felt the tension ease off a little. God only knows what those bastards will do to the baby. New York has bomb disposal units. What do they want with you?"

"I didn't tell you, but the government sent me to Boston University."

"What for?"

"I've always been interested in defusing bombs. Headquarters put out a communiqué asking for applicants to train in robotic bomb defusion, and I applied."

Nick shrugged. "I feel like I'm losing my right arm to Boston University."

Clancy leaned back in his chair. "It was fascinating. The laboratory was enclosed in glass. We wore white outfits. They'd been working on the experiment for three years."

"What did you do there?"

"The scientists were instrumental in developing a bomb-deactivating robot that responds to human muscle movement. It senses impulses from the body to control the robot that in turn defuses the bomb. It's similar to a remote-controlled toy car, but with a camera within the mechanism. They named it Prometheus after a mythological Greek god."

Nick rubbed his chin thoughtfully. "Lost you to a Greek god, huh? When do you leave?"

Clancy grimaced. "Tonight. Want me to apologize to J.J., for all the strings he had to pull to get me here?"

Nick sighed. "No, I'll take care of it."

"I could come back, but I doubt they'll go for it a second time."

Saddened and disappointed, Nick shook Clancy's hand. He tried to muster a smile. "Good luck," he said, "see ya around. He picked up his jacket, slung it over his shoulder, gritted his teeth, and hurried outside. Inhaling deeply, he thought, *You're a pro, man. You've gotten through worse situations.* He walked briskly, trying to clear his head.

A voice called out. "Hey, what's the rush?"

He stopped short.

The Russian wolfhounds, Natasha and Boris, jumped up to greet him.

Franny's face paled. Her eyes widened with anticipation. "I know that look," she said. "Give me an express yes or no. Is it bad news about little Nicky?"

His reply was a split-second motion of his head, accompanied by a "No."

"Thank God," she said. "So, why the long, mopey face? Your memory gone bye-bye again?"

"*That* is not funny."

"Oh c'mon, Nick. Lighten up."

"How come you're so friendly? Lately, your attitude toward me has been piss-poor. In fact, you've been downright bitchy."

"Moi?" She shrugged. "Yeah. I guess I have. We're all going through tough times. Maybe I'm growing up."

The dogs brushed up against him. "Don't," he said.

She waved her hand. "They're just being playful."

"I was talking to *you*, Franny, not to the dogs. Don't you ever grow up."

He's starting to sound like the old Nick, she thought. *Even his dress code is back to where it used to be, Jeans, sweatshirts, Reeboks, instead of Hugo Boss pants, Polo shirts and Gucci loafers.* "If it's not Nicky, what is it?" she asked.

He pointed to the gazebo. "Let's sit over there. I only have a minute. Have to get back to work." *God, she's so pretty*, he thought.

The gazebo—interlaced with a mix of cream, white and deep-red vibrant colors of trumpet vines mingled with lavender clematis blooms—sheltered the couple.

Nick spread his arms out against the back railing. *I'd love to grab her and kiss her, but I know better. She has Matt and I've got Cassie.*

"Gonna tell me what's wrong?" she said.

"Clancy is going back to New York. He's needed there."

"What a bummer," she said, thinking of the nights the telephone had rung, and he was out the door in the blink of an eye, not knowing when he'd return, or if he might not. She sighed. "Yeah, déjà vu. You guys are on call 24/7. Who's his replacement?"

"I have the two men from the Santa Fe headquarters, but I was counting on Clancy. I don't know who I can get to replace him."

She sat up. "I'll apply for the job," she said.

"Very funny."

"I'm serious."

He turned to leave. "Save the jokes for later, will you? Times a wastin'."

She took hold of his sleeve. "Don't you fucking walk away from me. I'm serious."

"Franny, please. I have to get back."

She blocked him. "I'm not one of the dumb bimbos you're used to dealing with, Nick. I'm smart. I run a business, I read the papers, I know what's going on in the world. And don't forget, I am the baby's biological mother."

"Franny, I know all that, but..."

"Fuck but," she said. "I could be your man Friday, sort of a secretary and confidant, and you can trust me. You don't have to pay me." She sat back down. "Look, I need some relief. I'm going nuts worrying about the kid. Cassie and the Sinclairs are the best, but facing them and their grief-stricken faces day in and day out is starting to freak me out."

The thought of being close to her again overshadowed his judgment, but he caught himself. "I'll think about it. We'll see."

"'We'll see' means no. It's what my mother said when she wanted to appease me."

"Okay, okay. Let me go. I have to see what's going on. We'll talk later."

"Don't give me one of those, 'don't call me, I'll call you,' spiels."

Annoyed, he said, "You don't know what you're talking about. Just cool it, will ya?"

She watched him turn and jog to the cottage. Running her fingers gently through the flowers that covered the gazebo, she watched until he was out of sight then sat down.

Natasha and Boris nestled at her feet. They looked up at her as if to say, "What's she up to?"

Franny bent over and stroked the dogs. "He doesn't know it, kids, but he'll come around."

CHAPTER 84

As Desi waited for Raymond, his partner in crime, to show up, he scanned the room, watching the people anticipating an announcement to board. The Santa Fe Municipal Airport's "Hacienda Taverna Pub" bustled with travelers, and the bartender hustled to bring in as many tips as he could. Desi strained his neck past the liquor bottles, trying to get a closer look at his image in the bar's mirror. Pleased with the Tommy Hilfiger plaid checkered shirt, tan Dockers, and Florsheim loafers, he smiled at his reflection. *No more gringo*, he thought. *With the ransom money you will be a king back in Havana. With this clean-shaven face and store-bought clothes, they'll never know it's me.* He smiled again at his likeness. *You clean up good, man. You a pretty good-looking guy.*

The tequila bottle caught his eye. *Si, I promised I would cut down on the booze, but what the hell. One little drink isn't going to hurt. Who will know?* He glanced around to see if Raymond was in sight, then hopped up on a bar stool next to a well-dressed middle-aged woman. He raised a brow at the bartender. "Tequila, two fingers," he said. "No, make it three fingers."

Raising her voice above the hubbub of the customers, the woman spoke into her cellphone. "I don't have much time," she said impatiently. "The plane is already twenty minutes late. Stop asking me, will you? There isn't a direct flight from here. I'll grab a taxi." She listened for a few seconds then shook her head. "I'll see you when I see you. Goodbye!"

Desi watched as she placed her cellphone into her handbag, which hung precariously on the back of her stool.

Perfecto, he thought. He swallowed his drink in one gulp, looked at the check and put a ten-dollar bill on the bar. He stood, lightly brushed the lady's shoulder with his elbow, and said, "Excuse me." He slid his hand into her purse, removed her cellphone and exited the bar. At the smoking area, he called Raymond.

Raymond looked at his cell phone. *Manahoochie, Mississippi? Must be a wrong number.* After two more rings, he answered. "Uh, huh," he said.

"Ray, this is Desi. Why you not answer your phone?"

"Why are you calling me, Desi? I told you no cell phones."

"I'm waiting for you. Something wrong?"

"Nothing is wrong. I had to lend a hand. Moving around to cover our tracks hasn't been easy, you know. I'm at the airport now. Meet me at the international ticket counter. We'll get some lunch and talk. What's with the number you called from?"

"I tell you when I see you. Adios."

CHAPTER 85

Nick tacked an index card of summative facts he had compiled to the bulletin board in his office at the Sinclair estate.

The Mayor and Santa Fe Criminal Division are giving J.J. a lot of heat, he mused. *J.J. is exasperated with the media, and the nosy bystanders who camp outside the estate are making him crazy. Thank God, with his clout he was able to convince them that I'm capable of handling the investigation with the two agents assigned to me. I told them I was considering another person, but who? Damn you, Clancy! I need you. The more people that are involved, the more fucked up this will become.*

He stuck the pushpin into the index card and put it on his bulletin board along with his other notes. Captain Knickerbocker's words flashed through his mind. "If I were on a kidnapping case, I wouldn't trust my own mother.'"

He let go of the index card and sat on his desk. *It would've been nice to have someone like Clancy but...* He thought of Franny. *No, that's crazy. It's not professional.* He ran his fingers through his hair. *On the other hand, she has an innate ability to sniff out the truth.* He clicked his teeth. *Cassie might not like the idea. On the other hand, she's too upset to care.* Studying the cards on the board, he tried to convince himself he would be doing the right thing. *Dashiell Hammet wrote about Nick and Nora Charles. And Faye Kellerman has Peter and Rina Decker, a husband-and-wife team.* He stroked his chin. *Of course they're fictional, but so what. Who says it can't work?*

Raymond used the cell phone Desi had stolen and called the number he had been given at the time he had asked for the ransom money.

Nick picked up the call. "Pagliara here," he said.

Raymond put a handkerchief over the phone to disguise his voice. "Are you ready to do business?" he said.

Nick thumbed a button to alert the agents to pick up the phone and trace the call. "You got me," he said. "Talk."

"You guys are pretty good, but we outsmarted you," Raymond said. "You found the cabin but no one was there. Too bad."

"You're going to outsmart yourselves," Nick said. "You want the money and we want the baby." He envisioned the baby. Controlling his emotions, he asked, "You realize if the baby is hurt, there will be no money. You and your partners will be dead meat."

"Don't threaten me. The baby is fine. Incidentally, the five million we originally asked for has been doubled. That's not too much considering the old man has a fortune. And we know that you're the kid's daddy." He haughtily laughed. "Get the okay from the old man and then we can talk about when and where. Oh, by the time you trace this call, the phone will be at the bottom of the river."

CHAPTER 86

"Where'd you get this piece of shit, Nick?" Franny mouthed.

He waited until she let herself into the black 1997 Fiat, sat down with a thud, put his hand on the steering wheel and drove out of the estate. The brakes screeched as he hit them hard and the gravel parted as the car came to an abrupt stop on the shoulder of the road.

"Whoa!" Franny yelled. "You trying to get us killed?"

Nick looked blankly ahead into the windshield, unseeing. He tapped his fingers on the steering wheel. He grabbed her chin and spun her face towards him then blurted, "I don't think you realize what you're getting into." He released his hold on her. "I'm thinking it's not such a good idea my taking you on." His voice dropped an octave. "Yeah, I'm thinking you caught me at a weak moment."

"I'm sorry," she said. "It was really rude. I only meant that the car is old." She shifted uneasily in her seat. "Look, if I'm making you uncomfortable—you know, because of our previous relationship—take me back to the house and we can pretend it never happened. You didn't wanna do it anyway. I pushed you into it." Fingering the necklace that hung around her neck, she sighed. "I still think I could be of help to you."

"I don't think you know how dangerous this can be. I've had all kinds of threats. The crazies come out of the woodwork when this kind of public hoop-la occurs. I'd feel responsible if you were put in harm's way. And another thing, you're pregnant."

Realizing he was having second thoughts, she said, "Two months is nothing. I have a clean bill of health from my obstetrician." She touched his arm then quickly withdrew her hand. "Little Nicky is *our* baby, well, yours and Cassie's. Matt and I will take care of the expectant one."

His lips twisted wryly and his anger returned at the mention of Matt's name. "You're walking a thin line, Franny, a very thin line. If you're going to give me attitude I'll take your sorry ass out of here and dump you back at the estate. Do you understand what I'm saying?"

She drew back, instantly regretting her words. "Sure, Nick. Sure. I spoke without thinking. It's crazy. We're both out on the ledge. Ease up, will ya? Look, You've got enough on your mind. I don't want to add to your stress. I only thought I could be a help to you. If you feel I'm not working out, fire me."

A grunt was his answer. He exchanged a long thoughtful glance with her. "Fire you?"

She sent him an apologetic glance. "Give it a try. You won't be sorry, Nick." *This is the old Nick, the Nick I adored.* An instant of reflections whirled through her head. *What happened to us and the love we shared?*

Letting the tirade drift past him, he smiled inwardly. "Okay, the bastards keep moving. They've holed up in two locations and probably are looking for a third. They've been informed that we're going to meet their demands."

"We are?"

"But I have other plans."

"Like what?" she asked.

"You and I are going to track them down."

"We are? Just the two of us?"

"Yep." He reached into the glove compartment and removed a forty-five revolver. "You were an expert shot. Think you can handle this?"

She took the gun, released the cartridge, emptied the bullets into her other hand, then twirled the gun cowboy-style.

"Yep," he repeated, "just the two of us."

Her grin wide, her composure back, she thundered, "Fuckin' A!"

CHAPTER 87

A light drizzle covered the road.

"I changed my mind. I like this car," Franny said, the excitement of an adventure racing through her mind.

Nick couldn't curb the grin that curved his lips. "A minute ago you said it was a piece of shit."

"I say a lot of things. You of all people should be aware of that. You have to admit I'm not as flighty as I used to be." She didn't wait for his answer. "I think Matt has taught me a lot."

He flinched at the thought of Matt.

"That," she went on, "and the business venture and of course with the baby thing—it all, I guess, matured me."

The baby thing. That's mature thinking. He glanced to see if she was wearing her seatbelt.

"What?" she asked.

"Nothing."

"Can I ask where we're going?"

"You can ask anything, Franny. Let's put anything personal on the back burner for the present. We're just two agents on an assignment to find a kidnapped child."

"Gotcha."

He swallowed a smile. "Okay. This is what we know. The five million ransom has been upped to ten. J.J. has okayed it. The assholes are on the move again. We haven't heard from them."

"Probably because they're on the move. The bastards won't hurt little Nicky?"

"Who knows? If I were to make an educated guess, I'd say no. When I questioned Rosie I had the feeling she was hiding something. Her brothers used to work for the Sinclairs. They were caught stealing small items and were told to leave New Mexico."

"Now, there's a red flag," she said. "Cassie told me about that. Are they sharp enough to pull this off?"

"I doubt it. They'd need skilled accomplices to pull this off. If it is those morons, there must be others involved."

"How about the security at the estate? They must have access to all the nooks and crannies."

He smiled. "Very good deduction, Sherlock. I thought of that, checked every man that worked for security for the last two years."

"And?"

"Nothing, except for one man that has a record of excessive speeding tickets, but they were paid up."

She shrugged. "Even nice guys get speeding tickets."

"Fifteen is a bit too many."

"How come security hired him?"

"Could be a lot of reasons. Maybe he knew someone."

"Yeah. It's not always what you know but who you know. How about Nurse Riddle or the help at the estate?"

"Been there, done that."

"We've been going up and down hills for a while now. This dirt road is snaking around and around. There's hardly any room for an oncoming car, much less a truck."

"We're in the mountains, Franny, not on the Long Island Expressway."

Stretching upward, she craned her neck and looked down at the steep incline. Her eyes followed the plunge of the stones that the tires raked as they fell into the abyss below.

"We're almost at the top of this hill. From the map it should be downhill for a while. You seem anxious, Franny. What's up?"

"I'm not sure. I have this weird feeling."

The car reached the summit. Franny breathed a sigh of relief. "Look," she said. "There's a plateau with a picnic bench and table. Can we stop for a minute? The view must be breathtaking?"

"No! We don't want to be spotted."

"Just for a minute. Look, there's a cluster of trees. No one can see us from there. And besides I have to pee."

He offered his arm. "Need help?" he joked.

"I can manage," she said.

When she returned he was deep in thought, sitting underneath a group of thick, tangled acer trees, his long legs spread wide, a map between them.

"Nick, did you ever see such trees?"

Unhearing, he didn't reply but acknowledged her presence with a faint nod.

"They're real weird—the branches seem to be reaching out to grab us. Yikes! Like something out of a horror movie."

"What?" he asked.

"I was talking about the trees."

Ignoring her, he said, "Uh-huh. Come over here, I want to show you something."

She sat beside him. Too close for comfort, she shifted away.

His expression readable, he rolled his eyes. "Get over it, Franny. Making advances towards you is the last thing on my mind. To me, you're just one of the guys. And guys...I'm not into."

She moved closer.

With a marker, he penciled in a line and pointed to a route on the map. "This," he indicated with his index finger, "is where we are and this is where they holed up six hours ago. Here is where they might be headed."

"How do you know that?"

"They can't drive on just any road; they'd be spotted. The mountains are their best cover. Don't forget, we've got helicopters and police cars tracking us."

"I don't hear any whirlybirds and I haven't seen a police car since we left the estate."

"And why do you think that is?" he sing-songed.

She mimicked his voice. "Because it would alert the bastards."

"They want to get this over with and pronto. The longer they hide out the less chance they have of pulling this off. Getting the money and disappearing is their best bet. Right now, they have the upper hand."

She bit her lip. "Yeah. Little Nicky is their ace in the hole."

"Right," he concurred. "Have to hand it to you, Franny. Your thoughts about the security guy started me thinking."

"You mean about the security guy that works at the estate and had all those speeding tickets?"

"Yep. While you were doing your thing back there I called headquarters and asked them to run a detailed description on the guy."

"You think there's a connection between him and the brothers? They did have a vendetta against the Sinclairs."

"It's possible, and guess what?"

"What?"

"You steered me into it, Sherlock." He showed a "thumbs-up."

Her eyes gleamed with satisfaction.

Slipping the folded map into his breast pocket, Nick rose and extended his hand to help her up. Their bodies touching, he drew her to him, but she moved to the side. Quoting his words verbatim, she repeated his previous remark: "'Get over it, Franny. Making advances towards you is the last thing on my mind. To me, you're just one of the guys.'"

He nodded. "You're right. Let's go."

His cell phone buzzed. "What's up?" he said. "More to this Raymond dude than meets the eye, huh…and a wife abuser?" He clicked the off-button. "Well, Sherlock," he said smugly. "You are working out."

"This links the security bozo with Rosie's brothers," she said. "She seems like a sweet lady. Maybe she's not involved with them."

"Maybe she is and maybe she isn't," he said. "Get in the car and put your seatbelt on. This winding road can be tricky."

Nick drove the Fiat onto the dirt road.

Gazing out of the window, she remarked, "I didn't get a chance to view the scenery back there, but I sure can see it now. Wow, we're on top of the world! It's like being on the cyclone at Disneyland. What do you think the elevation is?"

"Reach into my breast pocket and look at the map."

"I'm not reaching into anything of yours. I'm not too sure I can trust you," she said, realizing the tension between them—remnant from the past—still lingered.

His outburst startled her. "What the fuck!" he cried.

She sat straight up. "What's wrong?"

"The brakes! The damn brakes! They're not working!"

"They worked before."

"We were going uphill."

"Use the hand brake."

"It's not functioning." He pumped down hard on the brakes but they went to the floorboard. "Shit, we're starting to pick up speed."

"Can we jump from the car?"

"Not a chance. We're going too fast, and not with your physical condition. Someone tampered with the brakes. They're gone."

Franny froze in her seat, too frightened to speak, her feet hard-pressed to the floor, clutching tightly to the handgrip.

The car roared down the steep hill uncontrollably, the scenery becoming one big blur.

The road curves kept coming at them faster and faster as the car careened down the hill.

Nick turned a ghostly white. He steered the car as best he could, but he had no control. He bumped the right side of the road, hoping it would slow the car down, but that didn't work. He shifted into first gear, thinking it would help. Then he turned the ignition off, but the car continued its wild plunge downward. In a frenzied, last-ditch effort he threw the gearshift into reverse.

Immediately, the transmission jammed. A loud clank resounded in their ears as the Fiat bucked like a rodeo bull.

The car spun around and landed on the edge of the embankment, the front wheels spinning in space, the back wheels wedged onto a split boulder. The Fiat teetered precariously as it hung suspended in mid air.

CHAPTER 88

The sun's rays baked down onto the makeshift shelter. It was their third move, and Angel's tension increased with each arduous change of location.

She fanned herself with an accordion pleated paper fan: a freebie that advertised an AAAA air-conditioning company's logo. She had picked up the fan while looking for a secondhand baby's bassinette at a local flea market.

Little Nicky's crying agitated Desi. "Angel!" he stormed. "Do something!"

"E`l tiene hambre," she said.

He yowled. "So feed the brat. Take him outside. We're waiting for a call from the police." He nodded at Vidal, Ray and the new accomplice, Johnny. "We need some quiet."

Angel held Nicky close and sniffed his diaper. Relieved to find no odor, she cradled him in her arms and gently rocked him back and forth. The wind gusted into the area as she opened the canvas flap, walked outside and sat down cross-legged on the hard earth. She wondered. *Do American babies smell different than Cuban babies?*

She bolted up as a loud crash resounded in her ears.

Desi, Vidal, Ray and Johnny ran out of the shelter.

"What the hell was that?" Vidal shouted.

"It came from over the hill," Angel said, pointing to an embankment.

"Desi," Ray shouted, "Come with me. "Vidal. You and Johnny watch Angel and the kid. Keep the motor running just in case." He pulled his gun from his holster and motioned for Desi to follow.

"Keep down," Ray said as they approached the hill. He peered over the rocky knoll. "A car hit something and is hanging over the cliff. Looks like the back wheels are caught on a rock formation. It's ready to drop into the canyon or maybe the river."

Desi raised his head. "Don't look too good for them. Somebody in the car." He squinted. "Looks like two people. They're not moving. Maybe dead."

Ray smiled. "Has to be the smart-ass detective. I had a buddy of mine fix his brakes so they'd leak. We better check it out. He may have let someone else use the car."

"We better get over there. The car is ready to fall."

Ray raised his gun. "Looks like the police are closer than I thought. Let's give the car a little push and send them over the cliff."

"Yeah," Desi agreed. "Then we better get back to the shelter and take off again."

Franny moaned. "Where am I? What happened?" She remembered Nick attempting to control the car as it sped down the dirt road and then smashed into—what—she wasn't sure. Her eyes focused on the steep ravine below, and then it hit her. "Oh, my God!" she cried. "We're hanging in mid air!" Fear gripped her. "We're swaying."

His hand was on hers. "Don't move, Franny. The car's caught on something and any movement might just send us down into the canyon or the river that runs alongside it. Are you hurt?"

"I don't know. I can't feel anything. I'm numb. Nick, you're bleeding."

"I'm okay. You don't feel any pain—I mean—your pregnancy?"

"I don't know. I'm too frazzled."

"Have to figure a way to get out of here."

She craned her neck, attempting to look out of the window.

"Franny, I told you the slightest movement could weaken the hold the car has on whatever it's hooked onto."

"It's not me, Nick. It's the wind. Shit, I'm afraid to breathe."

Cautiously, he reached into his pocket for his cell phone. "I'm going to call for help." The crunching noise started again as the car's wheels lost their grip on the rock that held it. The car pitched forward as it hung suspended above the wide-open abyss.

She gripped her hands tightly. Her knuckles turned white.

"You can't get to the phone can you?"

The car jerked slightly. The crunching noise sent a cold chill through Franny's body.

"I'm afraid to move."

"Nick."

"Yes."

"We're going to die, aren't we?"

Silence.

"Nick," Franny whispered, "the rearview mirror. Two men standing there. Call them!"

Nick eyed Ray and Desi. "No," he prompted. "They're probably the bastards that took the baby."

Franny paled.

The car started to lose its footing and slipped forward. Franny gasped.
Nick breathed a sullen, "Fuck!"

Franny squinted. "Am I hallucinating or are they coming closer?"

Nick watched Ray and Desi in the misaligned rearview mirror. "They're in back of the car."

❧

Ray's smile was evil. He put his gun away, rested his hands on the vehicle's trunk and turned to Desi. "Let's do it together."

Desi shook his head. "You do it. I want to stand at the edge and see the car explode when it hits the bottom."

An idea formed in Ray's mind. *I can pull this off without him, and have a bigger share of the ransom. Then I'll coldcock his wife and brother. Johnny and I will split the money. Splitting two ways is better than four. Maybe I'll get rid of Johnny, too.*

"Don't get too close to the edge, Desi. It's a long way down."

Desi walked to the cliff's edge and looked down. "This is gonna make one grand big bang. I hope it doesn't land in the river."

Ray removed his hands from the car and stealthily walked up to Desi. He raised his hands, intending to push Desi over the cliff, but Desi, sensing someone behind him swiftly turned and ducked.

Caught off balance, Ray lost his footing and plunged down the cliff.

Desi watched until Ray's body splattered on the rocks below, then he let out a loud howl. He unzipped his pants, removed his penis and urinated. "I piss on you," he shouted. "You no-good bastard." Then he walked to the swaying vehicle, kicked at the rear bumper guard and watched the wheels begin to disengage from the boulder. "Adios, amigos," he yelled.

Johnny shouted from a distance. "The cops are on our trail. Everyone's in the car. We gotta get outta here."

Desi yelled back. "Shit. I wanted to see the explosion." He gave the car one last shove then turned and ran toward the car Johnny was driving. "I'm coming! I'm coming!" he yelled and jumped into the moving vehicle.

"Where's Ray?" Johnny asked.

Desi shrugged. "You just drive, amigo. Ray—he don't feel so good."

CHAPTER 89

A horrendous shriek echoed through the fourth floor of the Lady of Our Mercy Hospital in Santa Fe, New Mexico.

The attending nurse ran to Franny's bed. "It's only a nightmare. Just an old-fashioned bad dream."

Matt was immediately at Franny's side.

"The sedation is wearing off," the nurse said. "She's coming to. I'll get the doctor."

Matt stood directly before her—a large, lean, somewhat menacing figure in her eyes.

Drawing a deep breath, he took hold of her hand.

The jolt of the horrid nightmare still fresh in her mind, her judgment unclear, she withdrew her hand. Tossing her head from side to side, she asked, "Did they find little Nicky? And with the next breath, "Nick? What about Nick?"

Matt tensed while waiting for her to acknowledge him. *Doesn't she see me? Why doesn't she say something? Damn him! It's always Nick! I bet she's going back to him. He must have convinced her to pick up where they left off. But that's the least of her problems. When she finds out she lost the baby, she's going to go berserk.*

Franny asked. "Is that you, Matt?"

He drew closer.

"I missed you, Matt."

Relieved, he leaned forward. "I missed you too. You have no idea how much. Rest, Darling. You've been through a lot." He took hold of her hand.

"What about Nick?" she asked again.

His face soured. "We don't know. The car dropped into the abyss and exploded. Just missed crashing into the river."

"Oh yeah, the river. Poor Nick. Cassie must be devastated."

He clamped his teeth together. *Who gives a damn about Nick or Cassie? Nick! Nick! Nick! What about me?* He stepped aside as the doctor rushed to her side.

"I see you're back with us," he said. "How you survived is a miracle."

"I hurt all over, Doc." Slowly, she reached down and felt her stomach. Her voice came out hoarse and strained. "What's going on? Did I have the baby? I couldn't, it's not time. The baby! Oh, my God! They took my baby!"

CHAPTER 90

From her hospital bed Franny watched a robin red breast on the ledge of her window pecking at a clump of twigs that had fallen from an adjacent tree. It had been two painful days of healing since she and Nick had the accident. The loss of her baby sent her into a deep depression, and anyone that entered the room was greeted with foul language and tossed vases, vials of medication, trays or anything she could get her hands on.

Matt, with the doctor's permission, was allowed into the room while she slept.

On the third day, Matt roused from the armchair where he had fallen asleep and walked cautiously to her bedside. With care, he said, "You're up. How are you feeling?" Her remote glance at him was less than cordial. Cautiously, he stepped back. His suspicions that Nick was in her thoughts troubled him no end. He thought, *Poor kid, she's been through so much, and she's so confused.*

"I can't tell you how happy I am that little Nicky is safe," she said. "I

337

keep dreaming about him."

"I was worried about you, Franny. But you seem to…"

"Have gone off the deep end? Yeah, I guess. I've been doing a lot of thinking. I figured I'm lucky to be alive. So what's the use bitching?"

"We can have another. The doctor said so."

"Forget it," she said. "I'm giving my insides a sabbatical."

"Are you sorry you let Cassie adopt Nicky?"

"Listen, I made a deal and I'm not going back on it. It's only natural for me to care about him. I am the biological mother."

He thought. *Yeah, And Nick's the father.*

"Have you heard anything new about Nick?" she asked. "It's been three days."

He edged closer to her and sat down on the bed. "A forensic team painstakingly examined the charred car and the area for rings or any other items belonging to Nick that might have survived the fire. Nothing was found. Not a trace of him."

"Here we go again," she said. "That idiot has pulled the disappearing act more times than Houdini."

"You need more rest. You're bruised and still in pain."

She shook her head. "I'm too wired. They doped me up with everything the hospital pharmacy had on the shelves. Between the pain killers, the sedatives, the uppers and the downers, there must be a fucking combat zone going on inside of me. I don't feel a damn thing.

"You know, Matt? When you experience something as traumatic as I did…" Her voice shook, broke, then stopped.

"Yes?"

She shuddered. "I mean, facing death, and losing the baby…"

He held her hand to his cheek. "I know. I know," he whispered.

"You don't. Not really. My perspective of how I lived my life keeps whirling around my brain." Her head bobbed up and down. "I've decided to be a better person."

"A better person?"

"I want to give of myself."

"If that's what you want, Darling, go for it. Does that mean you'll clean up on the cursing?"

"Let's not go overboard, Matt. I meant like volunteering, or adopting a child. Not a baby, but a kid that's had a rough time—an eight or ten year old. A child that nobody wants." She looked around the room. "It takes a rude awakening to discover how much you have, and how lucky you are to have it."

"It's called gratitude, Franny."

"What do you think?"

He opened his mouth as though he was going to say something, but he didn't. His mind was filled with today, not tomorrow, and there was so much of today they had to contend with. His look was ambiguous. "Sounds good to me."

"You're not happy with the adopting idea, are you?"

"Sure I am, Franny. But let's take one step at a time. Besides, the doctors say you can still get pregnant. That is, in time."

"Forget that for now. Where are Lily and Lew?"

"How'd you know they were here?"

"Are you kidding? She's my best friend in the whole world. She has to be here. Anyhow, I saw her, or dreamed she and Lew were here."

"Lew had to drag Lily away. You were out of your head, and she was carrying on. They're in the cafeteria."

"How about Cassie? She must be beside herself."

"J.J. and Ce Ce are with her. She's a basket case since she heard that Nick's missing. A rescue team is searching the Santa Fe River. There is a chance he landed in the river. He could be floating down and into the Rio Grande by this time."

Lily rushed into the room, followed by Lew. "Oh, thank God!" Lily gushed. "I knew you'd get through this." She embraced Franny.

"Hey," Lew said. Let me get a hug in, will ya?"

He looked her over. "What a mess you are, Kiddo."

Lily threw Lew an admonishing glance.

"Otherwise, you seem almost normal," Lew said. "I'm dying to know how you survived. All we heard was that you and Nick took a nose dive off of the cliff."

"That's not funny, Lew," Lily said.

"It's okay," Franny said. "I could use a few laughs. Pull up a seat, kids, and park. I think they have me on uppers. Well, the bastard gave the car a real hard push. I was petrified.

"Then Nick shouted: 'Open the door and try to catch hold of anything you can grab on to. It's your only chance.'

"I shouted, 'No, I can't!' He reached across, kicked my door and shoved me out. I heard the crunching noise of the tire again. The car was hanging by a thread."

She hesitated. Everyone leaned forward.

"I don't know how, but I was able to grip the roots of a tree or low-lying branches, I don't remember which. I guess the car hovered close to the cliff when the bastard pushed it.

"Don't know how I hung on, but somehow I did. Then suddenly an alien from space wrapped his arms around my waist and hauled me up and into a helicopter. Funny, but I don't recall ever hearing the whirlybird. In fact, I don't remember anything, but one thing I'm sure of—I was sure I was going to die."

Silence hung heavy in the room.

The door opened slowly and all eyes were on J.J. Stoop-shouldered, head hung low, hands clasped in front of him, he said, "They found a man's body in the Santa Fe River. The body was badly mangled, unrecognizable. They haven't made a positive identification yet, but..."

CHAPTER 91

The elderly man had his arm around his grandson. "We're not going to get many more days like this one," he said as he led his grandson down the rocky path and into the marshy-reeded water's edge. "Have to take advantage of them."

The lad pointed to the water. "Gosh, look at all those flies and bugs, and Grandpa, the fish are leaping at them. Maybe we should use a net."

"Think so?" his grandfather exclaimed. "Those bass are faster than a hummingbird's wings."

His hip-high boots made a sloshing *whish* as he stepped into the muddy water.

"Now, cast out like I showed you, Sammie."

Sammie miscast. The line sailed upwards and landed askew around the bend of the river.

"Reel it in, Sammie, and try again. Remember what I taught you."

"I'm trying, Grandpa, but it's hooked onto something."

"Okay. Let's have a look. Probably snagged on some branches."

They proceeded to where the hook had entrenched itself.

"Grandpa!" Sammie cried. "My line. It's hooked onto a man."

The elderly man acted quickly. "He tossed his fishing line down, untangled the body from the hook and the debris, and dragged the body onto the water's edge. Instantly, he tore apart the man's shirt and with closed fists started to pound on the unconscious man's chest. "Sammie," he shouted. "My jacket...the top pocket...pull the snap...grab my cell phone...call 911."

CHAPTER 92

The police cordoned off a restricted circle around Nick, screening him from the curious fishing enthusiasts who heard the ambulance siren.

On a stretcher, covered up to the neck with a blanket, an IV in his arm, Nick, ghostly pale, lay unconscious as the medics carried him up the incline to a waiting ambulance. One of the EMTs stubbed his toe on a protruding rock and stumbled. The stretcher jolted and Nick's left hand dropped.

Cassie, her hair disheveled, with J.J. at her heels, pushed her way through the onlookers. "He's dead," Cassie shouted. "I know it. He's dead."

J.J. turned to the medic. "How is he?" he asked.

The medic did not stop. "He's unconscious and barely breathing. Have to get him to the hospital real fast."

"Which hospital?"

"Santa Clara. Know him?"

"Yes."

"It's not customary, but you can ride with us if you want."

"We want," J.J. said, watching Cassie take Nick's hand and tuck it underneath the blanket.

In the ambulance, J.J. was on the cell phone calling his doctors, telling them to take his helicopter to the Santa Clara hospital. He turned to Cassie. "It's in God's hands now, Cassie. All we can do is pray."

❧

J.J. paced back and forth in the Santa Clara hospital hallway as Cassie sat sobbing. His eyes fixed to Nick's room, he waited impatiently for the doctors to come out. He tried to use his cell phone, but there was no signal.

"I'm going to find a telephone," he said. "There isn't any reception on my cell." He put his hand on her shoulder. "Will you be all right?"

"I guess. Bring back coffee."

"How about some food?"

"I couldn't."

The moment he left, the door opened and the doctors appeared.

Cassie sprang to her feet.

"What?" she said.

Dr. Portnoy spoke. "He's going to live, Cassie, but…"

"How bad is he?"

"He's in shock," Dr. Verker said. "Dr. Portnoy and I were fortunate to have the use of J.J.'s helicopter, and although Santa Clara has capable physicians, he insisted we attend to Nick. His excellent physical condition helped. The gentleman who found Nick and applied cardiopulmonary resuscitation deserves the credit for saving his life."

"Can I see Nick?"

The doctors exchanged glances.

Dr. Portnoy stroked his chin. "The fall from the cliff into the rapids

344

took its toll on him. He has a broken arm, a broken leg, a broken collarbone, and is severely bruised. He's not conscious. We took an MRI. Thank God, his brain is intact. Movement at this time is impossible. Be prepared for what you are going to see."

Cassie walked to Nick's door; she was halted by Dr. Verker's voice.

"One moment, Cassie," Dr. Verker called. "There are two nurses and a staff doctor who are attending to him." He spread his arms. "Looks like your father has taken over. An adjacent room for you has been prepared." He half smiled. "I'm sure I don't have to say more. Make this visit a short one." He held the door open for his colleague as J.J. appeared. "I'll be back later. Don't worry."

Cassie and J.J. hurried to Nick's bedside then stopped short. The hot coffee J.J. had brought for Cassie overflowed onto his shaking hand, but he didn't feel the scalding liquid on his skin. Setting the cup on the nightstand, he whispered. "All the way from the cafeteria I was thinking about that old expression, 'it never rains but it pours.' But this is more than just a rain shower. It's a flood."

Her mind flashed to the backbiting quarrelling she and J.J. had as she grew up. *We were always butting heads. Trying to outdo one another. Was it my fault or his? Anyhow, what's the difference? I'm sure he did it for my sake. Now, he's as gentle as a lamb.*

The only sound in the room was Nick's labored breathing.

Her hand shook as she picked up the coffee. "I need more than coffee, Dad. I may start smoking or drinking or maybe taking drugs."

They stood, their arms around each other, looking down at Nick.

"He'll recover," J.J. said. "And so will you. The man has gone through a lifetime of adversities. He'll make it through this one, too."

Cassie's head slumped. "I'm not so sure, Dad. I'm not sure at all. He might make it, but I'm not too sure about me. The rational person I was is somewhere in another galaxy."

"You'll see, Baby. The present is dismal now, but there's still the future. There is one thing on our side. And that's time."

She took a sip of the coffee. "Time?"

"Yes, time. It has wings. It flies by very fast."

"I suppose."

The door opened and a detective motioned for J.J. to step outside. Within a minute he reentered.

"Cassie, I've got some good news."

She glanced down at Nick then back to her father. "The only news I want to hear is that Nick will pull through…unless it's about little Nicky."

"It is. The police rounded up the kidnappers and the baby is okay."

She sighed. "Thank God. Maybe the rain is letting up."

"Desi's wife, Angel, jumped from the van with Nicky in her arms, and the police picked them up. I spoke to the captain about giving her amnesty. She took good care of Nicky."

"Can you do that?" Cassie asked.

Sounding like the old J.J., he replied. "I can do anything in this town, Cassie. I own it. Meanwhile, her children can stay with Rosie."

Nick opened his eyes, and then his mouth.

Cassie pulled back. "Look, Dad, his eyes are opening. He can't move his head." She walked to the foot of the bed. "If we stand here he will be able to see us."

Nick blinked and attempted a smile.

"Oh, Darling," Cassie said. "Thank God. Can you hear me?"

His smile broadened.

The attending physician moved quickly to Nick's bedside. "I'm Dr. Phelps," he said. "Do not move."

Nick muttered a groggy, "Okay, Doc."

"You're going to get well," Cassie said. "Oh, Nick, I'm so happy. We were so worried."

He tried to speak, but the words caught in his throat. His eyes closed. Within a few seconds he opened them. "Hi," he breathed. "I'm back."

Cassie's hands tightened on the frame at the foot of the bed. "Oh, Nick, this is the happiest day of my life. Little Nicky's safe and you are too…you're going to get well and…I love you so much."

He looked into her eyes and murmured, "And I love you too, *Franny.*"

CHAPTER 93

Holed up in her estate suite, Cassie had not eaten in how many days? A week…two weeks? She didn't know—or care to know. She had isolated herself, pulled the landline connections from the outlets and smashed her cell phone into tiny fragments with her spiked high heel the day she finally accepted that Nick preferred Franny to her.

Stale cigarette smoke hung heavily in the gloomy atmosphere as Cassie contemplated her future without Nick. Her newly acquired smoking habit was one of several she had adopted. Drinking was another.

The breakfast tray the chef had prepared sat outside her door untouched until the butler removed it and replaced it with lunch, then dinner, and again with breakfast.

Gone were her hopes and plans for the future. The clever, sharp, self-confident attorney who had rarely lost a case in court was on her way to becoming a reclusive drunk.

Hair disheveled, barefoot and clad in Dior silk pajamas that needed to be sent to the dry-cleaners, Cassie sat on an upholstered bay window seat and vacantly stared down at the estate's manicured gardens.

It would have been better if he had died. I wish he had. I knew all along something was not right. Back and forth, back and forth—loving Franny— loving me. Like a fool, I stood by him, oblivious that he would go back to her. "It's you I want to spend the rest of my life with," he said. "I'm going through hell. Trust me." Yeah, trust me. What a crock! How could I have been so blind? What was I thinking—that he could love both of us? And then in a moment of cleansing his soul, he had the nerve to tell me it wouldn't be fair to me, that Franny was the one he wanted to spend the rest of his life with. She snickered. *Pick one. Door A or Door B.*

The clipping sound of the gardener trimming the hedges drew her attention. She thought: Snip-snip-snip, and it's vanished. Now you see it—now you don't. Going, going, gone.

She poured another brandy and swallowed it in one gulp.

The knocking at the door jolted her from her thoughtful state.

"Cassie, Darling," Ce Ce called. "Please, can I come in? It's been more then a week and your father and I are concerned about you."

She placed the brandy snifter on the window ledge then shook her head, trying to focus. *I know I'm being selfish,* she told herself. *Putting my parents through my miseries. But I'm in no condition to see anyone.* "Later," she called out. "I'm going to take a nap. Later."

Ce Ce's overwrought voice spoke through the door. "You haven't seen the baby since he's come home."

Cassie picked up the snifter and drank. *The baby's safe and sound. He doesn't have a care in the world.*

J.J. attempted to rap on the door but Ce Ce grasped his hand in midair. "Let her sleep it off," she whispered. "What she needs is tender loving care, not a lecture." She leaned closer to the door. "Promise me, Cassie?"

"I promise, I promise," Cassie replied. She curled up on the window seat, the bottle of brandy nestled snugly in her arms. "Promise, promise, prom…"

❧

When Cassie eventually got up, she picked up the brandy bottle, stumbled to the bathroom and caught a glimpse of herself in the mirror. Shocked by her unkempt appearance, she sat on the hassock, sank her face into her hands and rested her elbows on the marble sink.

Slowly, she raised her head and spoke to her image in the mirror. "What's the use? There's nothing left for me." Feeling heartsick and detached, she fell into a whirlpool of depression that sucked her down and around and into endless darkness. "Why torture yourself? Why not take the coward's way out? But first, a drink. I need a drink."

The voice in her head said, *Feeling sorry for yourself, are you? You have everything anyone could want: beauty, brains and money to burn.*

Cassie crossed her arms over her chest. "What good are they if I can't have him?"

What good are you doing by drinking yourself into a stupor?

"The drinking and pills, they help ease the pain."

Her inner voice did not reply.

The vial of sleeping pills on the counter caught her eye. "Do you have the guts?" she asked the image in the mirror.

The image replied. *And you're supposed to be a top-notch lawyer? Pills are passé. Too slow. They'll find you, pump your stomach, and then where will you be? Go for something quick. One, two, three, and voila, you're history.*

She put her hands on the counter, pulled herself up and held the brandy bottle in the air. "Whoops," she exclaimed. "You're almost empty. Not leaving me too, are you? I must have a terrible affliction. Almost empty, Mr. Hennessy. Can't have that."

Wavering, she opened the door and peered down the hallway. *Ah, there's no one in sight. They're in the living room. I can hear them talking—discussing*

350

my fate—wondering if I'll come to my senses.

Tiptoeing down the hallway, unmindful of the brandy bottle scraping noisily against the wall, she staggered into the master bedroom, threw the bedcovers aside, and lifted the pillow on her father's side of the bed.

"Oh, there you are," she said. "You are here to see the end of my misery." She picked up the Smith and Wesson 9mm handgun J.J. kept for protection, held it against her cheek and breathed in its metallic odor. "Daddy always said you'd come in handy."

With her other hand, she tremulously attempted to place the brandy bottle to her lips but missed her mouth. The brandy trickled down the front of her pajama top. Her words slurred, she said, "Focus. You can do this." Then the bottle slid from her hand onto the parquet floor with a distinct clatter.

J.J. and Ce Ce suddenly appeared at the doorway.

Cassie, bleary-eyed, her mind spinning in different directions, gave a low whimper, a wave of her fingers at them, put the gun into her mouth, and pulled the trigger.

CHAPTER 94

After two weeks of healing and fighting with her conscience, Franny leased a furnished condo a stone's throw from the Santa Clara hospital where Nick was convalescing.

On the terrace, Franny asked Lily. "How do you like the condo?" An iced tea in hand, Lily sat eyeing her friend as Franny playfully stirred the straw of a Bloody Mary.

Staring blankly at Lily, she set her drink on the glass cocktail table and rocked back and forth in a rattan rocking chair. "I'm so confused," she said.

Reclining on a chaise lounge, Lily asked. "So what's new?"

Lily's sideways glance at Franny was guarded. "Before I get in over my head, can I ask you a personal question?"

Franny stopped rocking. "I don't believe it. Is there one fucking thing about me you don't know? If there's anyone in this world I can let my hair down with, it's you."

Lily nodded. "That's exactly why I'm being cautious."

"Don't tell me you're afraid I'll go into one of my hissy fits. I don't do that anymore."

Rolling her eyes was a given with Lily when it came to Franny. "Okay, I give up."

Franny's mouth tightened. She continued to rock. "Forget it."

Knowing Franny, Lily tried another route. "Something to do with Nick or Matt?"

Franny rocked faster.

"Want me to tell you?" Lily asked.

"Okay."

"On one condition. Put the brakes on the damn rocker. I'm getting queasy."

Franny complied. Sitting up, she said, "Like I didn't have enough going on. Matt's drifting away from me."

"Don't you have that backwards? From where I sit, you hardly talk about him. Nick seems to be the topic of conversation. Isn't that why you rented this condo? So you could be near Nick? You visit him every day. I'm sure that can not be going over big with Matt."

"He doesn't know."

"Fess up, Franny."

She started rocking again. "Matt's busy. Why should I bother him with details? He's gotta take care of business. The line doesn't get done by itself, ya know. That's why he and Lew left for New York."

Lily sipped on her iced tea, drew in a deep sigh and let it out slowly. "If I fall off the wagon and start drinking again I'm going to sue you for cause of action."

Franny stopped rocking. She threw her hands into the air, then stood, and sat next to Lily. Her head bent, she said, "Oh, Lily, I think I'm falling in love with Nick all over again. Don't know how or why, but it's just happening."

Lily shrugged.

"I feel so bad about Matt."

Lily raised her brows.

Franny dabbed at her eyes with a tissue. "I was thinking about what Nick had said—that he was in love with Cassie and me at the same time, and now…"

"Turnabout is fair play," Lily quoted.

"Not when it happens to me, it isn't. Lily, you always gave me the best advice. Help me out here. What do you think I should do?"

Lily stood and looked down at her friend. "Franny, this is one time you'll have to make your own decision. Have to grow up sometime. Stop thinking of only Franny." Her mind turned to Cassie. "I'm sure she's trying to pick up the pieces and make a new start." She waved a finger at Franny. "It could have been you."

"That's not the way I hear it. J.J. told me she's taking it extremely hard. Stays in her room and mopes.'

Lily waved a warning finger at Franny. "It could have been you," she repeated.

Feeling a sudden surge of adrenaline, Franny sat up. "You're right! If Cassie can pull a stunt like she did, I guess I can show some moxie and face up to…" She hesitated, and then feigned an insincere cackle. "Heh, heh. Imagine, getting so soused and then shoving a gun in your mouth. Fucking idiot. What the hell was she thinking? I bet the Sinclairs shit a brick, seeing her do it. I'm a little unpredictable, but hell, take my life…? I don't think so."

Lily rolled her eyes. She walked to the front of the terrace and looked out at the rows of corn in the distance. "A little unpredictable? I've seen you do and say things that would bring the men in white jackets to strap you in and take you away."

Franny joined her at the window. "Well, maybe. But if I were going to take the easy way out, I'd make sure the gun was properly loaded." She put her arm around Lily. "There's one thing I really, I mean *really cannot* stand, Lily."

"Uh-huh. And what might that be?"

"Anyone who can see right through me."

They both laughed.

CHAPTER 95

It was like being on the losing team before the game started. Franny gritted her teeth. With unsteady fingers, she punched Matt's numbers at the New York showroom. "Okay, here we go," she said under her breath.

Matt picked up the phone. A pleased smile formed at the corners of his mouth and his face lit up at the sound of her voice. 'Franny, Baby," he purred. "I've been waiting all morning to hear from you. I didn't want to call. I figured you and Lily were schmoozing, like always. What's happening? Feeling better?"

"Matt, I'm taking the redeye tonight."

He exclaimed, "Whoa! I'm dying to see you, but are you up to traveling?"

"I'm okay. There's so much I have to…ah…discuss with you."

His breath caught in his throat. *Here it comes,* he thought. *The old heave-ho. She's going back to him.* "What's this all about? Now that you've piqued my interest, at least give me a hint as to what you want to talk about."

"I can't do it over the phone. Please, Matt, don't make it any harder for me."

His face reddened as he slammed his fist on the desk.

"What was that?" she said.

"It was my fucking heart breaking. Let me guess. No! Let me tell you. Unpredictable, impulsive, fickle Franny has decided to go back to her husband. Right? Yes, right! Finally, what I've been anxious about for months has come to pass." Frustrated, he raised his voice. "Let me save you the tear jerking, the pitiful rationalizations, the explanations, and, oh yes, the nail-biting flight."

He slammed the phone down. *I'll get over it,* he told himself. *I'll get over it. But not before I teach her a goddamn lesson.*

"You buzzed me?" Emily, his secretary, asked.

"Yes, Emily. Get me a flight on the next plane leaving for Santa Fe, New Mexico."

CHAPTER 96

Matt settled back into the plush leather. Tapping his fingers anxiously on the arm of the seat, he mulled over the events of the day. His head throbbed.

The flight attendant interrupted his thoughts. "Good evening, Sir. I'll be serving you. My name is Stuart."

Matt looked up at him, eyeing his nametag. Ordinarily he would have clowned and said, "Stuart the steward, huh," and laughed as every passenger before him had. But Matt's mood was much too dismal. He waved a hand at the steward and snapped, "Get lost!"

The man backed away tactfully.

Matt shifted uneasily in his seat. *Who would have thought it? One minute you're sitting on top of the world and the next minute you feel like shit.* Staring at the couple across the isle, he snickered, his forehead rumpled like that of a bulldog. *In first class, everything should seem better,* he thought. *Champagne, caviar, all the goodies one could want.* The wonderful times he had shared with Franny flashed through his head. But they did not console or soothe the anger he felt for her, or the hurt. It only heightened them. He was more than just annoyed. He was bitter, vengeful, and unforgiving. If he had learned anything by living with Franny, it was the guarantee of uncertainty.

I should have known better. The bitch has robbed me of my manhood. Emasculated me. Cut off my balls. Nope. She's not going to get off that easily. Not this time. No more Mister Nice Guy. It didn't pay off. The lady's taught me a lesson. Now it's time for me to return the favor.

CHAPTER 97

Cassie had been wavering for days between mind-numbing depression and cowardly despair. She sat at the bay window of her bedroom, legs pulled up against her chest, hands hugging her knees, contemplating her next move.

Her Russian wolfhounds, Natasha and Boris, lay at the foot of the four-poster. Every so often they would glance up at her soulfully, give out with a poignant whimper, glumly look away then go back to their resting mode.

After a half hour of deliberation, Cassie made a decision.

The Hands-On Gun Shop, she thought. But how to elude her parents, the security, and the servants presented a problem.

Dad has the security personnel on red alert. Believes I'm desperate enough to take my life. He doesn't know how right he is.

Leaning down to pet the dogs, she thought: *He's smart but I'm just as smart. Thinks because my little mishap didn't get into the media that no one knows. It must be costing him a fortune to keep his daughter's suicide attempt quiet.*

Ce Ce, she thought. *I can get over on Ce Ce.*

Punching in her mother's extension on her new cell phone, she said, "Mom. I feel so much better. I've been thinking and thinking and I've come to the conclusion that I'm putting you and J.J. through hell—feeling sorry for myself—being selfish."

"You need a change of scenery, Dear. Start doing something. Maybe go back to the office, or get away and clear your mind."

"That's exactly what I've been thinking."

"We could go to Paris or Italy. You love Switzerland. You always said it was so peaceful there."

"No, Mom. Not now. Maybe later on." She wound an end of hair around her finger. "I was thinking of instant gratification, more like a shopping spree. It might help snap me out of this depression. It's always worked before."

"Wonderful idea, Cassie. I'm so happy to hear you speaking of getting your life together again. When do you want to go? Nieman's is having a fashion show for their new fall line. I was going to meet the ladies for a fundraising benefit, but I'll cancel."

"Don't cancel, Mom. I've caused you enough aggravation."

"But Cassie, J.J. absolutely forbids you going anywhere without... an escort. You understand, don't you, Dear?"

"Of course, I understand. Tell you what. Bentley could come with me. I won't feel like I'm a prisoner. He's not just a butler; he's family. I'd feel so much better with him."

"But J.J. said…"

Her tone softened. "We don't have to tell J.J., do we? He has enough on his mind. Remember the times I cut school and we had our secrets from J.J.? There really isn't any difference."

"I'm not sure it's quite the same, Cassie."

"Oh, Mom. I'm starting to come around. I'm fine. Really, I am. Isn't it worth my peace of mind? It will only be for about two hours. Pleeeease."

Ce Ce's voice faltered. "Uh…I suppose it's all right. You do sound more like the old Cassie."

"You're always so understanding, Mom. Tell Bentley to have the limo ready. I'll be down in ten minutes. Have to fix my face."

❧

Bentley held the limo door open as Cassie turned to wave to her mother, knowing she would be watching.

"Where to, Miss Cassie?" Bentley inquired.

"Let's start with the Riffraff Women's Boutique."

He glanced at her in the rearview mirror. "I know where it is, Miss Cassie. I've taken you there before."

This is better than a courtroom drama, she thought. *I get to be the lawyer, the judge, the jury and the executioner.*

The minibar caught her eye. *What I need is little pick-me-up.* "Bentley," she said. "I have to adjust my undergarment. I'm going to slide the screen. Okay?"

His eyebrows peaked.

"Don't worry, Bentley. I know you've been briefed. I'm not going to jump ship. You can lock the doors. As soon as I take care of business, I'll slide the screen back."

His expression showed reluctance. "Very well, Miss Cassie."

She unscrewed the cap on the scotch, put the bottle to her lips, took a hefty swig, replaced the cap, set the bottle back in the rack then slid the panel back into place. She unwrapped a stick of gum and chewed. "All done," she called to Bentley.

The limo phone rang. "I don't care who it is, Bentley. I'm not talking to anyone."

"It might be your mother or your father calling, Miss Cassie. I think I should answer it. You wouldn't want them sending security, would you?"

The scotch had calmed her anxieties. "You're right. Go ahead. And put it on the loudspeaker."

Matt spoke. "I'm trying to get in touch with Cassie Sinclair. Who am I speaking with?"

Bentley eyed Cassie in the rearview mirror and shrugged. "Miss Sinclair is indisposed. This is Bentley, the butler. Can I give her a message as to who is calling?"

"This is Matt, Bentley. You do remember me, don't you?"

"Yes, Sir. I hope you are well."

"I've seen better days, that's for sure."

"Hang up, Bentley," Cassie said. "I'll take it."

"Cassie, I was worried about you. I called J.J. and your home. All I got was polite jibber-jabbers that you're not available. What gives? Like I don't know." He laughed mockingly. "You should've seen it coming. I've known it all along. Don't ask me why I put up with it. Same reason as you did. The two of them deserve each other. You're not the only one that got dumped. Join the club. We're in the same boat—up the creek without a fucking paddle. Sucks, doesn't it?"

His banter sobered her. Little wheels of ideas started to form in her mind. "Matt," she said. "I've some shopping to do, but I would like to meet with you. Are you in the New York showroom?"

"No. I'm in a rental car, and guess where?"

"No games. I'm not into them at the moment."

"I'm at the entrance to the hospital where your ex-Lothario is recuperating. And guess who just walked up the hospital stairs to visit him?"

"Franny," she said.

"Bingo! Give the lady the pink Barbie doll a-sittin' right there on the top shelf. Yep, my so-called devoted lover, Franny—all gussied up for a scene from Romeo and Juliet—visiting with your Nick, who, 'promised to love you forever.' The two-faced son-of-a-bitch."

"Then, why in the world did you come to Santa Fe?"

"You may think I'm nuts but after getting the heave-ho from Franny, I was worried about you."

"Matt, come to the estate tonight at six. The folks will be glad to see you. Especially since you are going to make me better."

"I am?"

"You have no idea how much better."

CHAPTER 98

Bentley pulled the car up to the curb of the Riffraff Boutique. Cassie leaned forward. "Bentley, you can come inside while I shop, or you can wait outside for me. The boutique has an outdoor café. You can have a latté or lunch, or whatever until I'm finished. I'm leaving it up to you."

He unlocked the doors, stepped out of the limo, walked around to her door and held it open. "I'll be at the café, Miss Cassie."

"I'll make sure they send a waiter out," she said. "I plan to do a bit of shopping so why don't you have lunch."

Suspicious, Bentley said, "I'll be here waiting, Miss Cassie," He sat down, watched her enter the store, then turned and nodded at the security vehicle that was parked across the street.

The manager of the store greeted Cassie with a peck on both cheeks. "We've missed you," she said. "How's little Nicky?"

Probably missed my business is what she means, Cassie thought. But to her she said, "He's just fine, thanks. I've been busy, busy, busy. To tell you the truth, I'm in a hurry. I'm meeting a few old sorority sisters from college and I want to surprise them—shock them—with a totally new look. We always play these old dorm tricks on each other."

"How fun," the manager said. "What did you have in mind?"

"Something very hip, as we used to call it back then. But I'm meeting them…" she looked at her watch… "in fifteen minutes. I'll change here to save time."

The manager called to one of the salesladies. "Chantal. We have a project that needs immediate attention."

Within ten minutes, Cassie was transformed into another person. She stood in a private dressing room and admired herself in the floor-to-ceiling mirror. The tattered, stonewashed True Religion jeans, the Donna Karan, off-the-shoulder blouse, the six-inch Manolo Blahnik sandals, a change of makeup, and the jet black frizzy wig transformed her into an entirely different person.

"Keep my clothes for me, will you, Chantal? I'll be back to change."

Cassie hurried out of the shop, breezed by Bentley having lunch at the café, walked to the curb, and hailed a cab. Once inside the cab, she spoke to the driver. "Do you know where the Pawn Plus gun store is?"

The driver did not turn. He spoke into the rearview mirror. "Si, Senora. It take only un minuto. Is busy store in Santa Fe." He chuckled. "All peoples want to guard themselves."

"Wait for me," she said to the driver.

In the cab, she remembered a felon she had defended who told her about the gun shop and owner who sold you whatever you wanted with no questions asked. *I should have thought of this place before instead of using Daddy's revolver. If the lowlife clients I defend can use this place, I'm sure anyone can.*

The buzzer sounded as she opened the door of the shop. From behind the counter a burly salesman with a suspicious glint in his eyes placed both hands on the counter. He looked her over from head to toe. "What can I do for you, Ma'am?"

Cassie said, "I'm a friend of Maxie Freed. He said to ask for Hank." She looked down at the gun display in the enclosed glass case, trying to look nonchalant.

"Hank's my name, guns my game. What's going down with Maxie?"

"From what I hear, he's going straight."

"Good for him. That's what happens when you're young and get mixed up with the wrong crowd."

"Listen, Hank, can we do business? I'm in a hurry. The old man is…"

"Stop right there!" Hank said. "Not interested in your life story. What are you looking for?"

"Something small and light."

"Had any experience?"

"I can handle it."

"Got the cash?"

"How much?"

He grinned. "Usually a thou. But you being a friend of Maxie, five Benny Franklins." He called to a man in the back of the store. "Frankie, cover the front, will-ya." Motioning with his head, he said, "Back room. It's safer there."

Frankie yelled back. "Comin', Hank."

The cab driver dropped Cassie off two blocks from the Riffraff Boutique Shoppe. She walked casually to where Bentley sat, skirted past him and entered the store.

He nodded at the unconventional young woman as she cavorted past him. *My God*, he thought. *Looks like the Woodstock days are upon us again.*

He returned to sipping his latté then impatiently glanced at his watch.

In the store, Cassie retrieved her clothes, headed for the dressing room and called to Chantal. "Do me a favor," she said. "My chauffeur is sitting at the outside café. Be a dear and tell him I'll be out in two minutes, and put whatever he had on my charge. And Chantal, I won't have any use for this getup. They're so not me. I'll leave them in the dressing room. Keep them, or donate them."

CHAPTER 99

All through dinner J.J. kept a watchful eye on Cassie. For the first time in his life uncertainty plagued him. Her tranquil attitude, her forced laughter was not the Cassie he knew. It was agonizing, listening to Cassie and Matt talk about their problems so casually. Much too causally, he thought. *It's as if she were preparing a brief for a case she was to present in court, or rehearsing a part in a play. And what is Matt doing here? Are they consoling each other? True, they've both been hurt badly. Still, something's not quite right. Last week she tried to take her life and today…*

"You're very quiet, Dad," Cassie said. "Hard day at the office?"

Ce Ce attempted to make small talk. "J.J. always has a hard day at the office. I've never known him to come home and say otherwise. I suppose it's the only way he knows." She smiled at J.J. "Isn't that right, Dear?"

He forced a smile. "Yep, only way I know. When you've lived as many years as I have, it's not easy to change." He addressed Matt. "You must be going through some changes…uh…I mean at the showroom."

Matt raised a guarded brow. He sat back in his chair. "I take it you're referring to my breakup with Franny, not my work at the showroom."

J.J. shrugged. "Take it any way you want to. I understand what you and Cassie are going through. I haven't any advice, nor do I wish to tell you what to do. You're both adults. You'll work it out. Of that I'm sure."

"I think Matt and I will skip dessert." She stood and waited for Matt to follow. "If you'll excuse us..."

After they left, J.J. placed his napkin on the table. "Ce Ce," he said. "I've got this real bad feeling, real bad."

CHAPTER 100

Matt waited for Cassie to unlock the door to her suite. The dinner with her parents had been a grueling performance of playacting. From the smokescreen of pretense they had exhibited, he was sure they suspected something was amiss. Her parents had seen through their charade. Of that he was certain. He could only imagine the despair Cassie had felt when Nick told her he and Franny were getting back together. *Same horrific feelings I went through,* he thought.

He stepped in and closed the door behind him. It made an imperceptible click.

Cassie started to remove her suit jacket. She stood in the center of the room, staring listlessly into space, her face one of hopelessness as she let the bolero slip to the floor.

"That bad?" he said, bending down to pick up the jacket. He placed it over a chair, walked to the bar, filled two glasses of prepared iced Moet champagne, casually ambled back to where she stood and placed the flute in her hand. "How about we commiserate?" he said. "To us."

"What is there to toast, Matt?"

"We're two ships lost in the fog."

"Lost in the fog," she mimicked.

"That's exactly what we are, Cassie. Lost! Face it. You and I have been dumped. D-U-M-P-E-D!"

"Tell me something I don't know."

"Everything comes down to how you look at it."

Flute in hand, she walked into the bedroom and sat on the settee.

He followed her and sat close to her. Their glasses clinked. "To the winners, to the losers, and to the heartbroken; may the bubbly mend our sorrows," he said. "Drink up; we're going to drown them."

She shrugged. "Maybe you're right," she said, and this time managed a small smile. The bubbly went down easily, too easily. "Do you smoke?" she said.

"I guess you're referring to the essence of the gods—cannabis supreme. Haven't for a while. Let's make this a special occasion."

"Let's just do it," she said. "Forget the champagne. Pot and the bubbly do not mix. There's some fabulous scotch in the bottom shelf of the bar. I keep it there for special occasions." She nodded soulfully. "I guess this is one of them. Wouldn't you agree, partner?"

"Very special," he said and put his arm around her. "Now where's the weed?"

"In the top drawer of the vanity," she replied.

He stood, then turned and ran his finger lightly across her cheek. "I'm beginning to feel better already."

"It's in a plastic bag. There should be rolling paper in the same drawer." She rose and walked to her bathroom, then stopped. "I guess it's silly to ask you if you know how to roll a joint."

He didn't answer.

"I'm going to slip into something more comfortable," she said.

"Wait. One drink to set the mood." He filled two glasses with scotch whiskey and handed one to her. "Here's how," he toasted. "Now you can get comfortable."

His tie undone, his shirt unbuttoned, he sat at her dressing table and started to separate the seeds from the marijuana.

"You know your trade," she said as she re-entered the room dressed in a satin chemise.

He caught her image in the vanity mirror. "You are something else," he said, but thought, *Nick was one stupid bastard for ditching this beautiful woman. She has beauty, brains and all the money one could want. Forget the money, she's a knockout.*

Her eyes glistened as the lamplight revealed their deep green hue.

He held out a lit joint to her, but she shook her head. "I'll do the scotch after I have a few hits," she said."

"Never thought of you as a pothead, Cassie. You're full of surprises."

She studied him as he faced her. Her smile showed approval of his looks, his muscular build, and his cunning wit. "You never had the chance to really know me," she said. "It all belonged to one man."

He sighed. "Yeah. I read you. You with Nick, me with Franny. What a shame." He sat up. "What do you say, Cassie? How about we put them on the back burner. Okay?"

He handed her the joint. She inhaled deeply and lay back on the bed. He lay alongside her, took the joint from her hand and inhaled. Placing the joint in the ashtray, he gazed at her.

"Like what you see?" she asked.

"More every minute," he replied.

He refilled the glasses with scotch. "Drink up. I'm going to tell you something."

She sat up to drink, and then laid her head on the pillow. "You're in love with me."

He put his glass on the night table. "Yes, but not in the way you think." His lips puckered in thought. "I guess I could be…in time. You're quite a woman. How about you? Think you could fall for a smart ass like me?"

"Hand me the joint and I'll give it some thought."

He locked eyes with her. "I'm not feeling sorry for us, and the pot and drinks are not doing the talking for me.... I'm dead serious, Cassie. We need each other."

"Talk is cheap. You talk like you've gotten over Franny. Either you're just kidding yourself, or the liquor and pot are leading you down the primrose path." She rolled over and stood up. "You're kidding yourself, Matt. Now, if you'll excuse me, I'm going to visit the powder room." She picked up her glass of scotch and held it up to him. "It'll give you time to come back down to earth."

In the bathroom she opened the medicine cabinet, removed a vial of Ativan, placed three in the palm of her hand, changed her mind, added two more pills, swallowed them, and washed them down with the scotch. She fluffed her hair then reentered the bedroom.

Matt sat on the bed smoking a joint. "Thought you ran out on me."

"Why would I do that? We were just beginning to bond. Instant soul mates, a perfect merger of two spurned losers." She plopped down on the bed.

"Hey, what gives? Suddenly you're going south on me."

"I started to get depressed."

"What's wrong? Did you take anything?"

"Just a few Ativan. "I'll be okay in a minute."

"How many, and how many milligrams?"

"Three, five, ten. I don't remember."

He ran into the bathroom and spied the open vial of pills and others scattered on the counter. "Jesus," he yelled from the bathroom. "I'm calling emergency."

She waved a feeble hand of dismissal at him. "Don't, Matt. I'll be all right. Let me rest a minute."

Reluctantly, he lay down beside her. *I should call for help. On the other hand, I may be overreacting.*

He poked her.

Her eyes fluttered.

Good. She's not comatose or convulsing. I'll give her a minute, and then I'll wake her up.

Stealthily she reached underneath her pillow and took hold of the gun she had purchased at the Pawn Plus gun store.

Matt bolted up.

"Back away, Matt," she warned.

The gun at her head, she spoke calmly. "It's no use. Don't you understand? It's over. Maybe not for you—but it is for me. This time I won't miss." She smiled.

His breath caught in his throat. "Cassie," he pleaded. "Think what you're doing. We can work this out. I'll help you. It's not too late. We could make a fresh start. There's chemistry between us. I feel it, and I know you do too. Please, give me the gun."

"Maybe there is something, but it's too late. Funny how things work out. I really like you, Matt."

In a last ditch effort to stop her, he lunged at her and grabbed for the gun. A loud burst was heard through the house as blood splattered on the chartreuse velvet tufted headboard and matching striped wallpaper.

Blood rushed to Cassie's brain, and her mind reeled at the sight of Matt lying at the foot of her bed. She gasped at the sight of his motionless form, his eyes dead, open, an expression of horror on his face.

Woozy from the mixture of pot, liquor and Ativan, she held onto the four-poster for support, swung her legs off the bed, stepped over his body and dropped to her knees.

Shock filled every pore of her being. Her eyes looked at the trickling of blood that oozed from his injured chest, ran down onto his trousers, and pooled underneath him, forming a cherry red oblique pattern on the Oriental carpet.

"Oh, Matt," she sobbed. "It wasn't supposed to happen this way. You're not supposed to die. I am."

The shouting and banging at her door caught her attention. "Cassie! Matt! Open this door immediately or I'll break it down!" J.J. screamed.

"Not this time," she muttered. "Not this time." She picked up the gun and lay down next to Matt.

"Move over," she said. "Make room."

The gun at her temple, Cassie snuggled close to Matt. "See you when I see you, partner," she said and pulled the trigger.

CHAPTER 101

It was less than twenty seconds when Cassie shot up in bed.

Alarmed, Matt swiftly threw his arms around her. "You're okay," he barked. "I'm here. Relax. Take a deep breath. You had a reaction to the shit you took."

Shivering, she said, "I had the most god-awful nightmare."

He massaged her back. "It's my fault. I knew you were depressed. I shouldn't have let you smoke and drink. And the Ativan, that was a sure no-no. The mixture probably gave you the bad dream."

"It was so real."

"It was only a dream, Cassie. You could've overdosed. Lesson learned.

"I can't get it out of my mind."

"Like the shrinks say: want to talk about it? Could make you feel better."

"You're not going to like it, Matt."

Trying to keep the conversation light, he said, "Did I at least get laid?"

She shook her head. "Nothing that good. I shot you…and you…"

"…Died?" he finished for her.

"Not only did I kill you but I killed myself too."

"Well then, we're even." He pulled her down on the bed. "You're coming back? That's a good sign."

She knotted her fingers tightly around his neck, glanced up at him and studied his eyes. "You know something?"

He drew her close. "What?"

"I haven't thought about you-know-who. Maybe you were right when you said we have something in common."

"Me either." He ran his fingers slowly up and around her ears, then down her neck and flicked her lower lip with his index finger. "Lips sweeter than wine," he sang.

"Want to taste?" she offered.

He lightly touched his lips to hers. "Mmm. Rare vintage." He slid the strap down on her chemise, moved his hand onto her breast and encircled her nipple with the palm of his hand.

She moaned.

"I'm so hot for you, Cassie. You have no idea."

She sat up, removed her chemise and lay down beside him. Pursing her lips, she said, "As my English professor used to say: 'Show! Don't tell.'"

CHAPTER 102

Lily pulled up to the entrance of the Santa Clara Hospital, shifted into park, turned off the ignition of the Budget rent-a-car and turned towards Franny.

Franny frowned. "Don't say it, Lily." She held onto Lily's arm. "I know exactly what I'm doing."

It was Lily's turn to frown. "If I've heard that one time I've heard it a thousand times." She shook her head. "I wonder if other best friends have as chaotic a relationship as we do."

"Fucked up, you mean, and mostly because of me."

Lily's eyes widened. "Mostly? How about *all* because of you?"

Franny huffed. "You better take off. You don't want to miss your flight."

"Don't think you can brush me off in your usual way. I know your shtick. I have plenty of time."

"You can't park here. It's only for hospital personnel."

"I'll stay right here until they tell me to move. For God's sakes, Franny, stop avoiding the situation, will you?"

"Here it comes. Another sermon, and it's not even Sunday. Okay. It's no secret. Nick will be out of the hospital in a few days and we're going to start over. Is that what you want to hear?"

"For the most part, yes. And what about Matt? Or are you going to play the field?"

"If you're referring to Nick and Matt, I haven't decided yet. In fact, I haven't heard from Matt in over a week." She blew out a deep breath of annoyance. "Last I heard was that he spent time with the Sinclairs at the estate. I haven't been able to get in touch with Cassie. I wanted to know how the baby was doing, and Bentley said Cassie was going on a sabbatical."

Lily threw her a guarded look. "With the baby? Something's not kosher."

"No. Alone. He sounded like he was reciting what he was instructed to say." She checked her watch. "Anyhow, Lily, I'm going in to see Nick. You can stay here all fucking day if you want to."

"Okay," she sighed, but you have a lot of repenting to think about." She leaned forward to hug Franny.

Franny alighted from the car then leaned into the open window. "Stop worrying, will ya? Matt will understand. Nick needs me." She started to walk up the hospital stairs, turned on her heels and called to Lily. "And I need him too." She blew Lily a kiss and continued her climb, but Nick's words of the distant past stuck in her mind. 'I love you, Cassie, and I love you too, Franny.'

CHAPTER 103

Sitting in the waiting room outside Nick's room, Franny thought long and hard about her conversation with Lily. *If there's one person in this whole fucked-up world who will tell me the god-honest truth, it's Lily. Why do I argue with her? For years she's been trying to get me to calm down, act normal. And for as long as I can remember, I've gone the other way. What is it that drives me to rebel?*

Two nuns walked into the waiting room. They acknowledged Franny with a nod and a polite smile, sat down in the far corner of the waiting room and started to chat.

Franny thought about how curt she was with Lily. *She's right. I am selfish. I shook Matt off without thinking how much I hurt him. And now Nick is doing the same thing to Cassie. How did things get so out of whack?*

"Repent," she said aloud. "How do I do that?"

"I beg your pardon?" one of the sisters said.

"Oh, I was just thinking aloud."

The nuns went on chatting.

I wonder, Franny thought. *No, I haven't been to church in I don't remember when. A wedding? Maybe, just maybe I could give it a shot. Every hospital has a chapel.*

"Excuse me, sisters. Do you know where the chapel is?"

"Yes," one of the nuns said. "It's on the main floor. You can't miss it."

Franny walked into the chapel and sat in the first row of pews. *Where is everyone? Is this a hospital or what?*

A well-dressed elderly gentleman sat next to her, removed a pocket-sized book from his jacket and started to read.

Franny thought. *We're in an empty chapel and he has to sit next to me?*

He turned down the corner of the page, closed the book, folded it, and placed it in the pocket of his suit jacket. Catching her eye, he smiled at her. His smile was fatherly and cordial.

She returned a half-smile.

His sad grey eyes and lined face showed years of wisdom and sorrow. He nodded sympathetically at the troubled expression he read on her face. With a European accent, he asked. "You got somebody sick here?"

"He's not sick. Well, not really sick. He was in an accident, but he's healing."

"That's a blessing," the man said. "Better not to have to be in the hospital. You can get sicker here than before you came in." He gave a tired, forced chuckle. "So if he is getting better, why you look so worried?"

"It's hard to explain. There's a lot going on in my life right now, and I'm not sure of what to do." *Why am I even telling this man, a stranger, about my life?*

"Don't be embarrassed. I've lived so long I feel I can give advice. And ya know what? I don't charge. Not a penny. In the old country, I was what you kids call a shrank."

"You mean a shrink."

"I can look at a person and in one minute I know what's going on with them."

"Okay, Professor, what's going on with me? You have a crystal ball or do you read Tarot cards?"

He nodded. "*You* make jokes, but you're hurting. What's your name, my child?"

"Franny. Franny Pagliara."

"You such a beautiful lady. But so mixed up, like your name. You maybe got yourself caught between two gentlemen?"

Intrigued by his insight, she said, "So far you're 100 percent on target. What's your name?"

"Hershel Green. But you can call me Henny. The Green was cut from a…how you call it…oh, yes…a three-syllable name, after I left Germany. But that is not either here or there. The gentleman that mends here, he's married to you?" He didn't wait for an answer. "You feel troubled because you can't make up your mind whether he or the other one is the right one, and the guilt is making you crazy."

"Right again. 'Crazy' is the key word here. My problem is that I think too much and talk too much." She laughed nervously. "I hurt people. People I love. Gets me into all kinds of trouble, Professor."

"Henny."

"Henny," she repeated.

"Sometimes even when the hurt is over our head, we have to make a decision. Waiting only makes the pain more. I think you already made a decision. Stay with it."

"There's more," Franny blurted. "I had a baby. I gave it up for adoption. Now I want him back."

He nodded his head. "That's a problem. But that will also fall into place. Life has a purpose. First things first."

"I'm so overwhelmed."

He lowered his voice and looked at her as he slipped a hand over hers and squeezed it. "I'm only human, not a prophet or a saint. Existence here on earth, it is short. The time…it flies. You born…you ten…twenty…forty…fifty and soon poof…" He raised his brows. "People sometimes take longer to grow up; afraid to leave the nest, they stay in the same place. Grab happiness while you can, my dear. Now is your time to grow up, to fly."

Franny sat mesmerized. His words: "Now is your time to grow up, to fly" struck a chord in her brain.

"I see that you understand. Go with your gut feeling," he said. "Don't look back."

The tears welled up in her eyes and spilled over. It took a moment before she spoke. "This is a first. I don't know what to say. Suddenly, everything seems so clear."

His eyes lit up. "Ya know, every so often a stranger comes into our life. He tells you, 'this way, not that way.' How? Why? Who knows? Maybe it's God's will."

Franny leaned over and kissed his cheek.

He smiled, stood, and looked down at her. "Go…. Go to your husband and talk it through."

A glow illuminated the chapel as he shuffled past the empty pews, the book bulging in his jacket pocket.

Franny, her mouth open, watched in awe as the man trudged to the chapel door. He turned, gave her a knowing nod, a brief wave, smiled then faded away.

CHAPTER 104

It took Franny a good twenty minutes to compose herself. The man called Henny, who had come out of nowhere and seated himself next to her in the chapel, left her mystified, yet elated. And then, as he had said, poof, he was gone.

The two nuns were still chatting in the waiting room when Franny passed them on her way to Nick's room. They nodded. This time Franny gave them a wide smile.

As she entered the room, Nick's face brightened. "I was worried," he said. "I called you but your cellphone was not taking calls."

Leaning over his bandaged arm, she kissed him. "I turned it off."

He squinted at her. "Only time you don't use your phone is when you're in trouble, or about to be. What gives?"

"Stop the interrogation, Nick." A vision of Henny flashed in her mind. "Okay. The reason I turned the phone off was because I didn't want to speak to Matt."

"Franny, we made a deal. You would tell Matt and I would tell Cassie. She and I had a long talk. Did you know she tried to commit suicide?"

"Jesus. No."

"Matt's been with her."

"Matt? With Cassie?"

"He went to the estate, thinking you would be there. That's when she went ballistic."

Franny plopped into a chair. "You're right. You stuck to your end of our agreement. I'll call Matt."

His look was one of uncertainty.

"I know! I know! I know! I chickened out. But now I see things differently. I have a whole new outlook on life."

He rolled his eyes. "I have a feeling this is going to be one of your Frannyisms."

"Cross my heart, Nick. I met a man in the hospital chapel just before I came to you and I think I had an epiphany."

He swallowed a chuckle. "You in a chapel? Did he wear a flowing, ethereal white robe and have a halo and gossamer wings?" His chuckle emerged into a full-blown laugh.

Defiantly, she folded her arms across her chest. "If you're not going to take me seriously, I'm leaving." She turned to leave.

"Come back," he called. "I'm sorry. I know you can be weird but you're not a liar. We have certain matters to go over."

"Thank you for the left-handed compliment," she said, keeping a suspicious eye on him. "What's on your mind?"

"Nicky," he said.

"Yeah. I've been going nuts about it. Little Nicky is ours, but not legally. Not any more. Why did I ever give him up?"

"Let's not look back at what was, Franny. What's done is done."

"You're smart, Nick. Can't you think of something?"

"Cassie's a lot smarter when it comes to legalities. And then there's J.J. He has power and influential colleagues. We'd never stand a chance. Unless…"

"What?"

"I was just thinking out loud." He sat up. "I'm not sure."

"Don't leave me hanging, Nick!"

Silence.

"If you wanna live to see another day, Nick, you better tell me."

Ignoring her, he laid his head on the pillow again and closed his eyes. "Did you know that she's been seeing a lot of Matt?"

Franny walked to the night table and absentmindedly rearranged the roses in the vase. "Spurned, rebound lovers," she uttered. "And it's our fault."

His eyes opened. "We can't control where life takes us."

"But we can try to control how much harm we inflict on others."

"Come closer. We have to make things simple." He took her hand in his. "I'm beginning to think your story about the man in the chapel had an effect on you."

"It wasn't a story."

"Well, whatever the happening was, I do sense a change in you."

"Is that a good thing?"

"We'll see."

"I have to ask you something, Nick. It's been bugging me forever."

"Shoot."

"By any chance, you're not still thinking of Cassie…I mean…you're not still in love with her, are you?"

"Honestly, Franny, I do love her, but not in the way I love you."

"That needs an explanation, Nick."

"I don't think I can." He rubbed his chin.

"That is *not* funny. I'm serious. If we're going to pick up where we left off, we have to clear this up."

"Okay, Smartass. What about you and Matt? You professed your love for him, didn't you?"

"It's not the same."

He shook his head. "Did you get the telephone number of the man in the chapel? I think you're going to need him again."

"Do *not* joke about that. It happened and it had an effect on me."

He leaned forward and with a magic marker drew a heart with an arrow of Franny and Nick going through it, on the cast of his leg. "You still love Matt, don't you?"

She pursed her lips. "Guess so."

"I proved my point. Case closed," he said. "Listen, I'm getting out of here tomorrow. I was thinking of having another conversation with Cassie. There's tons of stuff of mine at the estate. Might be a good time for us to talk. She seems to have mellowed. Maybe it's the medication she's on. Or there could be something going on between her and Matt."

"You're thinking they may discover a need for each other?"

"I only wish. Could be the answer to all our problems."

"Gee, Nick. I'm not sure that's a good idea. You know the old saying about a woman scorned. And she'll never give up Nicky." She took the magic marker and wrote Cassie and Matt alongside Franny and Nick on his cast. "Ya know something, Nick?" she offered. "Stranger things have happened."

He gave her a long, tentative smile. "That's exactly what I was thinking, my love. Stranger things have happened."

CHAPTER 105

Matt dialed Cassie from the New York showroom. He didn't wait for her to speak but immediately said, "Don't tell me you're still in bed."

The night table clock displayed 7:00 AM. Her right foot found its way into a bedroom slipper as she looked for the other one. "Hold on, Matt." Her arm searched beneath the bed. Landline at her ear, she muttered, "There you are."

"There you are? I'm gone three days and you're already bedding a guy?"

Tying the sash on her robe, she laughed. "It may seem like three days to you, but it's been over a week now. And I was looking for my bedroom slipper. I'm not hiding a man under the sheets."

"Shit. Has it been a week, Cassie? The fall line has been giving me unbelievable agita. We are so damn late. The head designer is useless. He got into a fight with his lover and tried to commit suicide."

She sighed. "That's something I can relate to. It must be just about a month since I…"

He overrode her words. "I thought we were going to put that behind us?"

"Like it never happened, Matt?"

"Listen, Cassie. I'm up to my ass in work. And it isn't any easier with Franny not being here."

She snapped. "Get her back, if you need her so badly."

"I don't. I handled this whole division before and I can do it again! And speaking of attending to things, my friend, I've been receiving calls from Nick. He wants to talk with you. Says you're putting him off."

"I know he's been trying to get in touch with me."

"What are you hiding from? Unless…"

"I don't want him back, if that's what you're intimating. You and I made a pact, Matt. So far it's working. We're friends. You're happy, I'm happy. It's a good foundation for us. Please believe me. I'd be lying if I said I'm completely over him, but with your help I will be. Ease your mind. Yes, for a while I wasn't sure. But I'm on the mend. Scout's honor."

"We'll see. I know where you're coming from. I'm getting over Franny, but I'm not sure about you and Nick."

"Matt, we have to trust each other. Going back into court has kept my mind focused, and you *have* been my rock." She blew out a deep breath. "I know exactly what Nick wants."

"So do I. He and Franny, ever so discreetly, have been dropping hints, hoping you'll give little Nicky to them."

"They are his parents. Matt."

"What's this—a change of heart? Would you give him back?"

Hesitating, then finally, "I don't know. I might."

"Sounds like you will. It's your call. Besides, we can always adopt. And what about us? I'm not about to give up designing, and I'm certain you want to continue your law practice. Would you move to New York and practice here? My pad is big enough for two, or we could shop for an apartment."

"Slow down, Matt. You're throwing tomorrow at me when we haven't cleared up today."

He ran his hands over his face. "You're right. I'm sorry. It's all this pressure."

"And I don't have pressure? Jesus, Matt, I wouldn't know where to begin. Franny says *every* season is a calamity in the garment center. Want to compare notes?"

"Look, Cassie, I'm getting stared-down by the crew outside my office windows. Just this morning Lew decided that he's not happy with some of the fabrics and also the colorations. Everyone's on edge."

"What do you think about me flying up to see you? Always wanted to see what goes on in the garment center. I promise I won't get in your way. While I'm there, I can network with some local attorneys about practicing law in New York." She paused. "There's more."

He knew where she was coming from and it worried him. *I'm well aware of her mental state. She's been living through hell. She is not the hard-hitting lady who won practically every court case. It will take time to get back to where she was, if ever. Will she be strong enough to face Nick without the old feeling returning?*

"It has been a mess," he concurred. "What are you thinking?"

"I'm thinking that while I'm in New York, we could get together and resolve this entire fiasco with Nick and Franny."

"Are you sure about that?"

"We have to face them eventually."

"Now you're talking like the Cassie I knew. I'm proud of you. I'd love it. Listen, Lew's raising hell. I really have to go. I'll call you. We'll talk. Okay? Bye."

He hung up before she could say good-bye.

She placed the phone in its cradle, walked to the nursery and greeted the baby's nurse. "How's my little fella doing?" she asked.

"He's a darling, Miss Sinclair. Just waiting for his mother to pick him up. She picked up the baby and gently placed him in Cassie's arms. "Here you go, Nicky," she said.

A chill ran through Cassie as she locked eyes with the baby. *This is Nick's baby. He has Nick's name, Nick's eyes. Maybe he should be with his father…*

CHAPTER 106

Sitting on her boudoir chair looking into the vanity mirror, Franny watched Nick at the bar in the living room. She fluffed her kinky hair. "I hate my hair," she said. "No matter what I do, it frizzes up."

"Stop fidgeting. You'll be fine. We've had a good relationship with them."

"Yeah. *Had* is the strategic word here. Where are we meeting them?"

"They've taken a suite at the Plaza."

"How can you be so calm? And what are you doing?"

"Making martinis."

She stood, smoothed her dress, walked into the living room, placed her hands on her hips and posed. "So, how do I look?"

Nick placed the martini shaker on the bar and nodded approvingly. "You look fantastic."

"You're not just saying that to give me courage, are you?"

"Why are you so jumpy? Ten to one Cassie and Matt are onto what we're going to ask them."

"We? Uh-uh. You."

"Come on, Franny. Cassie and Matt seem to be getting their life back on track again. What happened to the new you? Has the epiphany with the mentor gone bye-bye?" He shook his head. "Okay. I'll broach the subject."

"You can joke around all you want to," she said blandly. "My mentor, as you so eloquently alleged, opened up a whole new world for me."

He shook his head. "Could be. Could be."

"What does that mean?"

"It means the man definitely had some kind of effect on you. You haven't used profanity in forty-eight hours. I'll broach the subject with Cassie."

She hesitated for a long moment then nodded as though confirming her thoughts. "If they won't give the baby back I..."

"You'll what? Go on strike? Kidnap Nicky? Get real, Franny. You knew what you were doing when you gave the baby to Cassie."

"That was then and this is now. For the first time, I'm thinking logically. I can't help the way I feel. I didn't know I was going to miss Nicky so much."

"Cassie will do the right thing."

"You think so, Nick? From your mouth to God's ears."

He walked to the bar, stirred the martini shaker, poured, and handed the cocktail glass to her. He toasted. "Here's to us and the life we will have together with Nicky."

She clinked his glass. "Amen. And to you, Henny, whoever you are."